# Slow
# Dance

........................

ALSO BY RAINBOW ROWELL
*Scattered Showers: Stories*

**THE SIMON SNOW TRILOGY**
*Carry On*
*Wayward Son*
*Any Way the Wind Blows*

*Landline*

*Fangirl*

*Eleanor & Park*

*Attachments*

# Slow Dance

........................................

*A Novel*

# RAINBOW ROWELL

*wm*

WILLIAM MORROW
*An Imprint of* HarperCollins*Publishers*

SLOW DANCE. Copyright © 2024 by Rainbow Rowell. All rights reserved. Printed in the United States of America. No part of this book may be used or reproduced in any manner whatsoever without written permission except in the case of brief quotations embodied in critical articles and reviews. For information, address HarperCollins Publishers, 195 Broadway, New York, NY 10007.

HarperCollins books may be purchased for educational, business, or sales promotional use. For information, please email the Special Markets Department at SPsales@harpercollins.com.

FIRST EDITION

Designed by Bonni Leon-Berman

Library of Congress Cataloging-in-Publication Data has been applied for.

ISBN 978-0-06-338019-6 (hardcover)
ISBN 978-0-06-338982-3 (international edition)

24 25 26 27 28  LBC  5 4 3 2 1

For my friends Kai and Paul,

time machines

# Slow
# Dance

· · · · · · · · · · · · · · ·

# ONE

# January 2006

THE WEDDING INVITATION CAME, AND Shiloh said yes, of course she'd be there.

Mikey was one of her oldest friends, and she'd missed his first wedding. She couldn't afford the trip to Rhode Island at the time. (She still couldn't afford a trip to Rhode Island.)

But this time he was getting married here in Omaha, right down the street—of course Shiloh would be there. Everyone would.

Everyone loved Mikey. He held on to people. Shiloh had never been sure how he managed it.

She checked *yes* on the RSVP card and wrote in, *With bells on!*

The week before the wedding, she bought a new dress on clearance. Deep-burgundy floral with a low-cut neck. It was meant to be tea length, but it came to Shiloh's knees. The sleeves were a little short, too—she'd just wear a denim jacket over it. (*Could* you wear a jean jacket to a wedding? A second wedding?) (It would be fine. She'd pin a silk flower to the chest.)

The wedding was on one of Ryan's Fridays. Shiloh waited until he picked up the kids before she started getting ready. She didn't want Ryan to see her wearing makeup. Or heels. She didn't want him to see her *trying*.

Maybe some people wanted to look good for their exes, to show them what they'd lost or whatever. Shiloh would prefer that Ryan never thought of her at all. Let him think he was too good for her. Let him think that Shiloh had gone to seed.

Shiloh was a thirty-three-year-old divorced woman with two children under six—maybe she literally *had* gone to seed.

Ryan was late, even though she'd told him she had somewhere she needed to be. (She should never have told him she had somewhere to be.)

He was late, and the kids had gotten tired of waiting. They were hungry and sullen when he finally showed up and blustered his way into the living room like she'd invited him in.

"They're hungry," Shiloh said.

And Ryan said, "Why didn't you feed them, Shy?"

And Shiloh said, "Because you were supposed to take them for dinner."

And then he said—

It didn't really matter what Ryan said after that. He was just going to keep saying the same old things for the next fifteen years of coparenting, and Shiloh was going to have to keep listening, because . . . Well, because she'd made a *series* of *serious* mistakes and miscalculations.

It was funny, almost, how poorly Shiloh had built her life—especially for someone who had once prided herself on her ability to make decisions.

That's something she'd decided about herself when she was a teenager. She'd thought she was good at making decisions because she *liked* making them. They felt good, they gave her a zing. If someone was lingering over a decision or seesawing between two options, Shiloh loved cutting in and settling the matter. The world would spin faster and with more clarity if Shiloh were in charge.

If Shiloh could talk to her teenage self now, she'd point out that deciding wasn't any good if you weren't deciding correctly—or even in the neighborhood of correctly.

Ryan finally left with the kids. And Shiloh tore the clearance tags off her dress. She put on makeup. She pinned up her hair. She stood on tiptoe to get her boots zipped over her calves.

She'd already missed the wedding, but she wouldn't miss the reception. No one would. Everyone would be there.

## TWO

THE RECEPTION WAS IN A rental hall on the second floor of a youth wrestling club. Mikey had married someone from the neighborhood this time, a girl who had been a year or two behind them in high school.

It was a plated dinner, with assigned tables. Fancy.

"Shiloh!" someone called out, as soon as she walked into the lobby. "We thought you weren't coming!"

It was Becky. Shiloh and Becky had been on the high school newspaper together. They'd been thick as thieves—they'd actually stolen a traffic barricade once—and they still talked sometimes. They were friends on Facebook. (Shiloh almost never logged in to Facebook.)

"I'm here," Shiloh said, mustering up a smile. There was going to be a lot of mustering tonight, she could already tell.

"You're at our table," Becky said. "It's practically a journalism reunion. Everyone's here. Oh god, wait—you *were* at our table, but we thought you weren't coming, so we gave your seat to Aaron King, do you remember him? He was a sophomore?"

"I remember him—it's fine."

"But you should still come say hi. Everybody's here."

"No one can say no to Mikey," Shiloh said.

"You're so right," Becky agreed. "Plus we all thought there'd be an open bar." She laughed. "Oh well."

Shiloh followed Becky into the reception hall. She held her head straight and kept her gaze fixed, deliberately not scanning the room for familiar faces. Anyone that Shiloh would recognize was going to have to *force* their way into her field of vision.

They got to their table. There was Becky's husband and Tanya—god, Shiloh hadn't seen Tanya for years. And Tanya's husband, yeah, they'd met, hi, hi. Hugs. Hi. Nia. And Ronny. Shiloh hated Ronny. At least, she used to hate Ronny—did she still hate Ronny? She hugged him anyway. People, all these people. From the same tiny part of Shiloh's life (it hadn't felt tiny at the time). All these people who knew her and remembered her. They were all eating salads and sorry that they'd given away her seat—but that was okay, Shiloh didn't mind. She'd pull up a chair later. It was good to see them, she said— and it really was. It was good to know now who was here, from the old days.

And who wasn't.

It made sense that he wasn't here—he was in Virginia, wasn't he? The last time Shiloh had heard, he was in Virginia. Maybe someone would mention it later . . .

*Of course* he wasn't here. He was in the Navy. He was probably on the ocean somewhere. Probably didn't get back home much. She'd heard once that he didn't get back home much . . .

He wasn't here, and other people were, and she could enjoy this now. Enjoy them. Enjoy *something*.

Shiloh didn't want to stand there hovering over her old friends while they finished their salads. She squeezed a few shoulders, then squeezed between tables to get to the one in the corner where Aaron King had been assigned to sit. (She actually *didn't* remember him.) There was a couple sitting there, surrounded by empty chairs.

"Mind if I join you?" Shiloh asked.

They didn't mind at all. They introduced themselves—Mikey's aunt and uncle—and told her they'd already eaten her dinner roll.

"We ate all of them," the uncle said. "We thought we had this table to ourselves!"

The aunt cackled warmly. "We were gonna eat your cake, too."

"You still can," Shiloh promised, sitting down. There was a white jar candle next to her plate, branded *Mike & Janine, January 20, 2006.*

Shiloh picked it up and sniffed it. Lavender.

She could look around now—now that she knew he wasn't here. It was safe.

The tables were set up at one end of the reception hall, and there was a dance floor on the other. Spotlights were already flashing onto a disco ball in the corner. Shiloh had been to three or four weddings here before, but this was probably the best she'd ever seen this place look. Someone had wrapped all the fixtures in Christmas lights. The chairs were swathed in tulle.

Shiloh *liked* weddings. Improbably. Still. She liked seeing people's best outfits. She liked beginnings. She liked the flowers and the favors and the little bags of Jordan almonds.

A lot of the other guests were people Shiloh vaguely remembered from high school . . . all of them looking a little older and fatter and knocked around by life to varying degrees.

It was easy to pick out Mikey's New York City friends. Art-world people. There was a woman in a bright yellow bandage dress and a man wearing black culottes and platform boots.

Shiloh used to take great pains not to be dressed like anyone else in a room—but she'd lost her edge. And she'd never had as much edge as these people. She felt dowdy in comparison. Thrown together. Even though she hadn't tried this hard in years.

She scanned the crowd for Mikey. She'd have to apologize to him for missing the ceremony. Maybe he hadn't noticed. He surely had plenty of other things on his mind.

Someone near Shiloh started tapping a fork against a wineglass, then other people picked up the clanging, everyone eagerly turning to watch the bride and groom kiss. Shiloh followed the wave to the head table.

There was Mikey. With his curly blond hair and big, goofy smile. He was wearing a white suit. That was obviously Janine next to him in the wedding dress. Then the bridesmaids in pale green satin. And the groomsmen. And Cary.

*Cary.*

Shiloh clenched her hands in her lap.

Cary was a groomsman.

Right . . . *Right*—that made sense.

Of course Cary was here.

Of course he wouldn't miss it.

## THREE

SHILOH HAD BEEN IMAGINING THIS moment since she got Mikey's invitation—but she hadn't known how to picture Cary. He wasn't on Facebook. He didn't turn up in Google searches.

She kept picturing him the way he'd looked in high school—in his ROTC uniform, weirdly—even though she'd seen him since then . . . At their five-year reunion. Standing across from her in the same old circle of friends. She and Cary had hardly spoken that day. Shiloh had brought Ryan to the reunion; they'd already been married a year. (They hadn't invited Cary to the wedding.)

Shiloh had been imagining this moment—the moment she'd see Cary again—for months, but even in her imagination, it wouldn't mean as much to him as it did to her. Cary wouldn't have been thinking about it all day. He wouldn't have been wondering, worrying, that Shiloh might be here. He wouldn't have bought a new dress, so to speak, just in case.

Cary looked good. Here. Now. From a distance. He looked sharper than the rest of them, less worn down on the edges. He looked tan. His hair was still so short . . .

He turned, almost like he could feel Shiloh watching him. She was too far away to say that their eyes met—or even to know whether he recognized her—but she smiled a little and raised her hand to wave. Cary waved back. He might just be waving because someone had waved at him.

Shiloh's hand dropped. Cary was still looking in her direction.

He stood up and moved behind the bride and groom. He was saying something to Mikey. He glanced up toward Shiloh again, then shuffled behind the bridesmaids' chairs and out onto the floor, heading toward her.

Shiloh straightened her jean jacket. (Why was she wearing a jean jacket?) Cary was wearing a navy blue suit; people must not rent tuxes anymore for weddings. He was walking toward her table now, and Shiloh stood up, then thought that she probably shouldn't have done that—like she was the gentleman, and he was the lady—but it would be weird to sit down now. She straightened her jacket again. Cary was looking at her like, *I'm coming.* And she nodded like, *I see you,* and smiled. She waved again, and he waved back. He was nearly there—the tables were packed too tightly, it was slow going. Shiloh wondered whether she should hug him when he got to her. She'd hugged nearly everyone at the other table, plus some of their spouses. She'd gotten very good at casual hugging.

"Shiloh," Cary said when he got to her.

"Cary." She smiled at him.

He smiled back.

He looked *good.* Even up close. Cary had blondy-brown hair and a heart-shaped face with a narrow jaw and a pointy chin. She'd only ever seen him clean-shaven. (Were you allowed to have a beard in the Navy?) He'd been built like a stick of gum back in high school, but he'd filled out now. He looked grown-up. Settled. He looked like he'd gotten out of North Omaha.

"It's good to see you," Shiloh said.

"Yeah," Cary said, nodding. "You weren't at the wedding."

"I wasn't," she agreed. "There was a mix-up with my kids." Did Cary know she had kids?

He nodded, he must know.

"You're a groomsman," she said.

"I guess I did so well the first time, I got invited back."

Shiloh hummed a laugh. "Do you have to give a speech?"

"No, that's the best man—Bobby. He's really drunk, so I'm excited to see how it turns out."

"Maybe you should prepare something just in case."

"I'll improvise."

Shiloh nodded. Then nodded again. "Nice suit."

Cary looked down. "Thanks. We had tuxes at the last one, but this time, Janine was like, 'You don't have to rent a tux, you can just buy a navy blue suit that you can wear again.'" Cary looked back up at Shiloh. "I don't think she realizes it's *way* more expensive to buy a suit than to rent a tux."

"She probably doesn't care."

"Yeah, probably not. It's her big day. I'm just an accessory."

"Did you fly in?"

"Yeah." Cary nodded. "Yeah."

"From Virginia?" Shiloh was pointing for some reason.

"From San Diego, actually."

"Oh." Shiloh moved her hand to point in the other direction.

"You were right the first time," Cary said, moving her wrist back.

She laughed, embarrassed. "North, south . . ."

Cary was laughing, too, a little bit. "East, west."

"Right, right."

"I *was* in Virginia," he said. "But I got stationed in San Diego two years ago."

"I thought maybe you were on a boat somewhere . . ."

"I do work on a ship," he said.

"Yeah?"

"Yeah." He nodded again. He was still kind of laughing. "But I live in an apartment."

"So, like, your office is on a ship?"

"Yeah."

Shiloh was still kind of laughing, too. Even though nothing was funny and everything was awkward. "I don't have any idea how the Navy works," she admitted.

"That's okay," he said. "Why would you?"

Yeah. Why would Shiloh know how Cary spent his days and nights? Or where he'd been? What he did, how he felt . . . "Well, I do pay your salary," she said. "So I should really be better informed."

"I've been meaning to talk to you about that . . ."

Shiloh huffed out a laugh. "Have you."

He was smiling right into her eyes. Shiloh had heels on, so she was a little taller than him. "Mikey says you're still in Omaha," Cary said.

She tucked a piece of hair behind her ear. "I am."

"He said you're in theater."

"I'm not in theater," she said quickly. "I work at the children's theater."

"That's *in* theater."

"It's mostly administration."

"It sounds interesting."

"It's . . ." Shiloh was shaking her head. "Very nonprofit."

"And you have kids. I mean, your own."

"I do," she said. "Two. A girl and a boy."

Cary was nodding.

"Six and almost three," Shiloh said.

"I should have asked how old."

"You're not obligated."

"Do you have photos?"

"Um . . ." *Did she?* She glanced down at her bag.

"It's okay," Cary said, looking apologetic. Awkward. "Sorry. I thought you'd want me to ask."

"I guess I never do that—show pictures. Because I never know what to say when people show *me* pictures of *their* kids, and I'm a parent."

"I usually say, 'Well, look at that.'"

"That's a good line." Shiloh laughed. More naturally. "It's not that my kids aren't cute or something. They're very cute—you'll just have to take my word on it."

"I do." Cary was smiling again. His mouth was closed, and there were deep lines in his cheeks. He'd always had a face full of lines—in his cheeks, under his eyes, in his forehead. Even in high school. Like he had a little too much face for the space. Cary crinkled when he was happy and creased when he was angry.

He was so familiar to Shiloh.

Standing *close* to him was so familiar.

They could be standing by their lockers. Standing by his mom's station wagon. Standing in line at a movie theater.

"It's so weird to be talking to you," Shiloh said. She tried to laugh when she said it—like, *Isn't it weird? Isn't it funny?*

Cary looked hurt. "It is?"

Shiloh felt her face fall. "It's so weird to be talking to you," she said again without laughing, "and not know, you know . . . *anything.*"

Cary pushed his tongue out over his bottom lip.

*And not know everything,* Shiloh thought.

A waitress swung around their table with a serving cart. She picked up two plates and looked at the elderly couple. "Chicken? Chicken?"

Shiloh looked at Cary. She had to make this less weird. This was their first conversation in fourteen years, and she didn't want it to end like this. She didn't want it to *end.* "Maybe we can catch up more . . ."

"Chicken?" The waitress was pointing at Shiloh.

"Yes," Shiloh said, "thank you."

"Chicken," Cary said, raising his hand.

The waitress dropped two plates on the table in front of them.

Shiloh turned to him. "Don't you have to sit at the head table?"

"No one will miss me," he said.

"I think you probably get special food up there . . ."

"Special chicken?"

"And free beer."

Cary pulled out her chair. "No one will miss me," he said again.

# before

THEY WERE SQUEEZED INTO THE front seat of Cary's mom's car because the back seat was always full of junk. Like, bags of stuff that his mom bought at the thrift shop and then didn't bring into the house until it was all broken from being sat on or thrown around. It was a bad cycle, but Cary tried to ignore it. Shiloh wondered if his house was like this, too. She'd never been inside.

Cary always drove, and Mikey sat in the passenger seat, and Shiloh sat in the middle. She leaned more on Cary, because leaning on Mikey would feel weird. And also because it wouldn't bother Mikey.

It bothered Cary. Shiloh messed with him while he drove. There was a hole in the seam of his Army surplus pants, on the outside of his thigh. She poked at it, and Cary tried to pull his leg away. "Don't rip my pants."

"They're already ripped."

They were going to see a movie—*Delicatessen*. Omaha only had one art-house movie theater, and the three of them saw pretty much everything that came there. Mikey was into arty stuff. And Shiloh was *kind of* into it . . . even though most of the movies they saw didn't make any sense, and they were usually sort of embarrassing. (European people smoking on balconies. Or having sex in dirty kitchens.) But the movies were confusing in a way that made Shiloh feel smart. Like, at least she knew enough to be there, on the cutting edge of something. Of the three of them, Cary was the most likely to walk out of the theater afterwards and say, *"Well, that was garbage."* But he still kept going along. He still kept driving. Kept covering Shiloh when she couldn't buy her own ticket. (Cary worked weekends at a grocery store.)

Cary always sat in the middle at the theater. Because he and Mikey had to sit together, to crack each other up. And because Shiloh had to sit by Cary, because she just did.

When *Delicatessen* was over, Cary said, "I could have used less cannibalism."

"Or maybe you could have used *more* cannibalism," Mikey said. "There's really no way of being certain."

"All right, sure," Cary agreed. "Either way, it had an unpleasant amount of cannibalism."

"I think the cannibalism was a metaphor . . . " Shiloh said.

"For what?" Cary asked.

"I don't know. I'm just saying I think it was probably a metaphor."

"Well, I'm hungry," Mikey said.

Shiloh laughed.

"Where can we go where they might serve us people?" he asked. "Also I only have three dollars."

Shiloh had one dollar. Cary had eight, but he had to save five for gas. They went to Taco Bell.

They each got a bean burrito and then a Nachos Supreme to share. Shiloh and Mikey ate most of the chips because Cary was driving. She tried to feed him some, but he just frowned and shoved her arm away.

Cary had bony hands. Swollen knuckles. Knobby wrists. Chafed-looking elbows. He looked like he wasn't getting the recommended daily amount of something. He was pale, and he had too many moles. Dark ones—even on his face. He was tall enough, and strong when he needed to be, but there was something stunted about him. Like maybe he got taller at the expense of some other vital function. Shiloh wouldn't be surprised to hear that Cary only had one kidney. Or that he was digesting his own intestines. He should let her feed him some nachos.

Cary always took Mikey home first, and then he'd take Shiloh home. She and Cary only lived a few blocks apart.

Shiloh lived right across from Miller Park. It was one of the grand old parks that were part of the original city plan. It had a playground and a swimming pool and a golf course . . . (Who in North Omaha played *golf*?) There had been a few gang shootings in the park. And a few regular shootings. It was illegal to drive through there at night. Shiloh always tried to talk Cary into doing it, but he never would.

Sometimes they drove around for a while before he took her home. They were high school seniors now—they could do pretty much whatever they wanted. And neither of them had the kind of parents who kept track.

Cary lived with his mom (she was actually his grandma, it was a long story) and his mom's fourth husband, who Cary wouldn't even call his stepdad.

Shiloh just had her mom. Her dad had never been in the picture. Like, Shiloh had never even *seen* a picture of him. Her mom had boyfriends that came and went. It was always a relief when they went.

Tonight Cary drove straight to Shiloh's house after Mikey's—but he backed into her driveway, so they could look out on the park. That meant he wasn't in any hurry to get home.

Shiloh didn't bother Cary as much when it was just the two of them. She still messed with him just as much, maybe even more—but Cary didn't *get* bothered. He'd let her fool around with the car radio and tug on his pockets. Sometimes she'd play with his hair.

Back in middle school, Cary had always needed a haircut. His hair had been lank and clumpy. Now he paid for his haircuts himself, and his hair always smelled like apples. He'd let Shiloh fiddle with his hair, but if she pulled it, he'd shove her hand away.

Sometimes Shiloh felt like she was disappointing Cary. Like, she was pretty sure he was usually *pretending* to be irritated with her. But underneath that, there were moments when he seemed *actually* irritated with her.

"Would you eat me"—Shiloh hooked a finger in a loop sewn into the pocket of Cary's cargo pants—"if we were stranded on a mountain, and I died first?"

"Pass," Cary said.

"Are you passing on eating me? Or passing on the question?"

"Both."

"I would probably eat you," she said. "Partly to stay alive. And partly as a way to keep you with me for the time that I had left."

He frowned at her.

Shiloh poked him. "Come on. What would you do?"

"You're dead?"

"Yeah, but I'm fresh. Half frozen."

"No, I wouldn't eat you. What would I have to live for?"

"A plane might see you the next day."

"Pass," he said.

She poked his thigh. "I guess the world will forget us both."

Cary grabbed her wrist and held on to it for a second, away from his leg.

# before

THIS WAS HOW IT WENT:

Cary and Shiloh rode to school together.

And when they got there, they stood with the same group of guys next to somebody's locker. Unless Shiloh was irritated with one of them. Then she went and hung out with the girls from journalism. Or she went to the journalism room and worked—Shiloh was editor-in-chief of the newspaper. Sometimes she stood out on the school's front steps with a group of sophomores and juniors, because she had a crush on one of them—Kurt. He lived in a nice neighborhood and was good at math.

Sometimes Shiloh had morning drama club. (With Cary.) Or morning science club. (Also with Cary.) And sometimes she had to get to school early because she hadn't done her homework and she had morning detention.

Once school started, she'd go to first-hour journalism, and Cary would go to ROTC.

And then he'd come down to the journalism room, because they both had study hall there. With Mikey. And the three of them would fuck around in the darkroom. (Like, platonically. Obviously.) Or they'd fuck around in the computer lab. Or, if they were on deadline, they'd work.

And then blah blah blah class.

And then lunch with Cary and Mikey and a bunch of other journalism people. Shiloh got free lunch, but she shared it with a girl named Lisa, in exchange for Lisa buying them both ice cream cones every day for dessert.

Then more class. French. Literature with Cary. Yearbook.

Always something after school. Play practice. Newspaper stuff. Mikey started an Amnesty International chapter, and they all joined. They wrote letters to the president of Chile, asking him to free political prisoners. Cary had ROTC junk after school sometimes, so Shiloh found other things to do. She was helping the art teacher rebuild the school mascot, even though Shiloh wasn't in art and she didn't have any school spirit. Kurt, the junior she liked, was on the men's volleyball team, so sometimes she went to the practices.

If Shiloh didn't have anything else to do after school, she'd hang out by the flagpole and wait for Cary.

If she wanted to, she could walk home by herself. But she never did.

## SIX

# before

CARY'S MOM HAD NEEDED HER car, so Shiloh and Cary were walking home from school. It was a forty-minute walk, and they had to go through rough neighborhoods where nobody knew them. (North Omaha was a collection of rough neighborhoods, but it was different when it was your own.)

Cary was wearing his ROTC uniform, which made everything worse.

Shiloh hated his ROTC uniform. She hated what it stood for—like, wars and killing babies, and the obvious Hitler Youth resonance—and she also hated it because it was so *ugly*. The boxy green poly-blend suit, the pale green shirt, the black polyester tie.

The pants didn't fit anyone correctly, especially not the girls. They were too wide at the bottom, and Cary's were too short—because he'd gotten his uniform while he was still growing. He was *still* growing.

People in ROTC had to wear their uniforms every Monday, even when it was hot, and they always sort of smelled. Like, in the car with Cary on a Monday morning, Shiloh could smell his uniform. The staleness. The old sweat. It's not like anyone ever had their ROTC jacket professionally cleaned. Cary had a bunch of ribbons and medals on his chest, and Shiloh was so grossed out by ROTC that she never even messed with them.

Shiloh hated that Cary was in ROTC. She *hated* it. She generally tried not to think about it—but she couldn't *not* think about it right now, because they were out of their neighborhood, and he was in his stupid uniform. The high-water pants. The short-sleeved shirt that drew attention to his bruised-looking elbows. He was carrying his jacket over his arm. Somebody had already leaned out of a car and shouted, *"What's up, Beetle Bailey?"* And that was probably the *nicest* bad thing that could possibly happen at the moment, but it was still so humiliating. It reminded Shiloh of the time she'd been walking home with Cary in junior high, and someone had driven by and yelled, *"Your girl has a fat ass!"* And both of them had been too embarrassed to even talk to each other for the rest of the way home—Shiloh could hardly *look* at Cary, and when she had, she could tell that he was just as mortified as she was.

"I don't know why you have to wear that all day," Shiloh said now. Ten minutes after *"Beetle Bailey!"* and with at least fifteen minutes left on their walk. They were finally on familiar territory, walking past the pawnshop and the liquor store and the barbershop where all the old white guys in the neighborhood got their hair cut too short. (Almost no one in the world did anything right. Everyone's hair was too long or too short. Everyone was too loud or too quiet. Nothing was the right color. Music was embarrassing. Movies were confusing. Shiloh hated it. She hated it all.)

"It's required."

"You could change your clothes after ROTC class."

"It's required that we stay in uniform all day."

"*I* would change," she said, "if it were *me*."

"You'd get a demerit."

"Perish the thought."

Cary didn't reply to that. He probably didn't think there was anything more to say. Shiloh felt like hitting him. She felt like tripping him. She felt like pushing him off the sidewalk.

"I don't understand why you want this all the time," she said. "Like, for your *whole life*."

Cary was joining the Navy after graduation. He'd already been accepted. He was going to get free college, Shiloh didn't know the details—because she didn't ask about it. Because she *hated* that it was happening.

"It's only six years," Cary said.

"Six years of following orders and . . ." Shiloh tried to find a way to say the worst of it. "And being a *tool*."

"There's nothing wrong with being a tool. Tools are necessary."

"A tool of . . . of a *corrupt* government."

He didn't say anything, so Shiloh kept going. "Like, you know that the military has committed atrocities. *Atrocities*. And you still want to be part of it."

"I'm not going to commit atrocities," Cary said flatly.

Shiloh had never said anything flatly. "You don't get a *choice*. They don't *consult* with you. It's not like there's an atrocity track and a non-atrocity track. Do you think the soldiers at My Lai *opted in*?"

"You don't know anything about My Lai," he said.

Cary knew all about it. He read military books and watched war movies. The teacher who headed up ROTC had served in Vietnam, and he told the ROTC kids real battle stories.

It was pretty fucked up that their school had two ROTC teachers, and they were in uniform all the time, and it was like they had their own *unit*, right at the high school! Why did public schools need military units? Starting in seventh grade? Twelve-year-olds in uniform! Doing rifle training! It was pretty shocking when you thought about it. It turned your stomach. Shiloh should write a column about it for the school newspaper.

Cary had been in ROTC since seventh grade. He was one of the highest-ranked high school kids in the entire city. He'd been awarded a ceremonial saber.

"I just don't understand why you'd give someone else agency over your life," Shiloh said. "Why you'd let them *use* you."

"Someone has to do it."

"Do what?"

"Serve."

*Serve. Oh my god.* She hated that word. She hated that way of thinking about it. Why should Cary *serve* anyone, why would he *want* to? "I mean, one," she said, "I question the truth of that. That someone *has* to do it. And, two, it doesn't have to be *you*."

"Are you suggesting that we don't need a standing military?"

Shiloh didn't know the difference between a standing and a sitting military, but yeah, she figured the whole world would be a lot better off without American boots on the ground. "I'm suggesting that we don't need to devote so much of our money and blood into dominating the world by force."

"Okay, John Lennon."

"I'm not being John Lennon."

"It just seems like, all you are saying is give peace a chance."

"I'm not John Lennon. John Lennon beat his wife."

"That wasn't very peaceful of him . . ."

"What I'm *saying*," Shiloh said, "is that we have a military so that we can kill people who disagree with us. And I don't understand why you want to be a *part* of that. You could *kill* people, Cary. You're going to work on a submarine with nuclear weapons. Nuclear weapons are an *atrocity*."

"The goal is to never use them."

"So we spend jillions of dollars on missiles, hoping we don't have to use them?"

"Yes."

"That's crazy."

"You don't know what you're talking about."

"I know that I don't want you to kill people!"

Cary stopped walking. Shiloh didn't want him to stop. They were about to cross Thirtieth Street, and there wasn't a traffic light, and they needed to focus and then make a run for it.

"Wouldn't you rather it be me?" he asked. His eyebrows were bunched over his yellow-brown eyes. "When you think about those submarines, and the bombers, and the machine guns . . . wouldn't you rather know that there was someone like me there, someone you trust?"

"*No.* I don't want you anywhere near there!" Just thinking about it made Shiloh feel out of breath. "If the military has to exist, if we're stuck with this situation, let someone else corrupt their soul."

"You really think it's going to corrupt my soul?"

"You really think that killing babies *won't* corrupt your soul?"

"I'm not killing *babies*!"

"There are no baby-free *bombs*. Bombs don't *discriminate*."

They were standing by the 7-Eleven on Thirtieth Street. And Cary was wearing his Beetle Bailey uniform and carrying his fifty-pound backpack. And Shiloh was wearing a vintage dress, something a big-boned housewife had worn in 1952, over long-underwear bottoms. And Shiloh was shouting, and Cary was *practically* shouting back, "I just don't understand who you think should protect this country! Whose responsibility it is!"

"Not yours!"

"If not me, *who*?"

"I don't actually care!"

Cary shook his head, and then he walked into traffic.

"Cary!" Shiloh screamed.

The street was four lanes wide, and he crossed them one at a time. People honked at him, and he ignored them. When he got to the other side, he kept walking.

It took forever for a break in traffic. Cary was long gone by the time Shiloh got across.

# SEVEN

"SO YOU'RE MIKE'S FRIEND FROM the Army?" Mikey's uncle was very chatty.

"From the Navy." Cary was very polite.

"What's that?" Mikey's aunt asked. "This music is so loud I can't hear myself think."

"I can't hear myself *eat*," the uncle said.

"The Navy!" Cary shouted.

"Well, we thank you for your service!"

"Thank you!" Cary glanced at Shiloh. He looked self-conscious.

"Does that happen to you all the time?" she asked, under the music. She was cutting her chicken. "Complete strangers just follow you around thanking you for your service?"

"You're just jealous that no one thanks you for your service."

"Your mom thanked me for my service last night."

Cary snorted, and then started to cough.

Shiloh touched his arm. "Are you choking?"

He shook his head and swallowed. "It's just lettuce."

"So you *are* choking?"

He shook his head again and reached for his water.

Shiloh watched him. She watched him too carefully. She was glad they were at this table in the corner of the room where no one would notice how wide her eyes were and how focused she was on him.

Up close, Cary still looked fresher-from-the-box than anyone else here. Maybe it was the sea air. Maybe it was not having kids.

They were both sitting a little sideways in their chairs, facing each other. He was heavier than she ever imagined he'd be. Not heavy, really. But there was no more rope and wire to him. There was a softness in Cary's cheeks now and around his pointy chin.

Shiloh felt like she was combing his face and body for changes, like her eyes were hands. Or maybe she *wasn't* looking for changes—maybe she was trying to find all the ways that he was the same. All the ways she recognized him. The ways he was still Cary.

Shiloh was fiddling with a napkin. Cary looked like he was trying to think of something to say. Shiloh should beat him to it—she should try to keep it light.

"How did you all meet Michael?" the aunt called across the table.

Cary turned toward her. "We went to high school together."

"You went to North?" the uncle asked.

"That's right." Cary looked down at his plate and picked up his fork.

"Mike went off to art school," the man said.

Cary nodded and started eating his chicken. Shiloh turned to her own plate.

"Have you all seen his art?"

"Yep," Cary said, "good stuff."

They'd seen Mikey's art. They'd seen it at the beginning, and they'd seen how it had evolved over the years. It was very abstract. Shiloh could never decide if she liked it—she could never decide if she *got* it. She could honestly never decide whether there was something there to get. But sometimes Mikey's art made her feel almost desperately sad. So it must be as good as the people in New York City and Tokyo and Phoenix, Arizona, said it was.

Mikey's first wife had been someone from that world. The art world. But now he was marrying a North Omaha girl and celebrating at a youth wrestling banquet hall. Shiloh felt like this was another Mikey project she didn't quite get.

"And how long have you two been married?" the aunt asked Cary.

"Oh," he said. "We . . ."

"We're not married," Shiloh said. "Just old friends."

"How long have *you* been married?" Cary asked politely.

"We're not married!" The woman was aghast. "That's my brother!"

"Oh, I'm sorry," Cary said. "I shouldn't—"

"We're not even wearing rings!" she protested. She was embarrassed. So was Cary.

"I mean, neither are we," Shiloh said, knowing only Cary would hear her. She nudged him with her elbow. "You could still move to the head table. Everybody up there is drinking champagne."

"I'll go if you go with me. We'll pull up a chair."

She shook her head. "So when did you get into town?"

"Today, actually. I missed the rehearsal dinner last night."

"How was the wedding ceremony?"

"Good," Cary said. "Standard. Walk down the aisle, stand at attention. Don't lock your knees."

Shiloh grinned. "I meant—how was it, in general. Not for you personally."

"Oh." He smiled. "Still good. Standard. Catholic."

"Was Mikey nervous?"

Cary looked thoughtful. "I don't know that I've *ever* seen Mikey nervous . . ."

"Me neither. Hey"—she leaned toward him—"do *you* remember Janine from high school?"

"Yeah. Mikey dated her senior year."

Shiloh smacked Cary's arm. "I didn't know Mikey dated someone senior year!"

He shrugged. "They were pretty quiet about it. Her parents were religious."

Shiloh was still shocked. "I can't believe he never *told* me—we were best friends!"

"I think *I* was his best friend . . ." Cary was being a shit.

"I meant the three of us."

Cary chewed a bite of chicken. He shrugged, still teasing.

"You guys never talked to me about girl stuff," Shiloh said, not managing to keep it light.

Cary'd had a secret girlfriend, too. Or at least a girlfriend that he never mentioned to Shiloh.

One day she was working on the ROTC section of the yearbook, sorting through photos of the military ball—and there was Cary, standing tall in his dress uniform next to some chubby girl in a shiny formal. Apparently the girl lived in their neighborhood. She went to parochial school. Her name was Angie.

To this day, Shiloh didn't know when Cary had started dating Angie. Only that they'd broken up sometime before graduation.

Shiloh had started to cry when she saw the photo—the *photos*, there were a dozen of them.

It wasn't because Cary had a girlfriend. (He was allowed to have a girlfriend.)

It was that he hadn't *told* her. It was that *nobody* had told her. Mikey obviously knew—he was the photographer.

When she'd stopped crying, Shiloh chose the nicest shot, where Cary's date looked the prettiest, and made it the biggest photo on the yearbook page. Cary was their school's commanding officer, and he'd gotten some award at the military ball. It made sense to feature him.

Shiloh hadn't dated anyone during high school—but she wouldn't have kept it a secret from Cary and Mikey if she had.

Cary cleared his throat. "So, you do what at the theater now?"

"I run the educational department," Shiloh said. Still thinking about Janine and Angie. "We offer classes—acting, playwriting."

"And do you act?"

"No," she said, like that was a silly question. Like she didn't have a master's degree in theater. "I mean, sometimes, in emergencies. We have a main stage with professional actors."

Cary was nodding a little too quickly. As if he were acknowledging twice as many things as Shiloh was saying.

"I don't even teach much anymore," she said. "It's a lot of bureaucracy. I sit at a desk all day." That wasn't exactly true, but Shiloh felt like she needed to make *explicitly* clear to him that she was nothing he had ever expected her to be.

If Cary was combing Shiloh for sames and differents, he should see that she was *wholly* different. That her final form was nothing like her larval stage. And not in the good, butterfly way.

"You live out west?" he asked.

"I used to live out west." In the suburbs they grew up hating. "I live here now. I mean, in the neighborhood—with my mom, actually." Shiloh tried not to wince as she said this.

Cary looked genuinely surprised.

It took all of Shiloh's strength not to bow her head. She smiled. "In the same old house."

Cary looked bewildered. "By the park?"

"By the park."

When Shiloh and Ryan had separated, they couldn't afford to keep their house out west—Ryan was a high school drama teacher—and their home equity didn't amount to anything once it was split between them.

Shiloh's mom had been wanting to work fewer hours, but she was already struggling to pay her mortgage. It made sense for her and Shiloh to pool their resources.

So now Shiloh's kids were living in the same old crappy house where Shiloh had grown up. She'd tried to make it *less* crappy . . . (Another mortgage. They'd gutted the kitchen. Added a bathroom to her mom's room. Replaced some of the wiring.) But it was still the same house. The same neighborhood.

Shiloh was the same in all the ways she was supposed to be different. (And vice versa. Vice, vice versa.) And Cary might be the only person on earth, other than Shiloh, who could fully appreciate what a disappointment she was.

Because Cary had sat outside that very house with her while they plotted their mutually exclusive ways out.

*Look at me,* Shiloh thought now. *Really look at me.*

*I've been thinking about seeing you for months. Now look at me, see me. Get this over with.*

"So, you're—" Cary was frowning at her. "I mean, I heard that, um—"

"Heyyy, everybody." Someone was standing at the microphone on the dance floor. Mikey's little brother, Bobby. "Whazzuuuhhp."

He was holding a mixed drink in one hand and bracing himself against the mic stand with the other. It tilted.

"Whaaaazzzzzzuuuuuhhp," he said again, at greater length. A few people hooted. "I'm here to talk about my main man, my tin-can Sam, my . . ." The mic stand tilted the other way.

Mikey had stood up at the head table. He was looking at Cary. Cary was already on his feet, headed for the dance floor.

Bobby greeted Cary with open arms. "Carrrryyyy. Whazzzzuuuhp. I missed you, bud."

Cary wrapped an arm around Bobby's waist, propping him up. Cary was saying something too softly for anyone else to hear.

"Thasssright," Bobby said. His eyes were closed. "Thass*right*. We're here to talk about *Mikey*."

Cary gently took the microphone away. "We're here," he said, "um, both of us—all of us—to celebrate Mike and Janine as they make this commitment to each other . . .

"I was going to say 'as they begin their life together,' but—" Cary turned to the head table, where Mikey was still standing, his hand now resting on Janine's shoulder. Cary smiled. "I think that the love they share began a long time ago. So instead I'll say that we're here to honor their commitment and the promises they made today."

Shiloh winced a little. Of course Cary would get hung up on the *sacred honor* of it all. He'd always loved an oath.

"Janine . . ." Cary went on, in a clear, serious voice. "I've known Mike since I was twelve years old, and he's always been the guy who makes everyone else feel lighter."

"You are *correct,* Cary," Bobby chipped in.

"I think we all wanted to be around Mikey," Cary said, "because he brought the sun with him."

The whole audience was humming in agreement.

"But you're the bright spot in Mike's sky. You're the one who makes *him* feel lighter."

More humming. Bobby was nodding deeply.

"So thank you, Janine," Cary said, "from all of us who have stood in Mike's light, for bringing him so much joy."

Bobby held his glass in the air.

"And, Mikey," Cary continued. "You know I've never been married. I can't imagine the gravity of this day . . ."

Shiloh could practically *hear* every unattached woman in the room rev her engine.

"But I'm just so happy for you. And proud of you. You're the best friend I've ever had, and I'm honored to share this day with you. We all are. To Janine and Mike!"

"To them!" Bobby agreed, sloshing his glass in the air.

One of the bridesmaids ran onto the dance floor to hand Cary a flute of champagne. He held it aloft.

"Cheers!" Cary said.

"Cheers!" everyone answered.

"Cheers," Shiloh murmured. She held up her Diet Pepsi.

Mikey was making his way to the dance floor. He gave Cary a bear hug when he got there.

Shiloh had never felt so far away from another human being. From two human beings. Mikey and Cary, best friends. Still best friends. Always best friends. How did Shiloh fit into any of this?

Tangentially. That's how.

She wondered how her kids were doing. Ryan had promised to make popcorn tonight and let them watch *Hercules*. They were both obsessed with the Disney *Hercules* movie for some reason.

If Shiloh left now, she could possibly get fifteen hours of sleep before Ryan brought the kids back in the morning . . .

Or she could go hang out with Tom, her assistant and deskmate at the theater. He'd invited her over to watch this week's *Sopranos* . . .

Or Shiloh could stay here. She could drag a chair over to her old friends' table and try to catch up with everyone . . .

Was there any point in catching up if she was just going to lose them again?

If Shiloh had learned anything about herself, it was that she couldn't hold on to people. She could only really deal with the people directly in front of her. Her children. Her mom. Her boss. Her assistant. The teachers who worked for her. The kids in the theater programs. Their parents. The board . . . Christ, that was already too many.

The maid of honor was at the mic now, toasting Janine. She was telling a raunchy story about their trip to Mexico. Shiloh felt sorry for her. There was no good way to follow Cary. He was a forensics champion. He'd played Scrooge in their senior-year production of *A Christmas Carol* with a flawless English accent. (Shiloh had played the Ghost of Christmas Present, with a wreath of holly and icicles.)

Shiloh lifted her glass again when everyone else did. "Cheers!"

There hadn't been toasts at Shiloh's wedding. She hadn't wanted to do anything traditional.

She and Ryan got married in the university theater, just before Shiloh graduated from college. Shiloh had worn a dress from the costume shop. (Lady Macbeth's—was that bad luck? It was the only pretty dress in the shop that had fit her.)

It was a small wedding. Mikey had flown back for it.

Apparently the toasts were over. Mikey and Janine were going to cut the cake now. Cary was still standing near the dance floor, talking to Bobby.

All the little kids had gathered around the cake table, with the photographer.

Shiloh hadn't had a professional photographer at her wedding. Or a cake. What had they had instead? She couldn't remember . . .

No, wait—fancy cream puffs. They'd spent all their money on up-scale Lithuanian food and a band.

It wasn't so bad. As weddings go.

Ryan had also worn something from the costume shop—one of the Lost Boy costumes from *Peter Pan*. There was a photo of the two of them dancing at the reception. Ryan's mother had taken it. Ryan was wearing fox ears, and Shiloh was displaying a shocking amount of cleavage.

"I'm not going to make you keep your promise," Mikey's uncle said.

Shiloh looked over at him. "I'm sorry?"

"You can eat your cake."

One of the caterers was standing there with a trolley of cake slices.

"There are six people sitting at this table," the uncle told the waitress. (There were not.)

"No," Shiloh said to him, "I am honoring my commitment. The cake is all yours."

She got up and headed for her original table. She looked around for Cary. He was standing in a crowd at the bar. She recognized his stiff shoulders, the way he held his head. She'd wanted to see him tonight, and she'd seen him. She'd wanted to know if he was still himself, and he was.

"Shiloh!" everyone at her assigned table called.

She'd give herself an hour of reminiscing and catching up. That would still leave plenty of time to sleep.

# before

THE DARKROOM WAS SET OFF from the journalism room by a revolving door. You stepped through the doorway, then spun the opening around to the other side and walked out into a closetlike room.

There was only space for two or three people back there, and one of them was always Mikey. The other two were usually Cary and Shiloh.

Today when Shiloh spun the door around, the red lights were on, which meant that Mikey was developing something. Probably something totally unrelated to school.

He was leaning over the chemical bath, prodding at a photo with plastic tongs. Cary was sitting on a stool, working on homework. Shiloh climbed onto the stool next to Cary's and poked him with a pencil.

He smacked her pencil away.

She leaned over his notebook to see what he was writing. Math. His handwriting was cramped and square.

"It's time for lunch," she said.

"Lunch," Mikey said. "We need to buy prom tickets at lunch. Today's the last day."

"Who are you going to prom with?"

Mikey looked up. "The two of you."

Cary kept working on his homework.

Shiloh frowned at Mikey. "Haven't you asked someone?"

"Nah." He jiggled the tray of chemicals. "Cary, have you asked anyone?"

Cary shook his head. He was graphing sine waves.

"Let's just go," Mikey said. "We can't miss prom."

"I have so far," Shiloh said.

"Well, shit, Shiloh, now you *really* have to go." Mikey swished the tray. "Don't be one of those sad nerds who goes to alternative proms in their thirties, trying to fill the void."

She folded her arms. "I'm pretty sure that'll be the least of my voids."

"I got a white tuxedo at the thrift shop," he said. "I'm gonna decorate it."

"God be with you," Shiloh said. "I don't have a white tux. Or fifteen dollars to spend on a prom ticket."

"I've got you," Cary said.

"Cary's got you," Mikey echoed.

Shiloh grimaced. "I don't know . . . Don't you have to wear a big dress to prom? Like a crocheted-Barbie-Kleenex-box-cover dress?"

"Wear whatever you want," Cary said. "You always do anyway."

Shiloh wanted to wear some great vintage thrift-shop dress. She wanted to be the heroine of a John Hughes movie. Or maybe a John Waters movie.

But the fancy dresses at the thrift shop near her house were never more than a few years old. Glossy satin *gowns,* with big puffed sleeves and lace cutouts.

The week before prom, Shiloh's mom took pity on her and took her to a discount department store called Richman Gordman. Shiloh ended up with a stretchy blue wrap dress that looked more like something a forty-year-old divorcée would wear to a fern bar than something a high school girl would wear to prom. It was the only thing that fit Shiloh and also fit their budget.

Shiloh wasn't fat, exactly, but she was bigger than other girls her age—she was already *built* like a forty-year-old divorcée. At eighteen, she looked like someone who looked really good for having had three kids.

Plus she was too tall. Five foot eleven. Almost as tall as Cary.

"It'll be fine," her mom said. "We'll pin a silk flower on the chest, and you can wear my boots."

Her mom had a pair of calf-length, maroon suede boots with a wedge heel. They were *literally* something a middle-aged lady wore to bars. But they were still cool, and her mom had never let Shiloh borrow them before.

The night of the dance, Shiloh's mom did her makeup for her and rolled the front of her dark hair into one of those 1940s whorls. Shiloh's hair was long and heavy. It took a whole sheet of bobby pins and half a can of Aqua Net to wrangle it.

The overall effect was better than Shiloh had hoped. She admired herself in the hall mirror while she waited for Cary to pick her up. The dress and the boots and the hair didn't really *match,* but they were making a ragtag go of it. Shiloh had stacked her wrists with fake gold bangles, and her mom had pinned a silk calla lily to the front of the dress—she was right, it did help. Then she'd painted Shiloh's lips bright red. Shiloh had a tube of red lipstick in her purse to touch it up later.

Shiloh wasn't sure that she looked *attractive* like this . . . But she looked different. Different from herself and different from everyone else. That was the most important thing—Shiloh would shave her head just to look like nobody else. (Shiloh *might* shave her head when she got to college. She was still deciding. She needed to get there and scope out the shaved-head situation.)

She heard the front door open.

"Hey, Cary, you look nice."

"Thanks, Gloria." (Her mom made Cary call her "Gloria." He hated it, but it would be rude to call her "Mrs. Butler" if that wasn't what she wanted to be called.) "I wasn't sure whether Shiloh saw that we were here."

"You should have honked," Shiloh said, coming down the stairs.

"Slow down," her mom said to her. "You'll break your neck."

"I don't like to honk," Cary said, looking up at Shiloh. His eyes shifted, surprised. Shiloh couldn't read his expression—but she was happy to register with him.

Cary was wearing a black tux with a red cummerbund. Apparently all the guys rented tuxes for prom; you couldn't just wear a suit. (Well, you *could,* but Cary respected conventions.) His tux was too wide in the shoulders, and it was still polyester—but it looked way better than his ROTC uniform.

"Hang on," Shiloh's mom said, looking around the living room. "I'll get you money for dinner."

They were going to Kowloon, a sit-down Chinese place. Entrees were $7.95 and you got two crab rangoons plus egg drop soup.

"I've got it," Cary said.

"Save your money, Cary."

"You save your money, Gloria. I've got it."

"He's got it, Mom. See you later." Shiloh hugged her mom from the side, then pushed Cary out onto the enclosed porch. It was dark—the porch light was burned out. She closed the front door behind them.

"Hey, wait," Cary said. He caught Shiloh's wrist before she could walk past him down the steps.

She turned back to him. Thanks to her boots, she was a little bit taller than he was.

"I got you this," Cary said, holding up a plastic clamshell. "But I guess you already have a flower."

Shiloh squinted down at the box. There were flowers in it. A corsage.

"Oh god," she said, "was I supposed to get you a flower? And Mikey?"

"We don't need flowers," he said. "But we thought—I thought, well, girls always have them at prom."

"Then let's do it," she said. "Thank you."

Cary shook his head. He seemed upset. "No. Your flower looks better. You look good." He glanced down at her, then up again. "You look like a time traveler."

Shiloh reached for the corsage. Cary pulled the box away—"*Shiloh.*" She caught it anyway and tugged it out of his hand.

She cracked the lid open. It was a little bouquet with three white carnations and baby's breath, tied with a blue ribbon.

"Your flower is nicer," Cary said again.

He was right.

"My flower is fake," Shiloh said. "Hold this." She handed him the box and started unpinning her lily. She had to be careful—her mom had used two sewing pins.

Cary watched her. He handed her the corsage when she was ready for it.

It was hard to pin something onto your own chest. The corsage came with a long pearl-ended pin, and you had to get it just right . . . Shiloh stuck her finger and swore.

"Here," Cary said. "Let me." He took the carnations from her, and the pin, and leaned closer.

"I guess you've done this before," Shiloh said, thinking of the photo of Cary and Angie, and remembering the corsage on Angie's sleeveless gown.

"It would be easier with a light," Cary said. His head was bent in front of her face.

"Your hair smells like apples," she said. More quietly than she meant to.

"Hmm," he said, acknowledging her in his usual begrudging way.

Shiloh had been teasing Cary much less since she found out that he had a girlfriend. Not that the teasing would be *inappropriate* now . . . or *disallowed* . . .

But Shiloh had always felt like Cary was sort of her territory. The teasing had been part of their whole thing. The Shiloh-and-Cary of it all.

It was different now—pulling his hair, poking him, leaning on him—knowing that he was very officially someone *else's* territory. Someone who had *intentions.*

Shiloh didn't have intentions.

"There," Cary said, standing up. The corsage was pinned neatly to Shiloh's dress.

"Wait," she said, before he could back away.

Shiloh had slipped the silk calla lily into her purse. She pulled it back out now, un-squashing it, and reached for Cary's chest. "Does this go on your collar? Or to the side?"

He tucked his chin down to see what she was doing. "Oh. You don't have to—"

"I want to. Do you not want me to?"

He lowered an eyebrow at her. "Do you *care* whether I want you to?"

She let her hand drop. She shrugged. "I mean . . . yeah."

"On the lapel," he said. "Just below the bow tie but above the pocket."

"Which side?"

"Over the heart."

Shiloh reached up to her left.

"My other heart."

"Right." She smiled and shifted the flower over. It took her a second to get it attached. Cary kept his head bent to watch, probably worried she'd stab him. His hair was in her face again. "You still smell like apples."

"Hmm."

"Where do you put the flower when you're wearing all your ROTC medals?"

"No boutonnieres in uniform."

Shiloh nodded. She twisted the last pin back through his collar. *There.* The lily was a little bit crooked, but it looked good . . . It looked *really* good, actually. It classed up the tux.

She patted the flower gently. "Nice."

Cary stepped away from her then. He opened the porch door for her, and Shiloh started down the steps.

"Don't break your neck," he said, taking her arm.

"I'm fine. Don't I look fine?"

"You're walking like the Tin Man before Dorothy oils him."

"I'm *fine*," she said, letting him steady her.

They made it to the bottom of her steps, and Mikey got out of the car. "Hey, Shiloh, you look like somebody from *Blade Runner*."

"Thanks," she said. "You look . . ." Mikey had decorated his white suit with a black marker. He'd drawn bodies. Faces. Political slogans. "Like a wall in Keith Haring's neighborhood."

"I try."

Mikey was waiting to let Shiloh in first, so that she could sit in the middle, like usual, but she pushed him toward the car. "I'm in a dress," she said, like that mattered.

Mikey got in without complaining, and Shiloh got in, too, smushing him against Cary. "Huh," Mikey said to Cary. "You really do smell as good as Shiloh's always saying."

Cary just frowned at him.


Kowloon was full of other prom kids. Half the schools in the city had prom that night. Everyone else had come in pairs.

For Shiloh, it was just like any other night out with Mikey and Cary. Talking about movies. Talking about people at school. Egging each other on. Coming up with schemes.

The three of them were always planning something—the more absurd, the better. They'd spend hours imagining a scheme, building on it, trying to make each other laugh.

*They should run for class officers on a communist platform. They should come to school wearing matching skirts. They should sneak Dead Kennedys lyrics into newspaper editorials.*

At some point in the scheming, Cary and Shiloh would start to worry that Mikey was serious, and they'd try talking him down.

Sometimes he *was* serious.

Sometimes the three of them ended up executing one of their

schemes—Mikey, gleefully; Cary, conflicted; and Shiloh, desperately afraid of being embarrassed or getting caught.

*This* was a scheme, wasn't it? Going to prom together, without dates, dressed like they were from three different planets?

Shiloh was a little worried that Mikey might have something more planned for the prom itself—like, the Mikey version of spiking the punch. Getting the deejay to play klezmer music or unfurling a banner across the dance floor that said, *No blood for oil.* You just never fucking knew with him.

But once they got to the dance, Mikey did something even more surprising—he danced. He abandoned Cary and Shiloh as soon as they got through the door.

Shiloh had been expecting the prom to look like something out of a movie. The theme was "Under the Sea," just like in *Back to the Future.*

But the dance was in a hotel conference center, and the only signs of marine life were some seahorse-shaped balloons in the lobby.

Shiloh and Cary walked through a wall of blue streamers into the ballroom.

Shiloh was disoriented for a second. The room was dark. The music was loud. There were tables along one wall, but nearly everyone was dancing. Shiloh's ankles buckled. She started moving toward an empty table and collapsed onto a plastic chair.

Cary stood over her. "There's supposed to be punch," he said. "You want some?"

She shrugged.

He wandered away, punch-ward, and Shiloh looked out on the dance floor. It was too dark to really recognize anyone. Mikey stood out in his white suit, but everyone else blurred together.

Cary came back with two cans of Pepsi—"I guess they were worried about people spiking the punch"—and sat down next to her.

"We missed the golden age of punch," Shiloh said.

"When was that, the 1700s?"

"I was thinking the fifties."

"You over-romanticize the fifties," Cary said. Matter-of-factly.

Shiloh thought again about the vintage prom dress she would never find at a thrift shop. The wasplike waist she'd never have, anyway.

"Women in the fifties weren't allowed to open checking accounts," Cary said, like he could hear her dreaming.

"My mom doesn't have a checking account," Shiloh said. "She cashes her check at the grocery store and pays all our bills with money orders."

Cary watched her for a second over his Pepsi can. Then he turned his whole body toward the dance floor. Shiloh turned, too, kicking her feet up onto the chair next to her.

"Did you want to dance?" he asked.

Shiloh didn't even bother answering him, just threw him a face that he didn't bother acknowledging.

What a joke. Shiloh wasn't going to *dance*. First of all, she didn't know how—she couldn't even do choreographed dances, like the kind you learn at slumber parties. And second, she didn't *want* to know how. Dancing was stupid. The proof of that was right in front of them.

Cary sat with his hands in his pockets. He was antsy.

"*You* can dance," she said. Was that what he wanted?

Cary shrugged.

He probably wanted to dance with his girlfriend. Why hadn't he brought her?

A school dance is interminable when you aren't dancing.

Shiloh sat at the table with Cary. Some friends stopped by and asked her to watch their purses.

A boy from drama club sat with them for a while. He was on crutches—his date was dancing without him. After a few songs, he hobbled onto the dance floor anyway. Bouncing on one foot. Clinging to his crutches.

It was too loud for Shiloh and Cary to talk much. Every time the song changed, Shiloh would announce whether or not she liked it.

She wished that Cary was sitting closer. She wished she could amuse herself by pulling on his jacket or kicking the backs of his heels.

There weren't many slow dances. When "Open Arms" came on, Shiloh said, "I know Journey is a hessian band, but I love this song."

Hessians were kids with long hair who wore black T-shirts and smoked in bathrooms. Most of the other white kids at their school were hessians. Or hessian-adjacent.

"Journey isn't a hessian band," Cary said.

Shiloh leaned toward him to argue, but Becky, from journalism class, had just run up to their table. She was out of breath from dancing. "Cary, come dance—I need a partner!"

You couldn't slow-dance by yourself; even Shiloh knew that.

"I don't think so," he said.

"Cary, come on—*please*." Becky looked cute. She had on a slick purple dress with a ruffle over one shoulder. She'd taken off her shoes and was wearing little socks with pom-poms over her pantyhose.

"Go ahead," Shiloh said. "I'll be fine."

Cary frowned at Shiloh. "I don't need to dance."

"Yeah, but you don't mind." She'd seen pictures of him dancing. "Just go."

Cary sighed.

He got up and took Becky's hand, then walked with her onto the dance floor.

It was so weird the way people acted at dances . . .

Cary would never just *touch* Becky under normal circumstances. But now he had his arm around her waist, and he was looking in her eyes . . . It was *unbearably* intimate, all of this—how could they even *do* it? How could they *playact* love and intimacy? They were only holding each other because that's what you *do* at a dance. It didn't mean anything, they were just going along with the ritual. Shiloh hated it—she *hated* it. She couldn't even watch.

Sometimes Shiloh thought that she and Cary were the same, that they agreed on all the important things—but that was obviously not true. Because there was Cary with his arms around a girl he didn't even *like* in that way. Holding her close, even though he had a girlfriend. (Didn't he still have a girlfriend?)

The song ended, but Becky kept Cary out on the floor. She and another girl, another friend of theirs, were dancing around him.

Shiloh couldn't watch Cary slow-dance—and she *really* couldn't watch him fast-dance. She looked away. She was embarrassed.

After two songs, she was bored.

A little while after that, Cary dropped back into the seat next to her. He'd taken off his jacket and laid it over a chair. His face was flushed.

"Sorry," he said.

"It's fine. Keep dancing. You should be having the full senior-prom experience."

"And you shouldn't?"

"No, I am." Shiloh stretched her hand over her chest. "I'm having my *own* version. Classic wallflower scenario."

"I asked you to dance—you're not a wallflower."

She held up a finger. "I'm an intentional wallflower. I choose this adventure."

Cary blew air through his teeth. He didn't go back to dancing. "We could leave—"

"Yeah?" Shiloh sat up.

"—but I'm Mikey's ride."

She slumped back. "Right."

Shiloh was so relieved when the deejay finally announced the last dance. It was "End of the Road" by Boyz II Men.

Cary turned to her. He looked unhappy. "Will you please dance with me?"

"Why?"

"Because this is our senior prom," he said, "and the whole point of *being* here is to have this experience."

"What experience?"

"*This.*" He looked frustrated. "You get dressed up, you come to the dance, you *dance.*"

"It's just a ritual," she said.

He nodded. "Yes. Rituals are all we have."

"Speak for yourself, Cadet Colonel."

Cary pulled his pointy chin into his neck. "How did you know I'm a colonel?"

Shiloh folded her arms. "I read our school newspaper. I'm the editor."

Cary huffed. He sat back in his seat, away from her. "I should have known you'd be like this."

She glanced at him. "Like what?"

He didn't glance back. "Stubborn. Miserable."

"*I'm* not miserable."

He huffed again. "When I saw you, at your house, I thought *maybe* you were actually going to allow yourself this."

"I'm allowing! I'm here!"

Cary rolled his eyes.

Shiloh waved her hand out at the dance floor. "Everyone else here is dancing. You could be *with* them. Nothing is stopping you."

"That's why you don't want to dance, right?" He'd turned on her. His brown eyes were narrow. "Because everyone else is? It must *kill* you to have to drink water and breathe air, just like the rest of us."

Shiloh clenched her jaw. "I feel like you're being really unfair right now."

"Yeah, maybe." Cary shook his head. "This is our senior prom."

"You keep saying that."

"It's a *ritual*—"

"To manufacture sentiment," she said.

"No, Shiloh. To allow us an outlet for *actual* sentiment. We're all here to say goodbye."

"Hence the Boyz II Men."

"Yeah, *hence.*" He shook his head. Then he shook his head again.

His tongue was in his cheek—that seemed like a bad sign. (The phrase "tongue in cheek" should really mean "pissed off and thinking something hurtful.")

Cary shook his head some more. "We could have had a good time. Tonight. It could have been a memory."

All of a sudden, Shiloh could see it—the night they could have had, if she didn't care so much about making a fool of herself...

If she could have stepped over some internal threshold...

Out on the dance floor with Cary and Mikey. Holding on to Cary's shoulder for balance. Maybe taking off her boots. Dancing like a broken robot. Being silly to mask the fact that she couldn't be sexy or smooth. Slow-dancing with Cary—because that's what friends do at dances, right? They put their arms around each other. They stare into each other's eyes.

None of that was going to happen now. This was the last dance. End of the road.

Cary was angry. He was the kind of angry that sometimes led to him just walking away from her. Leaving. But he wouldn't leave her *and* Mikey stranded there, so he was stuck.

Here came Mikey now, running toward them. He caught himself on the edge of their table. "Shiloh, get up, come on!"

"Are you ready to go?"

"No, it's the last dance, and you have to get out there, or you won't have broken the spell. This whole night will have been for naught."

"What spell?"

"Cary and I swore we wouldn't let you be one of those horrible bores who think they're too fucking cool for high school. One of those girls who ends up with a beehive, in a punk band."

"I love those bands. You love those bands."

"Just get up, come on."

Shiloh turned to Cary. He still looked pissed. She stood up. She stumbled toward Mikey. She was three inches taller than him, even without the heels.

Mikey took her by the hand. They'd never held hands before. It was mostly painless.

Dancing wasn't.

Mikey put his arm around her. He smiled.

Shiloh couldn't move her legs. She really, honestly didn't know what to do with them. And she didn't like standing this close to Mikey.

Her cheeks felt hot.

There were tears in her eyes.

"Oh god," Mikey said, face fallen. "You *really* didn't want to do this."

She shook her head.

"I thought you just needed a big push to get over yourself."

She shrugged. It was impossible for Shiloh to imagine ever getting over herself.

"Yeah, okay," Mikey said, pulling away from her. "Let's just go."

# NINE

"IS CARY MARRIED?"

"I heard he was engaged."

"Shiloh would know."

"No—I don't know."

"You were just talking to him."

"Not about that, I guess."

"You guys don't keep in touch? That's hard to believe."

"You know how I am. I don't talk to anybody."

"I have poked you so many times on Facebook, Shiloh . . ."

"I'm not really there often enough to be poked."

"Why are you poking Shiloh, Becky? That's like making a pass."

"It's not a pass—it's a poke."

"Who says 'making a pass' in 2006?"

"Hey, it's 2006! Shouldn't we be hearing about our fifteen-year reunion? We never even had our ten."

"I heard we're not having reunions anymore. Tammy moved to Michigan."

"So? It's still her job to organize reunions. It's her only job."

"This is what happens when you vote for the *hot* one and not the *diligent* one."

"Let it go, Sylvia. You were never going to be class president."

"If I was, we'd be having a reunion this summer."

"You can still organize the reunion."

"Hell yeah—do it, Sylvia!"

"Well, that's not fair. All the work, none of the glory."

"Maybe we could have Tammy impeached?"

"Great idea, Shiloh. Sylvia, organize Tammy's impeachment."

"I can believe you'd lose track of the rest of us, Shiloh . . . but you and Cary?"

"When did you guys break up?"

"I never dated Cary."

"Really?"

"That's not right—is that right?"

"Yes, it's right. I would know who I was dating."

"Yeah, but he put up with *so much* of your shit."

"What shit, Ronny?"

"You know, general Shiloh shit. You were kind of high-maintenance."

"I wasn't high-maintenance. Was I high-maintenance?"

"No. Don't listen to him."

"Thank you, Sylvia."

"You maintained yourself. It was more like you demanded high maintenance from everybody else."

"I don't . . . Does that even make sense?"

"You were running 110 on a 220, Shiloh."

"Guys, don't be hurtful, let her be."

"It was a compliment."

"You got shit done, Shiloh. We were all scared of you."

"Not Cary, though."

"I always thought they were dating."

"They went to prom together."

"I can't believe Cary isn't married. He got kind of hot, right?"

"Tina!"

"That's what happens when you don't get married."

"Yeah, Cary still looks like a big Okie, but he's well preserved."

"Hey, Shiloh, don't look like that. We were just giving you shit."

"I know, I'm fine."

"You seem different now, anyway."

"Yeah, you seem calm."

"You smoke weed now, Shiloh?"

"No, I have two kids—I'm just tired."

"110 on a 220—you're probably burned out."

"We're all burned out."

"Not Cary, though, right? Look at him."

"Calm *down*, Tina."

"Not Mikey, either."

"Mikey's famous."

"Mikey's Mikey."

"I heard Mikey's first wedding cost thirty thousand dollars."

"I heard they served crab. I wish I could have gone. Shiloh went, right?"

"No, I didn't go."

"Really? I was sure you'd be there."

# before

THEY WERE SUPPOSED TO GO to a friend's house after prom. Somebody from journalism was having a party.

But Cary didn't want to go. And Shiloh wasn't going to go without Cary. She didn't feel like hustling another ride home. Among other things.

When they got to the party, Shiloh let Mikey out of the car.

"That's the last time I sit in the middle," he said, climbing out and stretching. "I'm a window-seat guy." He bumped his shoulder against Shiloh's. "Cut him some slack."

Shiloh made a face. *She* was the one who deserved some slack tonight. Where was her allotment of slack?

She got back into the car, worried that Cary might be thinking about driving away without her.

He didn't say anything on the drive home. Cary never talked just to keep things from getting awkward. If anything, he seemed fortified by silence. Shiloh played with the car radio, chattering to herself while she scrolled through the channels. "Gross, no . . . Oh. I like this song, but it's almost over . . . This'll do, I guess."

Cary didn't even pull into her driveway when he got there. Just stopped in front of the house and waited.

And waited.

Shiloh sat back in the passenger seat and looked out the window, up at her house. She felt heavy all of a sudden. Like she was made of concrete. Like she didn't have fully articulated joints.

She wasn't going *anywhere*.

If she got out of the car right now, that would be it, the end of the night—Cary would stay angry with her. He might still be mad when he picked her up for school on Monday.

*Why was Cary so angry?* Because Shiloh wouldn't dance? Because he'd been trying to do something nice for her? Even though she didn't *want* it?

He'd called her stubborn and miserable—well, he was right. That's exactly how Shiloh felt. Stubborn. Miserable. Immovable. She wasn't ever going to get out of this car. Cary was going to have to lean over and open the door, unbuckle Shiloh's seat belt, then shove her out into the street. Roll her right into the gutter.

There was no parking on the street in front of Shiloh's house. A car came up behind them and honked, then swung around. Some guy leaned out the passenger window to cuss at Cary.

Cary let up on the brake and drove around the block. Shiloh pretended she didn't notice. It was a long block. When they got back to her house, he pulled into her driveway and shifted into park. He left the engine running.

Shiloh didn't feel any lighter or more inclined to get out.

A song came on the radio that she hated. She contemplated changing it, but that would mean moving.

Cary knew she hated this song. He let it play out.

Shiloh shifted against the door. Her forehead hit the glass. She took a breath to say something, but didn't.

She waited. Then took another breath to say something, but couldn't.

She pressed her nose into the glass. "I'm not miserable," she mumbled.

"What?" Cary asked.

"I'm not miserable," she said, even more faintly.

He turned off the radio. "*What?*"

"I said—nobody's saying goodbye."

He turned off the car.

Shiloh kept her face against the glass. "I don't even know why you're mad."

Cary didn't say anything.

"I didn't mean to *ruin* your senior prom." Shiloh looked at him. He was staring up the driveway. His hands were still at ten and two. "You could have danced," she said. "You could have brought a date."

Cary nodded.

"Why didn't you?"

"Because I was going with you and Mikey."

"Yeah, but . . ." Shiloh blinked slowly, trying to keep her tear ducts in check. "But you have a girlfriend, right?"

"Yeah," Cary said quietly.

"So . . ."

"I already went to her prom."

"Oh," Shiloh whispered. "Was it cool?"

"It was fine. It was the same as ours."

"'Under the Sea?'"

"'Welcome to the Jungle.'"

Shiloh nodded. "You could have brought her to ours, too."

"I could have," Cary agreed.

"But?"

He sat back a little, settling. The seat creaked. "But nothing, really. Mikey wanted the three of us to go together."

Shiloh let her head rest against the glass again. "I didn't know it was *a whole thing*," she said.

"It wasn't a whole thing."

"I didn't know we were *making memories*."

He didn't answer.

"Can we listen to the radio?" Shiloh asked.

Cary turned it back on. He switched it over to the seventies light rock station—it was the only station they both liked.

She bounced her forehead against the window. "Aren't we always making memories?"

"No," Cary said. "The brain makes note of novelty. Broken patterns. The more we do the same things, the more they blend together."

Was that true?

How many nights had Shiloh sat in her driveway with Cary, listening to Lite 96? Too many nights to count. Or maybe too many to remember . . .

Was tonight just going to disappear into the rest of those nights? Sink into the fog of them?

Or would she remember tonight because it had been particularly awful?

She rolled her head back in Cary's direction. He had gel or something in his hair. It looked dark brown, not dark blond. And he'd shaved— she could tell because he had pimples along his jaw, not because his face was noticeably smoother. The silk lily had gotten flattened against his chest. Probably when he was dancing with Becky.

The idea that this moment was going to slip away from Shiloh— that it was just *flotsam*, temporally speaking—made it unbearable. She wanted to start something on fire just to make this moment, this night, stick.

What was the point of being alive if you couldn't hold on to the details?

"*I'm* always making memories," she said.

Cary rolled his eyes. "Your brain functions differently than every other human being's?"

"Yes." Shiloh said it with certainty.

He huffed out a small breath and shook his head.

Shiloh tried to tuck her left leg under her right. Her heel snagged on her pantyhose. She unzipped her boot and let it fall to the floor, then finished tucking her leg and sat back, turning a little toward Cary.

He was looking at her lap. "You couldn't walk in those boots."

She didn't argue.

"They looked good though," he said.

Shiloh pulled her bare foot deeper under her thigh.

Cary lifted his head up, almost to her face. "You looked good. In that." He turned back to the steering wheel, wincing. "You know, you looked . . . pretty."

"Well, then maybe you'll remember it," she said. "Because of the novelty."

He shook his head again.

"*Nobody's saying goodbye*," Shiloh repeated. More strenuously this time.

"That's what prom is," Cary shot back. "And honors night. Senior banquet, senior skip day. Graduation."

He was looking at her again. She was glad.

"Most of our classmates aren't even going anywhere," she said. "They don't have to say goodbye."

"*You're* going."

"I'm going to *Des Moines*," Shiloh said. "It's two hours away."

"And Mikey's going to Chicago. And I'm going—I don't even know where."

Shiloh didn't know what to say to that. It made her clench her fists. "Well, *I'm* not saying goodbye."

"Why not?"

"One, it's stupid. Because we're not, like, *done* with each other. Just because we've completed Nebraska's secondary-education requirements. And two, it's too early—I don't leave until August."

"Things still change, Shiloh, whether or not you participate in the rituals of transition."

She threw up her hands. "So you're just *done* with me? Because we're graduating?"

"I didn't say that."

"That's how it sounds."

Cary started to argue, but Shiloh cut him off—"We don't *have* to say goodbye. No one is *making* us."

"But we aren't going to see each other after this summer."

"So? And also—why not?"

"Because we'll be in different states?"

"Yeah, but—" Shiloh shook her head. She still felt like setting a fire. "We don't have to, like, take orders from time and space."

Cary laughed, genuinely. One loud bark. "Now you're immune to physics."

"People do what they want, Cary. We have free will."

He looked over at her, more amused now than annoyed. "Oh yeah?"

"*Yeah*," Shiloh said, heavy on the *h* sound, reaching her head forwards. "We could just . . . *keep* being friends."

"I can't even get phone calls in boot camp," he said. It came out sadder than Shiloh was expecting.

"I will write you letters," she swore.

Cary was looking down. His voice dropped. "I know you will."

"Furthermore," Shiloh said, "I have a very potent presence. Do you remember Mr. Kessler?"

Mr. Kessler was their ninth-grade English teacher. Cary nodded.

"He said a little of me goes a long way."

Cary snorted. His cheeks crinkled.

"So even though we aren't going to talk as often, it's still going to *feel* like you're getting *a lot* of me."

He peered up at her, lifting an eyebrow. "I'm just used to *so much* of you . . ."

"I get it," Shiloh said. "Your new friends might feel watered down in comparison."

"Mild," Cary said.

"Weak," she countered.

"Shiloh, I don't think you realize how much time we spend together now—"

"We're stocking up," she said, "to get through winter."

"—and how different it's going to be."

"It's a proverbial winter, Cary."

"Shiloh . . ." Cary said softly. Like he felt sorry for her. It was intolerable. She reached out and yanked on his collar—his head wobbled.

"Do you *want* to drift apart?" she demanded.

"No."

"Then don't. Be a man."

"A *man*?"

"Like, not a monkey," she said. "Use your man parts—your thumbs, and the region of your brain that processes written language. Make your own *decisions*, Cary. This is *America*."

Cary was laughing at her, with her. Softly. (She had him where she liked him.)

Shiloh moved her hand up and tugged on his hair. She pushed her fingers into the roots, trying to break up the gel.

"Ouch," he said, ducking his head away from her.

"Don't be done with me," she pleaded, poking his shoulder.

"I never said I was done with you. I was just trying to ground the conversation in facts."

"More like opinions," she said. "Assumptions." Shiloh made a fist in his sleeve. She chewed on her lip for a second. *"Don't be done with me,"* she said. Too intensely. *"Don't say goodbye."*

"All *right*." Cary was trying to twist his arm free. "Don't rip my tux."

"I'm not going to rip it."

"You marked up my jeans with permanent marker."

Shiloh *had* done that, she couldn't argue, but she wanted to argue anyway. She wanted to break something. She hung on to his sleeve.

"You don't have good boundaries," Cary said, like it was an observation.

Shiloh had nothing *but* boundaries with other people. She wanted to die when they bumped into her. She could hardly even hug her mom. "*Cary,*" she hissed.

"*What*, Shiloh?"

She pulled on his sleeve. His shoulders swayed. Shiloh wanted to set *everything* on fire. She wanted to remember him. Every little bit of him. She wanted to remember him even as she was *here* with him. To fix him into a single point. Past, present and future.

"I can do whatever I want," she said. "Don't tell me I can't."

"I'm not."

"I want to stay like this. With you. No matter what."

Cary's eyes widened. He seemed a little frustrated. "Yeah," he sighed. "Okay."

"Do you believe me?"

"Yes."

"Do you believe *in* me?"

"Jesus. *Yes.*" He wrenched her wrist away from his sleeve with his other hand. "Is that what you want to hear?"

Shiloh nodded.

Cary let go of her wrist.

She settled back into her seat and turned up the car radio.

He was still breathing kind of loud, like he was frustrated. Like—breathing as commentary.

"I like this song," Shiloh said after a while. It was "Babe" by Styx. "Even though Styx is lame."

"Styx isn't lame," Cary said. "Aren't."

He turned on the car engine, but Shiloh knew he was just giving the battery a boost so they could keep listening to the radio. He wasn't going anywhere.

Cary had probably had the full senior prom experience with his girlfriend. They probably had sex in the back seat. The girl probably cried. *Angie.* Maybe Cary cried, too. Because it was all coming to an end. Because he was going away. Because the two of them were going to drift apart, like people do.

## ELEVEN

THE BRIDE AND GROOM DANCED to a Cowboy Junkies song. Shiloh had forgotten about the Cowboy Junkies.

Shiloh wished she knew their story—Mike and Janine's. It had to be romantic. First love, reconnection . . .

The wedding party dance came next. Cary danced with a bridesmaid. The bridesmaids wore long column dresses—sage green, halter neck. They were all in their thirties. Women with children. Cary's dance partner looked like she'd been tanning a lot recently. He was holding her in two places. The standard places. The song was "You've Got a Friend" by James Taylor—it wasn't very danceable, even for a slow dance.

Shiloh had never understood the point of wedding party dances. She hadn't had one at her own wedding. She'd barely had a wedding party.

When the song was over, something fast started. Whitney Houston. Cary looked up in Shiloh's direction, catching her staring at him. She looked away.

"Cary!" Becky called out a few seconds later.

He was walking up to their table. Ronny pushed out a chair. "Have a seat, homes!"

"I can't," Cary said. "I'd love to—but Janine wants us to get everyone dancing. It's a snowball dance, so I have to drag someone back with me."

Shiloh was trying not to look at him, but it was too hard; she was only going to get so many opportunities before this night was over.

Cary glanced over at her. His eyebrow twitched.

"I'll go." Tina jumped up and took his hand.

Shiloh watched them walk away.

"I thought Tina was a lesbian now," somebody said.

"That was just a one-time thing."

"It was at least a two-time thing. Ask her ex-husband, ha ha."

"You can be both, you know."

"Both what?"

"A lesbian and, like, regular."

"Regular and unleaded."

"We should be dancing."

"I don't think we can go out there until we get tapped. Those are the rules."

"Oh, the *snowball dance* rules. Very strict."

The music stopped with an artificial screech, and the deejay called out, "Snowball!" Everyone on the dance floor went scrambling for a new partner. Tina and Cary were both headed back toward their table.

One of the groomsmen got there first. "Shiloh, let's dance."

"Go on, Shiloh. Those are the rules."

"I don't have to follow the rules," Shiloh said. "I didn't sign a contract."

Someone else got up to dance with the groomsman.

After the next "Snowball!" Shiloh was alone at the table. She put her hand in her jacket and felt her car keys.

"Hey," someone said.

She looked up. It was Cary, a little flushed from dancing.

"Hey," she said. "You still snowballing?"

He looked around. "No. I think Janine's plan worked. Everybody's already out there."

"You want to sit down?"

"Yeah. Unless . . ." He tilted his head. He lowered his eyebrows. "Would *you* like to dance?"

Shiloh's bottom lip was already in her mouth. She bit it. And then she nodded. "Sure."

Cary kept himself from looking surprised. Or maybe he really *wasn't* surprised—maybe he didn't remember Shiloh well enough to be surprised.

She stood up.

Cary didn't take her hand the way he had Tina's. He didn't touch her arm or the small of her back. They walked side by side onto the dance floor.

"I can't fast-dance," Shiloh said quickly. The Whitney Houston song was still playing. (*"Don't you want to dance, say you want to dance."*)

"Um, all right." Cary looked like he was problem-solving. "Do you want to just stand here and bounce? That counts."

"Uhh . . ." She glanced up at him. "I'll just nod my head, okay?"

Cary laughed, like she was being kind of pitiful. "Shiloh, why didn't you just say . . ." He shook his head, like it wasn't worth finishing. Then he put his left hand on her side and reached for her hand with his right. "We'll slow-dance—is that better?"

Shiloh let him catch her hand. "But it's a fast song."

"No one cares."

"Okay." She put her other hand on his shoulder. "Yeah, okay."

Shiloh had done plenty of slow-dancing over the last fifteen years. Well, not plenty—but *some*. Enough. She'd figured out that dancing was just affectionate swaying most of the time. That you could turn down your nerve endings and not get so worked up about it. She'd danced with Ryan at their wedding and at other people's weddings. She'd danced with his dad and his brothers. It wasn't mortifying. The intimacy didn't burn.

But this . . .

Cary's steady hand resting on her waist, just under her jacket. Her hand in his. He wasn't holding her close—but it was still closer than they'd ever been in high school.

. . . this was a lot.

He was smiling at her. Shiloh was wearing two-inch heels—they were nearly eye to eye. "I'm glad you came tonight," Cary said.

"Of course I came."

"You skipped the last wedding—"

"It was in Rhode Island. And I was pregnant."

"—and then I missed our ten-year reunion."

"We didn't have one," she said.

"Really?"

"Yeah. Tammy flaked. She moved to Michigan."

Cary frowned. "That's why I voted for Sylvia."

Shiloh laughed. "If you tell Sylvia that, she might organize the fifteen this summer."

"You gonna be there?"

Shiloh wrinkled her nose and shrugged. "I don't know. This is already a lot of reunion for me."

"Yeah, god forbid you see your old friends twice in one year."

"There's only so much to talk about . . ."

Cary was smiling. "There's fifteen years to talk about."

"Yeah, but all we ever *actually* talk about is high school."

He raised an eyebrow. "Is that so bad? Sparing a couple hours to commemorate four consequential years?"

"It was *high school*."

"The more you talk about the past," Cary said in his science voice, "the more you remember about it. The more it unfolds."

"And that's good?"

"Yes. It makes your life feel longer."

"That is some Yossarian mind-fuckery, Cary. *Everyone* wants to forget high school."

He was grinning. "'Everyone,' Shiloh? Since when do you care about 'everyone'?"

She laughed again. She realized she was squeezing his hand when he squeezed hers back.

A new song had started, an even faster one. A guy dancing near them Cabbage-Patched right into Shiloh. Cary pulled her a little closer. "Here," he said, steering them back, away from the center of the dance floor—and immediately into another couple.

"No, *here*," Shiloh said, tugging Cary's hand and shoulder, guiding him another way.

He followed her. "We're still dancing, right?"

"If you want to."

"I want to." He stopped them. "Here is good, by the wall. Away from the speaker."

"You know," Shiloh said, "we *could* just be talking comfortably at a table . . ."

"We could," Cary said. He didn't let go. "Dancing is better."

"Why?"

"Because you *can* talk when you're dancing, but you don't have to. And nobody else can interrupt."

"Somebody could cut in."

"Nobody's gonna cut in."

"You think that nobody else wants to dance with me?"

"I think that when two people are slow-dancing to 'Hey Ya!,' everyone leaves them alone."

Shiloh frowned. She looked around. "Now that you've called attention to the song . . . it's actually hard *not* to dance."

Cary smiled. "Oh yeah?"

"Yeah, sort of."

He pulled her closer and started to sway faster, in time with the music.

Shiloh laughed.

Cary held her tight, moving his shoulders back and forth to the beat.

Shiloh tried to move her shoulders, too. She was clumsier than him. She was laughing. And blushing.

"This better?" Cary asked. He was grinning with his mouth closed. His eyes were light.

Shiloh was laughing too hard (and quietly) to answer. Her face fell forward. She let him move her hand to the music. She rocked back and forth with him and tried to relax her neck.

"Hey Ya!" turned into "Groove Is in the Heart," and then, to Shiloh's dismay, Marky Mark and the Funky Bunch.

Cary kept them moving. It was easier if Shiloh didn't look at him—

but she couldn't *not* look at him. (Time was short.) She lifted up her chin.

He looked like he'd been laughing, too.

"Who *are* you?" she asked.

"I'm a grown man," Cary said, like that was an answer.

Shiloh laughed some more, letting her forehead rest on the far edge of his shoulder. She was glad they didn't have to talk, because this was a lot to take in. So much more than she'd been hoping for tonight—more than just a good look at him and a warm conversation.

And it wasn't over yet.

To keep it going, all Shiloh had to do was keep her self-consciousness at bay. (Her self-consciousness and her bone-deep desolation.) (She could be desolate tomorrow. And the next day. She could table her ennui.)

Shiloh was getting another hour with Cary. A bonus hour. In his arms.

Her teenage self could never have predicted—or even comprehended—how precious this would feel. That seventeen-year-old kid had a *glut* of Cary hours. All the Cary she cared to eat. Cary was her day-in, day-out. Her standard operating procedure.

Shiloh hadn't been able to conceive of a life without Cary . . . until that's what she had. A whole life without him, years and years, with no sign of that ever changing.

This night was an aberration.

This dance.

Shiloh closed her eyes and kept her shoulders loose. She kept track of everywhere that Cary was touching her.


When the music slowed down, Cary pushed away from Shiloh a little. He let go of her hand and put both his hands on her waist. The song was "Faithfully" by Journey.

"I love this song," Shiloh said.

"Great song," Cary agreed.

The hand he'd been holding was hanging at her side. Cary picked it up and put it on his shoulder.

"Thanks," Shiloh murmured.

His hand went back to her waist.

It was almost impossible not to make eye contact like this . . .

Shiloh wasn't great with eye contact.

"I don't understand how people dance with strangers," she said. "Just like—*Hi, sure, let's stare into each other's eyes for three minutes.*"

"We're not strangers," Cary said.

"Right. But I mean—we are. Practically."

He frowned. His frown was *inches* away from her mouth. "Practically?"

"We haven't talked in fifteen years—"

"Fourteen," he corrected her.

"Well, that's longer than we knew each other to begin with."

"You think that makes us strangers?"

"No," Shiloh said. "But also, yes? Like—cells get replaced in the human body every seven years. So that's two full iterations since 1992. You don't have any cells left that remember me."

"I'm pretty sure my cells remember you, Shiloh."

"Not from firsthand experience." She clenched her hands in the shoulders of his jacket. "Anything your cells know about me has been passed down from other cells through oral tradition."

"You're winding yourself up," he said. "Don't."

"I'm not winding anything."

"I might believe that, if we'd just met. If I didn't know what you look like *wound.*"

"I'm just saying—"

He looked tired all of a sudden. "You don't have to look in my eyes, okay?"

"I don't *have* to do anything."

Cary had stopped swaying. "Do you want to stop dancing?"

Shiloh stood very still. She shook her head.

"That's a myth," he said. "Some cells replicate quickly, but others stay with you for life."

"Which ones?"

"It varies, depending on the system."

"I was using figurative language."

"I'm not a *stranger*," he said.

"But you've changed . . ."

"So have you, Shiloh." Cary was looking very stern. "Show me how."

Shiloh's bottom lip was between her teeth. She slid her hands up his shoulders to his neck. She started swaying again.

Cary squeezed her waist and swayed a little closer.

You could slow-dance to anything, if you were motivated—and Cary was right, nobody would bother you. They would surely *gossip* about you . . . but Shiloh didn't care about gossip.

She pulled Cary even closer, too close for gazing. With her arms around his neck and her cheek right next to his. It was a truly *astonishing* amount of intimacy. (Maybe worse than eye contact.) Shiloh couldn't be this close to Cary and also talk, so she didn't talk. She closed her eyes. She corralled her nervous system.

The deejay played more slow songs as the night went on. It felt like the whole room was slowing down to keep pace with Shiloh and Cary.

In the end, it was Mikey who interrupted them.

Shiloh felt a hand on her shoulder and lifted up her head to see Mike standing there. "I'm not cutting in," he said. He put one arm around her shoulder and his other arm around Cary's waist. "I'm dancing *with* you."

Cary smiled at him. He had a special smile for Mikey. Amused. Delighted. Waiting to see what would happen next.

Shiloh looked at Mikey the same way.

"Congratulations," she said.

"I thought you stood me up again, Shiloh. Where were you for the ceremony?"

"I can't believe you even noticed!"

"Cary noticed."

"I'm sorry I missed it, Mike. I had babysitter stuff."

He hugged her waist. "I'm just giving you shit."

"Well, you look handsome," Shiloh said. "And your wife is beautiful. And I'm very happy for you."

He grinned. "And I'm very happy to *see* you—it makes me feel young to see you two together. Like I'm seventeen, and we're about to get gyros and go to Putt-Putt."

"We could do that," Cary said.

"All the Putt-Putts closed," Shiloh said.

"We could still get gyros."

"All right." Mikey slapped Cary's shoulder. "That's Plan B. Don't tell Janine that I have a Plan B."

"I still haven't met Janine . . ." Shiloh looked around. There was only one other couple still dancing. Some kids were chasing balloons across the floor. The lights had been turned up in the back of the room, and the waitstaff was packing up chairs. A few people were standing at the bar.

It must be so much later than she realized.

"What do you need help with?" Cary asked Mikey.

"Nothing. It's all taken care of. I think Janine and I are going to take off in a few minutes. I'm wiped."

"Do you need me to drive you?" Cary offered. "I haven't been drinking."

"No, me neither. I'm good. You guys stay. We've got this place—and the deejay—for another half hour. Make him play your favorite songs."

Now that Shiloh was aware of the room around her, she couldn't imagine dancing any more. She couldn't believe she'd done it at all. It was like she'd danced right through her dress reverting to rags and her coach turning into a pumpkin.

Also, she was thirsty, and she really had to go to the bathroom.

She started pulling away from Cary and Mike.

"I'm just going to run to the bathroom."

"Here," Mikey said, "give me a hug first. I'm taking off."

She hugged him.

"I'm going to be in Omaha all the time now. I'll call you, Shiloh."

She squeezed him. "I'd like that."

The bathrooms were in the lobby, by the doors.

When Shiloh came out, Cary was standing there talking to someone. She stood on the other side of the lobby waiting for him.

He already looked sad when he walked over to her. "You heading out?"

"Yeah," she said. "I never expected to stay so long."

"I'll walk you to your car."

"Thanks."

Cary held the door for her and followed her to the parking lot. It was cold out, but Shiloh hadn't wanted to wear a coat.

They both stopped at her car.

Cary was scratching the back of his neck. He seemed nervous.

Shiloh knew what she wanted from this moment—but she didn't know how to make it happen. She wasn't practiced in the alchemy of changing a night into another kind of night. And she was historically bad at transitions.

"It was really good to see you," she said. Lamely.

Cary looked up, sharp. "Shiloh, can I verify something?"

"Sure?"

"You're living with your mom, right?"

"Yeah."

"And that's because you're no longer married?"

"That is correct," Shiloh said.

Cary nodded. "I'm sorry to hear that."

She shook her head. "It's okay."

"Is it?"

She laughed. There were tears in her eyes. "I mean, no, it's been a disaster."

"I'm sorry," he said again.

"Thanks. You're engaged, right?"

"*No*. What? Who said I was engaged?"

"Becky. She said she heard—"

"No," Cary said. "I've gone on three dates with someone."

"Total?"

"Lately. Before this wedding. I went on three dates with someone."

"Okay," Shiloh said, "well, I hope that turns into something for you."

"*No*." Both Cary's hands were on his hips. "I mean, I'm not engaged. I don't have a girlfriend. I've been on three dates with someone. Recently. That's the extent of my current commitments."

"Okay, Cary."

Cary reached a hand up to Shiloh's cheek.

He gave her a few seconds.

Then he kissed her like he'd been thinking about it all night—like maybe he'd been thinking about it for fifteen years.

Shiloh did her best not to ruin it.


Okay . . .

Okay.

So this was a kiss. A good kiss.

What made a kiss good, Shiloh decided, wasn't technique. It was wanting it—and she *wanted* this. She wanted *him*. She'd never wanted anyone else as much or as well.

Shiloh had wanted Cary before she'd even known how to recognize want. Before she had words for it. Before she had some sense of these things and their dimensions.

She'd *longed* for him—and she'd thought it was something else, some other feeling. She'd thought that someone else would come along someday and *that person* would show her what love and desire felt like. That future person would be real. In a way that nothing in high school ever could be. No one in North Omaha.

Shiloh was going to get away from this place, and *then* her life was going to begin, and everyone in the new, *real* life was going to be better than everyone who came before.

Maybe she'd never said that out loud. Maybe she'd never even thought it through until just now—the mechanics of her misunderstanding.

Shiloh had wanted Cary before she knew what that meant—and now it was too late for her to ever truly have him.

But Shiloh *was* getting this kiss . . .

And maybe she would even get this night. A bonus night with Cary. A break from destiny. An out-of-continuity adventure.

God, he felt so good. So deliberate. There was no question who was kissing who at the moment. Shiloh was *being* kissed. She was receiving it, taking it. Being told. Cary probably didn't trust her enough to steer just now—and he was correct. Shiloh did not have a steady grip.

Her hand came up between them and gently brushed the front of his shirt. Fumbling.

When Cary finally pulled away, Shiloh's chest was heaving. Cary's eyes were black.

"Let's not say goodbye just yet," she said.

"Okay," he agreed.

"We could . . ."

He nodded. "Yeah."

Shiloh pushed her chin forward, and Cary kissed her again. It was still so good.

"Did you drive?" she asked.

"No. I came with—"

"I'll drive. Where are you staying?"

"Oh," he said. "With my mom."

"Oh," Shiloh said. "Of course." She'd been imagining a hotel room. Should they *get* a hotel room? Going back to an existing hotel room felt different from obtaining a room at midnight for a one-night stand.

"Do you have to get home?" Cary asked. "Your kids?"

"They're not there," she said, making up her mind. "Come home with me? I mean—" She cringed. "I know how that sounds—"

"It sounds great, Shiloh."

Shiloh laughed. It was awkward. "Yeah?"

"Yeah," he said.

She pulled her keys out of her jacket and waved at her car. "I'm just here."

Cary nodded.

She unlocked the doors with the button. Then they both stood there. She felt like maybe she should open the door for him—maybe he was waiting to open the door for her?

She jerked toward the driver's side, opening her door. Cary went for the other side.

As soon as she sat down, she apologized. He was picking up papers from the passenger seat. Shiloh took them from him. Her work bag was on the floor; she grabbed that, too. "Sorry. No one else ever sits up here." She threw everything in the back, between the booster seats. Jesus Christ, reality was already making a harsh reappearance, wasn't it?

Cary sat down and reached for his seat belt. "Don't worry about it." He glanced over at her and smiled. "I've never been in the car with you before."

He meant with her in the driver's seat. "My mom wouldn't let me get my license in high school," she said.

"I know."

"She said it would affect her insurance."

"I remember."

She smiled at him. "Remember you tried to teach me?"

He smiled back. "Yeah."

Shiloh turned to the steering wheel, self-conscious now. Fortunately her house was only a mile or two away—and once they were on the road, Cary didn't actually watch her drive. He paid attention to the streets and houses.

"My mom says the neighborhood has gotten worse," he said.

"Everything has gotten worse. Everybody has a gun."

He hummed. "I wish she'd move." He looked over at Shiloh. "Sorry. That was insensitive."

"No, I get it—it's okay. How old is your mom now?"

"Seventy-three."

"How's her health?"

"She has emphysema."

"I'm sorry, Cary."

"She'll never move," he said, looking out the window again. "She has three dogs."

Shiloh laughed. Cary's mom had always had too many dogs. And too many kids. And too many relatives who needed a place to stay.

"Is she by herself?"

"No. My niece lives there with her kids. Angel."

Shiloh nodded. She remembered Angel.

Shiloh badly wished that she still lived in the suburbs—so that she wouldn't be driving Cary through such familiar territory.

She pulled into her driveway.

"You took down the fence," he said.

"It fell down."

"It looks good."

Shiloh thought about asking him if he still wanted to go through with this. He already seemed different than he had in the parking lot. More stern. But she didn't actually want to give him an out—she didn't want to make it easy for him to walk away from her.

She got out of the car. Cary was right behind her. Following her up the steps. Reaching in front of Shiloh to get the screen door.

His mouth was behind her ear. "Is your mom home?"

"I don't think so."

Shiloh opened the front door, bracing herself for the sight of the living room. She wasn't a complete slob—but she was a working mother with two kids and no desire to spend every free moment cleaning.

The living room was full of toys. Baskets of clean laundry. Potato chips.

"Sorry—" Shiloh started to explain.

Cary was still behind her. She felt his hand on her back. "Do you still have your old room?"

"No," she said. "I'm in the old spare room."

"Show me," he said.

Shiloh nodded.

They headed up the stairs. There were more toys on the steps. And books. Papers. There were so many coats on the end of the banister that it looked like a troll.

Cary stayed right behind Shiloh. She turned to him, to apologize again—but he caught her mouth and kissed her. He put one hand on the back of her neck and held her there.

Cary was good at this. He probably got so much practice . . .

He was a thirty-three-year-old single man. He still had his hair, he was almost six feet tall. He was smart. Kind. Probably not an alcoholic. And everyone knew the Navy had the best uniforms . . .

Cary probably had so much sex.

Like a *normal* amount.

The sort of sex people talked about in the advice columns Shiloh read online when she couldn't sleep.

First-date sex. Practically anonymous sex. Sex in bathrooms and cars. Hotel rooms. Sex without any ties or obligations at all.

Shiloh had never had that kind of sex. She didn't really want it, in an ongoing way.

She just wanted a little bit of it *now*.

Cary pulled away. He gave her space to keep climbing the stairs. She rushed up the rest of them. There were two bedrooms up here, plus the bathroom. Shiloh's door was open. Her room was the worst mess of all: Stacks of books. Bottles of lotion. Dirty mugs. Half her closet was spread out on her bed. "Sorry—" she said again.

Cary got in front of her, reaching behind her to close the door—then crowded her against it. "Shiloh," he said before he kissed her.

## TWELVE

SHILOH LET HIM PUSH HER head back into the door.

Her arms lifted up, hovered, and fell. She tried again and still didn't manage any contact.

Cary took hold of her wrists and set her hands on his shoulders. She wound her arms around his neck.

He kissed her.

Cary's chin was sharp with stubble. He smelled like layers of fading soaps and sprays. Like sweat. Like the champagne toast.

It had been so long since Shiloh had been this close to a person. (A person who wasn't her kid.) She *liked* kissing, but it was just so . . . *in your face*. Kissing was like eye contact, but worse. Kissing was carnal eye contact.

Cary pulled his mouth away. "Shiloh?" His voice was husky.

"Yeah," she whispered. "Yeah." She pushed her mouth forward. He met her more than halfway. She squeezed her eyes shut.

Cary was shuffling out of his jacket—Shiloh tried to help. He was warm beneath the wool fabric. His shirt felt smooth. His shoulders were broader than she'd expected.

The jacket dropped to the floor with a soft flop, and his hands came back to her waist. Shiloh hugged his neck again and pressed her chest against his.

Cary groaned—it made her shiver.

He tipped his head to kiss her more deeply.

Shiloh felt the arousal rising up in her, and it was such a relief. She could ride this feeling past all the other stuff. (The desolation, again. The ennui.) (Memories.)

She let it rise. She let it go to her head. She licked into Cary's mouth, and he surged forward, pressing Shiloh against the door, holding on to her hips.

*Yes*, she thought. *Cary*. And *please*.

Shiloh pulled her mouth away. It was difficult—Cary didn't want her to. "I want you," she whispered.

He surged into her again. She felt pinned. He was kissing her neck. "I want *you*," Cary said. "Shiloh. I always want you."

Shiloh closed her eyes. She could ride this feeling past anything. Past pitfalls and shipwrecks.

She let herself touch the back of his warm neck. His hair was so short . . .

He was trying to take off her jacket now—Shiloh still couldn't believe she'd worn this stupid jacket. She squirmed out of it.

Cary hummed and started unbuttoning her dress. The buttons were for show. "No," Shiloh laughed.

He looked up at her. "No?"

"No—*yes*." She touched his neck again. "They're decorative. It's just . . ."

"Oh," he said, and reached for the bottom of her skirt instead.

She laughed some more. Nervously. But also happily. She was happy. She was still rising. She lifted her arms. "Yeah."

He pulled the dress up over her head.

Shiloh couldn't even remember what bra she was wearing. (Her hopes for tonight had never been this high.) Surely it was a bra she'd had for years. Her panties were cotton and already riding below her belly.

She felt a little ridiculous for a second. Awkward. Imperfect. Exposed.

But then Cary pushed her back against the wall. He was kissing her neck. Sucking on it.

This was moving faster than Shiloh would have expected. (Had she expected it.) That was good. Momentum was good—it made it hard to stop. Shiloh might actually have this. *Him*.

Talk about bonus hours. Talk about breaks from destiny.

She closed her eyes against tears. "I want you," she said again.

"Shiloh, Shiloh," Cary said. He pulled her off the wall. Pulled her back toward her unmade bed. Shiloh had never seen him like this—is this how Cary was with the women he dated? Single-minded? In charge?

He fell onto the bed and brought her with him, kicking clothes and books off the bottom. Kicking off his shoes. Shiloh laughed. Cary took her face in his hands. He tried to look into her eyes. She tucked her head into his neck and kissed him there. He was so warm. He was sweating. He was taking off his shirt. Shiloh nodded. She helped. "I want you," she whispered. "I want this."

"I want you," Cary said. He sat up, on the edge of her bed, to take off his pants.

Shiloh took off her bra. Cary glanced over at her—then reached for her before he'd finished with his pants. They hung on one ankle. Shiloh didn't get a good look at his body. He was moving too fast, and the room was still dark.

She felt him climb on top of her. She felt her desire for him singing up through her veins, skating over her skin. It was happening fast. It was going to happen. She was going to have this.

Shiloh spread her legs. She was still wearing underwear. Cary touched her breast. He hummed.

"This is more than I hoped for," she said softly.

His face dropped over hers. He pressed their foreheads together. "God. Shiloh. I just . . ."

"I want you."

"Yeah," he said. "Yeah."

She started pushing her underwear down. He lifted off of her to help.

"Where . . . um . . ." He pulled her panties down her legs. "Condoms?"

"I don't—" Shiloh squinted against the dark. "I thought you'd have one. Like, in your wallet."

Cary sat back on his calves. "Why would I have a condom in my wallet?" He sounded amused. He was silhouetted against a window.

"It's a wedding, Cary. You might get lucky."

"I'm thirty-three years old."

"That's the prime age for hooking up at weddings."

Cary laughed. He shook his head, like he was shaking something off. Then he lay down next to Shiloh.

She turned toward him. She tapped his arm. "Don't stop."

"I'm not stopping. I'm re-evaluating."

She poked him. "God, no, don't re-evaluate. Let's just keep going. My tubes are tied."

Cary laughed—like that was a little too much. "Uh . . . no . . ."

"You could go get condoms," she said.

"I'm not going anywhere—come here."

Shiloh moved closer. "I could go."

He wrapped an arm around her. He kissed her shoulder.

"Maybe my mom has one . . . " she said.

"Jesus. No." He kissed her shoulder again.

Shiloh sat up. "I'll go to 7-Eleven."

Cary sat up, too. "At midnight?"

"I just . . ." Shiloh felt around the bed for her bra. "We're losing momentum."

"Do we need momentum?"

"Yes. We can't just . . . I've already turned into a pumpkin. The horses are field mice. If this is going to happen, I need it to happen quickly—and I *really* want it to happen."

Cary touched her side. "Hey. Lie down. I'm still here."

"But you won't be tomorrow." She was looking for her bra. "This is a window."

"A window?"

"Yes, a break from reality."

His hand fell away from her. "Lie down, Shiloh."

"In a few hours, you're going to sober up—"

"I'm not *drunk*."

"You are. Metaphorically. You're going to snap out of it. In a few hours, you're going to fly home and go on with your life—can't we just have sex before that happens?"

Cary sat up. He reached for his pants.

"Are you going to 7-Eleven?" she asked.

He huffed. "No. I'm leaving."

"You can't leave."

"I can, actually." He was standing up, pulling up his dress pants. "I . . ." He exhaled loudly. "Am not. Doing this. With you."

Shiloh felt tearful. She felt like she'd been tearful for a while now. "Doing *what*?"

Cary made that huffy noise again, that mean breath of a laugh. "Any of it. This was a mistake. I'm sorry, Shiloh."

"No—Cary. Please."

He didn't turn back. "I don't know why I thought you'd be different."

# before

SHILOH HADN'T ANSWERED THE PHONE when he called from San Diego, and there wasn't really time to send her a letter. Cary had to be in Orlando in four days. If he was going to trade in his plane ticket, he had to do it now.

He did it.

He'd stop in Des Moines. And if Shiloh could see him, she'd see him— and if she couldn't, or if she didn't want to, or if he chickened out when she answered the phone, he'd take the bus to Omaha. His mom would be glad to see him. His stepdad wouldn't be, but he'd live. They'd all live.

"Hello?" It was her.

"Shiloh?" He sounded too eager. He cleared his throat.

"Yeah?"

"It's Cary."

"Cary!" Shiloh sounded happy. Really happy. "Hi! I thought it might be you, but I wasn't sure. It's been— You haven't called."

"I couldn't call from boot camp."

"I got your postcards," she said.

"I got yours. Your letters."

Shiloh had been one of the only people to write to him in boot camp. He knew she liked sending mail. She used to send him postcards some-times even when they'd only lived a few blocks apart.

"It's good to hear your voice," she said. "How are you? Are you done now? Are you a full-fledged soldier?"

"Sailor. And no. Yes and no. I've still got training. 'A' School in a few days. But I'm done with boot camp. I graduated."

"You graduated? Do some people not graduate?"

"Yeah . . . some. It's kinda intense."

"Intense *how*?"

Cary didn't want to talk about how hard it was. Not at the moment. Standing at a pay phone. "Hey," he said. "I was thinking—maybe I could stop and see you on my way to training?"

"Yeah . . . that'd be cool. Am I on the way?"

"It's San Diego to Orlando. Everything's on the way."

Shiloh laughed. Cary's neck went soft. He rested his head against the top of the pay phone.

"When are you coming?" she asked.

"I was thinking . . . today?"

"*Today?*" She sounded surprised. Not necessarily in a good way.

"I didn't get much warning before I left—I tried to call a few times from San Diego. You don't have an answering machine."

"I know," Shiloh said. "Sorry."

"No, I'm sorry. I mean, it's okay if this doesn't work out." It had always been a long shot. "I'll go home. It's a short bus trip."

"No, Cary—stay. *Stay.* I can do today. I'm just surprised. When do you get here?"

"I'm at the airport."

"Oh my god, okay. Cary! This is amazing. I'm going to show you everything. I'm going to give you a campus tour. Should I come meet you? When does your next flight leave?"

"Not till Monday."

"Monday . . ." More not-good surprise. "Do you have someplace to stay?"

"Uh . . ." He closed his eyes. "I didn't really have time to plan anything. I was hoping I could sleep on your floor."

"We'll work something out," Shiloh said quickly. "I've got a roommate—"

"I can find someplace. I can go home."

"No. You can sleep on my floor, or I'll find you a floor. I've got friends in the boys' dorms who'll put you up if Darla feels uncomfortable."

"Your roommate?"

"Yeah. She's decent."

"If it's too much . . ."

"It's not too much!" Shiloh had already decided now, and he wouldn't be able to talk her out of it. "I'm really glad you're here, Cary. Do I need to come get you?"

"I can get to you."

# before

SHE CAME RUSHING OUT OF the elevator, and Cary stood a little taller. His mouth was dry. He swallowed.

Shiloh looked different. She'd cut her hair—it hung in a blunt shelf at her jaw—and she had bangs now. It made her look like someone in a foreign movie. And she was thinner. Her chin jutted out of her face. She was wearing a dress that Cary had never seen before—it was too tight over her chest and too short above her knees. She had on tights, but still. He wasn't used to seeing Shiloh's legs. He wasn't used to this Shiloh at all.

She looked impatient; that at least was familiar. *This* was familiar— the way she was standing, with her hands on her hips, looking around the lobby like she was trying to find something wrong with it.

She walked past him toward the door.

He grabbed her forearm. "Hey."

Shiloh jumped away from him, no sign of recognition in her eyes.

"Hey," Cary said again, softer.

Her eyes got big. And then her mouth opened. "Cary . . ."

"Hey," he said a third time.

He knew he was changed. He'd been worried about it the whole way here. The uniform. The hair. Everyone who came through the lobby had looked at him like he didn't belong here. Like he must be here for some strange and specific reason.

Shiloh's eyes were jumping all over him. His shoes. His tie. The single decoration that he got for showing up.

"*Hey,*" she said finally. Like his friend.

They'd never hugged before, so Cary didn't try to hug her. But he relaxed. He was relieved.

"I wasn't expecting . . ." She gestured at him. "Do you have to wear this?"

"No," he said. "I just . . . You go to boot camp with the clothes on your back. This is all I really have at the moment."

He could have worn his dress blues, but they would have called even more attention to him. He'd gone with the winter blues: Button-down shirt. Pants. Tie. All in a navy blue so dark, it may as well be black.

Shiloh was looking at his chest. She touched his shoulder quickly. Then tugged on his tie. He waited for her to say he looked like an SS officer. (Shiloh really knew *nothing* about military uniforms.) "It's nice," she said. "You look nice."

"Is there a reason you won't look me in the eye?"

She held on to his tie and laughed, still not looking up at him. "I'm kind of freaked out by *your hair.*"

Cary laughed. He was blushing. He picked up his duffel bag. Shiloh let go of his tie.

"Come on," she said, walking toward the elevator.

"Don't you have to check me in?"

"Nope. We're libertines here."

"Did you talk to your roommate yet?"

"I haven't seen her—but don't worry." They were the only people on the elevator. Shiloh pushed a button.

"You cut your hair, too," Cary said. "I thought you were going to shave it."

She touched the edges and frowned. "I chickened out. I didn't want that to be the thing that people know me by, like, forever. *The bald girl.* Like Sinéad O'Connor. So that I'd never look normal with hair again."

Shiloh's hair was dark, dark brown and very, very straight. It had always been long, as long as Cary had known her, and had always seemed a little too thick to be manageable. He'd seen her break elastic bands trying to tie it back. She had thick, dark eyebrows, too, and dark hair on her arms. Her mom said that her dad might have been Greek. *"My dad might have been anyone,"* Shiloh would say. Now that her hair was short, it looked even thicker. Like a wedge.

"You don't like it, do you?" She led him off the elevator, spinning to walk backwards, facing him.

"It looks fine," Cary said.

"But you liked it better before?"

"I don't have any opinions about your hair." He liked everything about her, however it was. That had been true since they met.

She spun to the front again. "I'm growing it out. I think it makes me look perky."

"What's wrong with perky?"

"Nobody takes perky seriously."

They were already at her door. Cary had never been in a college dormitory before. It was pretty much what you'd expect. Like a hotel.

Shiloh let him into her room. It was small. There was space for two beds, two desks, a rug, and a little TV.

"You can sit on the bed," she said. "Or the desk chair. Sit wherever. I don't have anything to drink. I could buy you a Coke."

"I'm okay."

She rolled her eyes. "Sit *down*, Cary."

"I'm waiting for you to sit."

"Oh my god," she said, sitting on the floor. Folding those long legs.

Cary didn't think he'd ever really seen Shiloh's legs before. They were as long as his and probably thicker. Sweet at the knees and the ankles. He sat on the bed, facing her, trying not to stare at them.

"Was boot camp terrible?" she asked.

He shrugged. "It was fine."

"You said people died."

"I said people didn't *graduate*..."

"What happened to them? Why couldn't they get through?"

Cary really didn't want to get into this. Boot camp was over. He was ready to leave it behind. "They took it too personally. They let it get under their skin."

"And you didn't?"

"No. It wasn't about me."

Shiloh laughed. "'*Boot camp, three stars. It wasn't about me.*'"

"Nothing in the Navy is about me," Cary said. "I'm just a component in a larger machine."

"I would *lose* my *mind*," she said, making a long face.

He smiled. "You would."

"But you haven't?" She seemed worried. She kicked a foot out, not quite touching him.

He shook his head. "It's what I expected." Regimented. Rigorous. Impersonal. Cary went to work, and then he went to sleep. And he tried to keep his head down in the moments between.

"You weren't homesick?"

"Um . . ." He wasn't sure how to answer that.

Cary missed his mom, but he didn't miss their house. He didn't miss his sisters—maybe he would eventually. He didn't miss school or Omaha.

He missed his first name. He missed Mikey. He missed driving. He missed regular clothes. Regular food. Godfather's pizza.

He missed Shiloh.

He'd known he was going to—but it was so much worse than he'd expected. Her letters made it worse. Everyone else had faded so fast. High school already felt like ancient history. But nothing about Shiloh had faded. If anything, her memory had taken on sharp edges. Even seeing her now made him miss her.

"I don't know," he said. "I guess. Tell me about all this. About college."

"I've already told you about it in my letters."

"That makes it easier," Cary said. "We're not starting from zero."

Shiloh smiled big at him. So he could see her bottom row of teeth. If he was closer, he'd see how crooked they were. "Good point," she said.

It was never hard to get Shiloh talking. Cary settled back against the wall to listen.

She told him about her roommate. About her classes. About her failed auditions at the campus theater. "They almost never cast freshmen."

She loved the dorms. She loved being on her own. She didn't miss her mom, much. Or the neighborhood. She missed Mikey.

She kept reaching for Cary as she talked. Just gesturing. Never making contact.

Cary had lots of practice listening to Shiloh talk. He could follow the thread of it even while his mind wandered. She'd tell you when she wanted feedback. *"That was a question, Cary."*

Shiloh had a nervous way of talking. Her sentences piled up on each other and spiraled. She'd chase an idea in several different directions . . .

It drove Mikey crazy sometimes. There were times when he'd say, *"No Shiloh tonight—I've got enough noise in my head."*

Cary had a much higher tolerance. You didn't have to spiral *with* Shiloh. You could just watch. You could just listen.

Even when she drove him crazy, he didn't exactly want less of her.

While she talked today, he tried to figure out what was different about her . . . Besides the hair. Besides the short skirt.

She seemed easier than he remembered her.

Less frustrated.

"You're happy here," he said.

Shiloh wrinkled her nose. She swatted at him, almost touching his leg. "What do you mean?"

"You seem really happy," Cary said. "You seem like you like it."

She smiled. "Well, I just . . ." She shrugged. "Yeah, I guess I do." She got up onto her knees. Her skirt inched up. She pushed her hair behind her ears, and it immediately slid out. "I kind of feel bad saying this to you, because of where you are, and where you're headed—but I feel like my time is my *own* here, you know? Like, my life is my own. So many freshmen hate it. They go home all the time—or they drop out. Becky was here, and she's already gone. And, you know, I *am* lonely sometimes. A lot. Actually. But . . . even the food. I can eat what I want, when I want. I'm responsible for everything. I've got this scholarship and my job, and I don't need to ask anyone for help. I don't ever need a ride, there are buses. You know?"

Cary nodded. "I'm glad."

"You're glad not to have to drive me around?"

"I'm glad you're happy."

She moved her legs, flopping back down onto her butt. "It's stupid, right? This isn't even a great school, I guess. It's just Iowa. But I still feel like I'm living *la vie en rose*. I'm, like, wearing a beret and smoking cigarettes and feeling like an adult human female."

"Are you smoking cigarettes?"

"No. Those were metaphorical cigarettes."

"Is the beret metaphorical, too?"

Shiloh kicked him and made contact. "The beret is real."

Cary laughed.

"Shut up." She kicked him again. She was wearing shoes with buckles.

"Stop," he said. "You're going to scuff my pants, and I can't wash them."

She grinned. "*You* have a little beret tucked into your belt . . . Don't think I haven't noticed."

"That's a flat cap. There are no berets in the Navy."

Shiloh climbed up onto the bed next to him, kicking off her shoes. "Let me see it on."

"I want to see you in *your* beret. Go get it."

She pushed his shoulder. "Let me see it, Cary."

"No. I'm not supposed to wear it indoors."

"Let me try it on, then."

He would like that, but it wasn't happening.

Shiloh's brown eyes were very wide and sparkly. Her tongue was peeking out of her mouth.

He pointed at her. "I know you're about to grab my cap. But I'm telling you now—don't."

She grabbed his finger. "Don't tell me what to do."

He pulled it away. "I'm not telling you what to do; I'm drawing a line."

Shiloh poked his shoulder. "When you tell me what to do, it just makes me want to do it."

"Because you're irrational and possibly need meds. Don't mess with my uniform."

"Is it a federal law?" she asked. "Like mail tampering?"

"Yeah."

"Liar." She pulled on his sleeve. "Is this messing with your uniform?"

"Yes."

She poked his arm. He ignored it. "I don't need *meds*," she said.

"You need something."

She poked him harder.

"*Stop*," he said. "That hurts."

"That doesn't hurt." She did it again. "Does that really hurt?"

"It doesn't feel good."

Her face fell. "I didn't mean to hurt you. I'm sorry." She patted his shoulder. "Cary, I'm sorry."

"Okay."

"Honestly," she said, petting him some more. "I'm sorry."

"Okay. Shut up. It's fine."

She smoothed his sleeve down. "Is this the uniform you wear all the time?"

"No. I've never worn it before. It's a little formal. But we can wear it when we travel."

"It's nice. I mean, it's nice on you. Can I take your picture?"

"Now?"

"Yeah," she said, "before I ruin your fancy uniform."

"I'm not letting you ruin it."

She stood up and got a camera out of her desk. It was a little pink point-and-shoot. Shiloh always had a camera.

Cary sat up straighter. "Like this?"

She was looking at him through the lens. "Yeah. I'll send you copies of these for your mom."

"I think I should stand up."

"Wait." The flash went off. "Okay, stand up. Look official."

Cary stood. He adjusted his tie.

"In front of the wall," Shiloh said.

He did what she told him to.

"Smile," she said. "This isn't the Civil War."

Cary smiled. "We have to take one together," he said. "We'll send it to Mikey."

"Yeah!" Shiloh looked around the room. "I guess . . . We can try it in the mirror." She stood partly in front of Cary, so they'd both fit into the long mirror on her door. She looked through the viewfinder. "I'm blocking you."

"It's okay." He laid his hand on her shoulder. "It's good."

"I hope Mikey doesn't hate my hair." Shiloh moved the camera off her face and snapped the picture. "I'm not sure that will turn out. Maybe Darla can take one of us later."

Cary watched her reflection. "And you'll send me copies?"

"Yeah."

She turned to him, slipping the camera into her pocket, and looked up at his head. "I'm used to your hair now. It took a minute."

She was an inch or two shorter than him in her stocking feet. He looked down into her eyes.

"I'm not used to seeing so much of your face," she said. "Did you cry when they cut it?"

"No. Some of the female recruits cry."

"They make the girls shave their heads?"

"They cut it to their collars. Like yours."

Shiloh touched the back of her hair, self-consciously. Then she reached up past Cary's cheek.

He didn't flinch. "Sorry there's nothing left for you to pull . . ."

She touched the bristly hair over his ear—freshly cropped just before graduation—and ran her fingers along his scalp.

She shivered.

Then she moved her hand to the top of his head. "Aren't you going to tell me to stop?"

He shook his head, just barely. "No."

Shiloh stroked his hair against the grain and shivered again, like she couldn't help it. He'd seen her do this before with velvet. With milkweed floss. One time, with the broken edge of a bowl.

She brought her other hand up and rubbed both of his temples. "You're lucky you have such a nice head."

Cary hummed a short syllable. He was just going to breathe through this.

"I do miss your hair though," she whispered. "It's a totally different color now. It's darker—hardly blond at all. That's weird, huh?"

He nodded.

She shivered from her head through her shoulders.

He put his hands on her waist to steady her. "Are you torturing yourself?"

"No," she said, defensively. "I like it."

She stroked with all ten fingertips from his forehead to the back of his neck. Cary cast his eyes down between them—he wasn't sure which game this was.

"Do *you* like it?" she asked.

He nodded.

"Your face looks different," she said. "Your eyes are so big now."

"My eyes are the same size."

"I've got eye-witness testimony to the contrary."

She stroked his scalp. Cary shivered. Shiloh laughed out a breath.

"*Eye*-witness," she said, "get it?"

He nodded.

"Cary . . ." she whispered.

He lifted his gaze to hers. She looked nervous. She was swaying a little.

"I missed you," she said.

"I missed you, too, Shiloh."

"I'm glad you're okay."

"It was just boot camp."

"I know, but still. Is it weird that I didn't even realize how much I missed you until I saw you again? Like, I saw you, and I realized I had a hole in my chest—when I'd thought all along I was fine."

"I'm sorry."

"No. I . . . I think I've just gotten used to talking to people who don't matter. And then I looked at you and remembered what it felt like to care about someone."

"Shiloh . . ." He squeezed her waist. "I've really missed you."

"You're lucky you have such a good head," she said again. "Such a good face . . ." She touched his cheeks. His nose. His chin.

He wasn't sure what game she was playing.

He wasn't sure this was a game.

Shiloh looked like she might cry.

Cary leaned forward and kissed her.

# before

IT WAS FEBRUARY OF THEIR senior year. They'd stayed at school late to work on the newspaper. Then Cary had dropped Shiloh off at home—it had been a whole production, she was in rare form—and now he and Mikey were going to play *Street Fighter* at Godfather's.

As soon as Shiloh was out of the car, Mikey changed the radio station. "You guys don't have to pretend for my sake," he said, "you know?"

Cary backed the car out onto the street. "No, I don't know. Pretend what?"

"That you're not a thing. Secret *lovers*"—he said it like *luvvahs*—"so to speak."

"What are you talking about?"

Mikey looked at him. "I'm just *saying,* you don't have to worry about my feelings. It won't be weird—I told you about Janine."

"I'm not . . ." Cary shook his head. "Shiloh and I aren't . . . that."

Mikey curled his top lip and looked confused. "Really?"

"Yes, really. Where are you even getting this? We're just friends."

"Yeah, but you're, you know . . ." Mikey bugged out his eyes. He could be just as dramatic as Shiloh sometimes. "Verrry focused on each other."

"We're good friends."

"She's very *tactile* with you, Carold."

"That's just Shiloh," Cary said. Mikey knew that was just Shiloh.

"She's not like that with me," Mikey said.

Cary shook his head again. "I'm like her dog or something. I'm her security blanket."

"So you don't have . . . *feelings*?"

"For Shiloh?"

Mikey rolled his eyes. "Obviously for Shiloh. I know you're not a robot."

Cary shrugged. "She's just messing with me because I let her."

"Why do you let her?"

Cary frowned at him. "Why do I let *you* hassle me? Because we're friends."

Mikey turned away, scratching his ear. "Yeah, okay. I hear you. I'll let it go. I mean, I am disappointed. I really wanted there to be an *undercover romance . . .*"

"You've got your own undercover romance."

He grinned. "I know. Don't tell anybody. Janine and I are *secret luuuu-vahs.*" He sang the last two words, like the Atlantic Starr song.

"Stop."

"Before I let this drop, like I said I would"—Mikey squinted like this next thing was painful for him to say—"Shiloh-is-crazy-about-you-and-that-is-my-professional-objective-opinion-that-I-would-bet-a-million-dollars-on."

Cary jerked his head toward Mikey, then back toward the road. "That's not true. She likes that guy—Kurt."

Mikey shrugged. "Eh. Kurt's nothing."

"She doesn't like me like that," Cary said. "And if she did, she'd lose interest as soon as I liked her back. She just likes to mess with me. She thinks it's funny."

"One *million* dollars," Mikey said.

Cary made a growling noise. "Okay, you can drop it now. For real. You're making it weird with her, and she's not even here."

"I'm dropping it, I'm dropping it."

Cary drove for a second, and then he slapped the steering wheel. "Also? I have a girlfriend!"

"I was wondering when you were going to remember . . ."

"Screw you, Mikey."

Mikey was cackling.

Cary shook his head. "Screw you."

# before

ONCE CARY STARTED KISSING SHILOH, that day in her dorm room—he couldn't stop.

He'd always *known* that if he started kissing Shiloh, he wouldn't be able to stop. That was one of the reasons that kissing her had always been such a bad idea.

You can't date your best friend in high school.

Cary couldn't have dated *Shiloh*.

There was nowhere for them to go with each other. The minute they started, they'd be at the finish line.

He already knew her so well.

He already loved her so much.

What were they going to do, get married?

What were they going to do if they *couldn't* get married? Destroy everything? Their friendship? Their shot at something bigger?

Cary wasn't ready for . . . whatever it would be between him and Shiloh.

And he wasn't even sure whether she *wanted* anything. He was pretty sure she didn't want what he had to offer her—which was everything.

Maybe someday, he'd told himself, they'd both be ready for this.

Maybe someday it would be appropriate to kiss her and never stop . . .

Was this the day?

Or had Cary just made a terrible mistake?

# before

THEY'D ENDED UP ON HER bed. Shiloh was in his lap. Cary's hands were on her thighs, just under her skirt.

She'd touched his tie, his tie clip, his single ribbon. She'd worried at his collar. She'd covered his ears with her hands and then pinched his earlobes.

He wasn't sure that she'd ever been kissed before, but she'd thrown herself into it—and Cary loved how eager she was. How happy she seemed. How absolutely Shiloh she was being about it all. Best-case-scenario Shiloh.

She pulled away from the kiss to look down at him. She was holding his face. He felt like he must be glowing—like he must have the dumbest possible smile, a cat with a face full of cream.

Shiloh was giggling and touching his lips.

She jumped when the door opened. Cary grabbed on to her hips.

Shiloh stood up quickly. Cary sat up. Wiped his mouth. Adjusted his shirt.

A pudgy blond girl walked in. She looked at Shiloh. Then at Cary. She raised her eyebrows. "Hello."

"Darla—this is Cary, my high school friend. Cary, this is my roommate, Darla. She's from Iowa City, and she's pretty wonderful."

"I am?"

"It's nice to meet you," Cary said. He knew his face was bright red.

Shiloh stepped closer to her roommate. "Could I talk to you . . . " She tipped her head toward the door.

"Sure . . ."

They stepped out into the hall.

Cary stood up. He looked in the mirror. He wasn't sure what would happen now. Would he and Shiloh get to be alone some more? Maybe he could take her out, he was really hungry—would that be a date? What would it be like to date Shiloh? What was even *happening* right now?

She and Darla came back to the room almost fifteen minutes later. Cary had found some crackers on Shiloh's desk. He was eating them. He stood up when the door opened.

"Darla's going to take our picture," Shiloh said.

"Okay," he said. And then to Darla—"Thank you."

Shiloh gave Darla the camera and came to stand by Cary. He put down the crackers. He let his arm come around her shoulders.

"Do we look good?" Shiloh was smoothing her hair. "Make sure we look good."

"You look great," Darla said.

Cary swallowed. He hugged Shiloh. The flash went off.

"Take another one," Shiloh said.

Darla did, then handed back the camera. "And now I am going to go study," she said. "For thirty-six to forty-eight hours."

She quickly grabbed some clothes and picked up her backpack. Shiloh looked embarrassed. Cary *was* embarrassed.

"Thank you for your service," Darla said at the door. "My grandpa was in the Navy."

"Oh," Cary said. "Thank you. I mean—thank him and you."

Shiloh walked Darla out.

She was frowning when she came back in.

"How'd you make that work?" Cary asked.

"She's staying with someone down the hall, and now I owe her something big and unpleasant that is yet to be determined."

"That was nice of her, I guess?"

"Cary, sit down."

He sat in the desk chair.

"No, sit over here, with me." Shiloh sat on the bed.

He came to sit next to her.

She looked antsy. Her fists were clenched.

Cary braced himself.

"I'm not sure what we're doing," she said. "You're on your way to Orlando, right?"

"Right."

"I don't even know when I'll see you again. Do *you* know when I'll see you again?"

He shook his head. "No."

"Will it be months? Or years?"

"It will be months," he said. "Or years."

"I can't ask you . . ." she said.

Yes, she could.

She threw up her hands. "What is this anyway?" She motioned between them, panicky. "*This?*"

"I don't know, Shiloh. I didn't plan it."

Cary hadn't *exactly* planned it . . .

He'd known that he needed to see her. He'd thought he might tell her, if the moment was right, what her letters had meant to him. What *she* meant to him.

Shiloh looked like she was winding up at one end and coming undone at the other. She was biting her lip. "This doesn't have to be . . . Cary, maybe this isn't . . . You've gotta . . ." She mimed a plane lifting up with one hand. "*Phew.* Take off. You're just taking off. You don't even know where you'll be. But I'll be *here,* right? So . . . it doesn't have to be . . ."

"Okay," he said, wanting this to stop. "Yeah. I'm sorry."

"No! Don't be sorry. I'm not sorry. I'm just . . . trying to be realistic, I guess. Am I being realistic?"

"Yeah." He nodded. "This is probably not the time for us . . . to . . ."

Shiloh nodded hard. "Right."

"Do you want me to leave?"

She grabbed his arm. "*No.*"

Cary huffed out a helpless breath. "Well—what do you want, Shiloh?"

Her face fell. It killed him. That was all it took to kill him.

"I want *you*, Cary. I guess I just want to be here with you. Anyway."

He nodded.

"Do you want that?" she asked.

"Yeah." His voice was gruff.

Shiloh moved her hand down to his. She squeezed it. This was the first time they'd held hands. Maybe ever.

They sat there for a while. Cary didn't know what was supposed to happen now.

He felt like he'd gotten the tiniest peek into the world he wanted. Like a door had swung open and then immediately closed.

But somehow he was still with Shiloh, still connected to her.

When she looked up at him, he could see she'd been crying.

He didn't think twice—he kissed her.

# before

THEY WERE BOTH CAST IN the fall play, their senior year of high school.

It was a mystery. A comedy. Cary was the bumbling detective. Shiloh was the lead, an old lady whose diamond necklace had disappeared.

Cary's mom had hurt her back that year. She fell on some ice. She'd already had enough problems before that—she smoked too much, she had high blood pressure. Now she was stuck on the couch between cortisone shots, and Cary was doing everything. Picking up her meds and dropping off bills. Running his older sister and her kids to the store. He still had his job at Hinky Dinky and all of his schoolwork. He probably shouldn't have gone out for the play—but he wanted to. And Shiloh wanted him to.

He missed a bunch of rehearsals. Then he took too long to get off book. A couple of the supporting players made snide comments about it. Cary thought about dropping out. Shiloh wouldn't let him.

Their first performance was great. Shiloh was hilarious as the old lady. Hunched over to seem smaller. With baby powder in her hair.

On the second day, they had two performances—a matinee and an evening show, plus Cary had to get up early for ROTC.

He was off his game that night. He missed a cue in the first act. And then he caught himself spacing out a few times onstage. He hadn't eaten dinner. He was tired.

There was one moment, after the intermission, when he realized just in time that he had a line—because Shiloh was staring at him, like she was waiting.

Cary sputtered out, "We'll trust the science, Mrs. Gadby. We always trust the science."

Shiloh's eyes got wide. The other people onstage kept going with their dialogue. And Cary realized he'd just said a line from the *next* scene. He'd skipped over a ton of exposition and a few major clues—and the other actors onstage had followed him right off the cliff.

They were deep into the wrong scene now. Everyone was making big, scared eyes at each other, like they didn't know what to do but keep going.

The scene eventually wound its way back to Shiloh.

She held up a finger. "Just one moment, Inspector . . ."

Shiloh brought them back to where they'd left off, but somehow accommodated everything else that had just happened in the scene.

She was completely improvising, and inviting Cary to improvise with her.

He locked his eyes on hers. He spoke in a Scottish accent. Between the two of them, they hit every point that they'd missed, and she made sure he still got to deliver his big joke: "Good lord, woman—not the perambulator!"

Cary just looked in Shiloh's eyes and followed her. And everyone else onstage followed her, too.

Shiloh didn't leave the stage for the next scene, so there was no time to strategize. They all just walked out there and let her steer them past the repetition until they were back on track.

The audience didn't notice.

Cary felt so mortified by his mistake. So ashamed of himself.

He thought he'd spoiled the whole show.

But Shiloh caught him. She held him. She carried him out of it.

After it was over, the actors who might have been angry with Cary were all too impressed with themselves to point fingers.

# before

"WE SHOULD HAVE SEX," SHILOH said. She was lying in his arms, on the bed in her dorm room. They'd been kissing for hours. They'd been kissing all day. They'd been kissing like they'd both realized that they should have been kissing all along.

Cary was feeling a little drunk from it. "What?"

"We should have sex. I've never done it."

He pulled his head back. "That's not a compelling reason."

Shiloh lifted herself up onto her elbow, resting her head on her hand. Her lips and chin were red from kissing. "It feels pretty compelling, from my perspective."

"We just talked about how I'm leaving," Cary said, "and how we don't know when we'll even see each other again."

"*Exactly.* This is our chance." She touched his neck. Her eyes were big and brown. "Please, Cary. I don't want to go on being someone who hasn't done this." She looked down at her hand. "And I want to do it with you."

Cary cleared his throat. "Why me?"

She looked up into his eyes again. "Apart from the fact that we're currently lying in my bed? Because I *know* you. And I trust you. I probably trust you more than anyone else on earth. I know you won't hurt me."

"Of course I won't hurt you."

She smiled. "And I like you. And you like me." She hooked her finger in the neck of his undershirt and pulled. "You like me, right?"

"Yes." His voice was flat. "I like you."

She twisted his shirt in her fingers. "I'm always going to remember the first time. And if it's with you, I know I won't regret it."

Cary tried to take that in without actually taking it in, without letting it mean too much. "You might still regret it," he said. "You should wait and do this with someone you love."

Shiloh sat up more. Her voice got louder. She pulled harder on his shirt. "Do you really think that's necessary? Most of my friends are doing it with"—she made a noise like *pfft*—"*whoever*, honestly. And besides, sex is just a *thing*, right? An activity? It's not magical. Or holy. It's just bodies. Biology. You don't need true love to unlock your vagina—virginity is a construct, Cary."

"I only agree with fifteen to twenty percent of what you're saying," he said. His T-shirt was cutting into the back of his neck.

Shiloh kept going. "And if love is an important factor . . . well, I probably love *you*. Like"—she let go of his shirt to wave her arm—"I don't know what else to call this." She lowered her eyebrows. Her voice dropped to a mumble. "There's nothing you could do to get on my bad side, Cary. There's no time that I don't want to see you . . ." She tugged at the hem of his shirt, still looking troubled. "It's like I've already made a permanent home for you in my heart."

Cary didn't trust himself to speak.

Shiloh lifted her head suddenly. She poked his stomach. "Wait. Are you saying that *you* don't want to have sex with someone unless you're in love with them?"

Cary couldn't look away from her face. "I'm not saying that. Exactly."

She shrugged. "I mean, you've already done it, right?"

"Yeah."

"With Angie?"

He didn't want to hear Shiloh talk about Angie. "Yes."

"Do *you* regret it?"

"I . . ." He didn't even want to *think* about Angie. "I don't want to talk about my previous experiences. Is this a job interview?"

"*No.* I'm not expecting you to be an expert. That's not why I want this."

"Good, Shiloh. Because I'm not an expert."

She made a fist in the fabric over his stomach. (She was *ruining* his T-shirt. He was glad he'd taken off his long-sleeved uniform shirt.) "But you know the steps," she said, "right? You won't get embarrassed."

Cary exhaled, disagreeably. "I'll probably still get embarrassed."

"But you won't embarrass *me*." She pushed her fist into his stomach. "Like, you won't do anything to humiliate me. I know you wouldn't."

"Of course not."

She was looking down at his stomach, biting her lip. "You won't laugh at me or judge me or tell stories about me."

"Shiloh . . ." His voice was so low, it cracked.

Her voice was low, too. "I know you wouldn't do that, Cary."

"Come here." He pulled her down against his chest. He pressed his face into her hair and cupped the back of her head. "Listen to me: You should have sex because you *want* to. Not as some sort of damage control."

"I *do* want to."

"You sound scared."

She looked up at him, pushing back against his grip. "That's the point—I don't *want* to be scared. I want it to be, like, lovely. And worth remembering."

Cary took a deep breath and let it out slowly. Every cell in his body felt divided. "I don't know . . ."

"What don't you know?"

"This is just *strange*," he said. "I feel like we're passing a resolution. Sex is supposed to be more organic than this."

"How do you know? You're no expert."

"You're trying to *manage* it."

"Cary, we're just talking."

"No." He pulled his hand away from her. "You're maneuvering. You're always maneuvering. It's not even chess—it's more overt than that. You're always making plans."

Shiloh frowned. "Sorry I'm not *organic* enough for you. Let's just go back to kissing, and then we can *accidentally* have sex like everyone else in the world."

She tried to kiss him. He caught her jaw and held it. "You want to have sex with me because I make you feel safe. That's what you're saying, right?"

"Yes."

"Well, that's kind of an insult, Shiloh."

She looked shocked. "Why is that an *insult*? There's nothing better than feeling safe. And probably nothing more rare."

Cary sighed. He felt himself losing this argument—or losing the will to argue. "Sex is supposed to be exciting."

"Look at all you have to teach me . . ."

He sighed again.

"You *don't* think it would be exciting, Cary?"

He was so lost. "I didn't say that."

"You're not saying anything!"

"That's not true." Cary shook his head. "Sometimes, in our history, that's been true. But it's not true right now."

Shiloh let her head drop to his chest. "Do you really not want to? If you really don't want to, I'll stop." She was giving in. Sometimes Shiloh gave in as soon as she'd won.

He couldn't see her face. He touched her cheek. He ran his fingers through her hair. "I just don't want you to regret this."

"Cary, honestly . . . I've never regretted anything with you."

This was all very dumb. Shiloh didn't have condoms—she didn't even know anyone who might have a condom.

Cary ended up walking to a convenience store. "This is going to take at least twenty minutes," he said. "You'll probably be asleep when I get back."

"I am *not* going to be asleep."

He bought condoms and Cherry Coke and Pringles and lip balm. When he got back to Shiloh's dorm, he stopped to use the bathroom on one of the boys' floors. He was still in uniform. The only other guy in the bathroom looked at him like he was a cop. Cary washed his face and dried it with a paper towel.

When he knocked on the door to Shiloh's room, she was still awake. She'd taken a shower and put on an old-fashioned nightgown. The only light was a reading lamp, and the stereo was on, turned low.

The first thing she said was, "Don't make fun of me."

"I'm not going to make fun of you," Cary said. "I'm going to kiss you."

She held up a hand between them. "First I want to tell you that you don't have to go through with this."

"Neither do you, Shiloh."

Her voice dropped. "Please, Cary. I want to."

So did he.

Cary had had sex before—in the back seat of his mom's car and on the couch in Angie's basement. Never in a bed. And never with all the time in the world.

And never with the girl he loved.

He worried about disappointing Shiloh. He knew what she didn't: that this was going to be so much faster than she expected, and so much quieter. It really was just bodies and biology, and Cary knew he didn't have the hang of it yet. He wasn't an expert.

They did it the first time with her nightgown still on.

Cary was worried he would hurt her, but she didn't cry or wince. The whole thing took a few minutes. Shiloh laughed when it was over, and she wouldn't stop kissing his face.

"You okay?" he asked.

"Yeah. Are you okay?"

The answer was no. Cary felt hot inside, and messy. Like his true feelings were going to flood in and destroy everything. Being with Shiloh was always hard work—managing his emotions, managing her excesses. This was too much. His safeguards were failing.

He sat up and took care of the condom. He handed her the Cherry Coke.

She was softer, after. She'd gotten what she wanted, and she hadn't decided what she wanted next. This was Shiloh in a rare moment—without an agenda.

He took off her nightgown, and they kissed some more.

Shiloh's body was different than he'd imagined. (He'd spent a lot of time on this.) She was smaller in his fantasies. More like the girls he'd seen in magazines. More like a doll.

In life, in her bed, she was Shiloh-sized—and all skin. He couldn't get over how long she was. Their bodies met at every angle. He wanted to see her in the light.

The second time was better.

It lasted longer. Shiloh looked in his eyes more. She made more noise.

It felt so good that he lost track of himself. Shiloh must have lost track, too. "I love you," she said to him, while he was still inside of her. "I love you, Cary. I love you."

They were the best two days of his life.

Holed up in Shiloh's dorm room, between boot camp and whatever came next.

They ordered pizza and ate it in her bed. They watched *Star Trek* reruns.

Cary got glimpses of Shiloh's body in the sunlight. Her shoulders, her knees. Her bare feet.

She was less self-conscious at night—they had two nights together. Cary tried to catalog and file away every minute.

They'd said that this was . . .

What had they said? Exactly? What had Shiloh said?

That their timing was bad. That they couldn't be together if they weren't going to *be* together.

But she was so happy. She was clearly happy. And affectionate. She kept touching him and kissing him. Everything was so easy.

There were moments—*hours*—when it felt like they'd finally arrived, like they'd finally made their way to each other. Like all their previous interactions had finally clicked together in a sensible way. Wasn't this where Shiloh and Cary had been heading all along?

And even though they'd said—Shiloh had said—that this wouldn't work and couldn't happen, it clearly *was* working. It *was* happening.

They couldn't undo it now.

They couldn't know how good they were together and pretend otherwise.

"I love you," Shiloh kept saying between kisses. "I love you, Cary."


An hour before Cary had to get on a bus, he went down to the men's floor to take a shower.

When he got back, Shiloh had showered and changed, and she was making her bed.

"I found one of your socks," she said, "and now I'm worried that something else might be missing. You only have six socks, right? Total?"

"I have six pairs. I'll be fine."

She kept cleaning and straightening. She seemed upset.

Cary was upset, too. He sat on her roommate's bed, watching her. Not sure what to say. He didn't know how he was supposed to walk away from her.

"I can get phone calls now," he said.

Shiloh laughed harshly. That hurt for a second, but then he saw that she was trying not to cry.

She wanted to walk to the bus stop with him. It was a couple of blocks away.

"I never gave you that tour of campus," she said.

"I saw what I came to see," Cary said.

Shiloh laughed again, less horribly.

When they got to the bus stop, they turned to each other. There was no telling how much time they had left before the bus would get there.

"Shiloh," he said, "I need you to be serious for a minute."

"I know." She couldn't look at him.

"This weekend . . ."

She lifted her chin. "Cary," she said. "This doesn't have to be . . . *anything*."

"It's already *something*."

"Yeah, but it doesn't have to be. It could just be an island of good. For us."

"An island?"

"I know how you are, about honor and obligation. And I'm just— I'm setting you free, okay? You don't owe me anything. This was just one great weekend between friends. You know what I mean?"

Cary felt very cold. His peacoat was in his seabag. "I think I know what you mean."

"Nobody's coming after you with a shotgun, Cary. You didn't sign a mystic contract with your penis." She pushed on his upper arm. "Go start your new life, it's okay."

"Is that still what you want?"

"Do I want you to start your new life, free of obligation and regret? Yes." She turned her head toward the road. "There's a bus coming—is this your bus?"

"I don't know."

She grabbed on to his arms. "I'll write you, okay? Will you write me back?"

"Yeah."

It *was* his bus. Shiloh didn't kiss him goodbye or make it easy for him to kiss her. She touched his shoulders and elbows and patted his bag.

The last thing he felt was her hand on the small of his back.


She did write to him. The same sort of letters that she'd written before. About her classes and the plays she was in.

Her letters made Cary feel insane.

He sent postcards back.

He called her a few times. It was hard to catch her in her room. She couldn't afford long-distance calls, so he told her to call him collect—but he wasn't always around to take her calls.

When they did talk, it was strange. He was never alone in his barracks.

He wrote her a letter once, saying how he felt—trying to say what he really felt.

Her next letter was exactly the same as all the others.

Nine or ten months after Cary saw Shiloh in Des Moines, Mikey told him that she had a boyfriend.

Cary stopped writing to her.

He realized that she'd already stopped writing to him.

## TWENTY

SHILOH COULDN'T REACH HER DRESS, and there were no blankets to pull up over herself.

"You hoped I'd be different?" Her voice came out thick. She was surprised it came out at all. "That's funny, Cary. I hoped you'd be the same."

Cary was fastening his belt. He was facing away from her. Straight-backed. Bare-shouldered. Shiloh found his shirt on the bed and threw it in his direction.

"I'm sorry," he said again. "This was a mistake."

She crossed her legs and pulled a pillow in front of her chest. She was crying now. She tried to stop. "Yeah, I guess that's how you've always seen me."

He jerked his head around. "*What?*"

"Don't look at me," she said through tears.

"Jesus Christ," Cary said, like this whole thing was too much for him. "I don't even know what you're talking about . . ." He bent over and felt around the floor. A few seconds later, he held her dress out behind his back.

Shiloh grabbed it. "I'm just agreeing with you. You're right, I haven't changed—I'm still someone you'd regret sleeping with."

"That's not— I don't *regret*—"

She pulled the dress over her head. "You just said that you did! Which I kind of already knew, but thank you for explicitly confirming it."

He turned to face her. "That's not what I meant. I meant— I meant I'm not going to be your—" He was so upset, he was sputtering. "Your sexual *safety blanket* again."

"There was never anything *safe* about you, Cary!"

"You're giving me whiplash, Shiloh!"

"Go, then. Fly away home. Your shirt's on the floor."

"You—"

There was a soft knock at the door. "Shiloh? You in there?"

"*Shit,*" Shiloh whispered.

Cary groaned. He started looking for his shirt.

"I'm here!" she called. "I'm fine, Mom."

"Because I've got my gun and a cell phone, and I've already dialed the nine and the one."

"She doesn't have a gun," Shiloh said, moving quickly past Cary to crack open the door.

Her mom was standing there in pajamas, looking worried. "I heard a man's voice."

Shiloh held the door mostly closed and slid past it into the hall. "It's fine," she said quietly. "It's Cary."

Her mom's eyes got big, and she mouthed, *Cary?*

Shiloh nodded.

"*Cary?*" her mom called out. "*Is that really you?*"

"Hi, Gloria," Cary said from behind the door. He sounded miserable.

Her mom pinched Shiloh's upper arm. "You brought *Cary* home from the wedding?" She was whisper-hissing. "I didn't think you had it in you!"

Shiloh pulled her arm away and rubbed it. "Okay, well . . . I need to get back in there now and finish arguing with him."

Her mom tsk-ed in disappointment. "Oh, honey, don't argue with Cary. You don't get to make new old friends, you know?"

"Yeah." Shiloh nodded again. "Okay."

"I know you're out of practice, Shiloh, but the point of bringing men home isn't to argue with them."

"I thought you were worried about my *safety*."

"Well, I was, but that's when I figured any man in your bedroom had to be a home intruder . . ." She frowned. "*Should* I be worried? Are you okay?"

"I'm fine. Don't worry." Shiloh slipped back through the door. "Good night, Mom."

"Good night." She craned her head after Shiloh. *"Good night, Cary! Don't argue with my daughter! You can't go making any new old friends!"*

Shiloh closed the door. Cary was fully dressed and sitting on her bed. He'd turned on the reading lamp next to her pillow. You could see now what a mess her room was.

"I'm sorry," she said. "She wasn't expecting me to have a guest."

Cary ignored Shiloh's apology. His face was under control, but you could tell he was upset because his nostrils were twitching. "I don't regret sleeping with you," he said. "I just don't want to go through it all again."

"That still sounds like you regret sleeping with me."

*"No—"* He took a breath, then tried again, in a more level voice. "No. I meant, I don't want to go through what happens next. When the window closes, and you go back to your real life."

Shiloh felt on display. Braless and barefooted. She crossed her arms. "Are we talking about now or then?"

Cary's eyes flashed. "Both! I'm never a real option for you, Shiloh. I thought maybe tonight would be different—that we could meet each other in a new place, that maybe you still had feelings for me . . ."

"I have nothing *but* feelings for you."

He laughed, joylessly. "You've already decided I'm a one-night stand!"

She felt so confused. *"Isn't* this a one-night stand? Aren't you only in Omaha for the night?"

He glared at her. "Is that the only reason you're interested?"

*"No."*

"Because you only seem to be interested in me when I'm walking away."

*"Cary."* She shook her head. "That's not fair."

"You pretended like it never happened!" His voice was extra quiet, like he was trying not to shout.

She jabbed a finger at him. "No, *you* pretended like it never happened!"

"You couldn't *wait* to tell me it was nothing, Shiloh. Before we even had a chance."

"I was giving you an *out*! Which you immediately took. You didn't even kiss me goodbye!"

"That's not how it happened!"

"Don't tell me how it happened—I was there!"

"You micromanaged every moment." He was looking away from her, counting on his fingers. "*You* decided we should have sex. *You* decided what it meant. You told me how to *feel*."

She scoffed. "I sound pretty terrible—why are you even here?"

He looked at her again, seething. "You said it was *nothing*."

"No, Cary, I said I *loved* you!"

"I loved you, too!"

"You didn't say that—you've never said that."

"I wrote you a letter!"

"You broke *up* with me in a letter."

"How could I *break up* with you? We were never together!"

"That's what I thought," she said, "but you sure fucking did it anyway."

"Don't swear at me."

"Don't tell me what to do."

He stood up. "I won't. This is— I'm going home now. You don't have to drive me. I'll walk."

Shiloh started crying again. She couldn't let Cary walk away—but there was nothing she could do to stop him. There was nothing she could say. She didn't have any pull with him anymore. What pull she'd had, she'd used up to get him here.

She scrubbed at her eyes with the back of her wrist and sat down on the bed. "I was giving you an out," she said again, with less fight.

Cary was standing at the door. He looked back at her. "How do you know that I wanted an out?"

"Then or now?"

"Either."

She laughed. "Cary, I'm divorced, I have two kids, and I live a million miles away from you. I didn't want you to think I was living in some fantasy world where tonight would lead to something."

He shook his head. "You decided all of this without me . . ."

"I was just being realistic."

"Oh my god, Shiloh, that's exactly what you said back then."

"How do you even *remember* what I said back then?"

He had one hand on the doorknob and one on his hip. "You don't think that weekend *stands out*?"

Shiloh let her head hang forward. "I don't know what to say . . . I don't know what you want from me."

Cary took a deep breath.

"Nothing," he said.

## TWENTY-ONE

RYAN BROUGHT THE KIDS BACK before breakfast. (Pick them up after dinner, bring them back before breakfast.) He had rehearsals that day, even though it was Saturday.

Ryan taught theater at a suburban high school—which was about as demanding as directing a show on Broadway. Seriously. His school put on five shows a year, plus banquets, club meetings, competitions, elementary school tours . . .

Shiloh tried to accommodate his schedule because it was the path of least resistance—the path of least Ryan.

They'd been granted shared custody of the kids. Shiloh had pushed for the greater share. Ryan said she had outdated and problematic ideas about the importance of mothers versus fathers. (Well, duh.)

The judge had taken Ryan's side. Fifty-fifty. Shiloh usually ended up with more than that. Ryan's schedule—and general temperament—meant he was always asking her to take extra hours and days and meals. It was hard for Shiloh to complain about something she'd fought for.

She was still asleep when he rang the doorbell Saturday morning.

"I've got it," she heard her mom call.

Then Shiloh heard the front door open . . . Heard the kids come in . . . Heard Ryan talking to her mom . . . *inside* the house. Shiloh groaned and rolled out of bed, getting dressed as quickly as she could in dirty jeans and an old cast T-shirt from one of the shows at her theater—*Old Yeller*.

Junie ran up to Shiloh on the stairs. "Dad's making pancakes!"

Shiloh looked up.

Ryan was grinning at her. Shiloh's mom was standing behind him, making big *What the fuck?* eyes.

"I promised them pancakes," he said, "but I didn't have eggs, so I said I'd make them over here."

"Um . . ." Shiloh frowned. "I don't know if we have eggs."

Junie was pulling on Shiloh's shirt. She was six and tall for her age. And she'd inherited both of her parents' flair for the dramatic, compounded. "We do!" she said—she *exclaimed*. "I already checked, and we only need one egg. That's the recipe."

Shiloh looked at Ryan again. He was giving her his best *Come on, Shiloh* smile.

Ryan's smiles were very effective, as a rule. He was very charismatic. Very attractive, to most people. Even to Shiloh sometimes. (Even after everything.)

Ryan looked like the smart-alecky sidekick on a teen sitcom. Still, at thirty-six. He was short, with dark hair and crinkly blue eyes and a smile that tugged up more on one side than the other. (This was possibly a learned behavior.) It was like Paul Rudd, Adam Scott, Jason Bateman and John Cusack had all pooled their distinguishing characteristics into one Midwestern high school drama teacher.

Shiloh worked very hard not to despise Ryan at a cellular level; her kids had too many of his actual cells.

She wrinkled her nose. "I don't think that's a great idea."

Ryan tried out a different smile, a softer one. "It's just pancakes, Shy."

"I want pancakes!" Junie said.

"I think Dad has to get to work," Shiloh said firmly. "He has rehearsal."

"Noooo," Junie whined.

"Noooo," Gus echoed. Gus was almost three. Most of what he said so far was just an echo of Junie.

"Yep!" Ryan finally relented, swooping Gus up into his arms for a hug. "Mommy's making pancakes. She makes the best pancakes anyway. *Mmmwah!*" He gave Gus a big kiss and then set him down, reaching for Junie. He had to pull her away from Shiloh's legs. "*Mwah, mwah!* You guys be good for Mommy. I'll see you Tuesday. I love you."

Gus had started to cry. He'd been doing that lately whenever one of them said goodbye. You'd think Gus would be used to this arrangement—Shiloh and Ryan had separated when he was just a few months old.

But Gus seemed newly rattled by the instability. He cried over everything. He'd bitten someone at daycare. And after six weeks of potty-training, he was less potty-trained than ever. Even *mentioning* the potty chair sent him into tears.

Shiloh went to pick him up. It was an excuse not to walk Ryan out. "Come on, Gus-Gus. Let's make pancakes."

"I'll text you about next week, Shiloh. See ya, Gloria!"

"Goodbye, Ryan!" Her mom waved.

As soon as Ryan was out the door, her mom followed Shiloh into the kitchen. "Why does he come inside every time? It's like he needs to piss all over the place, so it smells like him."

"Mom. You know the rules. Not in front of the kids."

Her mom took Gus from Shiloh's arms. "Gus-Gus isn't a kid. He's my baby."

"Not a baby," he pouted. Gus was big for his age, too. But he was still round like a baby, with chubby arms and legs, and a little dimple in his chin like Spanky from *Our Gang*. He had fine dark hair and round brown eyes. He looked *of* Shiloh and Ryan, but not really *like* either of them.

Shiloh got out the eggs and the milk. "Do you want pancakes, Gus?"

"No! Want *Hercules*!"

"You have to ask in a nice voice," she said. "You don't yell at Mommy."

"*Hercuuuuleees*," he said, like he was begging for it on his deathbed.

"Junie!" Shiloh called out to the living room. "You guys can watch a DVD."

Shiloh's mom set Gus on the floor, so he could toddle away despondently.

Shiloh had had big ideas about not letting the television raise her children. But then she'd actually had children. And then she'd gotten divorced. And now every day felt like something to get through alive. Something to try and stay awake for.

At least her kids were being raised by actual children's programming, and not *Match Game* and *Days of Our Lives,* like Shiloh had been.

"I was hoping you still had Cary squirreled away up there," her mom said.

"Uh, no." Shiloh started on the pancake batter. "He left right after I talked to you."

"Oh, I'm sorry, honey."

"It wasn't you—it just wasn't a great idea, I guess. We were both drunk on nostalgia."

Her mom leaned against the counter. She was shorter than Shiloh, with shoulder-length strawberry-blond hair that she colored herself. She worked at the airport bar and was already in her uniform—black slacks and a silky black blouse with the top two buttons undone, a small gold crucifix hanging on a gold chain around her neck. "I always thought you were sleeping with Cary back in high school."

"And I always told you that I wasn't."

"I didn't believe you. I thought you were going to make me a grandmother at thirty-five—you were here all the time by yourself."

"We were usually on the porch."

Her mom laughed. "Do you remember that time I walked in—"

"Yes."

"I was *sure*—"

"We were just friends. When do you have to be at work?"

"Eleven," her mom said. "Time for you to take a shower and a breath if you want."

Shiloh tried not to assume on a regular basis that her mom would help with Junie and Gus—she wasn't one of those hungry grandmas who couldn't get enough of their precious grandbabies. But she was more enthusiastic as a grandparent than she'd ever been as a parent. Shiloh had had to keep herself entertained as a kid. But her mom played dolls with Junie. She read board books to Gus. She'd take them both to the park across the street on her days off.

Shiloh's grandmother used to watch Shiloh every day after school.

Maybe her mom just saw this as the circle of life. The circle of single mothers. From that perspective, Ryan was the most active father in *generations*.

"Thanks," Shiloh said. She finished the pancakes, eating the most misshapen ones herself, over the counter.

Then she went upstairs to take a shower. The bathroom was a mess of dirty clothes and bathtub toys. Smears of toothpaste. She was relieved that Cary hadn't had to come in here last night. She cleaned up the worst of it while she waited for the water to get hot.

Then she stood, blank-headed, in the shower, trying to sweep away thoughts of Cary as soon as they rose up. Shiloh had already lain awake for hours the night before thinking about him.

It had been very *Cary* of him to imply that he wanted more from her—only *after* they'd passed the point at which any more could happen.

It was like waiting for someone else to clear the table and then saying, *"But I was going to eat that pizza."*

Was Cary right about Shiloh being headstrong and manipulative? Yes. Obviously. Was he right that she'd been too quick to judgment? Yes. Always.

But when had Cary *ever* indicated that he wanted something more with Shiloh?

Even last night, during his grand stand, he hadn't shown her any cards. *"What if I didn't want an out?"* he'd said. Yeah, what *if*, Cary?

Shiloh shouldn't have pinned all these deep, romantic feelings on seeing him again. (She should never have bought a new dress.) Maybe she lacked the imagination to see herself with someone new. Ryan was gone, and Shiloh had gone back to the only other person she'd ever loved.

She *did* have other opportunities—of this sort. There was a single dad who volunteered at the theater who'd invited Shiloh to go on a bike ride . . . He was only *slightly* creepy. And one of the costume makers at work, a woman, had asked Shiloh out to a concert after her divorce was final. Shiloh could probably manage to have sex again . . .

With someone who had far less destructive potential than Cary Saunders.

She'd opened herself up to the person with the *most* power to hurt her—even Ryan couldn't affect her like that anymore—and he'd torn through her like a tornado through a trailer park.

Shiloh wrapped herself in a towel and went to get dressed in her bedroom, digging out another theater T-shirt and another pair of jeans.

She picked up the books that Cary had kicked off her bed. Shiloh had a bad habit now that she slept alone of stacking books, and sometimes dishes, in the bed next to her.

She gathered up the work papers and dirty coffee mugs on her bedside table. She threw away Kleenexes and cough drop wrappers. She made a pile of clean clothes to put away and threw dirty clothes out into the hallway. The washer and dryer were in the basement.

She was reaching for her tights from the night before when she saw it, kicked under her bed—a man's wallet.

She picked it up and sat on the bed. The wallet was brown leather, worn slick from riding in Cary's pocket. She didn't have to open it to know it was his—but she still did. She looked at his driver's license in the clear plastic window. *Cary Roderick Saunders. Brown eyes, brown hair.*

Shiloh pulled her hair into a thick bun—even though it was still wet and heavy and would give her a headache—and headed downstairs. "Mom? Cary left his wallet. I'm going to run it over to him."

Her mom was painting her nails in the small dining room between the living room and the kitchen. "Oh, *really . . .*"

"I'm sure it was unintentional. That smells toxic, by the way—open a window."

"It's too cold to open a window. Come right back, all right? I have to leave soon."

"I will."

"And don't argue with him!"

Shiloh found a long cardigan buried under the kids' coats at the end of the banister and stepped out of the house.

She almost got in the car, but then decided to walk. Cary's mom only lived a few blocks away, and the neighborhood felt pretty safe on a Saturday morning.

Shiloh hadn't realized that Cary's mom was still in her old house. (Shiloh was always coming and going; she never really saw anyone from the neighborhood.) She was relieved to hear that his mom was still alive—her health had been precarious even when they were in high school.

Shiloh walked briskly, rubbing the leather wallet in her pocket.

This didn't have to be painful. Cary might not even come to the door. Shiloh could keep it low-key.

She got to the house, and it looked exactly like it had in 1991, like the same kids had left their broken Little Tikes toys out in the front yard. The house was big and gray, with cracked siding and a chain-link fence that had seen many better days. Shiloh let herself through the gate, keeping an eye out for dogs.

They must all be inside—she heard them go crazy when she stepped onto the porch. She knocked on the door.

"I'm coming!" a woman called.

"Mom, I've got it," Shiloh heard Cary say.

"I said *I've* got it." The door opened.

Several dogs hopped up onto the screen door. Cary's mom was standing there. She was a heavyset woman with short, curly gray hair. She looked a little thinner these days—and more fragile. She was wearing an oxygen tube.

"Hi there," Shiloh said. "Is Cary here?"

His mom smiled. "Is that Shiloh?"

"Yeah." Shiloh smiled, too. "Hi, Lois. How are you?"

"Honey, look at you! Come on in." Lois's voice was breathy. "Cary, it's Shiloh."

She held the door open, and two of the dogs started jumping on Shiloh.

"*Mom,*" Cary said. He sounded frustrated.

"Come in, honey." Lois touched Shiloh's arm. "Don't worry about the puppies, they like people. What can I get you to drink? I've got iced tea and Diet Pepsi."

Shiloh let herself be herded into the living room. It smelled like cigarette smoke in here—but less like dog than she was expecting.

Shiloh had never been inside Cary's house. The living room was crowded with stuff. Too much furniture, and piles of clothes and papers. The coffee table was *brimming* with pill bottles and drinking glasses, and a certain kind of decorative angel figurine—Shiloh thought maybe you could buy them at the Hallmark store. There were at least fifteen of the angels on this table alone.

Cary was on the landline, with the receiver tucked between his ear and his shoulder, and one hand holding the base of the phone against his hip. He was reaching for the dogs with his other hand, pulling them away from Shiloh and one-by-one shutting them behind a door. (Where they one-by-one went ballistic.)

"They weren't hurting anybody," his mom said, irritated with him, and settled with a *"Phew"* onto the couch. "Sit down, Shiloh. What a treat to see you, honey. Cary told me you work at a theater."

"I teach theater," Shiloh said. "To kids."

Cary was still trying to get the dogs shut behind the door. The phone cord was stretched to its limit. There was a photo portrait of him, from when he first joined the Navy, hanging by his head.

"Isn't that just perfect!" Lois said. She seemed genuinely delighted. Cary's mom had never been anything but sweet to Shiloh, the few times they'd met. "You were always such a good actress."

"Thank you."

"I loved watching the two of you up there in those plays. Do you remember when Cary was Mr. Scrooge?"

"Of course," Shiloh said. "He was so talented—I'm sure he still is."

Lois laid a hand on Shiloh's thigh. "Can I get you a Diet Pepsi, honey? Or some iced tea? Cary, get Shiloh something to drink."

"I'm really okay," Shiloh said.

His mom sighed and gestured toward Cary. He was wearing jeans and a long-sleeved T-shirt, and his hair was sticking up a little. "He's trying to get my electric bill sorted out . . ."

Shiloh caught Cary's eye and mouthed, *I'm sorry.* She slid his wallet out of her pocket so he could see it, and shrugged.

". . . but it's Saturday," Lois went on, shaking her head. "And they've got nobody answering those phones."

"Have you tried to take care of it online?" Shiloh asked.

"She doesn't have a computer," Cary said. "And she's not set up to pay online."

"I told him they're not gonna turn the power off when they say they will, anyway," Lois said. "This can all wait till Monday."

"I won't be here Monday," he said.

"Angel will take care of it."

Cary rolled his eyes.

"I didn't mean to pop in," Shiloh said. "I should go."

"Shiloh! You have to wait for Cary to get off the phone—you kids haven't even had a chance to visit."

"Cary can call me when he has time." Shiloh set the wallet on the table next to her. "I'm so glad I got a chance to see you, Lois." She reached out and squeezed Lois's hand.

"Well, if you have to go so quick . . ."

Shiloh stood up. She looked at Cary. He was watching her. His jaw was clenched.

"Um . . ." Shiloh wasn't sure whether he'd want any helpful advice from her right now—but decided to offer it up anyway. "They've got a customer service window. You could go pay in person."

"On a Saturday?" he asked.

"Till noon."

"Well, there you go," Lois said. "You can go when Angel brings back the car."

Cary was rubbing his temples, staring into space. He looked a million years old—he looked eighteen again.

"I could take you," Shiloh said.

Cary looked up at her, his eyes widening.

"You don't have to do that, honey," Lois said. "We can wait for Angel."

Shiloh held his gaze. "I don't mind—if you don't mind. I'll have to
bring my kids."

Lois clapped her hands, smiling. "I didn't know you had kids, Shiloh.
How many?"

Shiloh smiled back. "Two." She looked at Cary again and gently
shook her head. "I don't mind."

Cary nodded. He hung up the phone.

## TWENTY-TWO

"NO CAR," GUS SAID. "NO bye-bye."

"Yes bye-bye." Shiloh snaked Gus's arm through his coat sleeve. "Maybe we'll go to McDonald's."

"*I* want McDonald's," Junie said.

Shiloh's mom frowned. "You just had pancakes."

"Quiet, Mother, I'm bribing them. Put on your shoes, Junie."

"You're taking him *where*?" Her mom was still frowning and blowing on her nails.

"To pay his mom's electric bill."

"Oh." She frowned for a new reason. "Well, you better hurry—the window closes at noon."

Shiloh zipped up Gus's coat. "I know." She grabbed her purse and headed for the car. "Come on, Junie!"

"I didn't know we had *errands* today," Junie said, following Shiloh out onto the porch, dragging her feet. Her hair was cut in a short bob. It was thick and straight like Shiloh's, and it moved like a figure skater's when she shook her head.

"We're doing someone a favor," Shiloh said.

"Who?"

"My friend Cary."

Junie folded her arms. "You don't *have* a friend named Cary!"

Everything Junie said was over-emphasized and over-emoted. If you didn't know her, it seemed like an act. If you knew her . . . well, it still seemed like an act, but Shiloh was used to it. She opened the door on Junie's side. "You don't know all my friends."

"Yes, I do, Mommy. Who *don't* I know?"

"Cary, for one. Get buckled up."

Junie climbed into her car seat, sighing loudly.

Gus had started to whimper. "No bye-bye."

"Yes bye-bye," Shiloh said, setting him down in his car seat. "We'll go for a drive, we'll get French fries, and we'll do something nice for someone. It feels good to help people."

"Doesn't your friend have a car?" Junie asked.

"Nope."

Shiloh got behind the wheel and put in a Disney sing-along CD. Even Gus couldn't resist a Disney sing-along. Hopefully Cary liked *Hercules.*

Did Cary like kids?

She'd only seen him around his nieces and nephews and his mom's boyfriends' kids—and he'd never been happy about it.

When Shiloh got to his house, Cary was waiting on the porch with Lois. He'd put on a navy blue hooded sweatshirt. He started helping his mom down the steps.

Shiloh got out of the car. She opened the gate for them.

Cary's face was flat with stress. "She's got to go to the bank first."

"I need to get a money order," Lois explained. She was more breathless when she was walking. She wore her oxygen canister in a bag over her arm.

Shiloh went to the front passenger door. Cary brought his mom over to help her in. It was slow going.

"Are you coming, too?" Shiloh asked Cary.

He nodded. "I'm sorry."

"It's okay," she said. "I'll just have to move their car seats."

"Oh. I wasn't thinking . . ."

"Hello, angels," Lois said, looking into the back seat.

Shiloh opened Junie's door to try to figure everything out.

Cary was right behind her. "I can just sit between them."

"I don't know," Shiloh said. "It's pretty tight."

"It's a short trip. I mean—" He looked at her. "This is your car and your kids, sorry."

"If you want to try . . ."

Cary turned to Junie, who was riveted by his sudden appearance.

"Suck in your legs," he said, and climbed over her.

"Oh my lord," Junie said.

Cary was hovering over the back seat, moving books and toys off the narrow strip between the boosters.

"I'm so sorry," Shiloh said. "Sweep all that on the floor. Are you—"

He wedged himself between the seats, his body at an angle. "I'm in, I'm fine."

She laughed a little. "I'm not sure you're getting out."

"Oh my *lord*," Junie said again, in case they hadn't heard her the first time. She was making her eyes huge.

"Okay," Shiloh said, closing the door. By the time she got around to the front, Junie was introducing herself.

"I'm Juniper, and that's my brother, Gus."

"Juniper—what a beautiful name," Lois said. "I'm Mrs. Cass. But you can call me Grandma Lois, everybody does."

"You can call me Junie."

"And that's my baby boy," Lois said, "Cary."

Junie looked like she was pretending to try not to laugh, with her hand over her mouth. "Cary isn't a boy's name!"

"It's my name," Cary said.

Junie raised her eyebrows into her hairline. She had Groucho Marx eyebrows, just like Shiloh. All she needed was a cigar.

"Mom banks at Commercial Federal," Cary said to Shiloh. "Is there one on the way?"

"I like the one on Saddle Creek," Lois said.

"There's one on the way . . ." Shiloh tried to picture it. She didn't want to take wrong turns in front of Cary.

Cary was sitting mostly sideways and bracing himself on his mom's seat.

"You should be up front," Lois said. "There's more legroom."

"I'm fine," he said. "I'm grateful for the ride."

"God knows I owe you a ride," Shiloh said. "I owe you a thousand rides."

"Are you really my mommy's friend?" Junie asked, feigning disbelief.

"We went to school together," Shiloh said.

"They were *best* friends," Lois added. "Birds of a feather." She was twisting in her seat to look at Junie. "You look so much like your mommy."

"No," Junie said. "I have brown hair, and Mommy has black hair. And I have blue eyes, and Mommy has brown eyes."

"You look just like her," Cary said, looking down at Junie, unsmiling.

"No!" Junie said, covering her face.

"No!" Gus echoed, whimpering.

"Don't mind Gus," Shiloh said. "He's going through a blue period."

"We don't mind Gus." Lois patted Shiloh's arm. "He's perfect. I've got some candy—can they have candy?"

"No," Cary said.

"Let Shiloh decide." Lois was already reaching for her purse, struggling against the seat belt.

"It's diabetic hard candy," he said.

"It's not diabetic," his mom grumbled. "It's sugar-free."

Gus's whimpers were getting louder.

"Actually," Shiloh said, "if you don't mind Disney music . . ." She turned up the CD. "They like to sing."

Junie was aghast. "Mommy, I can't sing in front of people!"

"That is patently untrue," Shiloh muttered.

"I don't mind singing in front of people," Lois said. "I know this one." It was "The Bare Necessities." She started singing, much louder than Shiloh was expecting. *"Forget about your worries and your strife."*

Gus stopped crying to stare at her.

Junie started laughing. "I think Gus likes your voice!"

"You better sing with me," Lois said.

Junie started singing, hiding her face.

They kept singing all the way downtown. Junie very quickly forgot that she was hiding. She asked Cary if he'd like to sing, too.

"I'm sorry," he said seriously. "I have too much on my mind."

After two songs, Lois said she had to catch her breath, so Shiloh sang with Junie instead.

When they got to the bank, Shiloh had to double-park to let them out. Cary leaned forward. "This might take a few minutes," he said to Shiloh.

"Do what you need to do. We'll be fine."

He nodded. "Mom, wait for me to help you out." He turned to Gus. "Gus, I'm climbing over you this time."

"No!" Gus said.

Cary did it anyway, but then couldn't open the door.

"Shit." Shiloh put the car in park. "I've got to let you out. Hang on."

"Oh my good LORD," Junie said.

Shiloh opened the back door, and Cary practically fell out of the car.

"Sorry," she said, turning off the child-safety lock.

He looked up at her. "Stop apologizing. You're saving the day."

Cary hurried over to help his mom, who hadn't waited for him and was stepping out into the street.

They should have made a plan to meet again—Shiloh should have given Cary her number. There was nowhere close to park. Shiloh decided to just circle the block. But then Gus pooped his diaper.

"Mommy," Junie said, clutching her throat. "I can't even *breathe*."

Shiloh drove until she found a parking lot, then changed Gus under the hatchback of the car. Junie complained the whole time. Shiloh tried to talk to Gus about the freedom of potty-trained living. He alternately cried and ignored her.

Then they drove around some more to find a trash can. Shiloh rolled all the windows down, and Junie was sure she was going to freeze "to *death*."

By the time they got back to the bank, Cary and his mom were standing outside. He was trying to shield her from the wind.

"Sorry!" Shiloh called out, before they were even in the car. "We had a diaper emergency."

"I know all about those," Lois said breathlessly. Cary was getting her settled. "Don't get hit by a car," she told him.

He climbed over Gus again.

"Sorry," Shiloh said.

"We'd just walked out," Cary said. "Electric company next?"

"Yep."

The power company was only a few minutes away, and there was parking. Lois stayed in the car while Cary went in to pay the bill. Shiloh turned up the heat.

"I'm lucky to have a son like that," Lois said, watching him walk away. "That boy's never had an irresponsible day in his life—he was still taking care of me when he was in Japan."

Shiloh smiled. She wasn't sure what to say. Gus started crying again, angrily. Junie was trying to hand him a book. He slapped it away.

"Gus," Shiloh said, "I know you're unhappy, but you have to be kind."

Lois turned as much as she could to look into the back seat. "Should we sing some more, Gus?"

"No," he snarled. "Don't talk to me!"

"Poor Gus," she said, and then to Shiloh—"Are you sure they can't have candy?"

"They don't need candy," Shiloh said. "I'm already bribing them with McDonald's."

"Grandma Lois," Junie said politely, "would you like to go to McDonald's with us?"

"I love McDonald's," Lois said.

They decided to listen to Disney songs again, and everyone but Gus sang along. He seemed mildly mollified by that.

Cary's step was noticeably lighter when he walked back toward the car. Shiloh got up and let Junie out of her seat so that Cary could climb in more easily.

"All good?" she asked.

"Yeah," he said, sounding relieved. "Thanks."

He got into the car.

Junie climbed in after him. She covered her face. "I forgot your name," she said.

"It's Cary."

She dropped her hands. "Cary, would you like some McDonald's?"

"Yeah," he said. "I really would."

Even Gus cheered up once they were in the McDonald's drive-through.

The kids got Happy Meals. Cary got a Big Mac and an orange drink.

"What's an *orange* drink?" Junie asked.

"It's the best drink," he said.

"Well, I will have to try it sometime."

They listened to Disney songs on the way home, and everyone sang. Even Cary. It had been a million years since Shiloh had heard him sing—but she'd heard him sing a million times. She tried not to catch his eyes in the mirror.

"Don't sing with your mouth full," Cary told Junie.

Gus liked "Go the Distance" best, and no one minded if they listened to it three times in a row. Everyone in the car just seemed relieved, generally speaking.

When they got to Cary's house, Lois had to use the bathroom, so they didn't spend much time on goodbyes.

"I'm going to invite you over for fried chicken," Lois told Junie.

"Okay," Junie said, "thank you."

Shiloh didn't get out of the car to help. Cary seemed to have it under control.

He looked back at her when he got to the porch.

She waved.

"It feels good to help people," Junie said primly.

Shiloh nodded.

# before

SHILOH WAS HOME ALONE WATCHING a *Newlywed Game* rerun when Cary came to her front door. (It was the end of her junior year, and her mom had decided that they couldn't afford cable. Shiloh watched *so many* game shows.)

Cary was standing there in his Hinky Dinky uniform, and he was holding a baby. He had another kid with him, too—his niece Angel. (She was actually his half sister.)

"Hey," Shiloh said, opening the door.

Cary's white button-down shirt looked wet. So did his khakis. His tie wasn't tied.

"Are your clothes wet?"

"I need a favor," he said. "A big one."

"Okay . . ."

"I've got to go to work, but there's no one to watch Angel and Jesse. I can't miss another shift."

"Okay . . ."

"Will you watch them? It's four hours."

"Um," Shiloh said, "sure. I mean . . . I don't think I know how?"

"Just keep them from dying," he said.

"I'll try? I mean—yeah, I'll try."

Cary held out the baby. Shiloh took it. Him. Awkwardly. Cary handed her a bottle.

"Does this one need diapers?"

"Angel has them—but I just changed him." He looked down at the little girl. Shiloh couldn't tell how old she was. "Angel, be good for Shiloh. Help with Jesse."

Angel nodded. She seemed shy. She had the blondest hair Shiloh had ever seen.

"Cary," Shiloh said, "why are your clothes all wet?"

He rubbed his forehead. "The dryer's broken, my mom took the car, I've got to be at work in thirty minutes."

"Did you try ironing them?"

Cary frowned at her.

"It won't get them dry," she explained, "but it'll get them a lot less wet. And it's faster than the dryer."

He shook his head. He seemed overwhelmed.

"You can't walk a *mile* in wet pants," Shiloh said. "Come in."

He did.

"The iron's downstairs." She pointed at the basement door. "By the washer."

"I'm just supposed to iron them?"

"Yeah, slowly. But not too slowly. Like, you can still burn the fabric if you're not careful."

"I'm just going to walk," Cary said.

"I'll do it," she said. "Trade you. Baby for pants."

"He's not really a baby," Cary said. "He's two. You can give him Cheerios."

"I don't have Cheerios."

"I'm not taking off my pants, Shiloh."

"I'll go downstairs, and you can throw them down."

Cary sighed. Shiloh shoved the baby into his arms.

When she got downstairs, she plugged in the iron. "Come on, Cary!"

His pants landed with a wet whump at the bottom of the stairs.

"I have ten minutes!" he shouted down to her. "Tops!"

"I'll do my best!"

Shiloh focused on the inseams of his pants, where the damp would be most uncomfortable. Wisps of steam came up from the fabric.

Shiloh had done this for almost a year when their dryer was broken and her jeans weren't drying fast enough hung over the banister.

She was a little worried she might scorch Cary's only work pants . . . but so far, so good.

Shiloh didn't hear her mom come in, but she did hear her say, "What the hell is going on here?"

"Shiloh?" Cary sounded panicked.

"Mom!" Shiloh ran to the end of the steps. She knocked over the iron and ran back to it. "Mom!" she shouted. "I'm just ironing Cary's pants!"

"Why isn't Cary ironing his pants?"

"He was afraid of burning them! Can you give him a ride to work?"

She could hear them talking upstairs. Cary must be *dying*. Was he hiding behind something? What was there to hide behind upstairs?

*"Mom!"* Shiloh shouted, more insistent. "Will you give Cary a ride?"

"Yes!"

"Cary, I'm going to put your pants in the dryer for twenty minutes!" There was time enough now. Her mom threw his shirt down, too.

Shiloh didn't actually see Cary before he left. She stayed in the basement and brought his clothes up to the top step when he had to go.

Her mom gave him a ride to work, then came home and helped Shiloh keep Angel and Jesse alive. Her mom gave Jesse a bagel.

"Cary said he could have Cheerios," Shiloh said. "Not a bagel."

"Oh, that's right, Shiloh—you had a dozen siblings once, but I killed them all with bagels."

Her mom picked Cary up when his shift was over. "I guess it's the least I can do for that kid. He does drive you to school every day."

Jesse needed a new diaper by then, but Shiloh decided to let Cary worry about it.

"I owe you," Cary said, when he came in for the kids. With his red necktie knotted neatly at his throat and his name tag on.

"You don't owe me," Shiloh said. "You could never owe me."

## TWENTY-FOUR

SHILOH DECIDED TO TAKE THE kids to the grocery store while she had them in the car and they were sated.

"I didn't sign up for all these *errands*," Junie said, like she'd heard someone say it that way on TV.

Gus fell asleep on the drive home, and Shiloh couldn't decide whether to risk waking him by carrying him inside, or to sit in the car with him and let him finish his nap. She opened the front door for Junie and moved the groceries to the porch.

As Shiloh was coming down the porch steps, Cary was walking up her sidewalk. She stopped in her tracks, genuinely surprised to see him. "Hey . . ."

"I didn't thank you," he said.

"I'm pretty sure you did."

He shrugged. He still wasn't wearing a coat. "Thank you."

"You're welcome." Shiloh came down from the last step. "You can always call me, you know—if you ever need help back here."

Cary nodded his head. He looked away.

"This . . ." Shiloh said. "Last night . . ." She didn't know how to say this. "It doesn't nullify, from my perspective, the fact that you could *call me*"—her eyes were suddenly full of tears—"if you ever needed help."

Cary was looking up the road, toward his house. His hands were on his hips.

Shiloh wiped her eyes.

"I spent the whole morning arguing with her . . ." he said. He sounded almost wistful. "I've been trying to get access to her bank account—she gives everybody money and then can't pay her bills. I have to send her wires, like she's in a foreign country." He ran his hand over his hair. "But she signed the papers at the bank just now."

"That's great," Shiloh said.

"It's a huge relief. We're talking *years* of arguing about this . . . The guy at the bank might turn me in for elder abuse—I think he thought I was scamming her—but I'm so relieved right now, I don't even care."

Shiloh nodded.

Cary glanced over at her. "You left your car door open."

"Gus is still in there," she said. "He's asleep."

"Oh." He looked wrong-footed.

"I'm going to carry him in."

"I can get him for you."

"I'll manage," Shiloh said. Then she realized that accepting the offer would get Cary inside her house, at least for a few minutes, and not walking away from her. "But . . . I guess if you don't mind?"

Cary walked to the back seat. Shiloh met him there. "If he freaks out," she said, "just hand him to me."

Cary unbuckled Gus and smoothly transferred him to his arms. Gus stirred and lifted his head, making that panicked face kids make when you move them while they're sleeping. His arms and neck contracted. He whined. Then he settled on Cary's shoulder, relaxing again.

"Do you remember where my mom's bedroom is?" Shiloh whispered.

Cary nodded.

She shut the car door and jogged ahead of them to open up the screen.

Cary walked straight through the living room and dining room, past Junie, into Shiloh's mom's room, and laid Gus down onto the bed.

Shiloh patted Gus's back. "It's okay, Gus-Gus."

He stayed asleep.

She and Cary walked out of the room and left the door ajar.

"Will he roll off the bed?" Cary asked.

Shiloh shook her head.

Junie was in the living room, playing with her toy kitchen. The living room had more toys than furniture. (And it had a lot of furniture.)

"Cary," Junie whispered, holding her hands to her cheeks. "You're in my *house*."

He frowned with his eyebrows, like he was just realizing that was true.

Shiloh took hold of the back of a dining room chair. "Do you . . ."

Cary looked at her.

"Do you want a cup of coffee?" she asked.

He looked at her for another second, his expression flat.

Then he nodded.

Shiloh released the back of the chair.

"*I* could make coffee," Junie said.

"We'll both make coffee." Shiloh walked into the kitchen. To her relief, Cary followed.

She filled the coffeemaker with water. Shiloh never drank coffee this late in the day.

Cary stood near her without touching anything. "This room is different."

"We've been redoing it piece by piece." Shiloh had put in new red Formica countertops and painted the cabinets pale yellow. She was saving up for new linoleum.

"You weren't lying . . ." Cary said.

She looked up at him. She was scooping out the coffee grounds.

"Your kids are cute."

Shiloh laughed, relaxing slightly. (Very slightly.) "Thanks. Sorry about Gus. He's just . . . in a rough spot."

"I don't mind Gus," Cary said.

Shiloh nodded. She felt tearful again. She dumped the coffee into the filter.

"They're younger than I expected," he said.

"Oh." She shrugged. Closed the lid of the coffeemaker. Pressed the button.

"You must have had a difficult time of it," he said. "Recently."

"Huh," Shiloh said, like a badly formed laugh. "Yeah."

Junie came rushing into the kitchen with a plastic teacup. Shiloh held a finger over her mouth as a reminder. "Gus is asleep."

"Here's your coffee," Junie stage-whispered to Cary. "Do you like sugar?"

"Yeah," he said.

"Good, 'cause there's sugar in there."

"Thank you."

"Thank you, Junie," Shiloh said. "Give us some space to talk, okay?"

Junie's face fell. She probably thought Shiloh and Cary were going to argue—that was the only time Shiloh and Ryan ever asked for space. (Actually, she and Cary *might* be about to argue . . . )

Junie turned back to him—"Tell me if you need more sugar!"—then ran away.

Shiloh watched the real coffee dripping into the pot.

"Shiloh . . ." Cary said.

She looked up at him.

He was holding the toy cup like it was actually full of coffee. He seemed nervous. "It occurs to me that I wasn't really considering where you might be in life. When I . . ."

She waited.

". . . asked you to dance."

Shiloh nodded. A few tears spilled out.

"All I was really thinking about was myself," he said. "And how it would feel to see you again."

Her bottom lip was in her mouth. She bit it.

"I'm sorry," Cary said.

"I'm sorry, too," Shiloh replied, immediately. "I was . . ." She shook her head. "Wrong. Selfish. Bullheaded. Unfair, insensitive . . ." She shook her head again and pressed her lips together, trying hard not to cry. She covered her eyes with her fingers.

Cary touched her upper arm.

She dropped her hands to look at him. His face was full of feelings, but Shiloh wasn't sure which ones.

"You were only some of those things," he said. "To varying degrees."

She laughed—and gave up on trying not to cry. "Do you still want coffee? Or was that . . . I mean . . ."

"I want coffee," he said.

Shiloh laughed again and wiped her eyes on her sleeve. "Good. Me too." She reached for two mugs. "Do you really take sugar?"

"Yeah."

"Cream?"

"If you have it."

"I have it."

She poured two mugs of coffee, then held one out to Cary. "Trade you."

He looked down at his hand, like he'd forgotten about the toy cup, then smiled, passing it to her.

Shiloh's sugar bowl was shaped like an apple. She pushed it in his direction and went to get the cream out of the fridge. "Your mom's a sweetheart," she said.

Cary sighed.

Shiloh handed him the cream. "Who takes care of her when you're not here?"

"Well . . ." His forehead creased. "She's never alone. Angel's living there now, with her kids." He poured cream into his coffee. Shiloh took the carton from him when he was done. "And Jackie"—that was Cary's biological mom—"you know, she's never far. There was another woman staying over there for a while, a neighbor, maybe? I could never get to the bottom of it."

Shiloh leaned a hip against the counter, picking up her own coffee. She blew on it, feeling the heat blow back onto her face.

Cary looked troubled. "It's hard to say whether they're taking care of Mom or whether she's taking care of them. I know they all take advantage of her . . ." He shook his head. "But if she's getting her prescriptions and getting to her doctors' appointments, can I really complain?"

"It sounds like you worry about her a lot."

He raised his eyebrows, as if that was an understatement. He was taking a sip of coffee. "I tried to get her out to California a few years ago . . ."

Shiloh watched him.

"She'll never leave Omaha."

"Almost no one does," Shiloh said. "You're an outlier."

"I guess so. Even Mikey's back. Part-time anyway . . ." Cary looked up at her. "Will you see him? He says you never see anybody."

"He's been all over the world," Shiloh said, like that was her excuse.

"You should get together with Mikey," Cary said.

She frowned. It wasn't really Cary's business. "Okay."

"You can't make new old friends . . ."

"Oh." Shiloh laughed through her nose. "Well. Okay. Good advice. Thanks." She drank some coffee. "Do you guys get together? You and Mikey?"

"We try. He came to see me when I was stationed in Tokyo . . . I think he just wanted an excuse to go to Tokyo."

"How long were you there?"

"Three years."

"Where else have you been?"

Cary smiled a small smile. "Virginia. Florida. Canada. San Diego for a little while now."

"Will you stay in San Diego?"

"They move me around every two or three years. I don't really get to choose . . ."

"I guess that's baked in, huh?"

"Yeah." He smiled down at his coffee. "Not a whole lot of individual determination in the Navy."

"But you choose to stay in, right?"

"I'm gonna stick it out until I can retire."

Shiloh nodded.

Cary leaned back against the counter—in the L-shaped corner of it, so he was facing her. He took another drink of coffee.

Junie peeked her head into the kitchen. "Mommy. I'm *so sorry*," she whispered, slapping her forehead. "I forgot your coffee."

"I was wondering . . ." Shiloh said.

Junie came in with a teacup. "Black. Just like you like it."

Shiloh took the cup from her. "Thank you."

"Would you like more coffee, Cary?" Junie asked.

"I'm good. Thank you."

"Ring the bell for service!" she said, running out.

"*Shhhhh!*" Shiloh hissed after her.

"She really does look like you," Cary said.

"Don't tell her that. She's desperate to look like her dad."

"*Does* she look like her dad? That doesn't seem possible."

"I don't know. Kids are like water—you see other people's faces pass over them. Sometimes she'll smile at me, and I swear she looks just like my mother." Shiloh squinted at Cary. "You don't . . . I mean, did you say? Do you? Have kids?"

"No." Cary pulled his chin into his neck. "I mean." He shook his head. "No."

Shiloh laughed. "Sorry."

"I've never been married," he said.

She looked down at her coffee.

"*And* I don't have kids."

Shiloh was still holding Junie's coffee cup. She set it aside, with Cary's. "Was that intentional?"

"I don't think so . . ." He frowned. "Some people might say it was intentional."

Shiloh could never raise just one eyebrow—but she made her version of that expression, peeking up at him.

"It just hasn't gone that way," he said.

"It still could. You're only thirty-three."

"In my prime hooking-up years."

Shiloh rolled her eyes.

"We'll see," Cary said, more quietly.

She tried not to smile. "Is the problem that your life, your lover, your lady, is the sea?"

"You nailed it."

She grinned at him. "That really sucks for you."

He gestured at her with his mug. He was smiling, too. "I didn't know that you wanted kids."

She raised her eyebrows. "Well, I didn't want them at eighteen. But then . . ." She shrugged. "I was married, I was settled at my job—my *fertility* was waning. It felt like the next thing."

"That sounds practical."

"I didn't want to miss out on a chance to make my life feel bigger," Shiloh said. As soon as she said it, she winced. "What a rude thing for me to say! I'm sorry."

"It wasn't rude. It's how you felt. Is that how you feel now—like they make your life feel bigger?"

"In *some* ways." She tipped her head, considering. "I suppose I feel more invested in the world now . . ."

Cary was holding his mug to his mouth, but he wasn't drinking. "You weren't invested before?"

Shiloh shrugged again. "Eh. I felt like a short-timer before. You know, like I was doing my time, clocking in and out . . ."

"Clocking in and out of humanity."

"Exactly," she said. "But then I had kids, and now I worry a lot more about *everything*."

He was still smiling, a little. "I remember you already worrying a lot about everything . . ."

"Really? In high school?"

"Yeah," he said. "You made me join Amnesty International."

"*Mikey* made you join Amnesty International."

"Mikey never made me do anything." Cary pointed at her. "You told me that we had to write letters to the president of Chile because we *could.* That if *you* were ever disappeared by the government, you'd like somebody, somewhere, to do what they were able to. Even if it was just write a letter."

"I don't think those letters did any good," Shiloh said.

He shook his head. "Almost assuredly not."

"I don't know . . ." she said. "Having kids rewrites your programming. You can't really remember what the world looked like to you before you had them." Her voice dropped an octave. "That's probably some biological imperative to make sure you don't leave them by the side of the road."

One of Cary's cheeks dimpled. "I'm not sure that's an endorsement of parenthood . . ."

Shiloh laughed. "Me neither. Somebody should tell you beforehand that it's more like being mind-captured than falling in love—they take over your whole head, and that's that. You don't ever want anything as much as you want to make them happy."

"It sounds like you're doing a good job, Shiloh."

"Ha!" she said. "I thought I'd introduced you to Gus . . ."

Cary held his head at an angle. He raised his shoulders, sympathetic. "I think 'making your kids happy' is more of a journey than a binary proposition."

"Like America's journey toward justice."

He laughed. "Yeah. Actually."

She smiled down at her cup.

"I told my mom I'd come right back," Cary said softly. "I'm leaving tomorrow."

"Oh." Shiloh looked up, shifting her weight away from the counter. "Well. Thanks for coming by. This was . . ." The tears again. "This was really nice."

"I could . . ." Cary was looking at her with his brows drawn low. Like he was puzzling something out. "We could do more of this, later."

Shiloh pulled her lips down at the ends, surprised. "Do you want to?" She shook her head, closing her eyes. "I mean. I'd love that. I'd love to."

"Yeah?"

Her eyes were open. "*Yes.* Cary. Come back later?"

"Okay." He smiled. "I will."

"The kids go to bed at eight thirty. You can come before then, but it's a whole thing."

"I'll come after." He looked down at his coffee. "I'm going to be up all night anyway thanks to this coffee."

"Oh my god." Shiloh took his cup away. "Me too. I can't have caffeine after noon."

He was smiling. "I'll be back."

# before

CARY, AT NINETEEN, IN HIS black uniform, was the most handsome man Shiloh had ever seen.

She didn't recognize him at first—and it wasn't because he was so changed (though he *was* changed). It was because she forgot what it felt like to look at Cary.

She hadn't looked at anyone she really cared about in months—and Shiloh more than cared about Cary. Cary's face cut right through her, always. She'd become inured to it in high school—he'd sliced her open every day for years, sometimes several times a day.

As soon as she saw him standing in her dormitory lobby, she felt that old urge to touch him. (An urge she'd never once resisted.) Within seconds, she was tugging at his tie. Brushing her hands against his arms.

She could hardly look at his face. His hair was so short, there was no avoiding his golden-brown eyes, his long nose and pointy chin. The deep lines in his cheeks when he even thought of smiling.

The Navy uniform seemed to boil Cary's whole body down to its essential components: Sharp, square shoulders. Slim legs and narrow hips. Adam's apple. Knobby wrists.

Why did the military need to make its recruits look so clean and vulnerable before they taught them to commit atrocities?

Shiloh wanted to touch him everywhere at once. To test and check him. (*Are you Cary here? And here and here?*)

She'd forgotten how to be normal around him. Their version of normal. She didn't know where to stop.

When he finally kissed her, Shiloh felt all her internal architecture collapse—everything she'd ever told herself about how she and Cary fit together and what they were meant to be.

He kissed her, and she realized that she was always going to kiss him back. That she would have kissed him back at thirteen. At fifteen. After any day of school. At prom. At graduation. When they'd said goodbye last summer. At no point would Shiloh ever have refused him. At no point *could* she.

Cary could have what he wanted from her, if he ever wanted it. She was an unlocked door. An open book.

It was her first kiss.

In her dorm room. That day. She was nineteen, too.

It wasn't a kiss that changed anything, externally.

Shiloh was still in college and hoping for something bigger and better than the life she'd left behind.

And Cary was *very definitely* still in the Navy. Contractually obligated to walk away from her.

Cary had always been walking away from Shiloh . . . He'd never taken his eyes off the prize, as long as she'd known him.

There was no future where she told him she loved him and he told her that he'd stay. There was no future where he followed her or turned back for her.

There was possibly a future where *she* chased *him* . . .

Shiloh's brain was busy during that first kiss. (Her brain was always busy.) She was choreographing her fall. Calculating the softest landing.

What *could* she have with Cary? What could she have that day? Or ever? How much life could she squeeze from one weekend?

Having sex seemed like a no-brainer.

Shiloh couldn't imagine more ideal laboratory conditions for losing her virginity. She loved Cary. She trusted him. She was wildly, manically attracted to him.

Plus she knew—she'd been told—that you'd always remember your first time. What better way to pin Cary in her memory? To make him indelible?

Shiloh still felt like she was proving a point: Cary couldn't *make* her forget him by leaving.

It was too soon to have sex. She hadn't even acclimated to kissing. (He should never have let her take the wheel.)

Shiloh couldn't really absorb all the sensations—and Cary was too close for her to keep him in focus.

Feeling him actually inside of her body, feeling him actually *connected* to her . . . It was more intimacy than Shiloh could begin to process.

The first time was fast and incalculable.

The second time, she started to feel it. To understand what was happening. To recognize Cary's face above hers. All her self-discipline came unraveled. All of her anchors lifted out of the ground. She held him too tight. She kissed him excessively. She told him she loved him, again and again.

Shiloh didn't have an orgasm. (She thought that might just *happen*? Incidentally? It didn't.)

But, still, every part of what *was* happening felt so right . . .

Maybe Shiloh had been wrong.

Maybe she and Cary *weren't* meant for separate skies. Maybe the future could never offer anyone to rival him. Maybe the two of them fit—were *meant* to fit.

Maybe they could bend their paths toward each other.

Shiloh held his face in her hands. *"I love you, Cary. I love you."*

Cary had to take a city bus to the airport. He was starting a more specialized training program in Florida—nuclear science. He told Shiloh that aircraft carriers had their own nuclear power plants. Just floating in the ocean. She'd had no idea.

Cary had enlisted for six years. (Two more than usual.) Eventually he'd be assigned to a ship—or possibly a submarine. Imagining him under the water, in the dark, in close quarters, made her feel panicky. She'd pinched his thigh while he explained it to her.

Cary was getting on a bus, and then on a plane, and then the Navy was going to bury him alive for six years.

And *still* Shiloh was bending toward him. Trying to imagine them together. Wanting him to ask her to imagine it.

He didn't ask.

Cary didn't bend—in general, as a person.

He didn't change his mind.

He wasn't going to accommodate Shiloh.

He was just going to leave.


She wrote him letters.

He sent back postcards.

He said that he tried to call.

He wrote her one letter, about six months after that weekend.

"*Shiloh, you'll always be so special to me. You'll always be in my heart. What happened between us meant a lot to me. You should know that it meant a lot to me.*"

Shiloh felt like she was being wrapped in tissue paper and set in a shoebox, like she was being shoved under Cary's childhood bed.

She'd already met Ryan.

A few months later, they were dating.

## TWENTY-SIX

SHILOH STARTED BEDTIME EARLY. SHE gave the kids warm baths and Sleepytime tea.

Gus fell asleep easily, even with a nap. Maybe Shiloh's mom was right about three-year-old hormones; Gus ate and slept like a teenager.

Junie fought bedtime every night, but Shiloh wasn't having it tonight. "You don't have to sleep," she said. "You just have to close your eyes."

"My eyes are so *boring*," Junie said.

"If the inside of your head is boring," Shiloh said, "only you can fix that."

Cary got there at eight forty-five. He knocked softly.

Shiloh had taken her hair down. It fell to her waist, still damp. She'd changed into a V-necked, mulberry-colored sweater and nicer jeans. She knew they were just going to talk and be friends, but Cary should know that Shiloh still owned real clothing.

Cary was wearing what he'd been wearing earlier. But his hair looked nicer. He looked like he'd shaved. It hurt Shiloh to notice.

He was holding a bottle of wine. He held it out to her as soon as she opened the door. "I didn't want to come empty-handed," he said, "but I don't actually think I should have any of this."

Shiloh took the bottle. "I'll save it."

"Yeah, enjoy it with your mom. Or, you know, whoever."

She moved out of the doorway. "Come in, Cary."

He stepped inside. Shiloh had decided *not* to spend the whole evening frantically cleaning; Cary had already seen her house. She'd made Junie clear the toys out of the living room, while Shiloh thoroughly cleaned the bathroom . . .

And then they'd made a cake.

It was sitting on the coffee table on a milky-green glass pedestal, next to a pot of lemongrass tea.

"That looks incredible," Cary said.

"Sit down and have some."

"Did you make this?" He sat on the couch. It was royal-blue corduroy.

Shiloh sat on an easy chair. "The kids and I made it. It's an excellent way to keep them both occupied. Junie likes to measure, and Gus likes to dump things into bowls."

Cary frowned at the intact cake. "Did you make cake with your kids and not give them any?"

Shiloh laughed. "There were cupcakes, too."

He looked a little embarrassed. "Okay, that makes sense." He reached down and pulled his sweatshirt over his head. He was wearing a red-and-gold plaid button-down shirt underneath.

Shiloh cut him a slice of cake. She had a fancy silver-plated cake server, the kind you'd get as a wedding gift in 1958. Ryan had let her keep all their fussy kitchen stuff and thrift-shop silverware.

Cary picked up his fork. "What kind of cake is this?"

"Hummingbird," Shiloh said. "I should warn you—it's got a ton of stuff people don't like. Pineapple, bananas, pecans, cream cheese icing. I think that's why nobody makes it anymore."

"Why'd you make it, then?"

"Because I can."

"I don't mind pineapple and bananas—and what else?"

"Pecans."

"I'm in." He got himself a bite.

Shiloh poured him a cup of tea and served herself some cake. "We're so lucky to be able to eat tree nuts," she said with vigor.

"Do your kids have allergies?"

"No, thank god and knock on wood. It's a jungle out there."

"This cake is *delicious.*" Cary's mouth was full. "It's like carrot cake."

"Yeah, but no carrots."

"Seriously." He was smiling. "It's so good."

"Don't be too impressed. There's no art to baking a cake—it's just following instructions."

Cary leaned back, settling into the couch. "Then why do most cakes taste significantly worse than this?"

"Because most people refuse to follow instructions?"

"Well, that's true. You have me there."

"There's no caffeine in the tea," she said, pointing. "It's lemongrass."

"You didn't have to do all this, Shiloh."

"I boiled water, Cary. Relax."

Cary *looked* relaxed. He looked happy. The cake had been a good decision. Even if the sink was full of dishes.

Shiloh sat back in her chair and ate her cake, letting herself watch him. He knew she was watching him . . . He was smiling at his plate.

"What do you do?" she asked.

His eyebrows twitched down. "When?"

"In general. What's your job?"

"I'm a line officer," he said. "I help run a ship."

"Like an actual warship?"

"Yeah." He nodded, like it was nothing, focused on the cake. "A destroyer."

"A *destroyer*," Shiloh repeated. "But you don't live on it?"

"Sometimes I live on it. During a deployment."

"In a little room?"

His eyes flicked up to her. He looked amused. "In a little room, yes."

"I thought you were going into the Navy to do nuclear-power stuff."

"That's where I started. I'm trained in that. But I went a different route when I got my commission."

"Because you didn't like it?"

He shrugged. "I wanted to do something new."

Shiloh twisted her lips to the side. "I keep trying to picture your life, and I can't."

"Most people can't imagine living on a ship. You get used to it."

"Do you know I've never seen the ocean?"

Cary looked up, stricken. "What? Why not?"

She laughed. "Um, because Nebraska is the most landlocked state in the union? Has your *mom* seen the ocean?"

He was still stricken. "My mom won't drive west of Seventy-Second Street—how have you *never* seen the ocean?"

Shiloh was embarrassed. "It just hasn't happened, I guess. I only get invited to conferences in Chicago and Orlando and Indianapolis."

"Orlando is close to the ocean."

"Yeah, I was gonna go . . ." She shrugged with her fork. "I was tired."

Cary was frowning at Shiloh. She could tell he wanted to fix this for her, but he really couldn't.

"I'll take the kids someday," she said. "Junie says she wants to see the whole world. But not Australia. And not space."

"Why not Australia?"

"Snakes. Spiders."

"Yeah," he said, "okay, legit."

"Have *you* been to Australia?"

He nodded. "It reminded me of California."

"You'll have to tell her that you survived." Shiloh smiled at him. She had the urge to kick him. "You've been to Tokyo, you've been to Australia—have you been to Europe?"

"I have. That's one thing the Navy is good at. You get around." He picked up the mug she'd set out for him. It was a souvenir from Pioneer Village in Minden, Nebraska. Ryan had also let Shiloh take all of her tchotchkes and random old junk. His new apartment looked like one of the artier Ikea showrooms. Junie said it was *"so clean"* and *"so nice"*— *"like someone on TV lives there."*

Shiloh would rather *not* live in an Ikea showroom. She liked old things and bright colors. She liked having too many throw pillows and too many coffee mugs. She liked rugs. And macramé wall hangings. She liked everything to be a little too much.

She thought of Cary's mom's house . . . with its boxes and bags of detritus. Shiloh should have picked up more before he came over. He was probably desperate for a clean surface.

"What do *you* do?" Cary asked.

"I . . ." Shiloh blew out her cheeks. "I told you already, right? I'm an administrator. I hire teachers, I work on educational programming, sometimes I teach first graders how to do improv . . ."

Cary smiled. "How'd you get that job?"

"Would you believe it's the only place I've ever worked?"

He looked like he *didn't* quite believe it. "Really?"

"Yeah, I got hired there out of college as an actor-slash-teacher. It was seasonal at first, then full-time. And nowwww"—she drew out the *W*—"here I am."

"And you like it?"

"I don't know," Shiloh deflected. "I'm lucky to have a full-time theater job, especially in Omaha, Nebraska. I have health insurance. And I get to wear jeans to work." She looked down, scrunching up her face and shaking her head.

"What's wrong?" Cary asked.

"It's just *embarrassing.* I kind of hate to tell you all this. I'd rather you remember me the way I was when we were young."

"Manic and relentless?"

Shiloh kicked him in the ankle. She wasn't wearing shoes. "Shiny and full of potential!"

He laughed. "You're still shiny."

She groaned. "Don't lie to me, Cary. It makes it worse."

"Can I have more cake?"

"You can eat the whole thing."

He cut himself a big piece. "You're still shiny," he murmured. He was laughing.

Shiloh watched him. She had plenty of cake left on her own plate. Her eyes felt big and warm. "You were so mad at me last night . . ." she whispered. (Because she could never leave well enough alone.)

Cary sat back, slowly. His face was sad when he looked up at her. "Yeah . . ."

"I'd like for us not to be angry with each other," she said, still being quiet. "From this point forward."

Cary was watching her, paying attention.

"Do you think that's possible?" she asked.

He exhaled and ran a hand up through his hair. "I guess we do pretty well when we're not . . . reaching for more."

Shiloh nodded.

She hated that answer.

It brought tears to her eyes.

"I never meant to hurt you," she said. "I never *knew* I hurt you."

Cary stared at her for a few long seconds. Then he said, "I don't think we should hold grudges over things that happened when we were nineteen. We were just kids."

"Yeah, but—" Shiloh was crying, she wished she wasn't. "Our *whole friendship* happened when we were kids. And I want to hold on to *all* of it."

He stared at her some more. There were lines in his forehead. "I felt like you used me," he said. "I wanted you to want more. But, Shiloh—that's on me, not you. You weren't obligated to want more."

Shiloh felt confused already. Again. "But I— I told you that I *loved* you."

"Yeah, and then you sent me packing."

"I didn't send you packing!"

Cary set his plate on the table. "I really can't argue about this anymore."

"We're not arguing—we're talking. We've never talked about it!"

He blew out a breath. "Okay. Let's talk." He gave her a stern look. "But don't yell at me."

"I didn't send you packing," Shiloh said again in a level voice. "You were already packed."

He looked annoyed. "In the sense that I had just enlisted in the

Navy, that's correct. I'd spent eight weeks in boot camp and the main thing I learned there was that I wanted to be with you. I couldn't get to you fast enough."

She frowned at him. "You never told me that."

He lifted up his hands. "I showed up at your door with my seabag and fell at your feet."

"You didn't *fall* anywhere, Cary."

Cary still looked annoyed, but now he looked fierce about it. He leaned toward her, over his knees. "We spent two days in bed, Shiloh— I was head over heels. I would have done anything for you."

Shiloh's mouth opened.

This was all news to her. Shocking news. She didn't remember that weekend perfectly, but she would have remembered . . . "You didn't *say* any of that."

"I would have had to interrupt you telling me it was nothing." Cary was cold. "I'm pretty sure you told me that sex was a construct."

"I know that I said—well, I don't think I said sex was a construct— but I know I said a lot of complete bullshit that weekend. I was just *scared*, Cary. I didn't want you to reject me."

"In what way was I rejecting you?"

"You'd never shown any interest in me before!"

He scoffed. "Shiloh, the whole world thought we were dating."

"Well, *I* knew that we *weren't*. You never made a move toward me in high school."

"How could I have gotten any closer to you than I already was?"

"Cary," she said, like he wasn't being fair.

He was upset. "You didn't *want* me to make a move, did you? I don't remember you ever giving me a hint or an opening."

"You had a girlfriend."

"I had a girlfriend for three months."

"Well, it wasn't me. It was never me."

Cary sat back. Forcefully. A needlepoint throw pillow fell off the couch. "I didn't want us to date in high school! I liked what we had, and I didn't want to ruin it."

"Okay," Shiloh said, relenting.

His legs and arms were tense, like his whole body was frustrated. "I thought we were *beyond* dating," he said. "That we would just *be* together someday, when we were ready."

Shiloh's mouth hung open. She felt like there'd been a hook in her throat, and Cary had just ripped it out.

He ran his hands through his hair.

Shiloh waited to find words, but all she could do was repeat herself: "You never told me that you felt that way."

Cary's shoulders sagged. "I thought you felt it, too. I hoped you did. And then . . . when I came to see you, you told me what you actually wanted."

"No," Shiloh said.

"No?"

"I was giving you an *out,*" she said. "I didn't want to spoil your plans. You had planned this *whole life* without me."

That made Cary stick his tongue in his cheek. "People in the Navy are allowed to fall in love," he said. "I wasn't going to *prison*. You're the one who wanted something different. You made your feelings really clear."

"And you *didn't*!" Shiloh was furious now and unable to contain it. "Not once! I know I said a lot of garbage, Cary, but I also know that I opened my heart to you. I *remember*. Was I supposed to read your mind?"

"You were supposed to read my actions!"

"Okay, well—you left."

"My actions before that."

"Oh my god . . ." Shiloh brought both feet up onto the chair and hid her face in her hands. She was too upset to talk.

Cary was in no hurry to break the silence. They sat there for long minutes, both of them breathing loud.

Shiloh kept thinking of new objections . . . Of all the things Cary hadn't said. And all the times he hadn't said them.

The night they graduated from high school, Cary and Mikey and Shiloh had stayed out all night on Mikey's back deck. Mikey fell asleep, and Cary and Shiloh lay there on a spread-out sleeping bag, looking up at the stars, then watching the sun rise—and Cary had never once said they were "*beyond dating.*"

They sat a hundred nights in Shiloh's driveway, a thousand afternoons on her front steps.

The day he walked away from her, she lost her best friend and her true love, and she still wasn't sure how she was supposed to have stopped him.

This wasn't a problem Shiloh could solve at thirty-three. At nineteen, she didn't have a chance.

She'd never had a chance.

"You're right," Cary said.

Shiloh lifted her head—she wasn't expecting him to be the first to speak.

Cary looked tired, like the fight had gone out of him. "I'm sorry," he said, meeting her eyes. Then he looked down. "I should have been more clear, when I came to see you—even if I still don't believe that you wanted to hear it."

Shiloh sat very still.

"I should have said . . ." His words sounded carefully measured. He was staring at his lap. "'Shiloh, I think that we're meant to be together. I know you don't want me to join the Navy and that this isn't the life you want for yourself. But I'm still yours, if you'll have me.'"

It was a terrible thing to hear . . .

Fourteen years after it was true.

Tears streamed down Shiloh's cheeks.

"What would *you* have said," Cary asked, before she'd gathered her senses, "if you had been being honest that weekend?"

He hung his head while he waited for her to answer.

It took a while.

Shiloh's voice was hollow when she finally found it. She looked at the ceiling.

"I would have said—'Cary, I'm in love with you, and I'm so scared to lose you. I don't know where I fit in your life. I'm yours for the taking, but . . . I don't think you'll ever take me.'"

Cary exhaled hard. Like he hadn't really wanted to hear that.

Shiloh could sympathize.

"To be fair . . ." She still couldn't face him. "I think it's taken me this long to put that into words."

"Yeah," he agreed quietly. "Me too."

Shiloh turned in the chair so she could lean her forehead on one of its arms. She'd gotten very practiced at long, terrible conversations at the end of her marriage. She had two or three favorite crash positions.

"Hey," Cary said.

"What."

"Look at me."

Shiloh looked up.

He looked utterly defeated. And incredibly handsome.

He held out his hand. "Come here."

She sucked on her lip for a second. Then she took his hand.

Cary pulled her onto the couch and put his arm around her shoulder, holding her close. He pressed his face into the top of her head and kissed her there.

After a minute, Shiloh wrapped an arm around his waist, curling against his chest.

Could she have had this? Then?

And since then?

No. Even if she'd gotten it right at nineteen, she would have fucked it up at some other point in the timeline. Shiloh had no confidence in her ability to hold on to someone else's heart.

Cary kept squeezing her long after her own arm would have given out. And then he just held her. He rested his head on hers, and put his other arm around her, too.

He kept exhaling long, expressive breaths. Like, *"What a mess."* And *"Jesus Christ."* And *"Here we are, I guess."*

Shiloh felt dozy. Crying always wore her out, and Cary's arms offered some temporary respite. She wasn't looking forward to whatever came next.

When Cary eventually lifted his head and touched her chin, Shiloh almost pretended to be asleep.

She looked up at him.

He looked sad.

He leaned forward an inch and kissed her.

Shiloh wasn't expecting it, but she kissed him back—and immediately started crying again.

Cary kissed her through it. Long, sad kisses, with his hand cupped around the back of her head. These were kisses without hopes or ambitions. They were apologies. Eulogies. Shiloh's tears slid into the corner of her mouth. Cary licked them.

When she realized that he wasn't stopping, Shiloh sat up a little, making her mouth more available. Cary hummed and squeezed her neck. She gripped one hand in the front of his shirt. He kissed her and kissed her. If she emptied her head in his lap, all that would fall out was his name.

They sat on the couch and kissed goodbye for an hour or so. In another context, it would have been wonderful.

Even in this context, kissing Cary was fairly wonderful.

He was gentle and attentive. He rubbed her back and stroked her hair. And he didn't mind being in charge—she could just let herself feel it all and respond.

Shiloh pulled back when her mom's headlights slid across the front picture window. She moved a few inches away from him.

Cary kept his arm around her shoulder. He rubbed his mouth.

Shiloh wiped her eyes. She adjusted her sweater. She tracked her mom's progress up the steps—the slam of the porch door, her keys in the lock.

Her mom startled when she saw Shiloh and Cary on the couch together. "Oh," she said. "Cary. What a nice surprise."

Cary nodded.

"We were just having some cake," Shiloh said. "Would you like a piece?"

"Thanks"—her mom leaned over to take off her ankle boots—"but I'm going to fall asleep as soon as my head hits the pillow."

That was a lie. She was going to drink a glass of wine and read half a romance novel.

"Good night," Shiloh said.

"Good to see you again, Gloria," Cary said in a gravelly voice.

"You too. You are welcome here anytime, Cary. Whenever you're in town."

Shiloh's stomach clenched painfully.

Her mom walked past the table and then stopped. "Is that hummingbird cake?"

"Junie and I made it."

"Okay, well . . ." Her mom leaned over and cut a slice of cake, plopping it onto her palm. "I will take a piece, but I'm still going to bed. Good night, good night."

"Good night," they both said.

She disappeared into her room.

Cary leaned forward to pick up his mug from the table. He kept his hand on Shiloh's shoulder while he took a drink.

"Do you want me to heat that up for you?" she asked.

"No. Stay here with me." He poured more cold tea into the mug and handed it to her. Shiloh took it and drank some. Cary picked up his plate—there was still a lot of cake on it—and sat back, finally letting go of Shiloh but still settling against her.

He held his fork out to her with a bite of cake.

Shiloh met his eyes over his hand. He looked pretty wrung out, honestly. But he still looked like he liked her. She took the bite, covering her mouth. "Do you have to get home?" she asked, even though the last thing she wanted was for him to leave.

"No," Cary said, "I have to eat this entire cake."

Shiloh smiled. She watched him eat a few more bites of cake, shaking her head when he offered her more. "So . . ." She tried to think of something practical to say. Something conversational. "You'll be able to manage your mom's bills now?"

"Most of them." Cary cleared his throat. He nodded. "Yeah."

"Will the rest of your family be mad?"

"Not in a way I'll have to deal with. They count on me to bail Mom out." He glanced up from the cake, frowning. "My older sister, Jenny, thinks I'm trying to get the house—I don't care about that house. Though I *am* going to sell it the minute Mom needs long-term care. So maybe Jenny's right about me."

"I've always wanted siblings," Shiloh said, "but I guess Mom and I at least have clarity. We know it's just the two of us."

He eyed her. "You seem like you're making it work."

"Yeah," she agreed, "better than I would have expected. We got a lot of our fighting out of the way when I was pregnant with Junie."

"Why then?"

Shiloh kept her voice down. "Because I was terrified of becoming just like her!"

Cary shook his head. "That was never going to happen. I knew you were going to be a great mom."

"*How?* You just called me manic and incessant."

"I said 'relentless.' And I knew, because you don't shirk. You like being in charge of things."

"You should talk, Cary."

He shrugged, like he was fine with owning that. "When'd you move back here?"

"Two and a half years ago," Shiloh said.

"Wow. Gus must have been . . ."

"Two months old."

Cary's eyes were wide with pity. (It had been an ugly, bloody time to get a divorce. That much was obvious.)

Shiloh smiled tightly.

"Is Gus his full name?" he asked.

"Yes."

Cary looked down, like he was trying not to laugh.

She elbowed him. "Don't make fun of my child's name. That's so rude."

"I'm *not*." He was still smiling with his mouth closed. "It's just very you of you."

"'Gus' is a good name."

"So is 'Juniper.'" Cary grinned. "You picked that one out in high school."

"This is *very* rude . . ."

He shook his head in denial, his eyes sparkling. "I like it. I like that you haven't changed."

She was affronted. "I've changed a lot!"

"No," he said, "you've grown."

"Oh, *pffft*, you don't know, Cary . . ."

"I don't know why you're arguing with me. It's a compliment." He tilted his head. "Have *I* changed?"

Shiloh looked at him. Her eyes got soft. She shook her head.

Cary smiled wide again.

"But you're still full of surprises," she said.

"Sure—because I could have grown in an entirely different direction."

"Yeah," Shiloh said. "I guess so."

Cary finished the slice of cake on his plate and set it down on the table. Then he sat back, holding his arm out. Shiloh leaned into him again, and he hugged her close. She could get used to this . . .

She was never going to get a chance to get used to this.

He tipped his head against hers. They were facing forward. Shiloh could see their reflection in the television. She watched them both get sad again.

All of their talking—and kissing—had helped them put their past in context. But it didn't do anything for their future.

"I've got a sea deployment in March," Cary said, reading her mind. That was in two months.

She turned her head to face him. "What's that mean to a civilian?"

"It means I'll literally be on the ocean for six months."

"Six months? That's so *long*."

"It's normal."

"Normal is long."

"I'm coming home for Christmas," he said. "Maybe you and Mikey and I . . . you know, we could get together?"

Shiloh's eyes flooded with tears. "I would love that."

Cary was telling her what they could have together. It was much less than Shiloh wanted—but still so much more than she'd expected a few hours ago.

He gave her one last squeeze, and then he stood up. He held out a hand to Shiloh, and she took it. She stood up with him.

Cary put his hands on his hips. "I'm glad I got to meet your kids."

"Me too. I'm glad we . . . ended up here, I guess."

"Me too." Cary leaned over and kissed her cheek.

"Let me get my keys," Shiloh said, her voice breaking.

"I'll just walk."

"It's too late, no."

"Shiloh, I'm a grown man and a Naval officer."

"Tell that to the kid with a gun who wants your cell phone."

Cary let her drive him home. She gave him one of her business cards before he got out. "Call me if you ever need a pair of hands in Omaha."

He nodded and put the card in his pocket. "Good night, Shiloh."

"Good night, Cary."

## TWENTY-SEVEN

MIKEY WAS AS GOOD AS his threats. A few months after the wedding, Shiloh was invited to his house—Janine's house?—for dinner.

Shiloh had a hard time finding a parking spot on their block.

Mike and Janine lived in a nicer part of North Omaha than Shiloh, a quiet neighborhood near the river. They had a big old house set back from the street and surrounded by trees. There was music playing outdoors, even though it was still cold. March.

Shiloh walked up the front steps. She was carrying the wine Cary had left at her house.

A couple was standing on the porch, quietly arguing. Shiloh could see the shadows of other people inside. She almost turned around—this was supposed to be a small dinner.

The front door was open. Shiloh opened the storm door and edged inside, head first. There were people sitting on the staircase, just inside the foyer. And people in the living room, eating cheese and bread and drinking wine. They all looked very comfortable and very interesting. Omaha interesting. Like, people who worked at artisan jewelry stores downtown or taught college poetry.

A couple of Mikey's paintings dominated the room—black and white, abstract, with photorealistic faces hidden in strange places. They were huge, propped up against the walls and nearly as tall as the ceiling. These must not be for sale—how would he ever get them out?

Shiloh was still thinking of turning around when a very pregnant blond woman walked into the room with a tray of more cheese. "Shiloh?" the woman said.

Shiloh looked at her for a second. "Janine?"

"That's me. Oh my god—Mike is going to be so happy that you came!"

Shiloh nodded. "It's great to finally meet you." Had they met in high school? Hopefully they hadn't met in high school. "I saw you from afar at the reception . . ."

Janine looked less glossy than she had at the wedding, but still very pretty. She had long blond hair and big blue eyes. Shiny pink skin. She was wearing jeans and a clingy black T-shirt with a blue blazer over it—like, Friday-casual pregnancy chic. It was working for her.

"Yeah, sorry . . ." Janine said. "I was so preoccupied that night. Then again"—she smiled—"so were you."

Shiloh laughed uncomfortably.

Janine set down the cheese and took Shiloh's arm. "Let's go find Mike."

They walked through the dining room and the kitchen. Shiloh liked their house. The furniture was simple, the walls were white, and there was art everywhere.

Janine led her out the back door. This is where the music was playing. There was a big fire pit, and people were gathered around it, wearing warm coats and stocking caps, and drinking beer.

Mikey was standing by the grill—cooking sausage, it looked like.

"Mike!" Janine called out. "Look who I found."

His face lit up. "Shiloh!" He reached out to her with the hand that wasn't holding barbecue tongs.

"Hey," Shiloh said, hugging him. "You didn't tell me this was a party."

He winked. "If I'd told you it was a party, you wouldn't have come."

"That is one-hundred-percent correct," Shiloh said, looking out at the yard and grimacing.

Mikey grinned. "I thought it would be good for you to meet some people. Some cool Omaha people. Artists. Writers. Thinkers."

"Mike, I work in community theater. My life is lousy with artists, writers and thinkers. *Literally* lousy. Like, I have to have my office sprayed twice a year."

"Wow," Janine said, looking at him. "She really is just like Cary. You weren't kidding."

Mikey shook his head, still smiling. "Two peas who won't leave the fucking pod."

"I left the pod," Shiloh said. "I'm here. I brought you wine."

He took it from her. "Thank you, Shiloh. You want some? You want a beer? Hot cider? You want a sausage? They're from Stoysich."

Stoysich was a local meat place. And Mikey was wearing a vintage sweatshirt from a defunct Omaha brewery. He was apparently getting back to his roots. Maybe Omaha got charming as soon as you left.

She sighed. "Sure. I'll take a sausage."

"I got these rolls at Orsi's," he said, picking up a bun.

"Stoysich, Orsi's. Is Warren Buffett here? Is Bright Eyes playing later?"

Mikey rolled his eyes and handed her the sausage. Janine had stepped away from them to talk to someone else.

"Hey . . ." Shiloh dropped her voice and nodded her head toward Janine. "Congratulations. I didn't know . . ."

"Didn't Cary tell you?" Mikey was grinning again. "Shotgun wedding."

"I'm happy for you," Shiloh said sincerely.

"Thanks," he said, also sincere and a little embarrassed about it. He bumped his hip against hers. "Thanks, Shy." He went back to the grill. "It was kind of an accident, if I'm being honest. But then we were like, *Fuck yeah. Let's just do this!* Like, probably this is the best thing that's ever happened, you know?"

She nodded. "Yeah. Good for you. I'll set you up with free toddler classes at the theater. We've got voice, movement, pop-and-lock dancing . . ."

Mikey pointed the tongs at her. "I have a feeling that's probably a great gift. Thank you. You're like one of the fairy godmothers who brings the good shit. The blessings."

"So you're really back in Omaha . . ."

"Yeah." He nodded deeply. "At least part-time. I need to be in New York sometimes, for the business stuff. And the parties. But I can paint here." He looked like he was sharing an epiphany with her. "I mean, I can *really* paint here. It's so quiet. And so far from anyone who wants something from me."

"That'll last approximately . . . when is Janine due? Two months?"

"Ha!" Mikey said. "*Right?* Right, right, right." He turned a row of sausages. "That's okay. I'm up for it."

"Yeah, you are," Shiloh said, encouraging. "You'll be a great dad."

He looked up at her, wrinkling his nose a little. "Do you really think so?"

"Yeah."

"Why? Be specific."

"Um . . ." Shiloh clicked her tongue a few times. "Okay. You're fun." She looked around—at the still-very-aggravating party scenario. "And you can lie with a straight face. That'll come in handy."

He pointed his tongs at her again. "You are going to have so much fun at this party. I swear to god, Shiloh."


Shiloh did not have so much fun at the party.

She stood by the fire pit and listened to people talk about whether the city would ever get streetcars and how to get a permit for backyard chicken coops.

Then she went inside and listened to people talk about a controversial foundation that was bankrolling tacky—but not the *good* kind of tacky—public art.

Then she went back outside and listened to the chicken coop stuff again. Apparently you had to be careful about raccoons.

These were all perfectly good things to talk about. These were probably good, interesting people.

But Shiloh was done meeting new people. For life.

Her mom was right, you couldn't make new old friends—but Shiloh wasn't in the market for new *new* ones either.

The prospect of meeting someone and small-talking and then following up with them . . . building tentative bonds, building trust, developing inside jokes . . . learning the names of their spouses, their kids, their coworkers . . .

Shiloh honestly couldn't imagine getting through all those steps.

She'd *never* done it before. Shiloh made friends in school and at work, with people she was trapped with all the time anyway. The idea of making friends in the wild? Inconceivable. And completely unappealing.

If Shiloh wanted friends, she'd rather reach out to all the people she already liked and rarely got a chance to see.

The party moved inside as it got colder. There was talk of charades. Shiloh was, of course, fucking *phenomenal* at charades. But she would rather swallow a tick than play charades with strangers. For *free*.

She found a spot by what was left of the fire and drank what was left of her apple cider.

She wanted to go home, but she didn't want to walk through the house and have to say goodbye to everyone. Maybe she could squeeze through the bushes on the side of the house.

The back door swung open. Shiloh recognized Mikey's silhouette.

He headed out toward her. She blew air into her closed lips.

"There you are," he said, when he got close enough.

"Here I am," Shiloh agreed.

He sat down next to her—she was sitting on a flattened-out log—holding his hands up to the fire. "You really hate parties, don't you?"

"I really do," she said.

"I thought maybe you'd like it once you were actually here and saw how nice it was . . ."

"Sorry, Mikey. I didn't mean to be rude to your friends."

"You weren't rude to my friends. Everybody likes you. One of our neighbors *really* likes you. He thinks you look like a young Cher . . . which is *very* generous in my opinion."

Shiloh smiled.

Mikey picked up a stick to poke at the fire. "You weren't being rude, but I—as one of your oldest friends—could *still* perceive that you weren't having a good time."

"What gave me away? Was it the sitting alone in the dark?"

He grinned. "It was, yeah. Then I remembered that time that you hid in the bathroom for an hour at Tanya's New Year's Eve party . . ."

"Her house had two bathrooms."

"I'm sorry," he said. "Next time we'll do dinner. For real."

"It's okay. It's probably good for me to get out, even if I'm not talking to anyone. And it was great to meet Janine—and to see you doing so well."

"Janine's the best."

"I can tell." Shiloh meant it. Janine seemed down-to-earth, laid-back. She laughed at Mikey's constant jokes without laughing *too much*. And he seemed totally besotted with her.

Mikey looked at Shiloh out of the corner of his eye. He was smiling. "So . . . how are things with you and our friend Cary?"

"Uh . . ." Shiloh shrugged. "We're fine? Why, what has Cary told you?"

"Cary hasn't told me anything—he's a gentleman. He won't ever talk about you. But you're no gentleman, Shiloh. Give me the goods."

She shook her head. "There are no goods."

Mikey tipped his head, squinting one eye. "Uhhh, maybe I'd believe that if I hadn't seen you filming a romantic comedy at my own wedding reception. Like, seriously. It was my wedding, but you guys got voted Cutest Couple."

Shiloh looked at the fire. She was embarrassed. It was probably rude to make a lovey-dovey scene at someone else's wedding. "I don't know what to tell you—nothing happened."

Mikey made another face. "*Nothing* nothing?"

"Nothing-ish," she said. "We just talked."

"I don't believe you."

"Okay, how about this . . ." She held out her arms. "We dug up our past and laid it all out on clean tarps, trying to figure out what sort of natural disaster had come through and destroyed everything."

Mikey nodded. He looked disappointed. "Okay, that I believe. That sounds like you. Both of you."

"What does that mean?"

"It means *you* overthink things—and Cary holds a grudge."

"I'm making it sound worse than it was," Shiloh said, kicking at a rock next to the fire. "It was good, actually. To clear things up with him. It was the first real conversation we've had in years."

Mikey shook his head, like that bothered him.

"*What,*" she demanded.

"I thought you guys finally got your act together that night. I was ready to take credit."

"We kind of *did,*" she said. "I think Cary and I are just supposed to be friends."

"Bull-shit," Mikey said, stretching out the syllables.

"You don't get to say that's bullshit."

"As the person who chaperoned you for five years, I absolutely do."

"What's that supposed to mean?"

He looked pained. "Oh, come on, Shiloh, you know what it means."

"Cary and I never dated in high school."

"Yeah, I know, but I don't understand why."

She shrugged. "We were friends."

"No." He motioned between them with his fire stick. "*We* were friends. You and Cary were caught up in some sexually charged will-they, won't-they fuckery."

"Well," she said, "I guess the answer is—they won't." That was the short answer, anyway.

"So you just danced cheek-to-cheek all night and then had a long platonic talk."

"Basically."

He poked at some coals. "What a rip-off."

"I don't know what you want to hear ..." Shiloh leaned forward with an elbow on her knee. "We're not teenagers anymore. I've got kids, Cary lives on a boat—and all of our shared experiences are from adolescence. Just because *you* married *your* first love—"

"Janine isn't my first love," Mikey said, quick to correct her.

"Cary told me you secretly dated in high school."

"We did. And it was nice. We were good friends. But no, we weren't in love—my first love was in college. She was a complete psychopath who made me sleep in my street clothes. And Janine . . . Well." He looked down. "Her first love died of cancer."

"Oh my god, really?"

"Yeah." Mikey frowned, breaking his stick off into the fire. "Her first husband. It was tragic."

"I'm sorry."

"Me too. If I think too hard about it, I get lost . . . *He* should proba-bly be here instead of me. But the thing is—*I'm really glad to be here.*" Mikey growled, frustrated, shaking his head. "Anyway. Janine and I never would have stayed together in high school. We were both only half-baked and double stupid back then. She broke up with me after prom because I didn't believe in Jesus. Now I paint, like, *actual* profan-ity, and she wants to have babies with me."

Shiloh was biting her bottom lip and laughing softly. "I feel like this proves my point—high school relationships aren't magical. They're not destiny."

"Pfff," Mikey said. "Janine and I had nothing on you and Cary back then. You guys were attached at the brain stem."

"Yeah ..."

Shiloh couldn't disagree. They *were* attached. They had something. But she didn't think that it meant . . . *anything* now.

She didn't want to spend her whole life trying to make it mean some-thing.

"I'm really glad that Cary and I finally talked," she said. "If you want, you can take credit for that. For resuscitating our friendship. He said maybe we could all hang out when he comes back for Christmas."

Mikey's high-beam face lit up again. "Heck yeah! That'd be great. We need to do that! We're never all three in the same place."

"I mean, I'm always in Omaha . . ." Shiloh frowned at him. "Did you really tell Janine that we're alike?"

"You and Cary?"

"Yeah."

"Yeah, duh. You're practically the same person sometimes."

"Uh," Shiloh objected, "we couldn't be more different! He's in the Navy, and I voted for Ralph Nader."

Mikey turned on her. "Are you fucking kidding me—did you *really* vote for Nader?"

She folded her arms. "I don't want to talk about it. I have some regrets. I have nothing *but* regrets. Which is another way I'm not like Cary."

"You guys look different on the outside," Mikey said. "Different packaging. But you're a lot alike on the inside."

"How?" Shiloh asked. "Be specific."

"You're both smart. You're both headstrong and . . . what's a nice way to say 'arrogant'?"

"There is no nice way to say 'arrogant.'"

Mikey shrugged with his eyebrows, like this wasn't his problem. "Also, you laugh at the same jokes."

"We laugh at *your* jokes."

"That must be why we all got along so well."

"Hmmm," Shiloh said doubtfully.

"You're not putting me off till Christmas," Mikey said. "I'm back in town now, and we're blood brothers."

# before

"WE SHOULD BE BLOOD BROTHERS," Mikey said.

"No," Cary said.

Shiloh made a face. "Haven't you heard of AIDS?"

"We don't have *AIDS*," Mikey said. "Has anyone in this car even had sex?"

Shiloh was sixteen. She hadn't done anything. She tried not to look at Cary to note his expression. They were on the way home from Family Fun Time, a big arcade out west. Cary was driving, and Shiloh was squeezed between them.

"People in movies are always becoming blood brothers and getting invited to circle jerks," Mikey complained.

"What kind of movies are you watching?" Cary asked.

Shiloh piped up—"What's a circle jerk?"

"No," Cary said.

Mikey elbowed her. "I'll tell you later. And for the record, I'm not proposing one. I'm just saying it would be nice to be *asked*. It would be nice to be invited into *some* sacred ritual."

Shiloh smiled at him. "Is this because we just saw *Dead Poets Society*?"

"Yes," Cary said.

Mikey turned toward them in his seat. "Wouldn't you like to be tapped into a secret society? What if all the other cool people are in one, and we don't know? You guys could be in one and not tell me. Are you already blood brothers?"

"No," Cary said.

Shiloh raised her palms and shoulders. "We might have taken a blood oath not to tell you . . ."

"*Fuck* me," Mikey said.

"What do you think people do in secret societies?" Shiloh wondered aloud. "I don't think anyone actually reads poetry."

"It's for rich people," Cary said. "They build bonds to enable future corruption and collusion."

"They get matching rings," Mikey said. "That's the shit, right? And secret knocks. Camaraderie. Lifelong allegiance."

"You can have my lifelong allegiance, Mikey," Shiloh said. It felt easy enough to say.

"What about Cary?" Mikey asked her. "Can you alleege with him? It's gotta be all for one and one for all."

She laughed. "Cary already has my lifelong allegiance."

"Fuck you guys," Mikey said. "I knew you'd left me out. Did you cut open your palms with a pocketknife?"

"No," Cary said.

"Did you clasp hands over a hobo fire?"

"What's a hobo fire?" Shiloh asked.

"He's making it up," Cary said.

Mikey pointed at Cary over Shiloh's lap. "It's a fire that hobos make in a trash can to stay warm! I didn't make it up. It's in *Fahrenheit 451*."

"I think he's trying to distract you, Mikey," Shiloh said, poking Cary's thigh. "Cary doesn't want to be our blood brother."

"Oh my god," Mikey said, dismayed. "You're right. What's up, Cary? What's holding you back? You love this knights-of-the-round shit."

"He's willing to pledge his life to this *country*," Shiloh said. "But not to you."

"It's getting worse and worse," Mikey said.

Shiloh tugged at a loop on Cary's Army surplus pants.

"What do you want from me?" Cary asked.

"Secret society," Mikey answered. "Right here, right now. Sacred bonds. Possibly blood."

"No blood."

"Mikey wants you to be his *best friend forever,*" Shiloh said.

"You too, Shy." Mikey elbowed her again. "We're getting robes—"

"No robes," Cary said.

"A secret knock, though, right? And a word that we say to each other when we need loyalty without question."

"It's not enough that I drive you people everywhere?"

"No!" Mikey slammed his hand on the dashboard.

Shiloh bit her bottom lip and giggled.

"All right, fine," Cary said. "Whatever."

"Clearly not 'whatever,'" she said. "You've already nixed blood and robes."

"You're welcome for that."

Mikey held his right hand in the air, like he was being sworn in. "Loyalty! Your sword in battle! Your shoulder in despair!"

"That's nice," Shiloh said. "I like that."

"Your vote," Mikey went on, "should I ever run for office."

"No," Cary said. They were at Mikey's house. Cary pulled into the driveway.

"All right," Mikey relented. "We just agree to have each other's back, in every circumstance."

Shiloh studied Mikey for a second. He could be a real goof sometimes. And he didn't know when enough was enough. But if he told her that he'd found a dead body in the woods, she'd keep it a secret for him. "Yeah," she said, "okay."

"Cary?" Mikey pushed.

Cary sighed and put the car in park. "Yeah. I have your back."

"You swear it?"

"I swear."

"And Shiloh's, too?" Mikey waggled his hand between them. "Are you guys good with each other?"

"You don't have to make me a blood brother just because I happen to be here," Shiloh said.

"Oh my god," Mikey said. "Shut up. You're baked into this, Shiloh."

Shiloh turned to Cary.

He was looking at her. "You've already got my sword, Shiloh. And my shoulder."

Shiloh's face felt hot. "Thanks, Cary. You, too—you know, already."

"Yes!" Mikey said. "Now we've got to shake on it or something. Are you sure we can't use blood? I just think the actual risk is very low, and then we'll have hairline scars to mark the occasion."

Shiloh could be talked into it . . .

"No," Cary said.

"Spit, then," Mikey said.

"Why spit?"

"They do it in movies—I don't know, I feel like it's a good compromise."

Cary shrugged. "Yeah, fine."

"*Really?*" Shiloh shuddered. "You're compromising on *spit*? I'd rather do blood than spit."

Mikey spat—excessively—in his palm and held it out.

Cary spat in his own hand, then clasped Mikey's. Mikey rubbed the spit into their grip. Cary rolled his eyes.

Shiloh was shuddering with every muscle in her body and making a gurgling sound.

"Come on, Shiloh," Mikey said, holding out his hand to her. "Let's do this."

"*Noooo.*" This had all taken a very bad turn.

"Wow," Mikey said. "You're just going to leave a lifelong bond sitting on the table."

"I can't do it," she said.

"Do it!" Mikey ordered. "Before our spit dries."

Shiloh held her left hand to her mouth and spat.

"Wrong hand," Cary said.

She groaned, still wriggling, and spat in her right hand.

Mikey grabbed her hand and shook it. It was wet. Shiloh stuck out her tongue and literally gagged.

Mikey pulled his hand away. Cary was looking at Shiloh, his expression flat.

"Complete the ritual," Mikey said.

Cary raised an eyebrow.

She held out her hand, still grimacing. Cary looked in her eyes. He took her hand and squeezed it.

"That's *it*!" Mikey shouted. "We're in *league*. You suckers are never getting rid of me. I am going to burden you with so many dangerous secrets."

Shiloh wiped her left hand on her leg.

"Don't wipe it off!" Mikey said.

"That was my wrong hand."

"You've got to let it dry for the pledge to set. Blood brothers for life."

"*Spit* brothers," Shiloh said.

## TWENTY-NINE

"RYAN CAME TO THE SHOW last night," Tom said. "Did he tell you?"

"To *this* show?"

"None other."

Shiloh was obligated to see all of the theater's main-stage produc-tions at least once. She always came with Tom, her second-in-command in the education department and her best friend during work hours. (Which made him her best friend generally speaking, too.)

Shiloh usually brought her kids to the shows, and Tom would bring his partner, Daniel, who worked in marketing at a huge furniture store.

The five of them were sitting in the back row of the theater tonight. Shiloh and Tom were sitting next to each other. The kids were sitting on either side of Daniel because he had jelly beans.

"Why would Ryan come to *Jacob Climbs the Food Pyramid*?" Shiloh asked. The play was an educational project funded by the Department of Agriculture. They'd brought in professional adult actors, but still . . . it wasn't the theater's artiest art.

Tom made a sad face. He had red hair and clear-framed glasses and an MFA in directing from Northwestern. His sad faces were always a little over-the-top. "I heard he's dating one of the actresses."

"Ah," Shiloh said.

"Do you want to leave?" Tom picked up his coat. "Let's leave. We'll say somebody got sick—Daniel can make himself puke just by think-ing about scrambled eggs."

"No," Shiloh said. "It's fine. I'm fine."

Tom made an even sadder face. He'd held Shiloh together with duct tape and baling wire during her divorce (which was *not* a part of his job description). He knew how not-fine she could be regarding Ryan. "Are you sure?"

"I don't mind puking to get out of children's theater," Daniel said amiably, handing Gus a jelly bean. "I've done it before." Daniel was Chinese-American. He had a very expensive haircut and always wore beautiful paisley neckties. Shiloh liked him enormously.

"Honestly," she said. "I'm fine."

Tom frowned. "Do you want me to tell you which actress?"

"No," she said. "Let me guess. It will keep me awake during the show. Who'd you even hear this from?"

"Kate. She's outraged on your behalf."

"Ah." Kate was the costume designer who'd asked Shiloh out a few months ago. Shiloh had said she wasn't ready to date.

Tom was a Kate advocate.

Tom was a Shiloh-moving-on advocate.

He didn't believe Shiloh when she said that she *was* moving on. That moving on as a divorced mother in your thirties could simply mean being less miserable. Enjoying a nice pear. Sleeping eight hours in a row. Wearing earrings. *"That's not moving on, Shiloh. That's just being happy in a sad way."*

Tom would probably love to hear about Shiloh's run-in with Cary . . .

If she had the heart to talk about it.

The play started. Gus climbed into Shiloh's lap as soon as Daniel ran out of jelly beans.

It was obvious which actress Ryan was dating. Shiloh called it as soon as the woman walked onstage dressed like a carton of 2 percent milk. She had dark hair and a big chest. Ryan had a type.

Before Tom could confirm, Junie said, "I know her—that's Jocelyn!"

After the play, they all walked across the street to a gourmet ice cream shop. "Ice cream is at the top of the food pyramid," Junie said confidently.

"That means it's the very best," Daniel said.

Tom and Daniel were both from bigger cities. They'd moved to Omaha eight years ago so that Tom could get a full-time theater gig on his résumé. The plan was always to move on.

Shiloh would be devastated if they ever did.

"What are you doing this weekend?" Tom asked while they were waiting for their sundaes. "Doesn't Ryan have the kids?"

"I am doing *so much*," she said.

"Oh," Daniel said, "are you going to enjoy a nice pear?"

Shiloh frowned at Tom. "Do you tell him every dumb thing I say?"

"Daniel and I have no secrets."

## THIRTY

IT WAS PROBABLY GOOD, ON balance, to have had children with someone who would eventually want shared custody.

Ryan had refused to leave the house the night that Shiloh tried to kick him out.

He'd sat on the couch with his arms folded. "I'm not leaving my children. I am not *physically* walking away from them. If you need to leave—leave!"

So Shiloh woke up the kids and strapped them into their car seats, both of them crying, while Ryan followed her around the garage swearing the whole time that he wasn't going to let her take them *or* the Subaru station wagon. Then he actually stood behind the car, so she couldn't pull out.

Finally Shiloh got out and told him that he was traumatizing Junie in a way that she may never recover from.

"Or maybe *you're* traumatizing her, Shiloh! By separating her from her father!"

They stood in the garage shouting at each other.

Somehow the story had shifted from *what Ryan had done* to *what Shiloh was doing.* This was about *her* hurting *him.* Ryan was a father, fighting for his family.

They only stopped shouting because Gus was screaming loud enough that they could hear him from outside the car—and Shiloh's breast milk had seeped through her bra and T-shirt.

"I'm not going to take them from you," she'd promised Ryan. "We'll work this out."

And they had. It went like this:

Ryan had the kids for two weekdays, then Shiloh had the kids for two weekdays, then Ryan had them for the three weekend days. The next week, it switched.

It was a chaotic way to split the kids fifty-fifty—Shiloh couldn't plan a consistent workweek around it—but it meant that nobody went more than three days without seeing each other. And when Gus was still breastfeeding, Ryan had let Shiloh have him every night.

Once Ryan realized that Shiloh wasn't going to keep the kids from him, the rest of the divorce came together smoothly. (Or came apart.) They sold the house and split their meager equity. Ryan earned slightly more money than Shiloh, so he paid a small amount of child support.

Of their shared belongings, he wanted everything they'd bought new, and she wanted everything they'd bought old.

They'd fussed over Junie's books and toys, and Gus's baby equipment.

*"The balls on this guy,"* Shiloh's mom had said. *"He should have his tail between his legs, taking whatever you give him."*

But Shiloh figured that in the long term, the kids were better off having a dad who would fight for them—who was willing to spend half his days taking care of them, all by himself.

She trusted Ryan to take care of Junie and Gus. He was sensitive and nurturing. He liked being a father.

Shiloh honestly believed that Ryan liked being a husband, too—he just wasn't very good at it.

Maybe Shiloh hadn't been very good at being a wife.


Shared custody meant that Shiloh's nights were either loud and frantic, or long and quiet. She stayed late at work when Ryan had the kids, and tried to do most of her errands and housework on those nights.

Ryan planned his longest rehearsals for his off nights. They both worked a lot of weekends and leaned on their families for help, but they'd agreed to be present as much as possible when it was their turn to parent.

That's what Shiloh hated about the arrangement—the feeling that she actually *wasn't* a parent on off days. That her kids only had a mother for half their life.

Ryan could say the same thing, Shiloh supposed, but she found her own loss more compelling. She was their *mother.*

*"You're doing your best,"* her own mother would say. (A woman who had never overly concerned herself with being present.)

But if Shiloh had been doing her best—her actual best—she wouldn't have made the choices that led her *here.* To part-time parenthood.

She'd wanted to stay home with her kids. Now she was only home with them two nights a week and every other weekend. If she thought about it that way, her whole life started to spin and swirl toward the drain. It was *intolerable.*

But what could she do, except tolerate it?

*Off, off. On, on. Off, off, off.*

When Mikey invited Shiloh over for dinner again, it wasn't hard for her to find a free night.

It was better this time. He'd only invited Shiloh and another old high school friend, someone who'd grown up with Janine.

The talk of the night was the incoming baby. Plans and logistics. Janine worked as a writer for a travel industry magazine. She was probably going to switch to freelance after her maternity leave. Mikey wasn't a superstar by New York standards—he claimed—but by Omaha standards, he was making a really nice living. They could manage it.

"I'm trying to talk other artists into moving here," he said over dessert. (Apricot torte from a local bakery.) "They could afford houses and studios—Omaha artists' colony!"

"No one loves a colonist," Shiloh said. "Our artist-to-sane-person ratio is perfect as it is."

Later that spring, Janine's sister threw a coed baby shower. Shiloh bought a set of vintage baby dishes at the antique mall—a little ceramic cup and bowl with lambs painted on them.

Her mother took one look at them and said, "Hopefully that's not lead paint."

Shiloh had inherited a love of old things from her mother, but her mom thought Shiloh went overboard. *"It's like you're buying every single thing we threw out when your grandma died."*

When the baby came, Shiloh told Mike and Janine to call her if they needed any help. But they both had big families, and Janine had her own friends. Shiloh went over to meet the baby—Otis—about a month after he was born. He was bald and healthy. Janine seemed exhausted. Mikey said he was going to take more time off work, maybe two and a half months. That was longer than Shiloh got at the theater for maternity leave.

Shiloh found herself feeling jealous of them. Not that she wanted another baby . . .

She was jealous of how *right* they seemed together. They were doing it right. They loved each other. (A fly on the wall would have said the same thing about Ryan and Shiloh . . . )

And she was jealous of what they were offering Otis. The attention of two parents. The same house seven nights a week.

Shiloh didn't like feeling this way. She was sort of glad that Mikey was too busy now to invite her to parties.

## THIRTY-ONE

SHILOH ANSWERED THE PHONE BEFORE she was awake. She thought it must be Ryan. "Hello?"

"Shiloh?" It wasn't Ryan.

"Who is this?"

"It's Cary."

"*Cary?* Are you okay?"

"I'm fine. I'm sorry I woke you. I, um— My mom—"

"Is she okay?"

"No. Actually. She fell, and she's been waiting for someone to come home. I think it must be bad for her to reach out to me, but she won't let me call 911—and now she won't pick up the phone."

"I'll go over there," Shiloh said. "I'll go now."

"Okay." He sounded relieved. "Thank you. There's a key in the mailbox. Not the actual mailbox. The old one, inside the porch."

"Got it."

"I really appreciate this, Shiloh."

"Don't worry about it. I'll call you when I get there."

"I know you don't like dogs—"

"I'll be okay."

"If it doesn't feel safe, just call 911. Call 911 if you have to, anyway."

"I'll call you when I'm there," Shiloh said again.

"Thank you," he said.

"Bye." Shiloh hung up and looked at the time—3 A.M.

The kids were at Ryan's. She threw on clothes and went down to tell her mom where she was going. "I'll come with you," her mom said.

Shiloh almost told her to go back to sleep, then reconsidered. "That might be a good idea, thanks."

Shiloh grabbed some cheese sticks from the fridge. Her mom walked into the kitchen, wearing a pajama shirt and sweatpants.

"Dogs can have cheese, right?" Shiloh asked.

When they got to Cary's house, there were no cars in the driveway. The dogs went nuts when they heard people on the porch.

"You talk to the dogs," Shiloh said, handing her mom the cheese sticks and fishing out the key.

Shiloh cracked open the door. "Lois? It's me, Shiloh." The dogs were jumping on the door, scratching at it.

"Go in," her mom said. "Be confident. They can smell fear."

"Thanks, Jerry Maguire. *Lois?*" Shiloh called. "I'm coming in!"

Shiloh pushed the door open. Her mom was talking to the dogs in baby voices, already handing out cheese. Shiloh hurried past them, into the living room. She should have asked Cary where his mom had fallen. Was she upstairs?

"Angel?" someone called from the back of the house.

Shiloh headed for the kitchen and carefully swung open the door. Lois was lying on the floor, against the cabinets. Her oxygen can had rolled away from her. Her baggy shirt was twisted up, exposing her stomach. The phone was sitting next to her, like she'd pulled it off the counter.

Shiloh got on her knees. "Lois, it's Shiloh. Cary called me. Where are you hurt?"

"Shiloh . . ." Lois said breathlessly. "I think I . . . I twisted my ankle, honey. If you could help me sit up . . ."

"It's just your ankle that hurts?"

"I'm an old woman, everything hurts. If you could just . . ." She reached out her hand. Shiloh took it. Lois's hands were soft and felt swollen. She was cold.

Shiloh reached under her shoulder, to lift her. Lois immediately gasped in pain.

"Lois, I think we should call an ambulance."

"No!" She shook her head. There were tears on her cheeks. "They can't come in here . . . The dogs . . . If Petey bites somebody, they'll put him to sleep this time."

Shiloh wondered if Petey was the one who looked like a pit bull or the one who looked like a Chihuahua. "I'll have them come to the back door, okay?"

"The back porch is a mess."

"That's okay."

"Honey, no . . . I want to wait for Angel."

"Lois, I can't leave you here. I promised Cary I'd take care of you."

"He worries too much," Lois said. "I shouldn't have called him, but I know his number by heart."

"Shiloh!" her mom shouted from the next room. "I'm waiting on the porch, I ran out of cheese!"

Shiloh got out her cell phone to call Cary. But then she looked at Lois again—pale and gasping—and called 911 instead.

Lois started to cry when she heard Shiloh talking to the operator. Shiloh held her hand. The operator told Shiloh how to check that the oxygen canister was connected.

Shiloh called her mom's cell phone and told her to make sure the EMTs went to the back door when they got there.

She tugged Lois's shirt down and slid her own hand between Lois's head and the cabinet. "I'm sorry," Shiloh told her. "I promised Cary I'd treat you like my own mother." She hadn't promised that, but she would have.

"I hate hospitals," Lois cried.

"I'm sorry," Shiloh said again. "I know they're going to take care of you."

"They don't care about"—she took a rasping breath—"fat old ladies on Medicare."

"We'll make *sure* they take care of you."

When the ambulance got there, Shiloh went to open the back door.

She struggled with the lock. And then the screen door wouldn't open because there was so much junk on the back porch.

"Shiloh?" Lois said. "Don't leave me alone."

"I won't leave, I'm here." The door finally gave. Something on the other side broke. The EMTs came through the refuse and into the kitchen.

"Shiloh?" Lois called. "Don't leave me!"

"I'm here," she said. "I'm not leaving. I'll stay with you."

The EMTs got Lois onto a stretcher. They were gentle, but she cried the whole time. One of them, an older man, was irritated that they had to take the stretcher down the back steps. "There's no light back here."

"The dogs . . ." Shiloh said.

When they got Lois outside, they asked if Shiloh was family. "That's my granddaughter," Lois said.

Shiloh got into the ambulance—they made her sit up front. Shiloh's mom said she'd leave a note for Lois's family. Shiloh gave her the keys to the car.

"*in ambulance,*" Shiloh texted Cary. She had a shitty cell phone; it took forever.

"*heading 2 immanuel ER
lois is in pain but awake
will call soon*"

Cary texted back immediately. "*Standing by for more information. Thank you.*"

The EMTs put Lois on more serious oxygen. They were trying to judge her pain, but she was still minimizing everything, even through tears. She told them she'd slipped on a wet spot on the kitchen floor, that it was nothing.

When they got to the hospital, the admissions people wanted Lois's personal information. Shiloh couldn't even remember Lois's last name. She called Cary. "We're at the hospital," she said. "Can I hand you over to someone?"

The woman behind the desk gave the phone back to Shiloh a few minutes later. "Your husband says he's going to call back with her insurance info."

"Okay," Shiloh said.

They let her go into the exam room with Lois. Shiloh sat by the bed and held her hand. Lois already had an IV, and they'd started her on pain medication.

It made Shiloh nervous, how urgently they were attending to Lois. Shiloh's other ER experiences—for the kids, and herself, and Ryan when he had appendicitis—had been a lot of sitting around and waiting.

Cary wanted to talk to his mom, so Shiloh held the phone up to her ear. Then she gave the phone to a nurse, so Cary could give Lois's patient history.

Shiloh went with Lois to radiology and held her hand on the way back to the exam room.

When the doctor eventually came in to say that Lois had fractured her hip in two places and would need surgery, Lois was asleep. Shiloh called Cary.

"I've left messages for my niece," he said, "and I finally got through to my oldest sister, but she's in Denver. She might send her kid."

"I'll stay as long as I need to," Shiloh said. "I'll keep you posted."

"I told the nurse you were family," he said.

"So did your mom. It seems fine."

"I'm sorry for all this, Shiloh."

"You can thank me," she said, "but you can't apologize."

"All right. Thank you."

The operation was set for seven thirty that morning, when the surgeon was scheduled to start her shift. Shiloh followed Lois to pre-op and sat with her as long as it was allowed. Then she went to wait in the special room set aside for family. She sent Cary a text. *"she just went back"*

"*Thanks,*" he replied.

"*did you get any sleep?*"

"It's afternoon here. Did you?"

"i'm fine," Shiloh typed. "where r u?"

"Singapore. For now. Do you have to work tomorrow?"

"not rly" Shiloh had decided to take a sick day. "fyi—i left dogs in house alone"

"Someone else will deal with them."

"mom + i fed them lots of cheese"

"Is your mom with you?"

"no but she came w/me to your house"

"What about the kids?"

"with their dad, it's fine"

"Thank Gloria for me."

"i will"

Lois was out of surgery and in recovery when Cary's niece Angel showed up. Shiloh recognized her from when they were kids.

Angel was in her mid-twenties now. She had shaggy blond hair and Cary's brown eyes, and she looked ragged and exhausted in a way that wasn't entirely explained by being at the hospital first thing in the morning.

Shiloh waved. "Hi. I'm Shiloh, Cary's friend. Your grandma just got out of surgery."

"Are you the one who brought her in?" Angel seemed suspicious.

"Yeah. Cary called me."

"She hates ambulances."

Shiloh wasn't sure how to respond to that. She decided not to apologize. "She was in the operating room for about two hours, but the doctor was in a good mood when she came out."

"I'll talk to the doctor," Angel said.

"Can I get you some coffee?"

"I can get it."

Shiloh nodded. She texted Cary:

*"angel's here. i think she'd like me 2 leave"*

"She's mad at me," Cary sent back. *"Not you."*

*"can she handle this? should i go?"*

"Yeah," he texted. *"My sister's coming, too. They'll all show up, I think."*

*"will they tell u what's happening?"*

"Begrudgingly," he sent. And then—*"You should go, Shiloh. I can't thank you enough for this."*

*"i'm still around,"* she said. *"call if u need anything, i mean it"*

*"Thank you."*

Shiloh picked up her purse. "I think I'm going to head out—unless you'd like me to wait with you. I don't mind."

"Nope," Angel said.

Shiloh called her mom for a ride home.

## THIRTY-TWO

SHILOH WAITED UNTIL THAT NIGHT to check in with Cary. She got confused looking up the time zones.

*"how's it going?"* she sent, after she'd put the kids to bed.

Cary didn't text back right away. He was probably at work. Shiloh took a shower and climbed into bed. She had a stack of plays to read for a youth competition. Her phone buzzed—Cary.

*"Not great,"* he'd sent. *"They think my mom had a heart attack."*

*"oh my god, i'm sorry. can i do anything to help?"*

*"No,"* he replied. Then—*"Thank you."*

Shiloh stared at the phone, biting her lip while she tried to think of what to say next.

*"I can't tell how bad it is,"* Cary sent. *"I guess the doctors aren't sure."*

*"u getting good info?"*

*"Yeah. Angel has been helpful. She and her mom aren't talking, so Angel has decided to ally with me. In a surprise turn of events."*

*"do u need allies?"*

*"And spies."*

*"i'm sorry, cary"*

*"I owe you one,"* he sent. *"Again."*

*"never"*

Shiloh watched her phone, waiting, but that was the end of it.


She checked in, again the next night. *"how's your mom?"*

Cary didn't text back.


"Shiloh?"

She recognized his voice this time. "Cary?"

"I'm sorry I keep calling you in the middle of the night."

She pulled the phone away to look at it. One A.M. "It's not that late. What's up?"

"I, uh . . ." His voice was faint.

"Cary? Is your mom okay?"

"Yeah," he said, louder. "Yes and no. She's, uh . . . still in the hospital. She's recovering. I'm in Omaha."

"Oh. Do you need a ride?"

"No, I rented a car. I'm just . . . My sister says I can't stay in the house . . ."

"Do you want to come over? I can make up the couch."

"Would that be okay?"

"It would be totally okay. Come now."

"Okay. See you in a few. Thank you." He hung up.

Shiloh sat up in bed and rubbed her face. Then she climbed out of bed. She was wearing a theater T-shirt. She pulled on some pajama pants and grabbed a bra from the top of the hamper.

Her hair was pulled up. Should she do something with it? Should she brush her teeth?

No.

She wanted to get to the door before Cary knocked, so she went downstairs and opened it. Then she cleared the toys and throw pillows off the couch. Junie's dolls and action figures were everywhere. Shiloh kicked them all into a corner. She heard Cary on the porch. When she looked up, he was standing in the doorway.

Shiloh smiled, carefully. "Hi," she whispered.

"Hi," Cary said quietly.

She motioned for him to come in.

He stepped inside and set down his bag, then shut the door so gently, it hardly clicked. He locked it.

Shiloh took a step toward him. "Come, sit down."

"I can get a hotel room," Cary said. "I wasn't thinking it through."

"You're already here. Sit down. What do you want to drink?"

"Nothing," he said.

"I'll get you water."

Shiloh went into the kitchen. Cary followed her. They both blinked when she turned on the light.

Cary looked awful.

Well. He looked very handsome. Straight-backed and square-shouldered, as usual. In a plaid button-down and navy blue windbreaker. But he looked haggard and pale. His eyes were bloodshot. He hadn't shaved, and she could see he had a little gray in his beard already.

She turned on the tap. "Did you just fly in?"

Cary nodded.

"I thought you were at sea."

"I was headed that way. I got emergency leave."

"How long was your flight?" She handed him the glass of water.

He drained it. "Long."

Shiloh took the glass and refilled it. "Have you eaten?"

"Yeah," he said, but he shrugged as he said it.

Shiloh glanced around the kitchen, thinking. "Would you eat toast if I made it?"

"Yeah," Cary said, with interest. "I would."

"Okay." She smiled at him. "Good. Go sit down."

He didn't. He followed her to the counter and sort of hovered while she started the toast—she had about half a loaf of good sourdough—and got out the butter.

"I could do cream cheese and tomato . . ." she said, opening the fridge. "Or peanut butter?"

"Peanut butter."

Shiloh grabbed the milk—and some strawberry jam and apple butter. The peanut butter was in the cupboard.

Cary watched her. Still hovering. Unsteady.

"You could sit down," she said.

"I'm fine. I've been sitting for . . . twenty-seven hours."

"You must be so jet-lagged."

"Not yet."

She spread Cary's toast with butter, then peanut butter, and immediately put more bread in the toaster.

Cary ate over his hand. She got a cloth napkin out of a drawer and handed it to him. "Milk?" she said, holding up the carton.

He nodded. He'd already inhaled the first of his two slices of toast.

When the bread popped up, she said, "Peanut butter again? I've got strawberry jam and apple butter."

"Apple butter. I never have apple butter."

Shiloh spread the butter extra thick and then the apple butter. She put more bread in the toaster.

"This is enough," Cary said, with his mouth full.

"I'll eat what you don't."

Cary ate his third and fourth slices more slowly. He still hadn't moved away from her. Shiloh made herself toast with butter and jam.

"Thank you," he said. "I was ravenous. All the restaurants in the airport were closed, and I just wanted to get home."

Shiloh took a bite of toast. She loved toast. She was happy for an excuse to eat it in the middle of the night. She took a sip of Cary's milk, then refilled the glass. "They wouldn't let you into the house?"

"My sister's there. Jackie. She's angry with me. I decided not to fight her on it—I don't even *want* to stay there if Mom isn't there. I hate that house."

Shiloh nodded, chewing.

"I'll get a hotel room tomorrow," he said. "I forget when I come back to Omaha that I'm an adult. I can rent a car. I can get a hotel."

"You should be able to go home," she said.

"What's home," Cary said indifferently. "My mom is home. The rest is . . ." He shook his head and shoved half a piece of toast into his mouth.

Shiloh put two more pieces of bread—the last of the loaf—in the toaster. "I wish my couch was more comfortable. It doesn't pull out."

"I'll be glad to have it. It's just one night."

When the toaster popped again, Cary said, "I'm full."

Shiloh buttered the last two pieces anyway and held one out to him. He took it. "This bread is really good," he said.

"I get it at a pretentious bakery where no one likes me."

Cary smiled. It was nice to see him smile. Shiloh brushed some crumbs off his chest.

"Thanks," he said. "I'd return the favor, but . . ."

Shiloh glanced down. She was covered in crumbs. She held her toast in her teeth and brushed off her T-shirt, then her pajama pants. "I'll sweep tomorrow," she said, taking the toast in hand again. "Or eventually."

Cary reached up to her chin and wiped something off with his thumb.

Shiloh looked away from him. She smiled with one side of her cheek. "I haven't gotten the bedding out yet. Let me do that." She finished the toast and washed her hands.

Cary watched her for a second. Then he screwed the lids onto the jam jars and picked up the milk carton. Shiloh thought about warning him that the fridge was a mess, but he'd see for himself in a second.

She went out to the dining room and leaned over the cedar chest. She'd found it at a garage sale. It made their sheets and pillowcases smell heavenly.

"You don't have to make up the couch," Cary said, behind her. "I think I'm going to sit for a while."

She stood up, hugging a pile of bedding. "Do you want some company?"

He nodded. "If you can spare it."

Shiloh sat on the couch with the sheets and blanket on her lap. Cary sat down next to her.

She turned toward him. They were basically the same height when they were sitting. "What time is it in your head?" she asked.

He groaned and ran his hand over his head. "Three o'clock in the afternoon."

Shiloh leaned against him for a second, humming in sympathy. "Have you been able to talk to your mom?"

"Not since the night she went in. That's why I decided to come home—the fact that she still wasn't talking. Or that they won't let me talk to her, I don't know."

"Has it always been like this? With your sisters?"

Cary was rubbing his temple. "It's gotten worse as Mom has gotten older, as there are more decisions to make. I'm gone, so they think that I don't get a vote."

"And you think . . ."

"I think I should get *all* the votes."

Shiloh smiled. "That seems fair."

"It *is* fair." Cary wasn't smiling. "I'm the only one who's thinking about her first. The rest of them only take care of her after they've gotten what they want. If it's convenient."

She shifted her expression. "Sorry. I didn't—"

He closed his eyes and pinched the bridge of his nose. "No. I'm sorry. I'm tired and humorless. And"—he shook his head—"worried."

Shiloh looked down at her lap, feeling useless. After a second, she took Cary's hand and squeezed it. He squeezed back and held on. She leaned her shoulder against his again, for a few seconds.

It was impossible for Shiloh not to think about the last time they were on this couch, kissing goodbye.

That goodbye seemed to have stuck. There was no danger of Cary kissing her now, nothing in the air between them—even though he had come to her when he needed help. Even though he seemed to want her right next to him.

Maybe they were moving into another phase together. Something like their first friendship. Constant intimacy, careful boundaries.

Shiloh realized she'd be okay with that. She'd want it, if that was on offer—

Cary, back in her life again. A place in *his* life. Shiloh liked being an emergency contact. She just wanted *contact*. She wanted to pull those old warm feelings through the empty years and into the present. She wanted to repot them here and find them a nice sunny window.

Did Shiloh want to be the person Cary called when he was feeling low? Or even *a* person he *could* call?

One hundred percent yes. One *thousand* percent.

Especially if it meant she could call him, too.

She stroked his hand with her thumb. Shiloh could manage not to kiss him. She'd managed not to kiss him for the best years of their friendship.

She would take Cary, as a friend. Halfway across the world but still in her sphere.

Cary's thumb started moving on her hand. His shoulder sank into hers. Shiloh tilted her head toward him—and then felt his head rest against hers.

She closed her eyes.

She could make this work.


"Shiloh?"

She startled.

"Hey . . . it's okay." Cary was sitting next to her. Her body was warm where she'd been leaning against him. "Why don't you go up to bed?"

"Sorry," Shiloh said, sitting up. "Sorry. Let me help you make up the couch."

"I've got it. Go to sleep."

"Yeah," Shiloh said, rubbing her face. "Okay." She stood up. After a second, she looked back at him. "Good night, Cary."

"Good night."

Shiloh went up to her room. She plugged in her phone. It was 3:30 A.M.

## THIRTY-THREE

IT WAS RYAN'S WEEKEND TO have the kids. Normally he'd pick them up Friday afternoon, from daycare. But he'd had a show that night, so he was picking them up this morning, on Saturday, instead. Which would have been fine . . .

Except Cary was still fast asleep on Shiloh's couch.

She kept the kids upstairs when they woke up. She got them dressed and started putting on their shoes. The plan was to take them outside fifteen minutes early and wait with them out there for their dad.

But Ryan decided to come *twenty* minutes early.

He knocked on the front door—*shave and a haircut, two bits*. (Ryan had made her hate "Shave and a Haircut." He ruined everything.)

"Okay," she said, "Daddy's here, and you guys are all ready. So we're going to go *straight out* the door without waking up Grandma."

"Very quiet," Junie whispered.

"Very quiet!" Gus shouted.

"Yep," Shiloh said, picking him up.

Gus immediately went stiff as a board. "No, I walk! Gus-Gus walks!"

"All right," she agreed, "Gus-Gus walks." Gus was still deep in his angsty period. Referring to himself in the third person was new. She let him slide to the floor. "Come on."

Junie beat Shiloh to the door and opened it—and Ryan, predictably, walked right in. "Hey!" he shouted, with his arms open. "Here come the beautiful people!"

"Daddy, we haven't eaten breakfast," Junie said. The little narc.

"Well, let's get you some breakfast," he said. "We're going right to the zoo."

There was no way for Shiloh to stand between them and Cary. She was stuck on the stairs behind Gus. So she very deliberately didn't look toward the living room. "They're all ready to go, Ryan. Why don't you get them packed up, and I'll grab some bananas?"

It was too little, too late.

"Cary?!" Junie shouted, pressing both hands on her cheeks *Home Alone*–style. "Are you sleeping at *my* house!?"

Cary had sat up, but his legs were under the blanket. He was wearing an undershirt. He still looked exhausted.

Ryan was staring at him, one eyebrow stuck in a raised position.

"Oh my lord," Junie said. "You're like Goldilocks, and I'm like Baby Bear."

"Cary . . ." Ryan said. "You're *Cary*."

"Hi," Cary said, not smiling.

Ryan grinned and took a step forward, holding out his hand. "Cary of the full-page yearbook letter."

"Hi," Cary said again. He held his hand out at the last possible second for Ryan to shake it.

"Let's get some breakfast," Shiloh said. "Come on, guys, into the kitchen. Ryan, can you help?"

"I'm Ryan," Ryan was saying. "Nice to finally meet you."

"I want peanut-butter toast," Junie said.

"You can have bananas," Shiloh said. "Or an oatmeal cup."

"Gus-Gus can have nananas," Gus said.

"Yes, you can," Shiloh agreed. "Ryan? Please?"

Ryan followed her into the kitchen. His eyebrow was still wedged into his forehead. "Cary, huh?"

"Will you get Gus a banana?"

"This seems like a good time for us to talk about the overnight rule," Ryan whispered.

Shiloh's head jerked up.

The overnight rule was simple: No overnight guests when the kids were in the house. Even Shiloh's mom had to follow it. "No," Shiloh said. "That's not what this is."

Ryan pointed over his shoulder with his thumb. "Goldilocks begs to differ."

She took a step closer to Ryan, dropping her voice. "He just needed a place to stay. His mom is in the hospital."

"You don't owe me an explanation, Shiloh. I'm happy to change the agreement. We said we would re-evaluate—"

"That's not what this *is*," she said again. "He was sleeping on the couch."

"Oh, is that an exception to the rule?"

"Maybe we should have McDonald's for breakfast," Junie said. "Cary loves McDonald's!"

"*Does* he . . ." Ryan said. He was going to have *aggressive* wrinkles around that eyebrow.

Cary appeared in the kitchen doorway, looking directly at Shiloh. "I'm going to take off. Visiting hours have started. Thanks again for the last-minute save."

"I hope you get to see your mom," Shiloh said.

"Tell Grandma Lois I said hi!" Junie said.

Cary glanced down at Junie. "I will, Juniper. Thanks."

And then he was gone. Shiloh heard the front door close behind him.

Ryan was staring at her. "Either you broke the rule," he said, "or we change the rule."

"We can talk about this later," Shiloh said.

# before

SHILOH HAD BEEN TRYING ALL day to get Cary to sign her year-book. All anybody was doing today was signing yearbooks and fucking around. The teachers weren't going to make seniors work on their very last day of school.

Cary put her off until last period, and then disappeared into the darkroom with her yearbook.

Shiloh had signed Cary's first thing. She wanted to claim a good spot—and she wanted to write something that would kind of embarrass him when other people saw it.

She'd signed on the theater page, over the background of a photo from *A Christmas Carol*. She made some crack about Cary joining the Navy and told him that she hoped his hair would always smell like apples. And then she'd written their favorite line from the fall play, the one they still said to each other sometimes: *"And that, Inspector Pierce, is the way the biscuit has crumbled."* Then at the bottom, in small letters, Shiloh tried to write something sincere. Something about how she wouldn't forget him.

She should have thought it through first, because she was writing in purple ink, and once she'd committed to the first part of the sentence, she just had to keep going with it. What came out was clunky and earnest and might end up embarrassing Shiloh more than Cary if anyone else bothered to decipher it—her handwriting was terrible.

Cary stayed in the darkroom for most of eighth period. He had Mikey's yearbook, too. When he came out, he wouldn't let them read what he'd written.

They all went to Zesto's with a bunch of other seniors, and Cary bought Shiloh a twist cone.

# before

*Shiloh,*
*I know that you're worried about going away and leaving high*
*school and home behind you.*

*You shouldn't be.*

*You are as intelligent and capable as anyone you will meet in*
*college. You are as intelligent and capable as anyone you will meet.*

*I know you to be brave and tenacious.*

*I know you to be perceptive and kind.*

*You'll be a talented actress if that's what you choose to do, but*
*those same talents could take you anywhere, really. I think it's up*
*to you.*

*You worry too much about your height—no one else minds it.*
*(If you would have joined ROTC, I would have taught you how to*
*stand straight.)*

*You keep telling me not to forget you.*

*When I think of high school, I will remember that every good*
*day started with you walking down your steps and getting into my*
*car. I will remember that every bad day ended with meeting you out*
*by the flagpole.*

*Your friend,*
*Cary*

## THIRTY-SIX

THE REASON THAT RYAN WANTED to drop the overnight agreement was because he knew Shiloh would keep following it anyway.

Shiloh wasn't going to bring some guy home when she had the kids. She wasn't going to introduce them to a new guy every week. She wouldn't introduce them to *anyone* until it was serious.

And that scenario wasn't even on the horizon, because Ryan knew that Shiloh wasn't dating. Ryan knew that Shiloh had never really dated anyone but him. And now she was thirty-three and a mother, and she only worked with women and gay men, and she didn't want to join eHarmony. She didn't want to go to bars. She didn't want to join a church or volunteer for a political campaign. She didn't want to make eye contact with people at Mikey's parties.

Shiloh didn't like *anyone*. Like, mathematically speaking. The percentage of people that Shiloh met and then liked was too close to zero to be statistically significant.

Was she going to follow in her mother's footsteps? Make their house a satellite location of Propeller Bill's Hangar Bar and Grill?

No, she was not.

And Ryan *knew* it.

*Ryan* would be the one to introduce the kids to his latest "friends." Junie and Gus had already had lunch with women and gone to the park with women, and rented movies and eaten popcorn with women.

Shiloh didn't need to add *breakfast* to that list.

Or midnight run-ins in the bathroom.

Admittedly—*admittedly*—Shiloh's romantic life held more potential for danger . . .

Ryan wasn't likely to bring home someone who would make a pass at Junie when she was twelve years old and just trying to get some cereal.

(A pass or worse. There was always the danger of worse.)

Shiloh would always have to be more careful than Ryan would.

Unless *she* dated women, too . . .

Not that women were always safe, even if that was an option . . . *Was that an option?*

Probably. It had probably always been an option. Shiloh knew she wasn't a lesbian, but she also knew she wasn't entirely straight. She was as intrigued by k. d. lang as she was by Jake Gyllenhaal. She'd just never gathered enough data to come to a firm conclusion about her sexuality.

Ryan knew that Shiloh barely had any sexuality left.

He hadn't *actually* been threatened by finding Cary *on the couch* . . . It probably confirmed Ryan's faith in Shiloh's chastity.

Shiloh wasn't going to renegotiate the overnight agreement; she couldn't trust Ryan's judgment. The kind of guy who would introduce his girlfriends to *his wife* didn't get to set the terms thereafter.

## THIRTY-SEVEN

SHILOH TEXTED CARY THE NEXT day, Sunday afternoon. *"thinking abt you + hoping you're getting good news"*

Cary texted back almost immediately. *"She's doing better than I expected. She's talking—some."*

*"that's great, cary. i'm relieved to hear it!"*

*"Can I call you?"*

*"now?"*

*"Yeah. Or whenever."*

*"sure, call"*

The phone rang a minute later, and Shiloh answered it. "Hi."

"Hi," Cary said.

"I'm glad things are looking up a bit."

"Yeah." He still sounded tired. "It's so much better to talk to the doctors directly. They think she had a heart attack in recovery, so they did emergency surgery to put in a stent. She just needs to heal now. As much as possible. Hey, Shiloh . . ."

"Yeah?"

"I need to apologize. I'm sorry I put you in that situation yesterday."

"Cary, no—"

"I wasn't even thinking."

"It was fine," Shiloh said. "Really."

"No, I'm sorry. I made your life more complicated."

"No," she said. "*I* made my life more complicated. And I don't mean last night."

"I need to remember that you're a mom now."

"Yeah, but I can still be your *friend*." It came out kind of desperate. "Cary, please let me be your friend."

He didn't say anything.

"I really liked being someone you would call for help," Shiloh said.

"Okay," he said softly.

She couldn't tell what he was thinking. "Did you get a hotel room?" she asked.

"Yeah. Near the hospital. I slept thirteen hours last night."

"Good."

"My mom can't go home any time soon. I need to find a rehab place for her, while I'm here."

"How long are you here?"

"I asked for fourteen days' leave—I didn't know what I was flying into. I'm hoping to see her through the transition."

"Well, call if you need anything."

"Thanks, Shiloh."

"And call if you're bored, Cary. Like, I know you have a lot to do. And maybe you have a lot of people here. But . . . don't sit alone in your hotel room, worrying—unless you want to. You can come over here and worry. Or I could meet you somewhere."

"Yeah?"

"Yeah," she said.

"Do you have the kids tonight?"

"No."

"You want to get dinner?"

"*Yes.*"

## THIRTY-EIGHT

CARY SUGGESTED A PIZZA PLACE where they used to go in high school.

Shiloh told him it sucked now and proposed an all-day breakfast place near his hotel.

She met him there at seven. She wore a sundress over boot-cut jeans with a cropped cardigan. Shiloh loved the dresses-over-jeans trend. Dresses had always been too short on her.

She almost wore heels . . . but something about heels would make this feel like a date.

She decided that eyeliner was platonic. Lots of people wore eyeliner every day. Not Shiloh—but Cary didn't know that.

He was waiting in a booth for her. In another plaid shirt. Flipping through the oversized laminated menu.

Shiloh smiled when she saw him. "Hey," she said, when she was still too far away.

Cary looked up at her. He smiled, too.

She squeezed his shoulder before she sat down across from him. "You look better."

He still hadn't shaved, but his eyes were clear. His hair was clean.

"Thanks," he said. "You look great."

"Oh, well . . . thanks. That's the bright side of not having the kids, I guess. I get to pretend I'm human."

"Does their dad have them every weekend?"

"No," Shiloh said. "That would be awful." She picked up her menu. "We split them fifty-fifty, actually. It's complicated. It's called two-two-three." She looked up. "This is more than you want to know."

"Fifty-fifty," Cary said. "Like, right down the middle?"

"Yep."

"I didn't know people actually did that."

"When we were growing up, they didn't. It was every other weekend. For dads."

Cary looked like he wasn't sure what to think. He wasn't smiling. "How do you feel about the arrangement?"

"I hate it," she said. "I *actively* hate it. But it's probably good, right? None of my friends grew up with their dads. I don't even know who mine is."

"Well. You know. Me neither." Cary turned back to the menu. "Though my mom is going to go to her grave without talking to me about it."

Cary had found some paperwork in junior high that showed his sister Jackie was his birth mother. His mom had probably never even been his legal guardian. His dad was unnamed.

"She's still never talked to you about it?"

He turned the page and shook his head. "Nope."

"And you haven't tried to talk to her?"

He sighed. "What am I supposed to say? Every version of 'I know you're not my mother' sounds terrible. And she *is* my mother. What do I get out of rocking the boat?" He looked up at Shiloh. "What are you ordering?"

"Hot turkey sandwich."

"There are ten pages of breakfast, and you're ordering lunch?"

"I like hot turkey sandwiches. And I never make them at home."

"I keep expecting one of my sisters to confront me with it . . ." Cary said, frowning down at the menu again. "Because daughters are legally closer than a grandson when it comes to making decisions about the house and long-term care. And my sisters know the truth—they were all teenagers when I was born. I'm sure Jackie would *love* to put me in my place . . . but then she'd have to admit to me, directly, what we are to each other."

"You've never talked to her about it, either?"

He looked up. "Again, why would I? She's a terrible sister; I don't need her to be my mother." He set down his menu. "I'm getting potato casserole with chicken and ranch dressing."

Shiloh laughed out a breath. "Aw, Cary, I'm sorry—it's all so messed up."

"No new tale to tell," he said.

"You know . . ." she said. "We grew up blocks away from each other, and neither of us know our dads . . . We could be siblings."

Cary laughed through his nose. "Lois and Gloria would never bring home the same guy."

Shiloh started laughing, for real. "Lois isn't your biological mother, dummy!"

Cary broke down, too, rubbing his forehead. "Oh god, you're right. I can't keep it straight."

Shiloh kicked him under the table.

He kicked her back. "I'm pretty sure Angel and I have the same dad," he said, more seriously. "We look alike, but we don't look anything like Jackie."

"Have you met *him*? Angel's dad?"

"Oh yeah. I've met him. And no thank you."

The waitress came to take their orders. Shiloh asked her half a dozen questions about other things, but still ended up ordering the turkey sandwich.

When the waitress was gone, Shiloh kicked Cary again. "They can't be all bad," she said.

"Who?"

"Your genetic contributors."

"I like that framing—but you're wrong."

"How could they be all bad, when you're so good?"


For all the time Shiloh had spent with Cary over the last few months, none of the circumstances had been normal. (Late nights, emergency phone calls.)

And even *this* dinner wasn't normal—Cary was deeply concerned about his mother. He wore it on every breath.

But it was somewhat normal. Sitting across from each other in a brightly lit family restaurant. It wasn't the sort of place you'd go on a date—unless you'd been dating for a long time.

Shiloh got to really look at him. She got to watch him while he talked and ate. Cary ate the same way he always had, and Shiloh couldn't even explain what that meant. Was it his posture? The way he frowned to show he was listening when his mouth was full?

Their conversation kept coming back to his mom, and what might happen next, and what he had to do while he was here.

Shiloh had known Cary for years before he'd opened up to her about his family, and he'd never been especially descriptive about his home life. He never told her stories. (Cary must have *stories*.) He had a very Walter Cronkitey way of discussing it all.

It was a relief that he was picking up with Shiloh right where they'd left off. As if she was still on the inside. Still a confidante.

They finished their meals, and Shiloh ordered tea. Cary got cheesecake. She leaned back in the booth and rested her feet on the seat next to him.

"I'm talking a lot," he said.

"You are," Shiloh said, smiling gently. "It's unusual. Unless . . . is this usual now?"

He smiled back at her. He shook his head.

"I like it," she said, tipping her foot against his hip. "I don't like how awful this is—but I like listening to you think out loud."

"There's no one else I could say all this to."

"I'm sure you have people who would listen."

"I'd have to tell them the whole backstory first," he said dismissively. "It's not worth it."

"You could sum it up . . ."

"No. I mean, it's not worth people *knowing* all that. It's not worth carrying my past around and handing it to new people. That's what I like about the Navy. Everyone who wants a fresh start, gets one. You are what you bring to the table."

Shiloh wanted to keep arguing her point—that understanding the fullness of Cary wouldn't be a burden. Didn't he talk to his friends or the women he dated about his family? And his childhood?

Maybe he just meant that there wasn't anyone *at the moment* who he could talk to . . .

"I think there are probably people in your life who would be happy to listen," she said. "But one of them is me. So . . ."

Cary rested his hand on her ankle and squeezed.

"Who's managing the *destroyer* without you?" she asked.

"The rest of the Pacific Fleet."

"Those good-for-nothings?"

The waitress came by with the check. Cary let go of Shiloh's ankle to pick it up.

Shiloh tried to take it. "Let me."

"No way." He held it out of her reach.

"Come on, Cary. I've never bought you dinner. I don't think I've even paid for my *own* dinner in your presence."

"I like that so much about us," he said.

She gave up.

They had to pay at the register. Shiloh waited in line with him.

"Thank you," Cary said.

"Don't thank me."

"You said I could thank you."

"Well, it's too much," she said.

Cary paid for dinner and bought them peppermint hard candy. He walked her to her car.

They stood there for a minute, clinking their candy against their teeth. Then Shiloh tugged on his sleeve. "You'll call me?"

"Yeah."

"Good."

## THIRTY-NINE

CARY TEXTED AGAIN ON WEDNESDAY. Shiloh was at work when she saw it.

*"Would you like to have dinner tonight?"*

*"i would,"* she sent back, *"but i have kids tonight, want to join us? i'm making split pea soup"*

*"Oh—I'm sorry. I must have done the math wrong."*

*"you did math?"*

He did *math*?

Shiloh reread the text a few times, still confused.

Then her office phone rang—there was a problem with the fall catalog of classes. It took fifteen minutes for Shiloh and Tom to sort it out.

She and Tom shared a long desk inside a big, open office where all the theater's full-time staff members worked, including the director. It was on the third floor, above the main stage.

Sharing a desk with any of her other coworkers would be untenable, but Tom was Shiloh's right hand—and sometimes her left, too. And occasionally her conscience.

Once they'd solved the catalog problem, Shiloh picked up her cell phone. Cary had texted back: *"You said you had 2–2–3 custody. I looked it up."*

Shiloh stared at her phone.

Another message popped up: *"I don't want to take you away from your kids."*

She sent a reply without taking a breath. *"that's why i invited you over"*

Cary didn't immediately text back.

Shiloh and Tom went to a meeting about a cooperative program with the public schools. The meeting was an hour long and extremely frustrating. Shiloh got testy with the schools' rep, and Tom made disaster eyes at her until she apologized.

When she got back to her phone, Cary still hadn't texted.

Shiloh had thought of half a dozen snippy replies—but she'd also recalled that Cary was probably texting her from his mother's hospital room.

*"it's ok,"* she sent. *"maybe some other night"*

Her cell phone rang. She answered it. "Hello?"

"Shiloh," Cary said. "I'm sorry."

"You don't have to come over, it's really fine."

"It's not that I don't want to—"

"It's that you don't want to run into my ex-husband?"

Tom was sitting across from her, typing. He raised his eyebrows without looking up and put on headphones.

"I . . ." Cary said.

"It's okay." Shiloh was rubbing one eye. "I don't blame you. It's not your mess."

"If it's okay, then why do you sound angry?"

"I'm not angry. I'm . . ." Her voice dropped. "Well, I know you don't want to hang out with my kids—but it feels a little extreme to google my custody arrangement just to avoid them."

"I like your kids, Shiloh."

"You don't *have* to like them."

"I'm just being careful." Cary sounded sad.

"I know." Shiloh rested her face in her hand. "I *do* know. I'm not angry. I won't be angry. How's your mom?"

"Better today."

"That's good."

"I found a rehab place for her."

"Oh, yeah?" Shiloh lifted her head. "That's great."

"I'll tell you about it tonight," he said. "When I come over for dinner."

Shiloh laughed out a resigned breath. "Cary, it's okay."

"It's your family," he said. "If you're comfortable, I'm comfortable."

"It's not about being *comfortable*—nobody wants to hang out with children unless they have to."

Tom looked up then, like he was done pretending not to listen. "I object," he whispered.

Shiloh put her hand over her phone. "Shut up, you get paid to hang out with kids."

"Not *much*."

"I take it you're not alone . . ." Cary said.

"I am never alone," Shiloh confirmed.

"How about this," he said, "I'll tell you if I'm ever not up for being around your kids."

She gave in. "Okay."

"Can I bring anything for dinner?"

"God no, from the hospital? Just bring yourself. The kids eat at six, but come whenever."

"Okay."

"Cary?"

"Yeah?"

"Ryan and I trade days all the time. Our schedule's a mess. You can't predict it."

"I won't try," he said.

"Bye."

"See you soon."

Shiloh set down her phone.

Tom cleared his throat, taking off his headphones.

She turned away from him, to her computer.

"Cary, huh?" he said.

"Cary," she confirmed.

"Cary like 'Carrie Anne, what's your game now?' by the Hollies, or Cary like 'Carey, get out your cane' by Joni Mitchell?"

Shiloh snorted. "The latter."

She heard Tom snapping out a beat. When she looked up, he was swaying from side to side on the other side of the desk. As soon as Shiloh met his eyes, he sang the first line of the Joni Mitchell song, giving it a jazzy swing.

Shiloh eventually joined in—she couldn't not. She could never really say no to a bit, and she and Tom loved to sing. He was a grown-up show-choir kid. She let him have the best line—"*Oh, you're a mean old daddy, but I like you.*"

"Cary, Cary, Cary . . ." Tom said when they were done goofing. "Sounds like a big old mess."

Shiloh swung back to her computer. "Yep."

"Good for you, Shiloh."

## FORTY

"I DON'T HAVE TO EAT dinner with you," her mother said. "I can go to my room."

Shiloh was cutting up a honeydew melon. "No, I'm saying—I *want* you to eat with us. So it seems more platonic."

"Does Cary think it's platonic?"

"*Yes,*" Shiloh said. "And when he walks in and sees you, he'll know that *I* think it's platonic, too."

Her mother took a piece of melon. "It's less of a mystery now, how the two of you never slept together."

"Just stay out here until I put the kids to bed."

"What happens then?"

"Well, at that point"—Shiloh was gesturing with her paring knife—"if you stay out here, it will seem like you're chaperoning us."

Her mom rolled her eyes. "Just wink twice when I'm allowed to go."

Junie came into the kitchen. "Mommy, I'm starving."

"You're not starving."

"I am." Junie clenched her hands in her bobbed hair. "I'm so hungry, I can't even *think*."

There was a knock at the front door.

"I'll get it!" Junie shouted.

Shiloh wiped her hands on her jeans. "Are you allowed to answer the door?"

Junie hung her head. "No."

Shiloh went for the door. Junie was right behind her. Gus was sitting on the living room floor, playing with plastic cars. He was just getting to the age where Shiloh could leave him alone for a few minutes. Like, he could still kill himself if left to his own devices—but it would probably take more than five minutes.

Cary was standing on the porch in a Navy baseball cap and a blue T-shirt. Shiloh opened the door and got a better look at him. He was wearing brown ripstop pants—Cary's pants always had several loops and pockets—and running shoes. Did Cary run?

"Hi," she said.

"Cary?!" Junie shouted. "What a nice surprise!"

He smiled at Shiloh. "Can I come in?"

"Yeah." She laughed and stepped back. "Come in."

He walked past her, taking off his cap and running his hand through his hair.

"Did you come for a visit?" Junie asked.

"Cary came for dinner," Shiloh said.

"That is *so nice*."

"I agree." Shiloh looked up at him. "I could feed the kids first, if you want?"

"Just do what you usually do."

"We usually all eat together."

"Let's do that."

"Okay," she said. "Come help me. How's your mom tonight?"

He followed her to the kitchen. "Better. Every day that she's better, I realize how bad it was when I first got here. She's sitting up now. She's eating."

"Is Grandma Lois coming for dinner?" Junie had trailed behind Cary.

"Not tonight," Shiloh said. "Junie, go wash your hands."

"Hey there, Cary," Shiloh's mom said, still eating the melon. "I'm sorry your mom's having a rough time."

"Hi, Gloria. Thanks."

Her mom wiped her hands on a towel. "I'll go get Gus ready to eat."

Shiloh nodded her thanks and got out a stack of mismatched china bowls. The soup had been in the slow cooker all day. She opened the lid.

"You really made split pea soup . . ." Cary said. He was washing his hands in the sink.

"Yeah?" Shiloh picked up a ladle.

"I thought that was a joke."

"Why would that be a joke? You don't like split pea soup?"

"I don't know that I've ever had it. Do kids eat pea soup?"

"I find that kids eat just about anything if they don't have other options. Your mom never made this?"

"My mom made . . . Well, she made sure there was baloney and Wonder bread in the kitchen." He shook his head. "That's not fair. She cooked sometimes. Spaghetti. She cooked when my sisters were younger."

"Gloria cooked when she wasn't working . . ." Shiloh said, ladling out a bowl of soup with lots of ham and potatoes. She raised her eyebrows. "Which was, you know, occasionally. I try to cook when the kids are here." She held out the bowl. "You don't have to eat this if you don't like it—but pretend to like it if Junie asks. There's bread, too." Shiloh handed him a spoon. "We sit at the table."

Cary walked out, but then came back to help her with the rest of the bowls and spoons. Shiloh got out the milk. "Cary? Do you want a beer?"

"No, thanks."

She took the rolls out of the oven and grabbed the butter.

Cary was standing at the dining room table. He waited for her to sit down, then took the empty chair between her and Junie.

"We don't say grace," Junie said. "We aren't a church."

"She means we don't belong to a church," Shiloh said.

Junie folded her hands. "But you can do it silently," she whispered. "Like at daycare."

"I'm good," Cary said.

The kids both ate their soup by dipping bread into it. Cary seemed hesitant about the soup—but he was eating it. His hat was hanging from the back of his chair.

Shiloh's mom asked Cary more questions about Lois. He told them about the surgeries and the rehab center. Shiloh's mom knew someone who worked there.

Shiloh watched him talk. She was distracted by his bare arms—

she hadn't seen Cary's forearms for fourteen years. (She hadn't gotten a good look at them that night in her bedroom.) They were less wiry than she remembered. More substantial. Lined. Tan. His elbows were still knotty and chapped-looking. She felt almost painfully fond of his elbows. Like she might cry if she kept looking at them.

Shiloh buttered a roll for Cary when he didn't take one for himself. She went to the kitchen to get the melon.

Gus was in a good mood, thankfully. He was usually in a good mood at dinner. He ate the butter off his roll and asked for more. Shiloh obliged him. The kids didn't get dessert on weeknights, so she let them eat as much as they wanted at dinner. Watching her kids eat was one of the happiest parts of Shiloh's day. That was probably biology working on her again. Her entire personality was dictated by hormones.

"This soup is great," Cary said. He'd eaten most of his bowl.

"Thanks," she said. "There's more if you want it."

"I'd take more."

"I'll get it!" Junie said.

"I'll get it," Shiloh said, standing up and reaching for Cary's dish.

"Want soup," Gus said. "Gus wants soup."

"Gus *has* soup." Maybe Shiloh shouldn't talk about Gus in the third person—was that reinforcing the problem?

Shiloh set another big bowl full of soup in front of Cary. He knocked his shoulder against her hip. "Thanks."

She touched his shoulder. "You're welcome." When Shiloh looked up, her mom was watching.


After dinner, Shiloh tried to get the kids to watch a video so she and Cary could talk. But Junie wanted to play a game—and she wanted Cary to play, too.

They ended up playing Chutes and Ladders while Shiloh's mom washed the dishes. (She didn't usually offer.)

Cary was quiet during the game. He let Junie run the show. Shiloh also usually let Junie run the show. Shiloh was an expert in playing Chutes and Ladders or dolls or even reading bedtime stories with one part of her brain, while another part of her brain whirred away on whatever was weighing on her at the moment . . .

Tonight it was Cary. As the game went on, Shiloh felt more and more regret about inviting him over and then making it hard for him to say no.

This wasn't a reasonable way to ask Cary to spend his time in Omaha—when he was so worried about his mother. Shiloh wasn't comforting him. Or supporting him. She was dragging him along on her single-parent marathon.

At eight o'clock, it was time to get the kids ready for bed. Junie made a big production out of saying good night to Cary, but she went upstairs without a fight.

"I'll get Gus rolling," Shiloh's mom said.

"No," Gus said. "Not tired. Not go to bed. No." He was already working himself into tears.

Shiloh's mom lifted him up and headed up the stairs.

"Grandma, no, you not know what Gus wants."

"That's for damn sure," her mom said.

Cary started packing up the board game.

Shiloh touched his forearm. "This was dumb of me." She pulled her hand back. "I don't know what I was trying to prove."

"What do you mean?"

"You were right to consider whether I had the kids tonight. I can't actually be a good friend and a good mom at the same time. Concurrently. On a weeknight. And you have enough on your mind . . . I should have seen that this would end up with you entertaining my kids. That we wouldn't have a chance to talk."

Cary peered up at her. "I didn't expect you to ignore your kids while I was here."

"I was wrong," she said.

He smiled a little, going back to putting away the game.

"What?" Shiloh asked. "Why are you smiling?"

"I'm thinking that it's still weird hearing you admit that you're wrong about something . . . And I'm also thinking that you *weren't* wrong, necessarily." He looked up at her. "I'm glad I came over. I haven't had a home-cooked meal in months—it's probably been a year since I've had a home-cooked meal cooked by someone other than me." He put the lid on the Chutes and Ladders box. "Now I know that I like split pea soup, I already knew I liked you and your kids . . . This was better than sitting alone in my hotel room. Or eating by myself at some Omaha restaurant that isn't as good as I remember."

She shifted her lips into one cheek. "Yeah?"

He nodded. "Yeah."

"Okay."

"All that said . . ." Cary glanced away. He sighed and scrubbed his hand through his hair, then looked back at her. "Do you want me to go now? Or can I stay and talk?"

She smiled. "You can stay and talk. I have to do bedtime though. It'll be half an hour."

"Can I have that beer?"

Shiloh was smiling too much, too big. She was glad her mom was upstairs. "Yes."

"I'm going to check my email," he said.

Shiloh got him a can of beer. She wasn't much of a drinker, not since her first pregnancy. But her mom drank red wine and Coors Light, so there was usually some in the fridge.

When Shiloh got upstairs, her mom had Gus's face washed and his pajamas on. The kids only took baths every couple nights or so.

"Did Cary leave?" her mom asked.

"No," Shiloh said. "We're going to talk awhile."

"Nice. Very platonic."

"It's not like that."

Her mom frowned at her. "It *should* be. You need to aim for the pins when it's your turn to bowl."

"Uh . . . yeah," Shiloh said. "Well. I've taken my shot. And look, I have two little pins who are ready for bed. Say good night to Grandma, Gus-Gus."

"No. Gus-Gus not go to bed."

It took longer than a half hour.

Shiloh's strategy as a single parent was to negotiate as little as possible—over food, sleep, television.

But Ryan was much more malleable, and the kids were constantly pushing at Shiloh's boundaries, looking for a tear in the fence.

Gus seemed to sense that Shiloh wasn't going to let him escalate to a full-blown tantrum with Cary downstairs. He pushed for an extra story, and Shiloh ended up lying in his bed, listening to him complain, until he complained himself to sleep.

When she finally went back downstairs, Cary was sitting on the couch. He had one leg bent, his ankle on his knee. His cap was resting on his other knee. His head was leaning back, and his eyes were closed. He was still holding the beer.

Shiloh hit a creaky stair, and he looked up. She waved at him. He sat up a little and waved back.

Shiloh sat down on the couch next to him. "You tired?"

"Still jet-lagged, believe it or not."

"I've never been jet-lagged."

"We need to get you out of Omaha."

Shiloh shrugged.

"I need to see Mikey's kid while I'm here," Cary said. "What's his name?"

"Otis. And I'm sure Mike will understand if you don't make it over."

"I want to, though. And I can't sit in my mom's hospital room twenty-four hours a day. I can't stand being there when Jackie and her husband, Don, are there—but I can't exactly forbid them from visiting. They're there every night."

Shiloh brought her feet up onto the couch, folding her legs and facing Cary. "Well, Otis is cute—fat, bald, no teeth—you won't regret meeting him."

Cary smiled. "I heard you've been hanging out with Mikey and Janine . . ."

"A little."

"*Good.*" Cary rearranged his hat on his knee, looking down at it. His smile faded into something more thoughtful. "Your ex-husband seems like . . . a handful."

Shiloh laughed, a genuine laugh. "Oh, he is that. Definitely. But I'm not going to say terrible things about him, because it just makes me look stupid."

"Sorry, I didn't mean—"

"No. You're fine. And you're correct. He's a lot. He's a high school drama teacher."

Cary laughed and looked up at her with his head still tipped down. "Really?"

"Yeah."

"Damn. Those kids got it from both directions."

Shiloh laughed and kicked him—she was wearing socks. Cary's hand immediately settled on her ankle.

He turned his head to her. "Did you meet in some production?"

"Yep. In college. *A Midsummer Night's Dream.*"

"What'd you play?"

"I was a tree."

"Was he Puck?"

"Shut up."

Cary laughed into his beer. "That's a yes." He lifted the can up to get the last of it.

"Do you want another beer?"

"No." He set the can aside. He started rubbing Shiloh's ankle.

"Why didn't you get married?" she asked.

Cary shrugged. "Just never got there."

"Did you ever come close?"

He looked at her for a long beat, like he was deciding whether to answer. "Yeah," he said.

"What happened?"

"We didn't get married."

Shiloh tilted her head, like maybe she could figure out the rest of the story just by squinting at him.

"I'm not great at it," he said.

"At what?"

"Um . . . relationships? I guess?"

"Does that mean you don't have them?"

"No, I have them. And then . . . I don't. Because I'm not great at them."

Shiloh wanted to argue, but she didn't have any ammunition for it. "Well," she said. "Me neither. Obviously."

"I don't know," Cary said, "you made it past the finish line."

"No, I made it past the *starting* line." Shiloh laughed.

Cary bounced his eyebrows. "See? What do I know."

She folded her arms. She felt relaxed. She was smiling.

Cary rubbed her ankle. "Are you going to tell me about your divorce?"

"Maybe someday."

He looked in her eyes. Waiting.

"It wasn't my finest hour," she said.

"I wouldn't figure."

Shiloh's smile felt tight. She dropped her eyes to Cary's hand on her ankle.

"It's my own fault," he said after a while.

She looked up. "What?"

"That I'm not in a relationship."

Shiloh waited to see if he wanted to say more.

"I shut down," he said. "And I have to be in control. And I'm never interested in the sort of women who put up with it."

Shiloh hummed faintly, acknowledging him. She knew she was giving him a soft look.

Cary pinched her Achilles tendon. He cupped her heel. He wrapped his hand around the bottom of her foot and pressed his thumb up along the arch.

"I think those are things you can change," she said.

"Nobody changes that much."

Neither of them felt like talking after that. Cary sat on the couch, holding Shiloh by the ankle. Shiloh rested her head on the couch and watched his hand.

## FORTY-ONE

SHILOH MET CARY FOR DINNER again.

And then he came over again, to have dinner with her and the kids. Shiloh made Monte Cristo sandwiches, with powdered sugar and rhubarb jam. Cary had never tried rhubarb. He liked it.

They watched a Disney movie. Gus was clingy and wouldn't leave Shiloh's lap.

She and Cary ended the night on the couch, talking. Not touching. When he said goodbye, his hand brushed over the back of her neck.

The next day, he moved his mom into the rehab center.

It was a rough transition. Cary was worried about her. He spent the night in her room.

He texted Shiloh a few times over the weekend. He was angry with his sister. He was angry with her husband. One of his mom's ex-husbands had resurfaced. Cary hated him.

Shiloh wondered if Cary had been this angry all the time back in high school—and she just hadn't fully appreciated it.

He was headed back to his ship next week, no matter how his mom was doing. He was frustrated about that. He was anxious. But he was also looking forward to it, Shiloh suspected.

There were moments when Cary seemed so strange to her. This grown man. With a life so far away that she hadn't really tried to understand it. He seemed colder than she remembered him. More remote. Packed too tight for her to ever tease him loose.

But then sometimes he was the opposite . . . Forthright and vulnerable. Cracked open in a way the old Cary never was. He was less contradictory in her memory—maybe she'd flattened him out over the years.

She and Cary seemed to be moving past . . . the past.

Shiloh was trying to fold it all in. To integrate: Cary as she remembered him from high school. The Cary in her dorm room. The Cary who came home with her after Mikey's wedding, with all of his revelations. This Cary. Who seemed to have forgiven her. Who kept grounding himself on her hips and shoulders and ankles.

"Shiloh! Get a sitter! We're going to Family Fun Time!"

Shiloh held the phone to her ear. "Mikey?"

"Yeah, Mikey. And Cary! The gang's all here. Let's do it, man. We're coming to get you."

"Now?"

"Now. Can you come?"

The kids were in bed. Her mom wouldn't mind. "Yeah. I can come."

"Bet!" Mikey said.

Shiloh was already in her pajamas. It was a Monday night. She changed into jeans and a short-sleeved flowered dress. Her hair was damp. She pulled it back into a long ponytail. Platonic eyeliner seemed in order. And big hoop earrings. She looked in the mirror. She still had some of her old bangles from high school. She loaded up one wrist.

She was sitting on the porch when Cary's rental car pulled up, and Shiloh broke into a grin when Mikey got out of the passenger seat.

"Hey, girl!" he called.

She stood up, laughing.

"I said we should make you squeeze into the middle, but Cary didn't want you to break the cupholders in his rental car."

"Killjoy," Shiloh said.

"I *know*. Here, you can sit up front." Mikey got in the back seat, and Shiloh got in the front.

"Hey," she said to Cary. He nodded at her.

"There's my crew!" Mikey said, slinging an arm around each of their necks.

Cary shook him off. "Buckle your seat belt. You're a father."

"How's Otis?" Shiloh asked.

"He's perfect," Cary said.

Mikey moaned. "He's trying to kill me. Jesus Christ!"

Shiloh turned in her seat. "That bad?"

"He never sleeps. So Janine never sleeps. She cries all the time. She's losing her hair. She sends me articles about postpartum psychosis."

Cary frowned. "Maybe we should go back to your house . . ."

"It's fine." Mikey laid his hand on Shiloh's shoulder. "It's fine, Shiloh—her mother's there. But also it's a *fucking nightmare!*"

"I'm sorry," she said. "It gets better, I promise."

"I don't know how you did this alone. There are two of us, and neither of us is working. We're just in his thrall. I'd say he was the son of Satan, but my mom says he looks just like me."

Shiloh laughed.

"He's a good baby," Cary said. "He's very stout."

"From draining my life force," Mikey said. "Thank god Cary showed up to spirit me away."

"He is a good baby," Shiloh agreed. "All babies are good babies."

Cary smiled at the road.


"Shiloh, get off your phone. Be present." Mikey and Cary were playing *Double Dragon*.

Family Fun Time was a two-story arcade owned by some religious people. The tokens were stamped with *Praise the Lord*. It hadn't changed much since high school. There was laser tag now, plus a bunch of new games—a whole corner was dedicated to *Dance Dance Revolution*.

Shiloh had been texting Tom about a work thing. (Tom had a BlackBerry and sent extravagant texts.) "What am I supposed to do?" she said. "What did I do in 1991?"

Cary reached into his pocket and pulled out a roll of tokens. "Go play *Centipede*."

"I do like *Centipede* . . ."

She found the machine at the other end of the floor—all the "retro" games were up here—and quickly dropped half her tokens into it. Shiloh wasn't any good at *Centipede*. She never had been. After that, she tried to remember how to play *BurgerTime*. She couldn't. She spent the rest of the tokens on *Space Invaders*.

Cary and Mikey were still playing *Double Dragon*. Shiloh stood behind Cary and tried to watch.

It was incredibly boring.

It had been boring in high school, too. But back then she was just happy to get out of the house.

Shiloh reached up and pulled Cary's hair. It was only long enough to pull at the very top. He shook his head.

She did it again.

"Stop," he said.

"Shiloh," Mikey said in a distracted voice, "did you blow through those tokens already?"

"Yes."

"You're worse than my five-year-old nephew—oh! *Snap!* I got you!" He and Cary both started pounding on the buttons.

Shiloh watched for a minute.

Then she poked Cary's side.

He reached back and scooped his arm around her waist. He pulled her up next to him and rested his hand on her back. He was still playing, absolutely focused on the screen and rocking his right hand between the joystick and the attack buttons.

After a few seconds, he needed both hands again. Shiloh stayed close to him and quiet. She turned her head to watch his face. His mouth was straight. The lights were dancing in his eyes. The game played electronic music, and the arcade was playing Christian rock.

"How d'ya like the taste of my *bat*!" Mikey shouted.

Cary laughed. Then his shoulders went tense. "There you go," he barked, "there you go, there you go—BOOM!"

Cary and Mikey sounded exactly like they always had. If Shiloh closed her eyes and pretended her lower back didn't hurt, she could be seventeen again.

They both whooped when they cleared the level.

Cary glanced over at Shiloh, like he was just now realizing how close she was. His face was red from laughing and yelling. He leaned in and kissed her cheek.

"Mother *fuck*," Mikey said. "Three of my fingers are going numb. This is my painting hand. I have a family to support."

Cary elbowed him. "Eyes up. Next level."

Shiloh bought herself popcorn and a Diet Coke and dragged a stool around the retro section, following Mikey and Cary from game to game. Then she had to find somebody to give her the key to the bathroom. It was tied to a chunk of wood.

When she came out, the guys were waiting for her in the lobby. Mikey was doing an impression of a *Double Dragon* villain, and Cary was laughing so hard his shoulders were shaking.

"We should go get a beer or something," Mikey said.

Cary looked at her. "Do you have to work tomorrow?"

"I can be hungover," she said. "The eight-year-olds won't notice."

"What would we have done in 1991?" Mikey asked.

Shiloh yawned. "We would have gotten Taco Bell."

"Oh *yeah* . . ." he said. "Let's make a run for the border."

They went through the drive-through. Mikey ate a chalupa and immediately lay down in the back seat. "That's all for me, folks. That's all she wrote. Wake me up when I'm dead."

Cary drove Mikey home first. Mikey made him get out of the car for a goodbye hug. Shiloh watched from the front seat.

Mikey threw his arms around Cary. "You take care of yourself, and you call me next time. I'm your man on the ground."

Cary said something that Shiloh couldn't hear. Their voices buzzed for a minute. Then Mikey gave him another bear hug.

Shiloh liked watching them hug. It was like watching Gus eat.

Mikey pulled away and leaned down to Cary's door. He pointed at Shiloh. "Pick up the phone when I call, Shy. Otis wants to party with Gus and Juniper."

Shiloh nodded. She yawned. "Maybe *I'll* call *you*."

She was still yawning when Cary got back in the car. Then she burped and made a face. Taco Bell.

Cary was smiling at her. "I'll get you home, Cinderella."

"I feel more like Rip Van Winkle."

"I like this neighborhood," Cary said idly.

"I like Mikey's house," she said. "I still can't believe he left New York for Omaha."

"It's a more comprehensible place to raise a family, especially if you had a happy childhood here."

Shiloh thought of Mikey's family and the little house he grew up in . . . His old neighborhood wasn't as nice as his new one, but it was a step up from Cary and Shiloh's. His parents still lived there. They were still together.

"I'd like to go to one of his art shows," she said. "Maybe he'll have a show here."

"Or maybe you could go to New York City or Chicago . . ."

"Or Munich?" That was the last place Mikey had had an exhibit.

"Or Munich," Cary said, smiling.

"I'm glad you guys called me," she said. "That felt like time travel."

"We'll do it again. I'll be back to see my mom."

She rolled her head toward him. "Are you gonna call me when you come back?"

He glanced at her like she was being weird. "Yeah. Don't you want me to?"

"Yes, I want you to." She poked his arm. "I don't want to go another fourteen years without talking to you."

He was already pulling into her driveway. "I don't want that either."

Cary turned off the car. They were both looking at their laps.

"When do you leave?" she asked.

"Day after tomorrow."

Shiloh hummed.

"I might not see you again before I go," he said.

She looked up a little. "Do you want to come in for a while?"

"No. You better get to sleep. I'm tired, too."

"Yeah." She squeezed his arm and opened her door.

"I'll walk you up," Cary said abruptly, getting out of the car.

He followed her up the steps and reached ahead of her to hold the porch door open.

They stopped on the porch. They could hear the TV. Shiloh's mom was probably in the living room—she didn't have cable in her room.

Shiloh looked up at Cary.

"Thank you," he said, "for everything."

She nodded. "I meant what I said—I don't want to go another fourteen years without talking to you."

"Okay."

"You're the best friend I ever had, Cary."

He was looking in her eyes. His cheeks dimpled. "You too, Shiloh."

Shiloh touched his chest pocket. She pulled on his collar.

Cary reached up and touched her cheek. He rubbed the bottom of her chin with his thumb.

The door opened, and Junie sang out, "Welcome hooome!"

Then her eyes got big and her mouth dropped open. It wasn't an act. She turned around and ran up the stairs.

Cary looked even more horrified than Junie had. "I'm—"

"Good night," Shiloh said, hurrying away from him into the house and flinging the door closed behind her.

Her mom was getting off the couch.

"What is Junie doing up?" Shiloh demanded.

"She couldn't sleep."

"Why'd you let her open the door!"

"I didn't! She heard you on the porch and rushed over to let you in."

Shiloh was already halfway up the stairs. She went into the kids' room. Junie was on her bed, rolled against the wall. The lights were off.

Shiloh sat on the bed. She touched Junie's back. "Junie?"

"I don't want to talk to you, Mommy."

"Okay."

Junie was crying. "I don't want you to do that . . ."

Shiloh rubbed between her shoulder blades.

"I don't want you to do that with Cary."

"I understand," Shiloh said. She wasn't going to make any promises—even if they were ones she could easily keep. "I love you, Juniper. I'm sorry I upset you."

Junie sobbed. "You're not supposed to *do* that."

*I am supposed to do that,* Shiloh thought. But it wasn't the right time to argue about it. Her skin was crawling with shame. Her gut was full of it.

"I don't want Cary to come over again," Junie said.

"Cary's going home," Shiloh said.

"Where does he live?"

"On the ocean."

## FORTY-TWO

SHILOH DIDN'T EXPECT TO HEAR from Cary that night.

But he texted her a couple hours after he left. She was still awake.

*"I'm sorry."*

*"you didn't do anything"*

*"That doesn't matter to your daughter."*

*"i'll worry about my daughter,"* Shiloh sent, frowning.

*"Sorry. I'm sorry."*

Shiloh sat up to type with both thumbs. She took the time to capitalize and punctuate. *"I'm not happy it went the way it did—but there's no good way to be a divorced mom. Or a kid with divorced parents. This sort of thing happens."*

She sat waiting for Cary to text back.

Finally he sent:

*"It didn't have to happen tonight. I feel like I broke something for you and her, for nothing, on my way out of town."*

The *"for nothing"* snagged in Shiloh's chest. *"This really isn't yours to worry about,"* she texted.

Cary didn't reply.

Shiloh lay back down, still holding on to the phone. She was exhausted. She hadn't washed her face. Her eyeliner felt tacky.

Her phone beeped. The text was so long, it got sent in two parts:

*"I was so angry with you after the wedding for saying you were giving me an out. But what you were really saying was that the stakes were too high for me"*

*"to even understand. And you were right."*

After a second, Cary sent:

*"I don't want to be the guy who makes your kids feel that way."*

# before

IT WAS HARD TO SLEEP with someone else in her bed. Was she just supposed to close her eyes and turn off? With someone else right there? With Cary right there?

The bed in Shiloh's dorm room was a twin. Cary was lying with his back against the wall. The only way for her to stay off the edge was to lie right next to him, with her head next to his on the pillow.

His eyes were closed . . . Shiloh couldn't tell whether he was asleep. Cary had so many moles on his face, it was impossible to keep track of them all. If he'd only had one or two, they'd stand out. But instead they registered as a field. He had one hidden in his eyebrow. Shiloh touched it. Cary's eyelid twitched. His eyebrows didn't have much shape, and they sort of faded out at the ends. Not like Shiloh's at all.

She touched his other eyebrow. His whole face twitched. "Go to sleep," he said.

"I can't," she whispered.

"Why not?"

"Because of you." She kissed his cheek.

Cary didn't react.

There was a bumpy mole on the side of his nose. She touched it. There was a scar on his cheek. It looked like he'd had a couple stitches. Shiloh kissed it. She touched the pitted line of it with her tongue, so she could feel it better.

"Dog bite," Cary said.

"How old were you?"

"Three or four."

She kissed it again. "I've got two," she said.

He opened his eyes. "Where?"

She pointed to a scar on the bridge of her nose. It was faint. You could feel it more than see it.

Cary rubbed it with his index finger. "How old were you?"

"Too young to remember the bite. I only remember my mom's boyfriend yelling at the dog." She lifted her face, so he could see the bottom of her chin. "And here." This was a nasty one—she'd had several stitches—but it was hidden, too.

Cary rubbed her chin with his thumb. "Same dog?"

"No. Later."

He pulled his hand away to show her a thick scar under his thumb.

"Same dog?" she asked.

He shook his head.

Shiloh took his hand and put her mouth over the scar, feeling it with her tongue. Then she gently bit the meat of his thumb. Then kissed the heart of his palm.

When she looked up again, Cary cupped her jaw in his hand and kissed her.

His kisses pushed her head back at first, like he was driving forward, gulping down his first drink of her. Shiloh let it happen. She wrapped her hand around his wrist and held on.

Cary was leaning on her. He was sleeping in a T-shirt and white boxer shorts. All his clothes were Navy-issued. It made Shiloh feel a little sick. They were making Cary anonymous. They were going to drop him into a sea of boys with the same shorts and haircuts, and Shiloh wouldn't even recognize him there—no one would. She tried to clench her free hand in his hair, but there wasn't enough of it left.

He climbed on top of her.

They were both still dressed. They didn't have this worked out—they weren't smooth. The condoms were in Shiloh's desk. She kept putting them away when they were done with them.

This time when Cary pushed into her, Shiloh held on to his neck with both hands. "I love you," she said. She kept saying it, like it was urgent that he know. Every time she said it, he kissed her.

When it was over, Cary rolled on his back and Shiloh rolled with him, resting her head on his chest. He was still wearing his T-shirt, and she could see the outline of his dog tags under the fabric. She had no desire to look at them.

Shiloh scooted up until she was peering down at his face. Her hair fell against her cheeks—she was still getting used to how light it was now. Cary smiled at her and rubbed the top of her nose. She held his face in her hands. "I love you," she said. "Backwards and forwards. Coming and going."

Cary's face got serious. He nodded. And lifted his head off her pillow to kiss her.


Before he left her dorm room, Cary tried to give her one of his dog tags.

Like she'd want a reminder that the government had tagged his corpse while he was still walking around in it.

"I don't need this," Shiloh said. "I already know who you are."

"Keep it safe for me," Cary said.

# before

HIS DAD DIED OF A heart attack when Cary was eight. That was Rod, his mom's second husband.

Cary's oldest sister—Mickey—was from his mom's first husband, who was also named Mickey.

His mom was married to Rod the longest, for twenty-three years. Rod was older than her. He retired from the railroad. He took Cary fishing and to the barber and to have breakfast at Harold's Cafe with the other old men.

Cary's sisters Jenny and Jackie were Rod's girls.

After Rod died, Cary's mom started dating their neighbor, a guy called Simple. That didn't last.

She was in her forties then. She went out on weekends to the bar down the street, the Walking Stick, and left Cary with a neighbor—a different neighbor—or with one of his aunts.

Men would come over. Men in the living room. On the porch. Eating fried chicken on the couch. Walking out of his mother's room in the morning.

His first stepdad was named Andy, and he was a drunk. His teenage son moved in with them. Cary was eleven. His sister Jackie had moved back home with her kids. Cary moved down to the basement.

Andy had other women. He eventually ran off with one.

Cary's mom went back to the Walking Stick, even though she'd never been much of a drinker. She didn't like to be alone. (She was never *actually* alone. You couldn't be alone in that house. The coming and going and crashing. Kids. Grandkids. Cousins. Dogs. Neighbors.)

Lyle was the worst of them all. He beat the shit out of everything he could reach.

Cary was in high school. He was a bag boy at Hinky Dinky. He put a padlock on his bedroom door, and Lyle broke it off with a baseball bat.

His mom married him.

After Lyle—he died in a car accident, he took the other driver with him—Cary's mom started to have more serious health problems.

Cary was in the Navy then.

He didn't know what company she was keeping.

## FORTY-FIVE

SHILOH WAS GOING TO WAIT a couple weeks, and then she was going to send Cary a text, asking how his mother was doing.

She wasn't sure he would text her back. She wasn't sure where they stood with each other.

She'd told Mikey that she and Cary were meant to be friends, *just* friends. But maybe they were meant to be less than that. Maybe all they had left to offer each other was discomfort.

People come into your life, and it's good, but it's finite.

There'd been good in her relationship with Ryan. She got something wonderful there—Junie and Gus. But the relationship ran its course.

When had her relationship with Cary run its course? When was the last time it was easy? Nineteen ninety-one?

She'd spent more years missing Cary than knowing him. All those years burnishing his memory with nostalgia.

Cary.

Shiloh got an email from Cary a week after she'd rushed after Junie and left him standing on the porch.

The subject line was *"Arrived."*

She opened it.

*"I got your e-mail address off your business card. I hope it's okay to write to you here. You can write to me at this address if you ever feel like it. We don't get cell service at sea."*

Shiloh replied right away from her personal email address. She asked about his mother and his flight. She asked him if he'd destroyed anything good yet.

Cary hadn't asked her any questions in his message. He hadn't said anything that obligated a reply.

Shiloh *only* asked questions.

He got back to her a few days later:

His mom had been adjusting to rehab when he left Omaha, he wrote, but he was still worried. His flight had taken a full day and ended with a helicopter ride. He was back at work now. He worked in Operations, and was almost never called to destruction. His hours were long, and he couldn't check his email every day, so she shouldn't worry if he didn't get right back to her.

Shiloh immediately clicked *reply*.

## FORTY-SIX

Cary, I still can't picture what it's like to live on a boat. Maybe I'll get a library book. Or stop by the Navy recruiter's office. Are you standing on deck all day, squinting into the sun? What do you do when you're not working? How long do you stay out there? On the ocean?

•

A typical deployment is six to nine months. This one is six.

I stand on the deck sometimes, but I don't look at the sun. (Are you looking directly at the sun, Shiloh? I wish you wouldn't.)

I don't get much downtime when we're at sea. But I read. I watch movies on my laptop. I play *Magic: The Gathering* with some people when our schedules align.

Most of the time we're either working or sleeping.

•

Cary, I watched *The Hunt for Red October,* and Jesus Christ, I'm glad you're not on a submarine!

•

Cary, I watched *Top Gun,* and I'm really glad you're not a pilot. Also that movie sucks. I watched *Hunt for Red October* again to rinse my brain out. I think *THfRO* might be the best movie ever made . . .

•

Shiloh, why are you watching Navy movies? And who was your favorite character in *Hunt for Red October*?

•

The Soviet second in command. Sam Neill!!!!

•

*"I would like to have seen Montana."*

•

Yes!!! I'm still not over it! I'm watching *Crimson Tide* next, but it can't possibly be as good.

I'm watching Navy movies because it makes me feel crazy not to be able to picture you in some kind of context.

Our theater is doing a play based on *Make Way for Ducklings*. They need me to play a duck.

•

You'll make a great duck. I thought you didn't act much anymore?

•

I only come out of retirement for the really big roles—like Mother Duck.

•

*Mother* Duck? You didn't tell me you got the lead!

•

I saw Mikey this weekend. He's looking less pathetic. Otis is sleeping four hours a night, which I guess is a big improvement. Mikey said he hasn't made any art since the baby was born. He seemed a little rattled—but still less desiccated than when you were here. Janine looks good, too. And Otis himself is, of course, perfect.

•

I'm happy that you saw Mikey and that they're getting more sleep. Mike's always wanted a big family. I wonder if this has changed his mind.

How are Juniper and Gus?

•

Junie is doing summer classes at the theater, so I get to see her during the day, which is wonderful. (Also the classes are free for me, so we're saving money on daycare.) Gus can take classes when he turns 4.

Junie is doing well. She likes to be busy.

Gus is . . . still having a rough time. Maybe this is just his personality and I should stop acting like it's a phase. (Can toddlers be emo?)

He still isn't potty-trained, and it really feels like he's decided not to be. Like a conscientious objector.

How are you, Cary? How's your mom?

•

I'm fine. I don't really think about how I am on deployment—there's always something else to focus on.

I've been able to talk via e-mail with the family liaison at my mom's rehab center. Mom's doing much better than they expected. Breaking a hip can be catastrophic for someone in her condition, but she's actually progressing. I think half of it is just getting her out of that house. She misses her dogs. But she doesn't have to cook or clean. I honestly don't think she *can* cook or clean anymore. She wasn't getting around well when I came home for the wedding. I'd like for her to move into an assisted living residence. But I don't know if I can sell that idea to her— not with my sisters and Angel lobbying against it.

I'm glad you get to see Junie during the day. (Do you never call her "Juniper"?) Wouldn't you have loved to take drama classes all summer long when you were her age?

Gus seemed like a good man to me. Knows what he wants. Isn't afraid to speak his mind. Devoted to his mother.

How are you, Shiloh?

•

I call her "Juniper" when she's in trouble or when I'm feeling very fond.

This is such great news about your mom—she has spirit! It must be so hard for you to manage everything long-distance. I'm glad you have a contact on the inside. What were these deployments like before email??

Would you believe that I am fine? And that I don't really think about how I am, because there's always something else to focus on?

•

Cary!! Did you send me a roll of film??????

•

Yes. You asked so many questions about the ship, I borrowed a camera and took some photos. I don't know how they'll turn out. Hopefully the film didn't get too hot in the mail. It can take a couple weeks in transit.

•

1. You can send mail from the ship??? How??
2. Does that mean I can send mail to *you*?
3. I can't wait to have this film developed!!
4. Cary!!!

•

1. Yes. Cargo planes come and go with supplies and mail.
2. Yes. If you want. Use the return address.
3. Like I said, I'm not sure any of the photos will turn out.
4. Shiloh!

## FORTY-SEVEN

SHILOH DROPPED THE FILM OFF at a one-hour photo place the next morning on her way to work. She went to get the prints over lunch.

Tom walked with her. She still hadn't given him the whole story. (Shiloh felt very protective of the whole story.) Tom knew that Cary had been emailing Shiloh, that they had a complicated history, and that Cary was in the Navy.

*"Oh no, Shiloh, I think he might be gay."*

*"He's not gay."*

*"Everyone I've ever met in the Navy is gay."*

Tom wanted her to look at the photos right away, but Shiloh waited until they were back at their desk and she had the privacy of a computer monitor between them.

The first photo was of the ocean. She smiled.

The next one was of a very small room with the skinniest bed Shiloh had ever seen—it had a roll bar, like a toddler bed. There was a small desk and some cabinets. There was no sign of Cary—or anyone—in the picture, nothing personal. But this had to be his room.

There were several photos of cramped hallways and rounded hatches. The walls and floors looked like metal, and there were exposed pipes and wires. Everything seemed a little too small. Was everyone on Cary's ship constantly squeezing past each other and ducking their heads?

There were three photos of a cafeteria-style tray—breakfast, lunch and dinner. Cary's hand was in the corner of one photo. Shiloh recognized his chapped fingers. The food looked like school food. At least there was plenty of it.

There weren't people in very many of the photos, and when there were, it was just their legs and feet or the back of their heads.

When Shiloh got to a photo of Cary himself, it took her by surprise. Someone else must have taken it. Cary was standing outside—probably on the deck of the ship. He was wearing blue coveralls and a baseball cap, and he *was* squinting into the sun. He wasn't smiling exactly, but it didn't take much to activate all the smiling lines in Cary's cheeks and around his eyes. There were three photos of him, taken all in a row.

"There he is," Tom said softly. He was standing behind Shiloh.

"There he is," she agreed.

"He's got a good face."

"He does."

"He looks like the mean teacher who ends up being on your side at the end."

"That's *my* thing," Shiloh said.

"That's your actual thing, on the inside," Tom said, "but from the outside, you're just a nice lady with interesting shoes."

"Jesus Christ," Shiloh said, "is that what it's come to? Is that who I am?"

He put his hand on her shoulder. "Don't let it get you down, Shiloh. Most people around here don't even have interesting shoes."

He went back to his seat on the other side of the desk.

Shiloh looked at the photos of Cary some more.

"You still just exchanging friendly emails?" Tom asked.

"Very friendly," she said.

"Well . . ." He looked thoughtful. "He did send you his G.I. Joe glamour shot. That's got to mean something."

Shiloh asked Cary a thousand questions about the photos. He sent her two or three answers.

*"Are these photos military secrets?"* she asked.

Cary said they weren't.

*"Can you picture life on a boat now?"* he asked.

*"I can picture it better,"* Shiloh replied.

## FORTY-EIGHT

CARY WAS SOMEWHERE IN THE Pacific Ocean. It was hard for Shiloh to know how far behind he was, on the clock. And his hours were so strange and varied—she could never predict when he'd have time to check his email.

It was a surprise to get an email from him as she was sitting in bed, already composing a message to him on her laptop.

Cary's message was short:

*"I haven't had a good day."*

Shiloh abandoned the silly message she was writing and replied directly to his email. *"Can you tell me about it?"*

*"No,"* he sent back.

*"Cary, whatever happened today, I know you were doing your best."*

*"How can you know that?"*

Shiloh paused for a second and sucked on her lip. Then she typed, *"Because I've only ever known you to do your best."*

She waited for Cary to reply. There was a delay sometimes. Internet on the ship was spotty. Cary had to send emails from a work computer because his personal laptop wasn't connected to the network.

A new message appeared. She opened it.

*"Shiloh? Can I ask you something?"*

*"Of course."*

She waited a few minutes. She felt anxious. She got up to pee and wash her face.

When she came back, Cary had sent, *"Was Junie okay? After what happened?"*

Shiloh frowned. She pulled the laptop closer. *"Yes. Cary, she's fine. I promise. Please don't lose sleep over that."*

As soon as she sent the message, Shiloh started typing a new one: *"It sucks for my kids to have divorced parents. But they do. It's reality. Their dad is already dating, and I could date someday, too. Theoretically. Junie's going to have to adapt."*

Cary didn't reply. Shiloh left the laptop open. She got under the covers and lay down. She kept the computer open by her face and refreshed her inbox every minute or so.

Cary's name went bold with a new message. She opened it.

*"You haven't dated?"*

Shiloh bit her lip and sat up a little to type. *"No. It's hard to picture that happening right now. My kids are so young."*

*"So are you,"* he replied.

She pushed the reply arrow but didn't start writing a message. A new email from Cary arrived before she could:

*"You should date, Shiloh. You should at least think about dating as something beyond a theoretical possibility."*

*"My mom dated. It sucked."*

*"You're not your mom,"* Cary replied. *"Or mine. Weren't you just telling me that Junie will have to adapt?"*

*"I feel like you've switched sides, Cary."*

*"I just don't like thinking of you alone. You deserve more."*

## FORTY-NINE

"SO HE THINKS YOU SHOULD traumatize your daughter with a stepfather . . . He just doesn't want to *be* that guy."

Tom and Shiloh were eating hors d'oeuvres left over from a fundraiser held in the theater the night before.

"I don't know what he wants." Shiloh shoved a stuffed mushroom in her mouth. "But *'you should date'* is very clearly not *'we should date.'*"

"It is not," Tom agreed. He was eating a cucumber sandwich. The bread looked soggy. "I had a stepdad. He was fine. He paid for my braces."

"I'm *years* away from a stepdad scenario," Shiloh said. "I don't even have any leads."

Tom glanced over to where Kate from the costume shop was getting a plate of cheese and crackers. "That's not exactly true."

Shiloh went to Shakespeare on the Green with Kate. It was fine. It was *Macbeth*. They both knew some of the actors. They collaborated on a picnic dinner.

Kate was short, with short blond hair and an elfin face. She was very cute, and she made a lot of her own clothes. She offered to tailor Shiloh's jacket so the shoulders would fit better.

She kissed Shiloh sometime during the fourth act, while Macbeth was visiting the witches and the air was thick with artificial fog. Shiloh managed to be still. Kate laid a small, rough hand on her cheek . . .

Shiloh liked it. She liked it a lot. The kiss confirmed a few things she had long suspected about herself. And she could imagine doing it again—she could imagine doing more.

But as much as she liked it . . . Shiloh didn't think that she liked *Kate*.

Not enough, anyway. She liked kissing Kate more than she liked sitting next to her. Shiloh gently declined another date.

Tom still declared the night a success.

"This is good," he said the next day, while he and Shiloh were clearing chairs out of a classroom. "This is great, actually. You just doubled the size of your dating pool."

"Yeah, but I'm not interested in *anyone*," she said. "So that's like two times zero."

Tom thought everyone would be better off in a relationship. He was sickeningly in love with Daniel (understandable) and a firm believer in monogamy and sharing mortgages—especially for straight people who could reap the full tax benefit.

When Shiloh had pointed out that she already shared a mortgage, with her mother, Tom said that wasn't a sustainable financial strategy. (It was very easy to talk about financial strategy when your partner made furniture-superstore money and managed your IRA.)

"I'm telling you," Tom said now, "this is a positive development— there are more datable women in the world than datable men."

"Says the guy who's never dated any."

Tom made a face. "I dated *tons* of girls in high school."

## FIFTY

Shiloh, thank you for the fudge. It's delicious. I'm not going to share it with anyone.

And thank you for the photo—that duck costume is genius.

How are you?

•

You're welcome! It took almost three weeks for that fudge to get to you. I hope it's still good. I wanted to send cookies, but the Internet was very discouraging on the matter.

Did you recognize any of the ducklings?

•

Cookies are hit and miss. I used to have a roommate whose mom would send snickerdoodles. Sometimes they'd mold or get crushed in the mail—but sometimes they were great.

This was really kind of you. Thank you. And it's great fudge. One of the people on my team commented on how smooth it is. (I did share some.) Apparently that's tricky?

Is that *Juniper*?!

•

It is tricky, but I've been practicing.

Do you have a roommate now? Your room looked so small.

It IS Junie! The director wanted a few actual ducklings to play ducklings. (Most of the ducks will be a type of puppet.) Junie's over the moon about it. Ready for her close-up, etc.

How's your mom doing? Will she be going home soon?

•

My current assignment means I have my own room.

Congratulations to Junie. I'm sure she'll be wonderful. She made such an impression on my mom . . . who I have great news about.

I've been colluding with the family affairs person at the rehab center. We've talked Mom into moving into their assisted living wing for a few months—we pitched it to her as extended rehab. My hope is that it will be permanent, but Mom's agreed to at least three months.

Angel has stopped fighting the idea. I think she likes having Mom's house to herself. That's a problem for another day.

How are you?

•

This is FANTASTIC news! You must be so relieved! I'm so happy for you, Cary. Good work!

•

Cary, one of our donors saw your photo on my desk and told me that you are a lieutenant commander, and that it's extremely impressive for someone your age.

I told him I wasn't surprised to hear this because you've always been talented and diligent. But actually I *was* surprised to hear this—Cary, why didn't you tell me that you're impressive?!

I'm even more proud of you than usual!

Our donor is a veteran and a conservative, and I think he was happy to see the photo, because he thinks we're all a bunch of pinkos who his wife gives money to. (He is correct.) So thank you for softening him up.

I was proud of you even when we weren't talking, by the way. Mikey would tell me small things.

I'm glad I can be proud of you directly again.

•

Thank you, Shiloh.

•

Cary, I've sent you something to congratulate you on all the promotions I missed. Tell me if it shows up moldy and crawling with worms. I'm experimenting.

•

You don't have to send me anything.

•

Are you asking me not to?

•

No.

•

Okay. Good. Tell me if it's gross.

•

Hey, Shiloh, today when I was supervising the watch, I realized that I've asked you twice how you were doing, and you haven't answered.
　How are you?

•

What were you watching for?
　I'm okay.
　I'm arguing with Ryan about whether he can take his girlfriend with him on vacation with the kids. They're going to Lake Okoboji and I'm already nervous enough about the water. (A 3-year-old doesn't need to be on a lake!) I don't want Ryan to be distracted.
　Plus if I say yes to *this* girlfriend and *this* vacation, it's like saying yes to all of them. It's pushing past a boundary.
　Ryan's whole family will be there. They go every year. They have a cabin. I used to go, too, and I hated it.

I was just going to say that I don't see the point of boats, but that's a stupid thing to say to you!

How about . . . I don't see the point of recreational boats. People literally just sit on the water and drink, and then some of them drown. I told Ryan I don't want him to drink when the kids are with him, and it turned into a big fight—even though I don't think he *will* drink much. Why couldn't he just say, "No problem"?

Also, my boss hates me.

Are you sorry you asked?

•

No.

Why does your boss hate you?

I also hate recreational boats.

•

He hates me because I hated him first.

•

Why?

And when do your kids leave? What'd you decide on the girlfriend?

•

I think my boss is bad at his job, and that he gets in my way. I don't hate him as a person—he's a kidney donor!—but I do hate him as a boss.

The kids left for Okoboji today. I said I'd relent on the girlfriend if Ryan promised he wouldn't drink. Ryan said that he never has more than two beers when he has the kids, and that I owe him more trust than this.

I'm just sad, I think. The kids will be gone for ten days. It's the worst part of summer.

•

I'm sorry, Shy.

What will you do while the kids are gone? Does this mean you get to take a vacation with them, too?

•

I'll work. Maybe paint the dining room, if I can get my mom to help.

I usually spread my vacation days over the whole year. Ryan has summers off, so he has big chunks of time to play with.

How are you?

•

Tired. We've been out here four months, which means everyone is in a groove—but also missing home. It's like the Wednesday of the deployment; we're past the halfway point, but the weekend is still pretty far away.

You should take your kids on a vacation.

•

You sure like to tell me what to do, Cary.

•

Do you ever listen, Shiloh?

•

Yes. I went on a date.

•

You *did*? How was that?

•

It was with a woman I work with. It was fine. I think she would have liked to do it again, but I wasn't interested.

•

Is that a new direction for you?

•

I guess so. I mean, I've only really dated Ryan. So anything is new.

•

Is this something you're interested in, generally speaking?

•

Are you asking me if I'm a lesbian now?

•

I'm not sure what I'm asking. I'm surprised.

•

I don't think I'm a lesbian—I might be bisexual. A nonpracticing bisexual. Not even an Easter-Christmas bisexual. It just really *all* feels theoretical at this point: I'm tired, and I don't like anyone.
    Don't tell me to date again, Cary. It's none of your business.
    Are *you* dating?

•

I'm on a ship with people I'm explicitly not allowed to date.

•

Me too. It's called *Spaceship Earth*.

•

Shiloh, I got your shortbread. Thank you. There are no worms, and only a few pieces got crushed. It's really, *really* good, but I can't figure out the flavor . . .

•

Earl Grey tea. Did the shortbread get stale? I vacuum-sealed it.

•

It's crispy and delicious. I've been dipping it in coffee, and this time I really *haven't* shared any. You're good at this.

•

Hey, Shiloh, I never should have told you to start dating. You're right, it wasn't my business. And I can see now that it was an especially messed-up thing for me to say, considering our history. I'm sorry.

•

It's okay, Cary. I knew what you meant—and you were probably right. I just don't have the heart for dating right now.

•

I ate the last of the shortbread today. Thank you again.

•

That wasn't me angling for more shortbread, Shiloh. I just wanted you to know that I ate every crumb, and I appreciate it.

•

Too late, Cary, I already sent you something different. Junie helped. She's fascinated by the fact that you live on a ship—I showed her the photos. She wanted to send you a decoration for your desk, like "a nice lamp or some flowers," but I told her it would fall off when the ship hit a wave.

Instead she drew you a picture.

I'm also sending you photos of Mikey and Otis. We brought Mike and Janine dinner, and my kids ogled the baby. Now Gus keeps telling me that he's NOT a baby, and I think I might have an opportunity to push this potty-training concept all the way home. Pray to your gods for me. Drop something into the sea for Neptune.

You never told me what you guys were watching, and I refuse to google it.

·

The watch is sort of a shift. It's how we organize ourselves and our time. But it does involve a lot of actual watching and monitoring—of the ocean and the ship.

My job is to supervise and oversee the larger choreography of the ship, to make sure all the different jobs are getting done.

You don't have to bake for me, but I'm grateful. I wish I had something I could send you.

I'll put Junie's drawing on my desk next to my Mother Duck photo.

·

Does your mom write to you, Cary?

·

No, but I can call her sometimes from the satellite phone. It's better now than it was when I enlisted—no e-mail back then and no cell phones, and my mom was never good at writing letters.

Shiloh—today while I was waiting for a meeting to end, I was thinking that you always wait for me to ask how you're doing before you tell me.

You can just tell me. I want you to just tell me.

I can't see your face to know when you're feeling down or bothered.

Just assume I want to know.

·

You sure do a lot of thinking.

·

Comes with the job.

•

Hey, Cary, you should assume I want to know how you're doing and what you're feeling, whether or not I ask.

It's hard to ask you about your feelings, for some reason. You have an intimidating face, even when I can't see it.

# before

SHILOH'S MOM HAD MADE CHICKEN and rice soup, and Shiloh had been eating it for three days. There was just enough for one more bowl tonight, if she added water to what was left.

There was a knock at the door while Shiloh was heating it up.

She wasn't supposed to answer the door while she was alone in the house—which was always. The only people who came to the door were Jehovah's Witnesses and people selling scam magazine subscriptions and the guy from the natural gas company who checked the meter.

Shiloh peeked out the living room window.

It was Cary.

She went to the door.

"Hey," she said.

"Hi." He just stood there.

Shiloh squinted down at him. She was in ninth grade, and she'd already been five-foot-eleven—taller than Cary—for a year.

Cary looked unsettled. He was wearing an old sweatshirt and camouflage pants with big pockets. His face was red, and his whole-wheat-colored hair was a mess. "Are you busy?" he asked.

"No," Shiloh said.

She and Cary had been friends since seventh grade. They walked to school together, and they talked on the phone. Sometimes they sat outside and talked. He'd never been inside her house.

It was cold out today, almost winter.

"I was just eating dinner," Shiloh said. "Do you want to come in?"

"That's okay." He shook his head. "I'll see you later." He turned around.

"Cary, no!"

He looked back at her.

"Just wait, okay? I'll be right back."

He nodded.

Shiloh left him on the porch and went into the kitchen. The soup was boiling. She poured it into two small mugs and got two spoons.

Then she grabbed her coat—a fancy pink wool coat from the fifties. It was very cute, but the sleeves only came down to her elbows. Women in the 1950s must have had cold wrists all the time.

When Shiloh got back to the door, Cary was sitting outside on the steps.

She went and sat next to him, holding out a mug. "Here."

He looked at it. "You don't have to feed me."

"I can't eat in front of you," she said, "and I'm really hungry."

Cary made a consternated noise and took the mug.

Shiloh started eating.

"Sorry I didn't call first," he said.

"It's okay. I wasn't doing anything. My mom's at work."

"She's a waitress at the airport?"

"She's more like a bartender."

Cary was staring out into the park across the street. "Hm."

"You have to eat at least one bite," she said, "or I'm still being rude."

Cary looked down at the mug. He took a bite. "What is this?"

"Chicken and rice. It was better three days ago. You okay?"

Cary shrugged. He was staring at the soup now. He didn't seem to be seeing anything, no matter where his face was pointed. The wind was blowing his hair all over. He needed a haircut, and maybe a shower.

Cary wasn't especially cute.

Like, none of the girls who hung out with Shiloh would ever think so. Nobody decent had a crush on Cary.

But Shiloh liked his face. She liked his weird eyes . . . They were gold on the outside and raggedly brown in the middle—but from any distance, they looked one color. Like maple syrup.

Cary's eyes were kind of small and pouchy. His chin was pointy. His top lip was thin.

His face didn't sound nice when you broke it up into parts. But it was nice altogether. She liked looking at him.

"My mom got married," he said.

Shiloh made a face. "When?"

"Today."

It was a Tuesday. "Was there a wedding?"

"No," he said, "they just did it. At the courthouse. It doesn't change anything—he already lives with us."

"Do you like him?" she asked.

Cary puffed out a harsh breath. "No."

"I'm sorry."

He shrugged.

"Where's your real dad?"

"He died when I was eight."

"Oh." Shiloh touched Cary's arm for a second. "I'm really sorry. Was he any good?"

"I think so, yeah. He was good to me." Cary looked down at the ground. He scrubbed a hand up through the back of his hair. "He was my grandpa, actually. My mom is my grandma."

That made sense. Cary's mom was older than everybody else's.

"She doesn't think I know," he said. He was still staring at the sidewalk.

"You mean, your mom doesn't know . . ." Shiloh paused. "That *you* know . . . that she's not your mom?"

Cary looked up at her without lifting his head. "Pretty much."

The wind was blowing Shiloh's hair into her mouth. She tucked some behind her ear. "How'd you find out?"

"It was . . . well, it was on the papers they sent home with us for free and reduced lunch." Cary looked in Shiloh's eyes. His eyebrows were pulled up a little in the middle. "My real mom is my sister. Like, my birth mom, I guess."

Shiloh worried at her lip. "Oh, wow."

"Yeah."

"And nobody knows that you know?"

He shook his head.

Shiloh looked down at her soup. She ate a few bites. "My dad could be anybody."

"What do you mean?"

"I don't know . . ." Shiloh shrugged. "He could be anybody. He could be that guy." She pointed at someone walking down the street with a bag of groceries. "My mom doesn't know who he is—I mean, I guess she *might* know and be lying to me . . ." Shiloh wrinkled her nose. "I don't think she knows."

Cary slid his chin to one side, frowning. It made his face look a little crooked.

"I don't talk about this at school," Shiloh said. "Obviously."

"Me neither. Don't worry."

She elbowed him. "I wasn't worried. I'm just . . . you know."

"Yeah." Cary took a bite of soup.

"So this guy's your stepdad now?"

Cary sneered. He swallowed. "No. I already had one stepdad. I don't need another one—I'm not going to start numbering them like British kings. This guy's just my mother's husband. He's . . . nothing."

"Does he have kids?"

Cary nodded. "They all have kids."

Shiloh watched him eat his soup. She was already done with hers. He tipped the mug up to his mouth to drink the last bits.

When he was done, she took the mug. "Wait here," she said. She went inside and put the dishes in the sink.

Then she went into her mom's room and scrounged around until she found a box of raspberry Zingers. There were four left. She took three.

Cary was still sitting on the steps. He looked cold.

"Look," Shiloh said, holding out a Zinger. "Do you like these?"

He nodded and took it. "Thanks."

They each ate one and split the third.

"I like the red ones better than the vanilla," Cary said.

"All Zingers are good Zingers," Shiloh said. "My mom buys them for herself and hides them—but she doesn't yell at me if I find them, because she feels guilty about being selfish."

"That's complicated. I didn't know I was eating stolen snack cakes."

"Yeah, now you're an accessory. She hides cigarettes, too. You want some?"

"No, thanks," he said. "My mom would just give me cigarettes if I wanted them."

Shiloh laughed.

"She's crazy," he said, "but she's generous."

"She likes this guy? Her husband?"

Cary rolled his eyes. "She likes everyone."

"Oof," Shiloh said, "I don't like *anyone*."

Cary looked at her without turning his head. He was smiling a little. "Smart girl."

## FIFTY-TWO

SHILOH RESISTED BAKING FOR CARY every time she had a few hours to spare. She resisted sending him candy and trail mix and Cracker Jack.

It was bad enough that she'd pinned his photo to the wall by her desk, right next to photos of her kids. She'd mentioned that in one of her emails because she felt guilty about it, because it felt like an over-step.

Shiloh wanted to warn Cary . . .

That she was thinking about him too much. That she was having her way with his memory. That if he were to send her another photo, she'd put that one up, too.

Cary should know that Shiloh could never be normal about him. He was always going to be her favorite. She was always going to want his attention.

He'd have to take himself away from her completely again if he didn't want that.

He was going to have to hide himself somewhere less accessible than the middle of the Pacific Ocean.

FIFTY-THREE

# before

SHE WASN'T AT THE WEDDING.

Mike and Janine said that she was invited, that she'd RSVPed yes.

Mikey was always telling Cary a little bit about Shiloh—like they were still part of some three-person team, even after all these years.

*"Shiloh got married—the wedding was a gas."*

*"Shiloh is working at the children's theater. That seems right, huh? You should call her."*

*"I saw Shiloh when I was home for Christmas—she's such a grumpy old man. She's a grumpier old man than you, Cary, despite being six months younger than you and a woman."*

*"Shiloh has a kid now, a little girl."*

*"Shiloh has two kids now. A boy, this time. I'm jealous."*

*"Shiloh is so hard to get in touch with, have you heard from her?"*

*"Tanya Bevacqua told me that Shiloh is getting divorced. I need to call her."*

*"Shiloh better come to my wedding. It's in Omaha this time, she has no excuse. Did I tell you she's single again?"*

Cary had never told Mikey why he and Shiloh weren't friends anymore . . . It would bother Mike too much. He needed everyone to get along. He needed everyone to be happy.

Cary flew home the day of the wedding. Mikey hadn't given him much lead time, and Cary had only been able to manage a couple days of leave. He'd barely get to see his mom while he was back.

He wasn't sure what he would have said to Shiloh if she'd come tonight. Maybe it would have been like their five-year reunion. They'd barely talked that day—just a few sentences when Cary first walked in and ran into Shiloh on her way to the bathroom. She'd asked him about his mother, and he'd asked her about graduate school, and that was it. If Mikey had been there, he never would have stood for it.

Shiloh had brought her husband to the reunion—some kid from the suburbs who was handsome enough to be on TV. (Probably not movies, but definitely TV.)

Cary wanted to gouge the guy's eyes out.

Sincerely.

He had no good thoughts. All bad urges.

He wanted to scream at Shiloh. He wanted to shove her husband into a wall.

He wanted to ask her how she could just stand there, alive and not in love with him.

How she could say what she'd said in her dorm room and then marry another man? What was the path from there to here? How could she explain it?

Cary held a grudge.

But that was ten years ago. And it had been fourteen years since he and Shiloh were together—and they'd only *been* together for two days.

Cary had grown up since then. He'd fallen in love with someone else. Then watched it fall apart. He'd moved around. Moved up. He'd made enough mistakes to recognize some patterns.

Cary had eventually stopped nursing his hurt feelings about Shiloh because he had other things to do. And now when he thought about her, there was no more gravel and broken glass mixed in—he just missed her. He wanted to see her. When he thought about the fact that she was divorced, his heartbeat picked up.

Mikey knew it.

When they sat down next to each other at the wedding reception, at the head table, Mikey said, "Have you seen Shy?"

"No," Cary said, "I don't think she's here." He'd scanned the church for her, and then the reception hall.

Mikey made a face like he felt sorry for Cary. "Sorry, pal. She's still a flake."

A lot of their other high school friends were at the reception. And Mikey was on cloud nine—he was so in love with Janine, and they were secretly expecting; Cary was one of the only people who knew. It was still going to be a good night, and Cary would have a full day to spend with his mom tomorrow. He had a list of action items for her.

He loosened his tie a little. He ran his fingers through his hair. He made eye contact with Shiloh.

*Shiloh . . .*

Sitting at the back of the room.

She waved.


Shiloh's hair was long again. Long enough to pull up. In high school, it had fallen almost to her waist—it was as thick as Cary's wrist when she wore it in a braid.

She was wearing flowers. She was always wearing flowers. She was waving at him again.

Intellectually, Cary knew that Shiloh was not in fact the most beautiful woman in the world.

Some of the boys in high school had called her "Sasquatch" when she wasn't around, even her friends. She was taller than most of them. She had broader shoulders. She had wider hips.

Her skin was darker than Cary's. Redder. But still like milk. Like pearls. Luminous. She had big brown eyes and eyebrows you could see from the cheap seats. A wide, wild smile. Her eyeteeth were too prominent, and her bottom teeth were a wreck—you couldn't always see them, but when you could, it made Cary weak.

He was halfway across the ballroom before he realized what he was doing.

He was going to end up on his knees, crawling to her.

## FIFTY-FOUR

"TRAVIS . . . *LIEUTENANT JONES,* WE'RE DONE here. Meeting over."

"Sir." Travis snapped to attention. He was about Cary's age, a good junior officer. He could be too jocular sometimes—too quick to joke when they were on task, it's why people liked him—but he was smart and creative, and he never blew Cary off.

"Are you with us today?" Cary asked.

"Yes, OPS," Travis said.

Cary was still getting used to that title—"OPS," said like "hops" or "crops." This was his first deployment as operations officer.

"Yes, sir," Travis added, glancing around the empty office. His eyes were red. He looked tired. They were all tired, but Travis looked especially done in.

The other officers had already moved on, back to their posts. "Are you okay?" Cary asked.

"Yes, sir." Travis nodded.

"No, I'm serious—are you okay?"

Travis rolled his eyes, like that was a complicated question. He looked tearful. "Sir, I just . . . some days it's harder to be away from home."

"Six more weeks, Jones."

Travis nodded briskly, blinking back tears.

"Is there a crisis?" Cary asked.

The man's eyes closed briefly. "No, sir. It's just . . . my son, sir. He's had a rough week. He's been given a rough lot in life."

Cary wasn't sure what to say. Travis had been in the Navy at least ten years. With a break for college. He knew about as much as Cary did about the realities of deployment. "How old is your son?"

"Fifteen, sir."

Cary tried not to widen his eyes. Travis was thirty-one, thirty-two tops.

"What's his name?"

"Corey, sir. He's . . ." Travis opened the work folder he carried. His family's photo was taped inside, across from a yellow notebook.

There was Travis, in his dress blues. He was a small guy with a smile that looked like a laugh. Pretty wife with red hair—a little older than Travis, it looked like. Three kids under seven or so, and a big adolescent boy who was already as tall as Travis and twice as wide.

Travis pointed at him. "That's Corey, sir. And that's my wife, Alicia, and Nevaeh, Travis Jr., and Jasmine."

In the photo, Travis had his hand on the older boy's shoulder. All the kids were smiling and wearing nice clothes. This was probably taken at a ceremony.

The ship pitched and caught Cary off guard. His shoulder hit the wall.

Travis gave him a surprised look.

"You have a beautiful family," Cary said.

"Thank you, sir."

"I mean it, Travis. You're lucky."

Travis knew Cary well enough to know that he wasn't married. He probably felt sorry for Cary. He probably should.

"Would a phone call help?" Cary asked. "I can get you on the sat phone later."

"No, sir, thank you." Travis smiled, rueful. "It was a phone call that fucked me up. Sir. I'll shake it off. I just . . . I'm here for them. I hate feeling like I'd be better off *there* for them."

There wasn't anything for Cary to say. "Six more weeks, Travis."

"Yes, sir."

## FIFTY-FIVE

Thank you for the postcard, Cary.

Is that a picture of your ship on the front?! This is going to sound strange, but it's smaller than I was expecting.

I showed it to Junie, and she wanted me to point to your "apartment."

Also, thank you for the engraved Zippo lighter. It cracked me up—and, no lie, I've always wanted a metal lighter. I love the way they smell.

I feel like this is the sort of lighter someone would have used to light my mother's cigarettes in 1978.

What else can you get with your ship engraved on it??? Silver flasks? Belt buckles?

●

Shiloh, I have sad news about the shortbread you sent. The package looked like it got mauled by a thresher. I had to throw out the cookies.

But Junie's drawing survived—please thank her for me. I'm pretty sure that's all of us at McDonald's, including my mom, right? I laughed out loud at the oxygen tank.

And I salvaged the photos, even though they were battered. Your dining room looks great. I like how you painted the chairs green.

Thanks for the picture of Mikey with Otis—babies change so fast, it freaks me out.

There were no photos of you, so I have to assume that you continue not to age a single day.

That *is* my ship. I could also send you patches, T-shirts, baseball caps and coffee cups. (I just thought of something else to send you. I won't spoil it.)

You said you want to know how I'm feeling . . .

I felt like my dog died when I saw that your cookies were ruined. I've never had someone sending me care packages this consistently, and I've appreciated it more than I can say.

I thought I was beyond caring about something like that; I've spent so much time at sea. But I'm not. Thank you.

We have about a month left out here, and everyone is itching to get home. We have to work not to be lax or get distracted. I have to work on it myself—and I have to watch for it in everyone else.

You're right, the ship *is* small. Three hundred people. This is the smallest ship I've served on so far. I wasn't looking forward to that aspect of it—but the assignment was good for my career. A step forward.

Living on a destroyer is like living in a small town compared to the big city of a carrier. You get to know each other better, faster. There's nowhere to hide. It's easier to spot weak links, but then it's also easier to notice when people shine.

I was worried about the job being too big for me to manage. It's a lot of oversight and supervision. Synthesizing information. Directing communication.

(Does that mean anything to you? I'm trying not to use jargon.)

In the past, I was the assisting officer. But now it's just me.

As it's turned out, it's been fine. I'm trained to do the work, and I do it. So I'm feeling relieved.

Don't send any more packages. There's a chance they won't get to me before our deployment ends.

I hope you're well, Shiloh.

•

Drat!!!!

I guess our luck couldn't hold with the packages. There were two kinds of shortbread, lemon and cardamom. And I'm sorry to tell you they were both *splendid*.

It makes me really sad to know that you haven't been getting care packages—though I can see that it wouldn't be your mom's strong suit. You probably send *her* care packages.

(Didn't you say you were engaged for a while? Was she not a mail person?)

I can't help but feel like it should have been me sending you care packages all along.

Now that we're talking again, I feel sick with regret over letting our friendship die.

It feels like such a *waste*.

Like—I get it. I GET IT. I know why it happened. I lived through it! I am at fault! But it just feels like a *spectacular* waste—to have had your friendship and lost it—especially now that I remember what it feels like to have you in my life.

The next time I send you something nice, give it to the 20-year-old version of yourself, and tell him I'm sorry I was such a dick.

•

Hey, Cary—I'm trying to talk about my feelings. But you should tell me if you want me to stop.

•

Don't stop, Shiloh.

•

Gus has used the potty chair all day today. Even at daycare. He even STOPPED WATCHING *BOB THE BUILDER* to use the potty chair. Unprecedented!

This feels like the first day of the rest of my life.

P.S. Cary, it only sort of makes sense when you talk about your job, even though I can tell you're trying to explain it the way you'd explain it to a 10-year-old.

•

Cary, I think about you almost every day when I drive home from work. I drive down Redick Ave.—the same way we used to walk home from school.

When I moved back home, all my childhood memories got sharper. Like I had moved onto the soundstage where my childhood was filmed.

Do you remember how we used to stop at the pawnshop, and you'd buy me Laffy Taffy? And then I'd make you listen to the terrible jokes printed on the wrappers?

•

Shiloh, I'm sorry, the last week has been nothing but long days and late nights.

First, let me congratulate Gus. Is he holding the line?

I *was* engaged. She was also in the Navy—which made some things easier and some things more difficult. I should have sent her more cookies.

I've gotten packages now and then, but you've always been especially great at mail. So the last few months have been a premium experience.

I remember the Laffy Taffy. Reading your e-mail made my molars hurt.

When I go back to North O, I feel like I get hit by wave after wave of intense memories. I can't imagine what it's like to live there. Is the nostalgia suffocating?

"Waste" is exactly the right word.

When I think about the last 14 years and everything I've missed in your life, I feel like I squandered something precious.

Like I was given something rare and valuable—a true blessing, an unearned gift—and all I had to do was hold on to it. And I let go.

I worry that it shows my true measure.

That I couldn't be trusted to get Frodo to Mordor.

I was young; is that an excuse?

There are 18- and 19-year-olds on this ship. They're like toddlers. I trust them to do their jobs, mostly, but I wouldn't trust them with anything else.

I can't believe that I thought I had it all figured out at that age—that I thought I had *you* figured out.

I should have done less thinking and more holding on.

What would I give 20-year-old Shiloh?

My attention. The loyalty I promised her.

•

Cary, you sent me a fanny pack with a Naval destroyer on it.

•

I'll be crushed if you don't wear it, Shiloh.

•

Too late, Junie has already claimed it. She's carrying scented markers and naked Disney princesses in it.

•

The intended usage.

•

Cary, it always feels lucky when you're online at the same time as me. Did you have a good day?

•

Yeah. No big mistakes. No big concerns. So busy that I hardly noticed time passing.

How about you?

•

Yeah. It's Junie's seventh birthday tomorrow. I've been baking the cake.

•

What flavor?

·

Hummingbird. Your favorite.

·

That is my favorite. Do you do their birthdays separately—you and
your ex?

·

No. Ryan and I do it together. We're having the party across the street,
at the park. That's what Junie wanted. It will be mostly family—Ryan's
siblings and their kids. These are the strangest times for me, because
it's *almost* like we're still a family. His parents still treat me like a
daughter-in-law. (His dad loves me.) And I'm in all the group photos.

I asked Ryan not to bring his girlfriend. This is probably the last
birthday party where I'll get away with that.

I am truly dreading the next fifteen years of parties.

I would never tell the kids this, but I feel like I'm serving out a sentence.

And I can't even complain about it, because I brought it on myself.

·

You can complain about it.

·

I'm going to miss having you as a captive audience, Cary. Maybe when
you get back to land, you can set me up with a handsome young guy
who's headed out to sea.

·

Or a lovely young woman?

·

Huh. Maybe. I don't know.

•

Is that still where your head is at?

•

You wondering if I've gone full Sappho since the last time you asked?

•

I'm just making sure I have the most current information.

•

I think I could probably date a woman. (This feels very weird to talk
about. Can you talk about homosexuality on a military computer?) Like,
I don't seem to have any emotional or physical objections? I feel very
enthusiastic about women, conceptually.

But, in reality, I can hardly stand *anyone*. Not at close range, anyway.

(I think this is getting worse as I get older . . . with exposure to
humanity.)

It's murder all day long trying to be patient with people and to give
them the benefit of the doubt. To remember that they probably mean
well, even when they don't *do* well.

And I don't like the look of them, either. (People.) (Human beings.)
Their clothes are embarrassing, and their voices are piercing, and I
never want to see their feet or their ankles or their knees or their elbows.

Maybe there are only five people in the whole world who I could
stand for more than ten minutes and who I'd also like to kiss—and
maybe one or two of them are women.

•

Is one of them still Val Kilmer?

•

One of them will always be Val Kilmer.

·

Shiloh, I'm coming home when my deployment is over. I have 20 days of leave, and my plan is to spend that time in Omaha, getting my mom's house ready for sale.

I'm going to stay with Mikey.

I know that you and I haven't had the best track record with face-to-face interactions—but I hope you'll let me take you out to lunch.

·

Cary!!

Of course!!!

I want to see you as much as you'll let me.

Please don't worry. We're going to be golden, I promise.

Tell me when you're coming. I'll bake you a cake.

## FIFTY-SIX

CARY HAD ONLY BEEN INSIDE the Omaha children's theater once, in junior high, on a field trip. It was a majestic old movie palace that had been refitted for live theater.

He was supposed to meet Shiloh here. She was going to show him around, and then he was going to take her to dinner. Mikey had suggested a Persian restaurant in the Old Market.

Cary had dressed up. Sort of. He was wearing navy blue pants and a button-down shirt. Mikey hadn't liked any of Cary's shirts, so he'd lent him one. It was a paisley pattern, and it was too tight—which Mikey said had been fashionable for years. *"It's fitted, Cary. That's the thing now. It's what they sell at the Gap."*

Cary walked into the theater. Shiloh was supposed to meet him in the lobby.

When he saw her at the far end, he almost started running.

Shiloh was talking to a man with red hair, waving her hands around. She was wearing a snug-fitting dress, and her hair was down, parted on the side.

Cary broke into a trot. "Shiloh."

She turned her head. Her face lit up. "Cary!" She rushed toward him.

He stopped when he got to her. He wasn't sure what to do next. She wasn't sure, either. She started laughing, raising her palms in a nervous shrug.

Cary held out his arms.

"Okay, yeah," Shiloh said, practically jumping into his arms.

She was hugging his neck—she smelled amazing. She felt amazing. He held on for dear life.

"I'm so happy to see you," Shiloh said, right in his ear.

Her dress was sweater material. Her hair slid over his fingers, and her dress slid over her back. He wasn't letting go. "Shiloh," he whispered.

She pulled away a little, squeezing his neck, then his shoulders, pressing her hands into his shirt. "You look great. You look unharmed."

"I am unharmed."

"I love you unharmed." She laughed, and he was close enough to see her bottom teeth. He hugged her again, and this time when it was over, she pulled away completely. "I want you to meet Tom," she said. "He's my only friend."

"That's not true . . ." the man behind her said, making an exaggerated sad face. He was a few inches shorter than Shiloh and wearing a gingham shirt. He held out his hand and winked. "I'm not actually her friend."

"I was going to say," Cary joked, "I thought *I* was her only friend. It's nice to meet you, Tom."

Cary wanted his hands on Shiloh again. He couldn't stop looking at her. He didn't think he'd ever missed her this much. Not even in boot camp. Not even after.

"I just tried to call you," Shiloh said. She seemed worried.

"My phone's in the car—is everything okay?"

"Well." She grimaced. "There's a play on the main stage tonight, and I'm directing—which is fine, I don't have to be there. But half the cast has norovirus. We *could* cancel, but the Boys and Girls Club is coming—and I can do the mushroom princess, I know all the lines. And Tom can do the hedgehog and the wolf . . ."

"Tom must have range."

"I do," Tom said. "Thank you."

Cary touched Shiloh's upper arm. "It's fine. We can go out after. Or tomorrow. Or both."

She looked relieved—also disappointed. "Are you sure? I'm so sorry. Wild horses couldn't have dragged me away from seeing you tonight . . ."

"This isn't wild horses. It's work. I'll stay and watch the show."

She smiled. "Yeah? You don't have to. There's a good Thai place right next door. And a coffee shop."

"I'll stay," he said. "I want to see the show."

His hand was falling away from her. Shiloh grabbed his wrist. "*Cary.*"

"Yeah?"

Her eyebrows were high. She looked like she was going to say something crazy. "If you're going to stay anyway, will you help?"

His voice dropped. "What kind of help?"

Cary was going to play the Old Oak Tree.

"It's mostly just standing," Shiloh had said. But then she'd handed him a script and two protein bars and left him alone at her desk to learn his lines. He was eating one of the protein bars now. He hadn't memorized lines in fifteen years . . . but he'd memorized plenty of other stuff in the meantime.

Shiloh's friend Tom had looked doubtful about her pressing Cary into stage duty. That made Cary want to say yes.

The Old Oak Tree really *didn't* have many lines. He mostly *did* just stand. And watch. And occasionally groan in the wind. He was supposed to have a deep, bark-covered voice. The show was for kids, but the cast was all adults. The script had Shiloh's notes in the margins. Her familiar, disastrous handwriting.

Cary kept getting distracted by his own photo pinned up next to her computer. He hadn't known how the photos would turn out when he sent her the film. He looked nervous in the picture. To his own eyes, he looked hungry. Maybe Shiloh hadn't noticed—she must think he always looked that way.

Tom appeared, covered in brown felt and pipe-cleaner needles. "Ready to make your debut?"

"My Omaha *children's* theater debut," Cary specified.

"Oh, sure, I've heard you've treaded the boards of the Pacific Theater . . ."

Cary laughed.

"Come with me," Tom said. "We'll get you in costume."

Cary stood up. "There's a costume?"

"You're a tree."

"I thought it was a set piece."

"It's both."

Cary followed Tom down halls and staircases. Everything was built like a warren around the stage and the lobby. Cary wished he had more time to explore.

They ended up in a dressing room, where a woman was waiting with a bundle of branches. "This is Kate," Tom said. "She'll take care of you from here."

Kate was cute. Small. Short, blond hair. A pierced nose. "You're Cary," she said.

He held out his hand. "I am."

She pursed her lips and nodded—he realized her hands were full. "I am *not* going to stick you with a pin," she said.

"Thank you."

Kate had Cary change into a long-sleeved brown T-shirt, and then she taped and pinned leafy branches to his arms. They were lighter than they looked.

"You stand inside the trunk," she said. "It's flexible. And there are places to rest your arms when you're not moving."

"That's clever."

"Well. Thanks. You're a little taller than the usual actor, so you might have to hunch to see out."

"Okay."

She frowned up at him. "Have you put on stage makeup before?"

"Uh . . ."

"I've got it," Shiloh said. She was standing in the door to the dressing room—all mushroomed up. She was wearing a short, full red skirt that looked like the cap of a mushroom, with white polka dots. The rest of the costume was a long-sleeved red leotard and white tights. Her face was painted white with red-circle cheeks. And she was wearing a cartoonish gold crown.

"That skirt is too short on you," Kate said.

"It's too small, too. I've got it pinned."

"Let me see if I can find some bloomers."

"I won't bend over in the meantime."

Kate squeezed past Shiloh out the door.

"Thanks!" Cary called after her.

Shiloh was grinning at him. "Look at you." She poked his shoulder. "Did you learn your lines?"

"Some of them."

"The makeup is simple. It's mostly just eyebrows. You want me to do it?"

"Sure."

Shiloh leaned past him to get a clean sponge. Her skirt pushed into his stomach. It was made of scratchy net with wire supports. It would look good from a distance, though. "Sorry," she said. "This is why we do makeup and *then* costumes."

She hovered over his face with the sponge and some tan-colored base.

"You look adorable," Cary said.

"You should see the real mushroom princess." Shiloh leaned past her skirt and rubbed the sponge over his cheek.

Cary put his hands on her waist to steady her. He closed his eyes. "I've been working on my tree voice."

"Let's hear it."

He let his voice drop and get gravelly. "*Something like this.*"

Shiloh giggled. "I like it."

"But the Oak Tree's supposed to be wise, right? So maybe more like . . ." Cary added an ounce of Jimmy Stewart waver. "*This is my faintly amused and world-weary tree voice.*"

Shiloh laughed. He squeezed her waist. "Even better," she said. "Close your mouth."

She was moving quickly, gently. After a second, he felt a cold, wet brush over his eye. "Your only important line," Shiloh said, "is *'Not my favorite branch!'* when Tom tries to break one off." She switched to his other eyebrow. "Otherwise, you can just stand there. I'll cover for you if you miss a line." The brush pulled away. "All done."

He opened his eyes.

Shiloh was looking down at him, smiling. "It's so good to see you," she said.

Cary wrapped his arms around her waist. He knew that he looked ravenous—did she?

Cary hadn't thought much about whether he missed theater. He didn't think about high school journalism much, either. Or quiz bowl. Or all the other things they'd kept busy with for four years.

But he *had* missed it . . .

The backstage whispering. The curtains. Everyone in costume, taking themselves seriously. Shiloh kept pushing him out of people's way. "Sorry it's so tight back here," she said.

"It's roomy compared to my ship."

Cary was onstage for the whole play. Tom helped him get situated in the tree costume before the curtain went up—it really was ingenious.

The story was about a young mushroom princess who longs to wander the forest . . . but she's stuck in the shade and under the supervision of an old oak tree. Friends were made and lessons were learned. The hedgehog was a riot.

Cary kept his eyes on Shiloh, which was, fortunately, in character for the Old Oak Tree.

She was by turns heartbreaking and hilarious—and absolutely believable as an eight-year-old mushroom princess. She telegraphed Cary's cues by looking at him, or nudging him. He thought he was mostly hitting everything.

The first time he used his tree voice, Shiloh giggled. So he made it even louder and sillier and more like Jimmy Stewart.

Cary gave one significant line at the wrong time. Shiloh caught it and batted it back to him for a second try. He fixed it.

An hour into the play, he realized that someone else would be the Old Oak Tree tomorrow, and someone else would be the mushroom princess—and he wouldn't ever get to do this again with Shiloh. Under the lights. In front of an audience. It made him want to wrap his branches around her and hold on.

When the curtain came down, Cary stayed onstage, attached to the set. The other actors—Tom, a woman who played a snake, a man who played a bird—all praised him. "Good thing Craig wasn't here to see this," they said. Craig was the usual Old Oak Tree.

The stage emptied out quickly. The tech people were resetting for the next day's show.

"Cary!" Shiloh shouted from the wings. "I'm going to come help you out of that. Don't move. Do you have to go to the bathroom?"

"No!" he called.

"You should! You're probably dehydrated."

She was back in a few more minutes with a bottle of water. "Sorry," she said. "I should have had Tom free you." She was unstrapping and untying him. "You were so good, Cary. So funny. I wish I could keep you. Honestly, I probably could have gotten one of the tech guys to play the tree—it's what Tom wanted—but you were genius. I knew you would be. I hope someone got pictures. You were *perfect*."

Cary was loose enough to step out of the costume without breaking anything.

Shiloh went to work on his arms, untaping the branches. She was still in full costume. One of her red cheeks had smeared. There was a hole in the neck of her leotard.

"You can keep me," Cary said.

She pulled the last branch away from his right arm. She looked up at his face.

Cary dropped to one knee.

## FIFTY-SEVEN

"CARY," SHE SAID. "NO."

Cary's eyes were wide and anxious. "No?"

"Not no," Shiloh said, feeling breathless all of a sudden. "Not no *specifically*. But no *generally*. What are you doing?"

"I didn't plan this," he said. He looked terrified.

"Okay, good." She reached for his arm. "Stand up."

"No," Cary said. "Let me finish."

Shiloh's heart was racing. She *couldn't* let him finish. "Cary . . ."

He swallowed. "Shiloh, I have five years left in the Navy. I know you can't leave Omaha. I know I can't offer you the life and partnership you deserve—"

"*Cary.*" Shiloh hadn't eaten anything. She had to go to the bathroom. She felt faint.

"—but I'm weak." His eyes were shining.

She touched his hair and shoulders. She pressed her palm over his mouth.

He pulled her hand away. He held it. "Shiloh, I love you—"

She stumbled down to her knees in front of him. Her skirt hit his legs. Cary dropped to both knees, too.

"Cary, stop—"

He didn't stop. "I don't want to spend another year—or another minute—without you. Without being what I'm supposed to be to you."

He reached into his pocket and pulled out a small velvet box.

"I thought you hadn't planned this!"

"I hadn't planned to do it now." He squeezed her hand. "Look at me."

She couldn't look at him.

"*Shiloh.*"

She looked at him.

"Will you marry me?"

At some point, she'd started crying. She laid her free hand on his cheek. "Cary, this isn't good."

"Why not?"

"Because you don't want this."

"I'm telling you what I want."

"I've got too much," she said. "Baggage. Sandbags. I can't follow you all over the world."

"I'm not asking you to."

"I'm *here*," Shiloh said.

"I know."

"For good."

"Shiloh, I know."

"And my kids—have you even thought about my kids? They're only getting older and less cute, and you'd have all of the responsibility but none of the joy—"

"Not *none*."

"They'll always be someone else's. And he's around, too." Her voice was getting quieter, and her words were coming faster. She couldn't slow down. "Marrying me is like marrying four people, and one of them is my ex-husband. He's clingy and manipulative, and you can't even complain about him, because the kids might hear. I only get half a life with my kids—you'd get a *quarter*. The bad quarter! And even if you give them your best, he'll still be the guy they call 'Dad.' It's too fucked up, Cary." She inhaled, too fast. She didn't wait to catch her breath. "You wouldn't be marrying a woman, you'd be marrying a *mom*. Someone who puts someone else's kids first in every situation—"

"Shiloh." Cary set the box down between them. He took her other hand. His voice was firm. "I've thought about your kids. I'm ready to take this on."

"How could you *know* that?"

"I don't know!" He sounded frustrated. "How *can* I know it? How can I ever know it without pushing ahead?"

"We haven't even dated," she said. "Couldn't we date?"

Cary looked disappointed. Hurt. "Do you *want* to date?"

She shrugged. She felt pathetic. "Why not?"

"*Because*. Because we already know what we need to know." He was holding her hands by the fingers. "There's no getting to know each other, Shiloh. You know me better than anyone. And I know *you*. If we're together, then it's already serious. I want to begin our life together."

Shiloh was sitting back on her calves. She was crying. She lifted her arm to wipe her eyes on her wrist. Cary didn't let go of her hands.

"What do you want?" he whispered.

She shook her head. "A time machine."

"I can't give you the past," Cary said. He squeezed her hands. "But we could have a future."

She sniffed. She tried to look at him directly.

His hair was pushed the wrong way, curling a bit over his forehead. He was making a stern face, and the eyebrow makeup made him look extra stern. His eyes were the same old spill of maple syrup. "I'm already yours, Shiloh. Do you want me?"

She nodded. Miserable. "Of course I *want* you, Cary. That's not the question!"

Cary was sitting on his ankles, too. "That's *my* question."

She jerked on his arms. "I just can't see this working out."

"Then I'm doomed," he said. "Because I only want to be with you."

Shiloh sighed.

Cary leaned forward, holding their hands up between them. "I only want to be with you, Shiloh. Please let me be with you."

"I don't think it's a good idea . . ." she said again.

"Do you have a better one?"

Her shoulders slumped. "No."

He rubbed her hands.

"Let me see the ring," she said. Desultorily.

Cary straightened, his eyes going a little wild, and let go of her hands. He picked up the box, turned it toward her, and opened it.

Shiloh leaned closer. The ring was silver with a round diamond. The band was intricate—twisted with filigree that looked like rope. "That's pretty," she said, already too interested. "I've never seen anything like that before."

"It's yours," Cary said. "If you want it."

She looked up at his face. He still looked so serious, even when he was desperate. (She knew he was desperate.) She tried to wipe the paint off one of his eyebrows with her thumb. It smeared.

"I want it," she said. "I want you. I just can't stop thinking of all the ways this could go bad."

"You think it'll go better with someone else?"

"It's more like—if it goes bad with someone else, it won't be so devastating."

"That's terrible logic, Shiloh." He was being gentle.

She felt her eyes filling again. "You told me you didn't want to be that guy! Remember?"

Cary's face fell. "I'm sorry—I panicked. I needed some time to think."

She sniffed. "I think *I* need some time to think."

"Okay," he said. He looked down. After a second, he closed the ring box.

"Wait—" Shiloh put her hand over the box.

He looked up at her, more with his eyes than his head. "Wait?"

"I can't not say yes to you," she said, rolling her eyes at herself, feeling her chin pucker, blinking out a few more tears. "If you're still asking."

Cary raised an eyebrow, confused. "I thought you wanted to think."

"I want to say yes, and *then* I want to think."

"Is that a tentative yes?"

"No." She shook her head. "It's more like a yes with an asterisk."

"What's the footnote?"

"It's like '*yes,*' asterisk, and then '*Let the record show I think this is probably a bad idea.*'"

He took her hand again. "But you still want . . . to be with me?"

"Cary," she said, chastising him, "I always want that. I'm obviously in love with you."

"Obviously?"

She nodded her head.

His eyes were wide again. "Shiloh . . . will you marry me?"

"Yes," she whispered. "Asterisk."

Cary whispered, too: "Let the record show you think this is a bad idea."

"Let the record show I'm terrified of losing you completely."

After a second he let go of her hand and opened the ring box. He took out the ring. "Do you want this?"

"Yeah," she said softly. She didn't hold out her hand, so he picked it up.

The ring slid easily over Shiloh's knuckles. She shivered. Her fingers were trembling. When she closed her mouth, her teeth chattered.

"You okay?" Cary asked.

She nodded. She held out her hand so they could both see. "It's pretty," she said.

"We can have it resized. It's white gold."

"It's pretty," she said again.

"Yeah." Cary's voice broke. He lifted Shiloh's chin, rubbing his thumb along the scar there. His eyes were searching, shining. "You want to try this with me?"

Shiloh nodded, without moving her head out of his hand. "Yeah. I do."

When Cary kissed her, he pushed her head back.

# before

RYAN WAS OLDER THAN SHILOH. He graduated two years ahead of her and got a job at a high school in Omaha, exclusively teaching theater. That was a coup—most drama teachers had to teach English, too.

They were long-distance while Shiloh finished school. Ryan drove back to Des Moines most weekends to see her. She got an apartment because he hated visiting the dorms.

Ryan loved his teaching job, but he was open to leaving Nebraska. Shiloh still wanted to get her master's degree, and there'd be more theater opportunities somewhere else—in Chicago, or even New York.

They were going to decide together on their next step.

The summer before Shiloh's senior year, she and Ryan were both cast in a theater-in-the-park show that a friend was directing for her thesis. It was a comedy of errors set in the 1940s—and drew surprisingly big crowds.

There weren't enough men in the cast, so Shiloh put on high-waisted pants and a pencil-thin moustache. Her hair was still bobbed. It was a very sexy look—she could tell because literally everyone in the cast paid more attention to her, male and female. She kept making the stage manager, a freshman girl from Bettendorf, blush.

Shiloh played the rake; she had all the best punchlines. Ryan was the shady mobster. They fought over the ingenue and both lost her to the fresh-faced soldier, played by another woman in the cast.

Shiloh and Ryan went shopping for rings that summer, in pawnshops and antique stores. She picked out a vintage ring with a small diamond and etched band.

She didn't know *when* Ryan was going to propose—but she wasn't surprised when he pulled her out of the curtain call one night. All the other actors stepped back, like they knew what was coming.

Ryan glanced out at the audience, to get them on his side before he went down on one knee.

Shiloh was already smiling so wide. She was stupidly in love with him... Charming, handsome Ryan. Always the best part of every show. Always the best-liked person in every cast. Ryan, who liked helping people with their lines. Who liked helping build the sets. Who was excited about teaching and wanted to travel and spoke a little Italian and a lot of Spanish.

Shiloh was lucky to catch his eye. She was lucky Ryan didn't mind being shorter than her. She was lucky that he didn't mind her energy or her opinions. That he loved the way they looked together.

Being with Ryan was so easy. It was going to be easy to love him. He was going to be the soft, bright center of her life.

When Ryan asked her to marry him—in a voice that carried— Shiloh bit her lip and looked at the audience, like she wasn't sure. Even though they all knew she *was* sure. They clapped and shouted. Shiloh laughed. She looked down into Ryan's blue eyes and said, "Yes."

The rest of the cast cheered and tossed confetti. One of their friends took photos.

It was perfect. It was everything she wanted.

# before

"SO YOU HAVEN'T *TALKED* TO Shiloh about this . . ." Mikey was standing on the other side of a jewelry case. He wore Otis in a sling around his chest—both Mikey and Otis seemed so accustomed to the sling that they didn't notice it. Mike supported the baby with a palm under his rump and held one of Otis's chubby hands.

Janine had gone back to work. Mikey was with Otis all day now. He was home when Cary arrived from the airport.

"No." Cary was looking down at the jewelry case. There were hundreds of rings, new and used. This place specialized in unusual jewelry. Antiques. Independent designers.

"Maybe you *should* talk to her . . ." Mikey said.

Cary sighed. "You said you'd help me pick out a ring."

"And I will. I will."

"This is pretty." Cary pointed at a ring. "Is this pretty?"

Mikey squinted at it. "It's pretty. Yeah. It's kind of normal. Shiloh's going to want something no one else has. Maybe a different gem? Like an emerald?"

"Emeralds are soft. I want a diamond."

"The ring isn't for *you*, Carold."

Cary looked up. He felt agitated. "I want her to know that I was ready to buy a diamond. She can trade it for something else if she doesn't like it, I don't care."

Mikey seemed concerned. He patted Otis's bottom. "Are you guys—I mean, Cary, does Shiloh know how you feel about her?"

Cary shrugged. "Yes. Yes and no."

"I pre-asked Janine. To make sure I had a clear landing."

Cary made a sour face. "What's the difference between pre-asking and asking?"

"You *hint*. You talk about the future. You give her a chance to tell you not to propose . . ."

"Shiloh can say no if she doesn't want to marry me."

"Okay. Well . . ." Mikey's eyebrows twitched. "That sounds painful."

Cary put his hands on his hips. "You think she's gonna say no?"

Mikey looked like he wanted to throw up his hands—but he was holding a baby. "I don't know what she's going to say! She told me you guys were just friends!"

"You've always wanted us to get together, Mike!"

"I still do! I'm just worried about you."

Cary sighed again. He walked over to a different case. "These are all used over here. I don't think she'd mind used."

"No, me neither."

They both stared at the case. Cary's eyes stopped on a silvery one with a decent-sized diamond and lots of lacy detail. There was something nautical about it. Cary pointed at it. "What about this one?"

"Oh, that's nice," Mikey said. "Kind of art deco, with the filigree?"

They asked to see it. Cary liked the ring even more up close. It looked old and a little fussy. He looked at Mikey. "That's it, right?"

Mikey looked like he was really thinking about it, which Cary appreciated. "Yeah. I think she'll love it."

They waited for the clerk to get the paperwork. Mikey looked worried, like someone watching his team lose a big game.

"I just feel like I've wasted so much time," Cary said, trying to explain himself. "I want to get right with her. And myself. I want to start living and dying in the right direction."

Mikey let go of Otis's hand and patted Cary's shoulder. "You're a good man, Cary."

# before

CARY MET BREANNA IN OFFICER training.

She was Mexican American. From Texas. Her older brothers were in the Navy, too.

She caught Cary's eye because she never complained. She was always doing exactly what she was supposed to be doing, just a little bit better than everyone else. She knew all the answers, even if she didn't say so. She didn't gossip or get involved in drama. She hated a mess.

Breanna was beautiful. She had thick, dark hair and a great smile. Busty enough that she was never happy with the way her uniforms fit. She loved to run, so Cary ran with her.

They couldn't date until after they finished their training. And then they were stationed in far-flung ports.

But they were both diligent, both focused—both interested. They did what they had to, to stay in touch. They tried to coordinate their leave time.

It was Breanna who asked Cary if he was ready for marriage. And then if he was ready to propose.

Cary wasn't sure. He wanted to be careful. There was a lot to consider.

About six months later, he bought a ring—platinum, diamond solitaire, two baguettes. And then he proposed to Breanna a few months after that, on leave.

She said yes.

But Cary got the feeling that he'd asked too late. He never felt like he could catch up, from then on. Breanna was always pushing forward, asking for slightly more than he could give.

It was easy to lose himself in his work. It was an excuse she understood.

Breanna broke up with him two years after he proposed. She did it over the phone. He wasn't surprised.

She sent him the ring—fully insured, registered mail—the next time he was on land.

## SIXTY-ONE

WHEN SHE AND CARY FINALLY stood up, Shiloh had a horrible feeling that all the actors and tech people were watching from the wings, ready to applaud.

But everyone was gone except for Tom, who was standing just off-stage, looking gobsmacked. "The house and restrooms are clear," he said, "and the under-eighteens have been signed out."

"Great," Shiloh replied. "See you tomorrow. Good work."

"Good night. It was nice to meet you, Cary."

"Thank you," Cary mumbled. "You too. Good night."

Cary and Shiloh were holding hands too tight, with their elbows too straight. He was letting her lead.

She dropped him off in the dressing room with his shirt, then went to change by herself in the women's dressing room.

Shiloh wouldn't say that she felt numb . . .

It was more like her ears were ringing in a full-body sort of way. When she got undressed, the diamond ring punched a hole in her tights. Shiloh laughed. This wasn't a dream, but it was just as nonsensical.

Cary was back in Omaha. And he wanted to marry her.

Shiloh had been trying so hard to manage her feelings for him for the long term: Sustainable friendship. No sex, minimal confessions.

And meanwhile, Cary had apparently been shopping for engagement rings. Beautiful, vintage engagement rings.

Shiloh still had her first engagement ring. It was too nice to throw out, but not nice enough to sell—and she felt like it should leave her with a note in its file: *This ring comes from a broken home. Personally, I don't blame the ring, but maybe you're superstitious. The good news, I guess, is I didn't die wearing it.*

Cary's antique ring might tell a similar story. She held it up to the lights around the dressing room mirror. The diamond seemed to float on a filigree bridge—straight lines, with a coil of rope winding through them. The band was only slightly too big. It wouldn't fall off her knuckle.

Shiloh washed her face. She changed back into her not-very-platonic knit wrap dress. (When Tom saw what she was wearing tonight, he'd called her "Backseat Betty.")

She put on her own tights—carefully—and zipped up her boots. She didn't take down her hair. There was spray glitter in it. She'd have to wash it out.

Cary was standing outside the dressing room door. Straight-backed. Pale. With makeup still under his chin and along his hairline. He reached for Shiloh as soon as she appeared—his arm around her waist, his eyes looking for hers.

"You hungry?" she asked.

Cary nodded.

It was too late to eat in a normal restaurant. They went to a diner a few blocks away that served loose-meat sandwiches at a stand-up counter.

Shiloh wanted to ask about Cary's mom. About his flight. About his plans.

But she just really couldn't manage it. They both gulped down their sandwiches and fountain Cokes. Cary wiped his mouth after each bite with a paper napkin. He wasn't talking either, and he was looking off into space, not at Shiloh.

When they were done, they stood outside the diner, holding hands.

"I still have my car," Shiloh said.

"I'll follow you home."

That made sense. He walked her to her car. Before she could get in, Cary kissed her. She kissed him back—desperately. As kisses go, it was the equivalent of shouting at your kid because they've done something reckless, but you're still so relieved they're alive.

*What were you thinking?* the kiss said.

And also, *Thank god, thank god.*

She held him as tightly as she could around the shoulders, and he held her around the waist. She stopped kissing after a while because it got in the way of holding him.

Cary was breathing deeply. "Shiloh, can I stay the night with you?"

"I . . . I think I need a minute."

"Okay."

"And the kids are home."

He pulled away. "The kids are home?" His face had fallen. "You should have told me. We could have waited to go out."

"I didn't want to wait—I missed you. And I would have had to come into work tonight anyway."

Cary nodded. Still troubled. Hopefully remembering that her kids were concrete, not abstract, and that he'd just signed up for fifteen years of hard labor.

She wouldn't hold him to it.

She was still going to offer Cary an out—probably several outs. As soon as she thought he might listen.

"Let's get you home." He opened her car door and touched her back as she got in. "Don't get too far ahead of me."

When they got to her house, Shiloh stopped Cary from getting out of his rental car. She stood by his door. He rolled the window down.

"Do you have the kids tomorrow?" he asked.

"Yeah. Do you want to come over for dinner?"

"Yeah," he said, then shook his head once. "Maybe. I have a meeting about my mom." He still looked strung out. Sort of dazed.

She touched his cheek with her left hand. He immediately put his hand over hers.

Shiloh laughed. At nothing.

Cary closed his eyes and kissed her palm.

"Okay, Cary," she said. "I'll see you when I see you."

"I'll see you tomorrow," he said. "Somehow."

## SIXTY-TWO

MIKEY WAS SITTING ON THE couch watching *Desperate Housewives* when Cary let himself in. He muted the TV. "Well?"

"She said yes," Cary said.

Mikey broke into a huge smile. "Yes?"

"Well . . . she said 'yes and.'"

"Like in improv?"

"It was more like 'yes but.'"

"But what?"

"But she thinks it's a bad idea."

"Why?"

Cary shrugged. "The obvious reasons. That we can't live together. That she has kids and it's complicated. That we haven't ever dated."

"Those are good reasons."

Cary nodded. "Great reasons. Smart girl."

"But she said *yes* . . ." Mikey said, like he was making sure that he got it.

"She said yes," Cary confirmed.

"Because she's crazy about you." Mikey grinned again. "And always has been."

Cary smiled. It felt like the first real smile he'd allowed himself tonight. "I think that might be true."

Mikey jumped off the couch to hug him.

## SIXTY-THREE

"ARE WE GOING TO TALK about what I saw last night?" Tom was waiting for Shiloh when she sat down at her desk.

"No," she said.

He raised an eyebrow above the frame of his glasses. "Because it *looked* like—"

Tom must have seen something alarming on her face. He stopped.

"Ohh-kay," he said. "I guess we're really *not* going to talk about it."

"Thank you."

"I'll just trust that you would tell me if you were, you know, suddenly engaged to a handsome sailor."

"That does seem like the sort of thing I would tell you . . ."

"It does, doesn't it?"

Cary sent her a text. *"I can come for dinner, if that still works?"*

*"yeah, come over—i get home at 5:30"*

Shiloh hadn't planned anything for dinner. She had fresh tomatoes and bacon. She stopped for bread on the way to daycare.

"Guess who's coming to dinner?" she asked the kids.

"Who?" Junie asked, already overcome with surprise.

"My friend Cary."

"Cary! He's home from the ocean?"

"Cary?" Gus repeated.

"Yeah," Shiloh said.

"Mommy," Gus said. "You friend is named Cary?"

"Yep. And he's coming to dinner."

"Well," Junie said, folding her hands in her lap. "I can't wait to see him."

•

Cary was late. Shiloh fed the kids and her mom—who had come home from the bar in a terrible mood.

"*What* is taking Cary so long?" Junie wondered. She hadn't ever mentioned the almost-kiss on the porch again. Even when Shiloh showed her Cary's photos and postcards.

"Mommy?" Gus said. "You friend is coming?"

"*Coming*," Cary texted. "*Sorry.*"

A half hour later, Shiloh heard his voice outside. It sounded like he was arguing with someone. She peeked out the window. Cary was standing by his car, on the phone—shouting.

"Stay inside," she told Junie. Shiloh went out through the porch.

"Jackie—" Cary was holding his forehead. "Jackie, you know that's not true . . . That's not true!"

He was walking in a circle. He saw Shiloh.

She waved.

Cary nodded at her, then looked away—then looked back at her, distracted and troubled.

Shiloh waved again, like, *It's okay, keep talking.*

"What other options?" Cary said into the phone, more calmly than before. "Tell me the other options."

He glanced back at Shiloh like he wanted to say something to her. But then he was shouting into the phone—"No— No— *Jackie*. This is reality! This is all we can do!"

A car was driving past Shiloh's house. It stopped. The woman in the passenger seat rolled down her window and yelled, "You planned this!"

It took a second for Shiloh to clock the woman as Cary's older sister Jackie. (His biological mom.)

Cary was still holding the phone. He looked shocked. "Did you *follow* me?"

"No, but I knew where to find you! I'm not letting you do this, Cary!"

Cary was walking toward the car. "It's not *me*! You heard the social worker—Mom can't get Medicaid until she sells the house. That's it! That's reality!"

"You don't even care!"

"I *do* care."

Jackie leaned farther out the window, rising out of her seat. She was about fifty, and she looked a lot like Lois. There was a man driving the car, also leaning toward the open window.

"You've got money!" Jackie shouted. "You've got a job! Angel has nothing!"

"This isn't about Angel," Cary said.

"It *is* about Angel!" the man yelled.

Cary clenched his fist. "Don, I swear to god . . ."

"You've always been so fucking selfish," Jackie said.

Cary laughed horribly. "*I've* always been selfish? *I've* always been selfish. That's rich." He glanced around. He glanced back at Shiloh for a second. His gaze hung on her. He looked gutted.

Shiloh should go in. It was probably humiliating for him, to have her watch this. She walked up the steps onto the enclosed porch but didn't go inside the house. She still wanted to monitor the situation.

"We either sell the house or Mom has to leave rehab." Cary kept raising his voice, then reining it in, then raising it. Shiloh had never seen him like this.

"She can come home now!" Jackie shouted. "We'll take care of her."

"You *won't* take care of her!" Cary shouted back.

"No, *you* won't take care of her!"

The front door flew open, and Shiloh's mom steamed past her, muttering, "That's it, that is *it*."

She got down the steps and pointed up the street. "You need to move the *fuck* along, Jackie!"

"Oh, fuck off, Gloria. This is family business."

"This is my property—and I *will* call the cops."

"And tell them what?"

"I'll figure that out before they get here." She turned to Cary. "You move along, too. Get inside—we don't fight in the yard!"

"Sorry, Gloria." Cary headed up the steps like he'd been given an order. He walked right past Shiloh, into the house. She followed him.

"Cary!" Junie exclaimed as soon as she saw him. "Are you okay? Was someone yelling at you?"

Cary looked bad. His face was bright red.

"Let's give Cary a minute," Shiloh said.

Her mom came in the door and slammed it. "I have kicked those shitheads out of my bar—and I will kick them out of my yard. I have no time for that woman."

Shiloh took Cary's hand. "Come on, come with me." She pulled him upstairs. He followed her.

As soon as they were in the hallway, she touched his shoulder. "Are you okay?"

"Shiloh," Cary said, abject and eyes half-closed, "you're not wearing your ring."

Shiloh was taken aback. "*Cary*," she breathed out. "Baby . . ."

She pulled the ring out of her shirt. She'd hung it on a silver chain with his old dog tag. "I just didn't want to talk to my mom and Junie about it yet."

Cary wrapped his hand around the ring and metal tag. He pushed Shiloh against the wall and pressed his forehead into hers. She brought a hand up to the back of his head and cradled him there. His eyes were closed. He was breathing hard.

Shiloh stroked his hair. "You're kind of a wreck, aren't you?"

Cary laughed through his nose, one wretched exhale. Shiloh thought he might be crying—that this might be what it looked like when Cary cried, like misery and heavy breathing.

She kept rubbing the back of his head. "It's okay. I've got you."

After a while, he moved his forehead down to her shoulder. His fist was still clutched around the ring. "I'm really helping my case here, aren't I?"

"What case?"

"The '*Shiloh, legally bind yourself to me*' effort."

She rubbed the back of his neck. "You just seem a little more . . . *frantic* than usual."

Cary lifted his head to look at her. He was still flushed. "I have seventeen days of leave. I need to get my mom's house on the market before I go. And I need to convince you to spend the rest of your life with me. Those are my two objectives. They're both of highest priority."

Shiloh laughed. It was gentle. She nudged his hair away from his face, even though it was too short to matter. "You don't have to deal with me right now, I'll give you an extension. I'm not going anywhere."

"*No,*" Cary said, frustrated. "*Shiloh.* No more extensions. No more waiting. I want the rest of my life to be about building something with you. I want to start that work."

"Okay," she said, kissing his cheek. "It's started. We've started. Look at me." He did. "We're engaged."

"Asterisk," Cary said, still wretched.

"The footnote now reads, '*This is an active, developing scenario. Both parties are at the table working toward a mutually beneficial agreement.*'"

Cary frowned. "That's too long for a footnote, and it doesn't sound celebratory."

"Let go of my ring," she said.

He did.

Shiloh smiled at him and tucked the necklace into her shirt. "Come hang out with my kids, and let me feed you dinner."

Cary looked in her eyes and nodded.

Shiloh led him downstairs. She'd been planning on not touching him in front of Junie and Gus. But the landscape of her worries had shifted. She held his hand.

Junie jumped up when she saw him. "Cary, are you feeling better *now*?"

"I am. Sorry, Juniper. It's great to see you."

"It's great to see you. I thought you'd never leave that boat!"

Shiloh's mom was on the couch. Cary looked penitent. "Gloria, I'm sorry."

"No, I'm sorry." She was holding a beer. "I shouldn't have stuck my nose in your business."

"I won't fight in your yard again. I promise you that was out of character."

Her mom rolled her eyes. "Your sister would bring out the worst in Mother Teresa."

"I'm sorry," he repeated.

Shiloh pulled him toward the kitchen. "The kids have already eaten."

"But we waited for you to have dessert!" Junie said.

"Mommy," Gus said, "Gus can have dessert? Gus can have ice cream?" He still hadn't abandoned the third person.

"Just a minute, Gus. Do you like BLTs?" she asked Cary. "Do you eat bacon?"

"I eat everything," he said.

"Good."

She cooked the rest of the bacon while Cary watched. She hadn't wanted it to get cold before he got here.

Shiloh had thought tonight would be about the kids. About reminding Cary that the kids were real people—and a real problem with his plan.

But now that he was here, Shiloh just wanted to make things easy for him. She toasted the bread and spread it with mayonnaise.

"That's so much mayonnaise," Cary said.

"Have you ever made a BLT?"

"No."

"No commentary, then."

She made them each a big sandwich and piled Cary's plate with potato chips and fresh cherries.

He watched her. Shiloh was pretty sure he wanted to kiss her. It made her blush.

They ate at the table, and Junie sat with them, asking Cary questions about the Navy. Gus kept bringing toys in from the living room to show Cary. "You name is Cary?" he kept asking.

"He's changed so much," Cary said to Shiloh.

"Yeah," she agreed. Gus had gotten taller, heavier. He was talking more. He was very nearly potty-trained—100 percent potty-trained at daycare.

"He seems a lot more upbeat," Cary said.

Gus was back with another toy car to show them. Shiloh smiled. "He's having a good night, aren't you, Gus?"

"Gus can have ice cream?"

"Yes," Shiloh said definitively. She had cake cones and strawberry ice cream in the kitchen. She got up and made cones for everyone but Cary, who said he was full.

Cary seemed to be coming back to life. "Oh," he said, "Juniper—I saw some humpback whales when I was on my ship. I took photos for you."

"*Hump*back whales?" Junie was agog.

Cary got his phone out of his pocket—it was a nice one, a Razr. He opened it and pressed some buttons. Then he handed it to Junie.

She gasped. "Where is its humpback?"

"That's just the name," Cary said. "Use the arrows to look at the photos. See if you can find the baby whale."

Cary stood up and gathered the dishes.

"Gus wants to see the baby," Gus said. He was in Shiloh's lap.

"Just a minute." Shiloh heard Cary running water and leaned back, so she could see into the kitchen. "Hey—what are you doing?"

"Dishes."

"I'll do them later."

"No, she won't!" Shiloh's mom was still sitting in the living room.

"I don't mind," Cary said.

"I see it!" Junie shrieked. She ran into the kitchen with the phone. "Is this the baby?"

"Yep."

Gus huffed. "Want to see the baby!"

"You have to be patient," Shiloh said, smoothing down his hair.

Junie came running back into the dining room. "Gus-Gus, look!" She held out the phone.

Gus reached for it. "You don't hold it. Gus holds it! Mine!"

Shiloh shook her head. "Not yours."

"Cary doesn't want you to touch his phone," Junie said bossily.

"Gus can hold the phone," Cary said over the noise of the water. "It's fine!"

Junie surrendered the phone with bad grace. Shiloh tried to supervise the transfer, but Gus had already grabbed it. As soon as he had it, he wailed, "Junie broke it!"

"Let me see." Shiloh pried his hands off the phone and looked at it. "You turned it off, that's all. He turned it off!" she called into the kitchen. "Sorry!"

"That's okay!" Cary called back. "Just turn it back on!"

Gus was whining in the base of his throat, like an engine trying to start.

"If you cry," Shiloh said, "you don't get to see the baby whale." The phone came back to life and asked for a PIN. "Just a minute, Gus." Shiloh set him down and walked into the kitchen, holding the phone out to Cary. "Sorry. It's locked."

Cary's hands were in the sink. "It's four-two-one-five."

Shiloh was surprised. "Oh. Okay." She typed in the code. "Like your old phone number."

"Yeah. Now you know my ATM code, too." He was gesturing toward the phone. His hand was sudsy. "Do you see 'Pictures' on the menu? You might have to scroll back to find the whales."

"Um . . ." Shiloh looked at Cary. He'd stacked the dirty dishes on the counter and filled the sink with soapy water. His sleeves were neatly cuffed at his elbows. He still looked tired. "I'll find them," she said. "Thanks."


Cary did dishes while Shiloh put the kids to bed. There were a lot of dishes.

When she came back downstairs, her mom had gone to her room, and Cary was on the couch.

Shiloh slowed down on the stairs when she saw him. She smiled.

Cary was watching. He smiled, too, and held out his hand.

Shiloh went to him and took it. She stood there for a second. "I've always wanted a man with dishpan hands."

"Don't be rude," he said.

"I'm being serious. I hate doing dishes."

Cary leaned forward. He fished the engagement ring out of Shiloh's shirt and left it hanging where he could see it. "You still have my dog tag," he said.

She nodded. "You told me to keep it safe."

He tugged on her arm.

"Junie's still awake," Shiloh said softly.

"Sit down," he said softly back.

Shiloh did.

Cary held on to her hand. He was looking at her bare fingers. "You kept my tag. And then you got it out last night?"

"This morning."

"And you put it on a chain?"

"It was already on a chain," she said.

# before

SHILOH'S MOM HAD NEVER MARRIED.

She worked as a waitress and then as a bartender.

She had Shiloh when she was twenty.

They lived with Shiloh's grandmother, who left them the house when she passed.

Shiloh's mom moved into the first-floor bedroom after that, and Shiloh stayed upstairs. Shiloh knew not to come downstairs in the morning if she could hear a man's voice.

When Shiloh was in grade school, her mom had a boyfriend named Grant who used to take them out to dinner at Bishop's and sometimes to the movies.

Grant was all right. He drank too much. He lasted about a year.

Most of the men came for the night and never came back. Her mom didn't go to their houses—or at least, Shiloh didn't guess that she did. Her mom came home every night.

She started dating Jack when Shiloh was in high school. He owned the bar at the airport. He was married.

Shiloh got the feeling that a lot of her mom's men were married. She wondered if her father had been married. If he'd come for the night and moved on.

Her mom didn't want Shiloh to get to know any of them. Not even Jack, and he'd stuck around for years.

The men who came into the house never got more than coffee and only came upstairs to use the bathroom.

There was a lock on Shiloh's door, and her mom started reminding her to lock it before Shiloh could wonder why.

# before

SHILOH STARTED HER MATERNITY LEAVE two days before the doctor planned to induce her.

She was already a week past her due date, and her back and right hip hurt too much for her to focus on work. She decided to bail out early and spend a couple days with Juniper.

Junie was three. She was happy to have Mommy home all day—but she wanted Daddy, too. "Daddy's at work," Shiloh said. "He's got a show tonight."

Ryan's spring musical—*The Wizard of Oz*—had its last show that night. They'd joked that the baby was waiting for his schedule to clear.

Junie kept asking for Daddy, so Shiloh told her they could bring Ryan dinner. Shiloh called and left a message, telling him they were headed up to the high school.

They got there an hour and a half before the show. There were kids onstage doing last-minute rehearsing. Ryan was onstage with them.

He spotted Shiloh and Junie as they were coming down the aisle. "Here come the beautiful people!" he shouted, grinning. Then he sat on the edge of the stage and hopped off.

A woman standing ahead of Shiloh turned around—it was Erin, a part-time production assistant who'd been one of Ryan's first students. She was in her twenties now. "June Bug!" she called out.

Junie ran into Erin's arms. Ryan brought Junie to weekend rehearsals—everyone here knew her.

Ryan put a hand on Shiloh's stomach and another on her back. He kissed her cheek. "How are you?"

"Upright," Shiloh said, leaning into him.

"You look gorgeous. Radiant. Fucking pomegranate lotus time."

Shiloh laughed.

Erin had picked Junie up and was holding her on her hip. "How are you feeling, Mrs. Cass?"

"Oh my *gosh,* Shiloh." Ms. Grand—Rachel—an English teacher who helped with productions, was standing on the stage. "You look like you're about to pop."

"I feel like Violet Beauregarde."

"I wasn't even mobile at forty weeks," Rachel said.

"I'm mobile," Shiloh said. "I have a team of people who roll me around."

"Mr. Cass?!" A woman was shouting from backstage. She walked out of the wing. It was Mrs. H, the music director. "Oh, hi, Shiloh."

"Hi, Naomi."

"Mr. Cass, when you get a second, we have a trumpet situation."

"If it's urgent," Ryan said, "call 911. Otherwise I'll see you in fifteen." He turned to Shiloh. "You want to sit down for a minute?"

She nodded. Ryan grabbed Junie and led Shiloh out to the front lobby, where they could sit and talk while he ate the burrito they'd brought for him.

They were only interrupted twice—by Kelly and Steph, the drama moms who ran the concession stands, and by Cassie, the high school senior who was playing Dorothy.

"Daddy's so *busy,*" Junie said, sighing. Shiloh and Ryan laughed. Everything she said cracked them up. (According to Erin, a preschool teacher, Juniper was very advanced, both verbally and socially.)

Ryan finished his burrito, then rubbed Shiloh's shoulders and neck for a few minutes. "You want to stay for the show?"

"I can't sit that long," Shiloh said.

He kissed her, still rubbing her neck. "Okay."

"I get kisses, too!" Junie said.

"Yeah, you do!" Ryan scooped her up and kissed her neck like Cookie Monster. "Take care of Mommy. She's about to do something magical."

Junie's eyes got big. "What?"

"Have a baby!"

"Oh, *that*," Junie said.

Shiloh and Ryan laughed again.

Ryan kissed Shiloh's cheek. "Love you."

"Love you, too. Have a good show."

Shiloh took Junie home and went into labor the next night, without any help.

Ryan always kept his phone in his pocket and slept with it on his bedside table. If he was texting someone when Shiloh walked up to him, he'd put his phone away and give her his full attention. If he wanted Shiloh to see a photo, he'd send it to her.

A few days after Gus was born, Ryan left his phone on the couch while he ran into the bathroom to help Junie.

Shiloh picked it up.

Shiloh would have guessed it was Mrs. H, the music director. But it was actually Ms. Grand, the English teacher. And Erin, his former student. (A recent development, he assured her.) And Kelly, the prettier of the drama moms—but only via text.

## SIXTY-SIX

RYAN HAD THE KIDS ON Friday, and Shiloh was anxious to be alone with Cary. He was already down to fifteen days of leave. (What could they solve in fifteen days?)

They were supposed to have dinner, but she called to see if he wanted to meet earlier—the theater was dead on Friday afternoons.

"Yeah," Cary said. "Definitely. But, um, I was just about to visit my mom."

"Ah, okay." Shiloh tried not to sound disappointed. "Call me after?"

"I mean . . . you could come along? If you want?"

"To see your mom?"

"You don't have to," he said.

"No," Shiloh said, "I will. I'd like to."

"I'm leaving Mikey's in twenty minutes or so . . ."

"Pick me up."


Shiloh was waiting on her steps when Cary pulled up. It was a hot day. She was wearing a navy blue eyelet dress and denim pedal pushers with metallic pink ballet flats.

She was thinking about her mother-in-law (her first mother-in-law? no, too soon), a suburban lady who worked as a school nurse.

She'd liked Shiloh just fine. She'd wanted Shiloh to stay. At Gus's first birthday, she'd sat next to Shiloh and said, *"Look at those beautiful children. They deserve two parents."*

Shiloh ran down the sidewalk before Cary could get out of the car. She got in the passenger seat—then gasped. (She sounded like Junie.)

Cary was wearing an all-white uniform. White pants. White short-sleeved shirt. White *belt*. There were ribbons on his chest and stripes on his shoulders.

"Look at you!" she said. "Are Fridays uniform days?"

"My mom likes to see me in uniform. I was going to change before dinner."

She poked his side. "I'll bet the nurses love you."

He smiled a little. "The nurses do love me."

She poked his thigh. She touched the insignia on his shoulder. Felt the gold embroidery. Ran her fingertips down the front of his shirt placket. The white fabric made his neck and arms look tan. "What is this uniform for?"

Cary had started driving. "Summer whites. For ceremonies. For visiting your mother."

"Are there winter whites, too?"

"There are winter blues, you've seen them."

"You're like an American Girl doll. You have your own wardrobe."

They were at a red light. Cary leaned over to kiss Shiloh's cheek. "I knew you'd make fun of me."

"This isn't making fun. This is sincere appreciation. I'm going to start requesting uniformed visits, too."

He smiled at her. Because she was implying future visits and a future. Because they were supposedly engaged.

They *were* engaged.

Sort of.

It had happened too quickly for Shiloh to process. Cary had said that he loved her—and she still hadn't quite swallowed it.

She still wasn't over the initial shock of seeing him again. Having him here. Touching him in small ways. If she thought about being engaged or being in love, Shiloh would start shaking her head.

She shook her head. She rubbed his thigh. "Is this polyester? I feel like the men and women of the military deserve better."

Cary caught her hand and squeezed it.


When they got out of the car, Cary produced a very impressive hat. White, with a black brim and a big gold anchor.

"You look like a cruise ship captain!"

"No, they look like me."

"Like Captain Stubing," she said.

"No."

The nurses and elderly people did in fact love Cary. If he ever felt bad about himself, he could just suit up and cruise a retirement home. He stood tall, with his hat in his hand. It took forever to get to his mom's room.

As soon as Cary knocked, Shiloh realized they hadn't gotten their stories straight. She'd been too dazzled by all that white polyester. What did his mom know . . . about Shiloh?

Cary's mom answered the door, standing behind a walker—and immediately let go of it to clap her hands. "Cary! You brought my guardian angel!"

Shiloh smiled. "Hi, Lois."

Cary leaned over to kiss his mom's cheek.

"You too, Shiloh," Lois said. "Come on."

Shiloh gave her a loose and gentle hug, careful of her oxygen tube and the walker. Lois looked much better than she had in the hospital. She was up and around. Her hair looked freshly colored. But she seemed frail compared to the day they all ran errands together. She'd lost more weight.

Lois patted Shiloh's back. "You are still so tall . . . Come on in and see my fancy apartment. I've got everything I need here."

Shiloh looked around. They were standing in a small living room with demure, neutral-colored furniture. Some of Lois's angel collection had made its way to the shelves and tables. There was a TV against one wall—Lois was watching a courtroom show. One side of the room was a kitchenette, with a half-sized fridge, a microwave and a freestanding counter.

"Sit down, Shiloh. I made some iced tea. And I have those cookies you brought me, Cary. Get Shiloh some iced tea and cookies."

Cary went to do what he was told. He set his hat on the couch. Shiloh sat down next to it.

"I have my own kitchen," Lois said, carefully easing herself down into a chair. "I make myself eggs sometimes, with the hot plate, but there's a dining room downstairs, so I've been getting lazy."

"That's not lazy," Shiloh said. "That's smart. This is a such a pretty room. I'm glad you brought your angels."

Lois looked at the coffee table. "Ha! This isn't even half of them. Angel—my Angel—says it's too much for the ladies to dust them all, so I had to pick my favorites. Did you know someone cleans for me? It's like I'm on vacation. I'm going to miss all this when I go home."

"I'm so glad you found this place," Shiloh said. "It seems like a really great fit."

"Oh, you know, Cary found it."

Cary was coming back into the living room with two glasses of iced tea.

"There he is," Lois said. "Isn't he handsome? That's my baby boy. Get Shiloh some cookies, Cary."

"I can't find them." He picked up the remote and turned down the TV.

"They're in the fridge. So the chocolate doesn't melt."

He went for the cookies.

His mom raised her voice. "Did Eliza at the front desk see your uniform?"

"I think so."

"We have to say hi to her before you go. Her son is in the Army." Lois looked at Shiloh. "Their uniforms aren't as nice."

Cary was back with a package of cookies and another glass of iced tea for himself. He stopped to open the blinds. Shiloh hadn't even realized how dim it was in here.

"That sun is going to heat up my rooms," his mom complained.

Cary sat next to Shiloh on the couch. "You have air-conditioning."

"I don't like to use it."

Cary frowned. "Please use it." He got up to check the thermostat.

"Sit *down,*" his mom said. "This is how he is, Shiloh."

"I know," Shiloh said. "He did my dishes last night."

Lois clucked her tongue.

"How does your hip feel?" Shiloh asked. Cary sat down next to her again.

"Oh, it's good, it's better," Lois said. "I go to rehab right here. Did you see Kathy down there, Cary?"

"I'm not sure."

"She's very pretty. Blond. She's a physical therapist. I told her about you."

"Mom."

"Shiloh, tell him," Lois said. "It's not good to be alone."

Shiloh turned to Cary. "It's not good to be alone."

Cary narrowed his eyes.

"You should be giving me grandchildren," Lois said.

"You have plenty of grandchildren," he said.

"None as sweet as you were, Cary."


They ate Lois's sugar-free cookies and drank iced tea. Lois kept thinking of things for Cary to do, and then she kept telling him to sit down.

They watched an episode of *Judge Judy.*

Then Lois wanted to take Cary downstairs to meet her friends. Cary made an excuse for Shiloh, so she could stay in the room if she wanted. She did. She watched another episode of *Judge Judy.*

When Cary and his mom came back, Lois looked wiped out. He helped her to her chair. "I think I'll just make myself some dinner tonight," she said.

"I'll go get you something and bring it back," Cary said.

"No. I'll be fine."

"If you don't eat it, you can have it tomorrow." He was already headed for the door.

"Cary—"

He was gone.

Lois sighed. She sat back. Her blouse was caught up in the arm of the chair. She struggled with it for a second. Shiloh leaned over to help.

"Thank you, Shiloh. You're a sweetheart."

"Did you see your friends down there?"

"Oh, yeah. I made sure they all met Cary. I've been telling them all about him. Isn't he handsome in his uniform?"

"He is," Shiloh said.

"He looks like his father."

Shiloh did the genetic math for a second and decided that was possible. "I'm impressed by how many friends you've made. I'd probably just hide in my room."

"There are some good old girls here. I'm going to miss them." Lois frowned.

"Do you want your iced tea?"

"I do want it, thank you."

Shiloh handed her the tea.

"Cary says I could stay here," Lois said. "But he says I'd have to sell my house to pay for it."

"Mmm," Shiloh said, listening.

"But what if I needed to go home? And what if . . . well, you never know when someone is going to need a place to stay."

Shiloh nodded.

"*You* know how it is," Lois said. "You live with your mother. Family takes care of each other."

"I think Cary wants to take care of *you*," Shiloh said, hoping she wasn't speaking out of turn.

"He's a good boy."

"He's a good man. You should be proud of yourself to have raised a son like that. And you should tell me your secret—my son is a *pill*."

Lois laughed. "No. He's a sweet boy. Shiloh, will you close these curtains?"

Shiloh got up.

"Do you think it's true," Lois asked, "that if I sold my house, I could stay here?"

"I don't know," Shiloh said, shuttering the blinds. "But I trust Cary."

Cary's hat came back on for the short walk to the car.

"Sorry," he said. "That was a long visit."

"It was a solid visit," Shiloh said. "I hate when people visit elderly people and are on their way out the whole time. That's how we always were with my great-grandmother. And Ryan's grandpa."

They got in the car. Cary dropped his cap in the back seat. "Is it okay if I change before we go out?"

"Is it against the rules for you to be out in your uniform?"

"No. It just draws attention."

"All the swooning gets on your nerves?"

He just raised his eyebrows for a second like, *Something like that.*

"We could get takeout," Shiloh said. "There's nobody at my house to salute you."

They stopped at a steakhouse on the other side of the park. Every meal came with mashed potatoes and a small salad with creamy Italian dressing, all packaged in Styrofoam containers.

When they got to her house, Shiloh moved the food to real plates, which Cary said was silly if she hated doing dishes so much. She told him to sit down—she sounded like his mother. Shiloh put his plate in the toaster oven and found a couple Fiestaware candleholders for the table. She got out the Zippo lighter he'd sent her to light the candles. That made Cary laugh.

When Shiloh brought out his chicken Parmesan, she frowned at his white shirt. "Why'd you order red sauce?"

"I'll be okay."

"Let me get you a bib."

"I don't need a *bib*."

"At least take off your fancy shirt."

He took off his uniform shirt and hung it over one of the empty chairs. He was wearing a V-neck undershirt. She gave him a big cloth dish towel to tie around his neck, but he put it in his lap.

When Shiloh went to get her own plate, she took the engagement ring off her necklace and slid it onto her finger.

Cary noticed right away. He raised an eyebrow and smiled at her.

"Your mom thinks she's moving home," she said.

"Yeah"—he picked up his salad bowl—"but she also doesn't want to leave her new apartment. I'm making progress with her. And I think I'm getting through to Angel. I sat her down and showed her the bank statements. The truth is, my mom can't keep that house if I stop helping with the mortgage. And I'm not going to subsidize a bad and unsafe situation."

"You're paying for the nursing home *and* helping with the mortgage?"

He'd taken a bite. He covered his mouth. "At the moment."

"Does Angel have a place to go?"

Cary swallowed. He was making a stern face. "I can't let that be my problem. I can't let *all* of them be my problem. It never ends, and nothing changes."

Shiloh touched his forearm. "I'm sorry. I don't know the whole story."

"It's okay. I mean, I'm willing to tell you the whole story—it's just a messed-up story." He took another bite. "You already know I'm white trash."

"Cary." She touched his arm again and squeezed it. "I grew up a few blocks away from you, and I still live here. With my *mother*. 'Ich bin ein Berliner,' as they say."

"It's not the same, and you know it."

She shook her head. "I don't think of you that way. I never have."

"Your mom does."

"That would be the pot calling the kettle trash. Also"—Shiloh poked his shoulder—"my mom likes you. She's been trying to get me to hook up with you since I was sixteen. If I tell her we're engaged, she's going to dump Gatorade over my head."

"'If,' huh?"

Shiloh felt her face get serious. "When."

Cary looked down at his food again. His cheeks and neck were flushed.

"Can I take a photo of you?" she asked.

"Now?"

"Just like this."

"I'll put my shirt back on."

"No. Unless you're breaking some Navy rule." Shiloh was already up. Her camera was in the living room. She checked that there was film, then stood by her chair. "Go back to eating."

"No."

"Just hold your fork. Look natural."

He picked up his fork. He lowered his eyebrows.

"You look really handsome," she said. "You look vivid."

He smiled a little, and she took a photo.

"Take one of us together," he said.

"How?"

"Sit in my lap."

"I'm too tall to sit in your lap."

"No you're not."

She walked over to him, and he pulled her down with his arms around her waist.

Shiloh sat on his lap and tilted her head against his, holding out the camera facing them. She took photos with the kids like this sometimes; she thought of it as a single-parent skill. "I'm going to take a lot because these probably won't turn out."

She did.

When Shiloh stood up, Cary's hands trailed after her. She sat back down in her chair, but she scooted closer to him.

"I think my mom thinks you're still married," he said. "Otherwise she'd have her eye on you."

"Oh, I'm sure she'd rather you marry someone who didn't already have kids."

"That would be hypocritical of her."

"Mothers are inherently hypocritical. 'Do as I say,' every one of us." Shiloh took a bite of her chicken-fried chicken and smiled at him. "I still can't believe how lucky I am to have caught you in costume. Can I try on your hat?"

Cary looked amused. "Why do girls always want to try on the cap?"

"What girls?"

"Girls in bars. They think it's sexy."

"*Is* it?" she asked.

His cheek dimpled. "Sometimes."

"Girls in *bars* . . ." Shiloh said, looking down at her salad and picking up a fork. "Never mind. I am never trying on your hat."

"It's called a cap. Or a cover."

"Hmm," she said, still thinking about Cary in a bar, looking like Tom Cruise in *Top Gun*.

Cary nudged her knee with his. "Why don't you ever say anything bad about the Navy?"

She looked up from the table. "What?"

"You haven't said *anything* negative. No passive-aggressive comments. No bald criticism."

"Why would I do that? That'd be very disrespectful."

Cary shot her a look. "Since when do you care about being disrespectful?"

"I don't know," Shiloh said sincerely. "But it must have kicked in at some point . . ."

"You don't have to be respectful with me."

"Cary, you're one of the only people in the world I actually *do* respect."

"Shiloh." He leaned over his chicken Parmesan. She pulled the plate away from his chest. "I *know* you hate that I'm in the Navy. You've always hated it. You want to fund the schools and make the military throw a bake sale."

"Are you quoting a bumper sticker that I had on my math book in eleventh grade?"

He nodded deeply. "Yes."

"Well . . ." She shrugged, then held up her fork. "*One,* I was an asshole in eleventh grade. Ask literally anyone.

"*Two . . .*" She shook her head. "Two is still that I was an asshole. I hadn't given any serious thought to geopolitical realities. I was just talking big—and taking the stance that matched my outfits."

Cary was listening intently. There was a line between his eyebrows.

Shiloh set down her fork. "I don't know . . . The military seemed like an awful life to me. I couldn't understand why anyone would opt into it—why *you* would opt in, when you were so smart and gentle and could do other things. I didn't want you to die in Kuwait."

"Very few Americans died in Kuwait," he said.

She rolled her eyes. "Well, I don't want you to die in Iraq or Afghanistan, either. Or really, anywhere, for any reason, other than extreme old age. So I guess that's a feeling I share with my seventeen-year-old self—fear."

Shiloh could hear her voice getting higher. "I don't like that you're in the Navy because it's *dangerous.* And because it means— Well, I don't know what it means for us, actually, because we haven't discussed it. But I know I only have fifteen more days with you before you leave again. So I hate that."

Cary's right hand was on the table. Shiloh took hold of it with her left, the one with the ring. "But I don't *hate* that you're in the Navy, Cary. I can't. It's so clearly who you are now. It's ingrained—it's practically embroidered. And I respect *you*. I'm grateful for you, I thank you for your service."

Cary's face crinkled. It was an almost laugh. "That's a first."

"Let me be sincere," she said.

His smile faded. "Sorry." He turned his palm up, so he could hold her hand. "So . . . you don't have moral and ethical objections?"

Shiloh blew air into her lips. Her head fell back on her chair. "I feel like I'm disappointing you . . . I hope you weren't in love with my teenage principles. They weren't exactly thought through."

She lifted her head and sighed. "I think I'd have to do a lot of reading to know whether I have ethical objections to the military beyond garden-variety feelings about torture and bombing civilians. I mean"— she raised her shoulders—"I feel really strongly that we should close Guantánamo. Is that something?"

Cary laughed.

Shiloh frowned. "I *do* morally object to you laughing about Guantánamo . . ."

"That's not why I'm laughing. I'm just surprised. With you."

"I haven't changed completely, Cary—I'm not, like, pro-war now."

"No one in the military is pro-war."

"I don't actually believe you," she said, "but okay."

Cary was still smiling, listening.

Shiloh bit down on her lips for a second. She hummed. "I'm worried that you think I'm still the way I was in high school." She shook her head a few times. "I used to be so *certain,* about everything. I felt like I could sort the whole world into good and bad, right and wrong. Now I'm . . ." She pulled his hand closer to her. "I'm never sure about *any-thing*. Everything is complicated. Everyone is flawed. Most things are a compromise."

She squeezed his hand. "Do you *want* me to be more vehement about things? Did you love that about me?"

"I love *you*," he said.

Was that the second time he'd said it, or the third? She shook her head again.

"Shiloh, I love you."

She looked into his eyes until she couldn't, then she looked down at her plate.

Cary stroked her hand with his thumb. "I'd be concerned if none of your opinions had changed since high school. And I'm relieved to hear that you don't hate the very *idea* of the Navy—"

"What I hate is the idea of being a Navy wife!" Shiloh blurted out. She let go of his hand to wave her own hand around. "I've been on the Internet, and there are blogs and support groups. It's a whole vibe, Cary, and I don't think I can do it!"

He laughed out loud. "You don't have to join a group."

"These women . . ." She covered her face with one hand. "They're very pretty and very devoted. They say things like 'my sailor.' They make T-shirts."

"Shiloh, you don't have to do any of that. Those are just . . . the same people who would blog and make T-shirts no matter where they were in life."

"You don't know. You're not on the blogs."

"I've met plenty of Navy wives and husbands. You don't have to do anything special."

Shiloh sighed.

He took her hand again. "Have you been googling your concerns?"

"I've done some googling over the last six months," she said, a little defensive. "The Navy wives have a lot to say about care packages."

Cary tugged on her arm. "Let's talk about this," he said, suddenly urgent. He lowered his eyebrows. "Brass tacks. Are you ready for that?"

Shiloh groaned. "I don't know . . . it's a lot to take in."

"I know, but—"

"I know, I know." She pulled her hand away. "You've got fifteen days to fix your whole life." Shiloh started eating again. Very purposefully.

"Talk to me, Cary. What's your plan? I love a marriage proposal that starts out *'I can't give you the life you deserve'*—so let's hear your pitch."

Cary took a bite, too. "Okay," he said, chewing for a few seconds. "I've been in the Navy for fifteen years. I can retire at twenty."

"Like, actually retire?"

"Yes."

"At thirty-eight?"

"Thirty-nine," he said, "but yeah."

"But they won't let you out before then?"

"They will, but I get military benefits at twenty years of service. That's almost half my salary, plus healthcare. Even if I get another job."

"Holy shit—that seems smart, Cary. You should definitely do that."

"But it means I go where the Navy sends me for the next five years."

Shiloh frowned. "Yeah."

"I'm in San Diego for another year or so. And then I'll get new orders—a new assignment. I'm guessing you can't move away from your ex . . ."

Shiloh shook her head.

"That's okay, that's good."

"That's good?"

Cary cocked his head. "Well, for the kids, right?"

"Yeah," she agreed.

"Okay, well . . ." He was sitting very straight. His chin was perfectly level. "That means a year of long distance, at the minimum. But you can come see me in San Diego, maybe one weekend a month? Sometimes two? When you're not on duty? I'm burning through my leave right now, but I could come back some weekends, here and there." He was being very businesslike. Like he'd worked up a spreadsheet. "And I can talk on the phone. Have you heard of Skype? We could Skype."

Shiloh nodded. "We could Skype."

Cary bolted down another bite. "And then, I can list preferences for my next duty station—that just means where they put me. And there are jobs here, at STRATCOM."

"In Bellevue?" There was a military base in the Omaha suburbs, fifteen minutes away. "Isn't that an Air Force base?"

"It's Strategic Command. It's a little bit of everybody. And people aren't tripping over each other to get stationed in Omaha—there's a good chance I'd get my request."

"There's a chance you'd be *here*?" Shiloh was crying all of a sudden.

"Hey . . ." Cary said gently. "Come here."

He pulled her back onto his lap. Shiloh sat sideways, it was still awkward.

She put her hands on his cheeks. "I didn't know that was possible."

"Well, we haven't talked about it."

"We haven't talked about *anything*, Cary! You proposed to me before we even went on a date! This is *crazy*!"

"I know, I'm sorry. I just want to be with you." He kissed her. "I'm tired of not being with you, Shiloh." He kissed her again. "I'm exhausted. I need to turn my sail into the wind." He kissed her until she pulled away.

"So you might live *here*?" she asked.

"Yeah. Maybe."

"With me?" Her voice broke.

"With you. I'll try."

Cary wiped her eyes with his thumb. His hands smelled like marinara.

"Well, that would be great," Shiloh said.

He laughed. "I agree. But . . . worst-case scenario, five years of weekends. Thirty days of leave a year. Maybe another six-to-nine-month deployment at sea. I mean"—he kissed her quickly—"*worst*-case scenario, if it's just not working, I leave the Navy."

"That would be dumb, right?"

He shrugged. "Well, yeah, but . . . we'll just take it as it comes. That's what I'm proposing."

"And in five years?"

"I move home. Not here. I gotta be honest, I don't even want *you* to live here. This neighborhood depresses the crap out of me."

"Are you putting my house on the market, too?"

"Oh, I've got ideas . . ."

"And you say I'm manipulative."

"We can live wherever you want," Cary said. "For the rest of our lives."

Shiloh ran both hands through his hair. "And you'll grow your hair out and let me braid it."

"No."

"Maybe," Shiloh said. "You're gonna owe me *big*."

"What do you think of my plan?" he asked in a soft voice.

She touched his ears, his cheeks, his eyebrows. "I still don't know what it's like to be with you," she whispered. "And I don't know how I'm going to find out."

"I'm sorry."

"And I think . . . if we're going to be married and living apart, you're going to have to start letting me in on your plans *sooner*."

He pressed his forehead into her chin. "You're right, I'm sorry."

Shiloh laid her cheek on top of his head. "But it's a good plan, Cary."

He looked up at her, dislodging her head. "Yeah?"

She nodded.

Cary shot his hand out to grab his cap and dropped it on top of Shiloh's head.

She shrieked and tried too late to cover her head, knocking the cap askew. "I'm not one of your girls!"

Cary hugged her. "Yeah, you are. You're my number one."

## SIXTY-SEVEN

"YOUR HAIR DOESN'T SMELL LIKE apples anymore . . ."

Shiloh's voice was muffled. Her face was pressed into the top of his head.

She'd knocked his cap onto the floor somewhere—Cary left it there. He finally had Shiloh back in his lap, and he wasn't letting her go this time. He needed both arms to hold her.

"It only smelled like apples," he said, "because the cheapest shampoo at Hinky Dinky was White Rain green apple."

Shiloh sighed. "It was so nice."

Cary ran one hand up her thigh, under her dress. She was wearing jeans. "It isn't nice now?"

She kissed the top of his head. "It's still pretty nice, Cary."

The way she was sitting put his face in her sternum. He could feel his dog tag under his cheek, under the lacy cotton dress she was wearing. Cary wished he had a free hand to unbutton it. He nosed between the buttons. He held her with an arm under her thigh and a firm hand under her bottom.

He felt ravenous. She *made* him ravenous. Hungry on top of hungry. It was a struggle to be rational when they were this close, a struggle to make sense.

"You probably want me to get off your lap," Shiloh said.

Cary almost laughed.

He shook his head, swallowed, and tilted his face back to look at her. Shiloh was a whole head taller than him like this. She was out of reach. "Kiss me," he said.

Shiloh waited a second. Her eyes wandered over his face. What could she be measuring—how much he wanted it? Whether he deserved it?

She kissed him.

Cary stretched his chin up to meet her. He moved a hand from her waist to the back of her head and held her there.

Cary thought of himself as someone with a lot of self-control, even before the Navy—but he was fresh out. He was done. He *wanted* Shiloh. He didn't want to *wait* anymore. He pressed her mouth into his. He tried not to press his cock into her thigh.

Shiloh's hands were in his hair, like she was trying to find enough to hold on to.

He thought of all the days and nights they'd sat hip to hip in the front seat of his car with her elbow in his ribs and her hand moving like an anxious butterfly over his leg.

All the times she'd sat next to him in the darkroom, playing with his hair.

Shiloh in her dorm room, finally open to him.

Shiloh on the night of Mikey's wedding, with her hands on his neck. Leading him upstairs. Her unmade bed.

Cary felt like he'd spent his whole life trying to close his arms around her and never quite succeeding. Even now . . . he had her on his lap, she was wearing his ring, and he still didn't feel sure of the situation.

Was he *there*?

Were they both finally there? At the start of something?

Could he stop trying to have Shiloh—and just *have* her? Be with her. Plan around her. Know she was his, even from ten thousand miles away.

Cary wanted to feel settled. He wanted to feel locked down.

Shiloh was a light in the distance. She was an ache he'd been feeling since he was thirteen. An itch. She was a finger hooked into every torn seam, tugging—and Cary was made of torn seams. Just a poorly stitched human being. He'd only known how to want Shiloh, never how to have her.

Could he just—

Could he finally—

*Relax?*

Could he push Shiloh down and hold her wrists? Could he put rings on all her fingers? Could he write his name and social security number on her body everywhere they fit?

Could he have a life here? Be a husband and some kind of father? Could he make a home between Shiloh's legs and at her table, and on his knees if that's where she wanted him . . . Could he rest? Could he finally *rest*?

Shiloh held on to his face so she could pull her mouth away. "Do you want to go upstairs?" she whispered.

Cary almost laughed. He almost cried.

*"Yes."*

## SIXTY-EIGHT

HER BEDROOM WAS CLEANER THAN Cary was expecting, but it still smelled close, like she needed to open a window. Shiloh's room smelled like incense and laundry and health-food store perfume. She'd worn patchouli oil in high school—Cary hated it then. Now it was one of a hundred things making him hard.

He pushed her to her bed. Pushed her down. Climbed over her. Held himself up with his hands by her ears, kissing her head back into the sheet. (Did she *ever* make her bed?)

He fell onto his side next to her and unbuttoned her dress until he could see his dog tag. Such a dumb thing. Juvenile. He rubbed the skin beneath it, around it. Shiloh had perfect skin. He pulled the dress farther open. He kissed her clavicle.

Cary had always been making the best that he could with his body. He was built from spare parts, he knew that. He had moles and eczema. He'd gone eighteen years without eating a fresh vegetable and then spent too much time in the sun. He was physically what the Navy made of him.

Shiloh was something finer.

Tall. Broad. Hair so thick you couldn't see her scalp. Skin that didn't freckle or burn. Her nose was long and perfectly straight. Her eyelashes were so dark, she always looked like she hadn't quite washed off her stage makeup. The only thing wrong with Shiloh was her crooked bottom teeth, and Cary wanted to touch them. He wanted to kiss them. He wanted to stick his dick in her mouth and cut himself on them.

(He'd built walls around these feelings once—those were gone now. Disassembled, along with all the reasons he and Shiloh couldn't be together.)

He kissed her. He kissed her again. Her hands were on his neck.

"I got tested," Cary said.

Shiloh looked confused for a second.

"At my last checkup," he said. "Just to be sure."

"Oh." Her forehead smoothed out. "Okay. I've been tested a lot."

That was strange; he let it go. "I also have a condom."

She smiled. "In your wallet?"

"Yes," he said. "Like a douchebag. There are more in the car."

Shiloh laughed and touched his cheek. "You're very prepared."

"I've had six months to think about this."

"Is that all you needed to fix everything—six months at sea?"

He nodded. Literally, yes, that was true. He could make any decision with six months to focus. He kissed her again.

"We're good," she said.

He kissed her.

"You're good, Cary."

His eyes welled up, he wasn't sure why. He kissed her again. He didn't trust himself yet to shove his tongue against her teeth. He unbuttoned her dress to the waist, then got on his knees to take it off. To pull it up over her head. He went right for the fly of her jeans and pulled those off, too. Shiloh's legs were too good. He wanted to fuck them. Didn't know how to fuck them. Thought about spreading them wide right now and moving the crotch of her underwear aside, so he could push in.

He kissed her back onto the mattress, then sat up to pull her underwear off.

She was ten miles long.

The hair between her legs was dark.

She was every centerfold.

Cary used to tell himself that it was wrong to think this way about a friend. To use her in his imagination. She drove him crazy . . . Pressed against him in the car. Draped over his desk. Sitting between his thighs once on a roller coaster.

Did it make it better or worse, he used to wonder, that he loved her?

Cary was so hard, he was seeing stars. He was hallucinating. He was making too much of this. It was just sex. (He'd never believed that.)

He stood up. He'd almost forgotten he was in uniform. He wished it was one of the better ones—he should have worn his dress blues. He pulled off his T-shirt. Got rid of his white pants. Decided to lose the boxers, too. He didn't want to stand up again.

Shiloh had lifted up onto her elbows. Her hair was still in a ponytail. Her eyes were big and shiny. He put a knee on the bed and leaned over her, unfastening her bra. In a second, he was going to see his dog tag hanging between her perfect breasts. In two weeks, he was flying back to San Diego. How many months before he could marry her?

When they did this at nineteen, Cary had thought he'd never be able to stop, that he couldn't live without it. How had he managed to *live*?

"Shiloh," he said, pulling the bra away. Her breasts were heavier than he remembered. There were stretch marks across her stomach. Her bottom teeth were crooked, and he wanted a way to fuck them.

"Cary," she whispered. She touched his neck.

Cary pushed her back with his body. Moved half on top of her. A hand on her waist. His cock on her hip.

Shiloh touched his shoulder. His nose. She shivered. He tried to kiss her, but she turned her head. He kissed her neck instead. He ran his hand along her bare hip and groaned. She was so beautiful—he should find a way to tell her.

He pulled back to kiss her mouth. Shiloh turned her head the other way. He kissed the other side of her neck. She shivered with her shoulders and her head. Her hands settled on his neck again and squeezed.

Cary pushed against her, moving more on top of her. He tried to kiss her, but she ducked her head and kissed his throat. Her shoulders seemed stiff. Her hands were too tight on his neck.

"Hey," he said. "You okay?"

Shiloh nodded. Her face was still under his chin. Cary tried to put some air between them so he could see her, but she stuck to him, squeezing his neck.

He pulled one of her hands away. "Shiloh."

She wouldn't look up. She shook her head like she was still shivering. "It's fine."

"You don't seem fine."

"You know how I am—what'd you call it, spastic and relentless? I get anxious."

Cary twisted his upper body, so he could pry her other hand away from his neck. "You don't get anxious with *me*."

Shiloh was lying on her back. Head turned away from him. Her eyes were closed. "I get *less* anxious with you."

## SIXTY-NINE

SHILOH FELT CARY MOVE HIS cock away from her.

It was a really nice cock. (Not that she was any kind of expert.) Thick and slightly curved. She'd forgotten that until she saw it again.

Cary had moles all over his chest and a tattoo over his ribs—Shiloh never knew that Cary had a tattoo, and she still didn't know what it said. He'd been moving too fast. There was too much to process. This was all just *a lot,* in general. Sex. And kissing. And apparently they were getting married.

"You can keep going," she said. "I'll catch up."

Cary laughed—but it sounded frustrated. Shiloh decided not to open her eyes.

"Move over," he said. "Put your head on the pillow."

They were lying at an angle. Shiloh's feet were hanging off the bed. She scooted over. Got right. Cary pulled the sheet up over them. She felt his hand on her waist again, rolling her so that her body was facing him. She went along with it.

"Shiloh."

Her eyes were open, but she was still looking down.

*"Shiloh."*

She looked up. Her eyes caught Cary's for a second, then dropped to the middle of his nose.

"You okay?"

She nodded. "I just get overwhelmed."

"Okay."

"It's easier if you sort of ignore me . . ."

"I'm not going to ignore you."

"Just for a little while."

"No."

Shiloh pushed her forehead into his cheek. She felt like crying.

Cary brought his hand up to her back. He rubbed between her shoulder blades. He sighed. After a second, he said, "What do you need?"

"I don't know."

"What's spinning around your head?"

She closed her eyes. She clenched her teeth. Cary rubbed her back.

"I want to light you on fire," she said.

"Literally or metaphorically?"

"Literally, I think?"

"Why?"

"So I can remember you."

"Huh . . ." He didn't sound alarmed.

She tried again: "I don't know what to do with you when you get close."

"What do you *want* to do?"

Shiloh touched his cheek. She touched his chest—it was hairy, she shivered. She touched his side, where his tattoo was. She poked his belly. He flinched.

"Are you really going to move back here?" she asked.

"Look at me."

Shiloh tried to look at him.

Cary looked stern, he looked handsome. She was thinking about the lines on his cheeks and the tan line at his throat and the fact that he'd stopped to buy condoms, and one time a bottle of wine—and another time Pringles and Cherry Coke. Cary was never empty-handed.

"I'm going to try," he said. "I'm going to do everything I can to be with you."

She shivered.

"Are you cold?"

"No." Shiloh shook her head. She wasn't cold, she was weird. She was running 110 on a 220. "I guess we're just going to get married, then."

"Only if you want to."

"I want to," she whispered. She found his ear. "Cary, I want you."

His hand tightened on her waist. "I always want you, Shiloh."

"You said that before."

"Because it's true . . . *Look at me.*"

Shiloh tried to look at him.

He looked handsome. He looked concerned.

"I love you," he said. (Was that the third time?)

She shivered.

"What do you need?" he asked again.

Shiloh didn't know what she needed, and she only sort of knew what she wanted. She didn't want this to stop. She didn't want Cary to leave or back out or change his mind.

She touched his rib. "Can I poke you?"

Cary nodded his head. "Yes."

"Can I pinch you?"

"Yes." He didn't blink.

"Can I bite you?"

His cheeks pulsed. "Yes."

Shiloh pressed her face hard into his shoulder. Cary. This was Cary. He was naked. They were both naked, it was distracting—it was mortifying. She felt like screaming. She felt like knocking something over. She was happy, but too full. Happy in a way that scratched. She couldn't take this all at once. She needed to build up her tolerance. She needed a circling approach.

She bit the muscle on the side of his neck—just hard enough to be too hard. It made her bones vibrate. Cary took a breath in through his teeth.

Shiloh moved her mouth down and bit him again—her whole body shuddered, and Cary exhaled with his throat tight.

She moved her mouth over his shoulder and did it again. Harder. All of Shiloh's muscles clenched until she let go—it was just a few seconds. Then she arched her neck back and pinched her shoulder blades together. Shivering, shivering.

When she looked up at Cary, his face had gone slack. He shoved her onto her back and kissed her.

Shiloh held on to his shoulders. She felt like someone had skimmed off her top layer of static. She stayed inside of the kiss. She smiled. Cary noticed. He kissed the corner of her mouth. "There you are," he murmured.

She looked in his eyes. "There you are."

The good thing about having sex with Ryan was . . .

Well, there were a lot of good things about having sex with Ryan. (Just ask the Southwest High School theater department!)

But one of them was that he was selfish.

You could say, *"I need this to not be about me,"* and Ryan would listen. He was happy for it to be about him.

When Shiloh told him, *"I'll catch up,"* Ryan went ahead. And sometimes she caught up, and sometimes she didn't. Sometimes she just went to sleep.

When they first started having sex, her nerves were always in the way. She couldn't initiate. She could only come if she was a little drunk and Ryan was a lot patient. (And sometimes if she pretended it was happening to someone else?)

And then Shiloh was pregnant and breastfeeding, and she stopped *wanting* sex. She'd still have it. And she usually enjoyed it once they got rolling. But her desire felt buried under a heavy blanket of snow. (Her clitoris was a groundhog that would occasionally peek its head out, yawn, and decide to go back to bed.)

And *then* Shiloh found out that her husband had slept with a dozen women while they were together. Going all the way back to college! Two people in the cast of that summer play in the park—the ingenue! The stage manager!

What did that make Shiloh, apart from a fool? (Could a woman be cuckolded? She *had* been wearing a suit . . . )

A fool. A naïf. An incubator.

Neurotic. Barely orgasmic.

Wasted—the way a resource is wasted. Like a faucet left on. Or food that rots before it gets eaten. Something left out on the counter.

What good had Shiloh's body ever had to offer?

What good did she have left?

What was sex, anyway?

She'd told Cary once that it wasn't magic. But that had turned out not to be true. Sex was a magic Shiloh couldn't master.

And he would know some of this—she would have told him!—if he would have taken *five minutes* to talk to her about it before he proposed.

They should have had sex first, and then Cary could have decided. She would have given him an out.

She'd still give him an out.


There were teeth marks on Cary's shoulder, but Shiloh hadn't broken the skin. She rubbed them with her thumb.

Ryan had drawn the line at biting.

Where did Cary draw the line?

Shiloh still felt de-staticked. Simplified, like a fraction. Cary was kissing her with his serious face. His hard-charging mouth. Shiloh felt swept along by it. She wanted to be.

Cary pulled away. He kissed her cheek. "I promise I got better at this," he said.

"I don't think I did," she said, taking her chance to be honest.

"You don't have to do anything but feel good." Cary kissed her ear, then her neck. Then her shoulder. He squeezed her hip. "Tell me what you like."

"I don't want to," she said.

"Why not?"

"Because then you'll do it."

He kissed her shoulder again. "Right . . ."

"And that will be it. I'll never figure out what *else* I like."

He pulled back to look at her face.

"I think there are a lot of things I *might* like"—Shiloh was still trying to be honest—"that I don't even know about."

He nodded. His tongue was in his cheek. Thoughtful, not angry.

"I feel like I don't know *anything*," she said.

"Don't get wound up," he whispered.

She touched his chin. "We should probably do this a few times and then revisit your brass tacks. You don't know what you're getting into."

"Shiloh, can I ask you a question?"

"Yes."

Cary looked very solemn. Like he was bracing himself. "Are you attracted to men?"

"In general?"

"Yeah."

"No," she said.

He started to sit up.

"But I'm not attracted to women in general, either!"

Cary was up on one arm, looking down at her.

"There's just you, Cary."

"And Val Kilmer."

"Only theoretically."

He dropped to his elbow.

"Practically speaking," Shiloh said, "I can't think of anyone but you."

Cary put his hand around her jaw. He sighed, with his eyebrows together. "We're not revisiting brass tacks. Not on my account."

"I might be bad at sex . . ."

"I know for a fact that you're not."

"That was old me," she said, "virgin me."

"I reject this at a conceptual level."

"What concept?"

Cary frowned. His eyes tracked up her face and down again. "Can I kiss you while you do this?"

"Yes."

He kissed her neck again.

"What do you reject?" she asked.

"The idea that you're bad at sex—the idea that anyone can be fundamentally bad at sex, especially women."

Shiloh lifted her head up off the pillow. "*Especially* women?"

He put his arm around her waist again. "Especially women."

"That makes it sound like you don't think women have any sexual agency . . ."

"I just told you that your only job is to feel good."

"That's *breathtakingly* sexist, Cary."

He moved his hand to her ass. He hadn't stopped kissing her. "Do you *want* another job, Shiloh?"

"Why should *you* give me a job? Because you're a man?"

"Because I'm the person you're having sex with."

She petted his hair. It was just long enough on top for her to lose her fingers in it. "All right, that's a good reason. Go ahead."

"Your job is to tell me to stop," he said.

"When?"

"When you want me to stop." He pulled on the back of her thigh, so that her knee was up on his hip.

Shiloh took a deep breath. "Roger that."

"Your job is also to give me directions if I need them."

"How will I know when you need them?"

"You'll know." He sucked on her neck.

Shiloh squeezed her eyes closed. She scratched his scalp. "It sounds like my job is to talk to you while you do all the work."

He pressed his cock into her stomach. "This isn't work."

She took another deep breath. "Some of it is work. You'll see. Everything with me is work."

"I know what I'm getting into."

Shiloh opened her eyes, she took hold of his cheeks—she pushed his face away so she could really see him. "*Do* you, Cary?"

Cary's face was flushed. There was hardly any gold left in his eyes. "When have you ever been too much for me?"

Shiloh kissed him then. She held on to the back of his head. She was crying. She didn't even need to bite him again—she felt static-free.

Cary stopped holding her. He pushed his hand between their bodies and slid his fingers between her legs.

Shiloh was crazy wet. At least that wasn't going to be an issue.

She kept kissing him while he pushed his fingers inside of her. He moaned. That made her smile—it seemed so un-Cary of him.

He rolled onto her, spreading her legs.

"Cary?" she whispered.

"What is it, Shy?"

"Could my job be to feel nothing?"

Cary's mouth was open. His eyes were mostly closed. "Give me more details."

"Could my job just be to feel whatever I'm feeling?"

His hand was on the inside of her thigh. "Can we agree on 'good' as a general direction?"

"Yeah." She nodded. She grasped the side of his neck.

Cary touched her vagina again. She was open. She was really wet— she could hear it. He pushed his cock in.

Shiloh wrapped her arms around his shoulders.

"Good?" he asked.

She nodded. "It's good." She nodded some more. "It's good."

"It's so good, Shiloh."


Cary had gotten better at sex. Shiloh tried not to think about the particulars.

If she thought too much about the last fourteen years, she'd cry. She was already crying. She cried a lot during sex. Ryan never minded; he approved of public displays of emotion.

Cary kept her on her back. He kept leaning over her to kiss her cheeks and her forehead. He kept grinding his pubic bone against her clitoris. She kept nodding at him. It was almost enough. It was enough to make her reach for his face and tell him over and over that she loved him. He made her sloppy.

Cary finished inside of her, and she could tell because he closed his eyes tight and groaned. Because she could feel him pulsing. Because his head dropped like she'd snapped his neck.

He drew his hips away and fell to Shiloh's side, immediately pushing his right hand into the mess of her.

He looked groggy. She wanted to kiss him while he looked like that. She did. His mouth was warm and loose. He pushed his tongue past her lips and rubbed her teeth. He rubbed her clit. When she flinched, he rubbed her a different way. She was close—but close was relative.

"This could take forever," Shiloh whispered.

"I've got fifteen days," he said.

She laughed. She closed her eyes. "I love you so much, Cary."

"I love you, too, Shiloh."

"That's the fourth time you've said it."

"I've said it more than that."

"No, you haven't."

He kissed her neck. He shifted to get more comfortable. "I'll say it more."

"You should say everything more. I love your voice."

"Yeah?"

She nodded. She tilted her hips back.

"Is that good?" he asked.

Shiloh nodded. "You do such good accents."

He laughed. "Do you want me to do accents in bed?"

"No. I'm just saying . . . I was just thinking . . ." She stretched out her neck. "*That's nice.*"

"Like this?" He kept rubbing her.

"*Yes.*"

"I like your voice, too, Shiloh."

"Thank you."

"Are you going to call me when I go back?"

"Yes." She was breathing hard. "I'll call you. *Cary, that's good.*"

"I missed you so much—I love you."

"Cary, don't you like breasts?"

"What?" He lifted his head up, but he didn't miss a beat.

"You haven't touched my breasts at all."

"I don't trust myself yet," he said. "They're too good. Sometimes I don't trust myself to touch you."

Shiloh started to come. She stretched her neck long. She held on to the sheet.

Cary found her ear. "You're so good at this."

## SEVENTY

CARY WAS TRYING TO GET the window open. He'd put on his white boxers.

Shiloh had gone to the bathroom to get a drink of water. She climbed back into bed. She was wearing a T-shirt that said, *Let's put on a show!*

"Is this painted closed?" he asked.

"I don't know, I've never been able to get it open."

He grunted a few times, shoving at the windowpane. "This is a fire hazard."

"Just leave it," she said. "It's hot out."

"I'm trying to get some fresh air." He grunted again, and the window budged. "A-ha." He worked it farther open. "You need a new screen. Do you have a fan?"

"Maybe in the hall closet?"

Cary headed out the bedroom door.

"Cary!"

She heard him open the closet.

"What are you doing?" she called.

"Getting the fan!" he called back. "This closet is a Charlie Foxtrot, Shiloh!"

"Come back to bed!"

He came back with the fan. "You need to keep the kids away from this; it has metal blades."

"That's why it was in the closet."

He plugged in the fan and set it up in the window frame. It made a choppy helicopter sound. The air blew in from outside cool and sweet.

Cary came back to Shiloh's bed.

"That's nice," she admitted.

He lay on his back and pulled her against him. His forehead was lined. Shiloh tapped his head and mimed pulling something out of his ear.

"What's that?" he asked, frowning at her.

"It's a list. It says, '*Fix Shiloh's window, repair screen, buy new fan.*'" She blew the imaginary list out of her hand.

"I'm going to do all those things."

"You've got bigger fish to fry, my friend."

He held her close to him and closed his eyes, humming. "We should get married now."

"That's not even possible . . ."

He opened his eyes. "It's possible. And you'd get spousal benefits."

"I've already got health insurance."

He started to say something, but she covered his mouth. "*Cary.* You're getting your way. Be happy for a minute."

His eyes were focused on her. They softened.

She kept her hand on his mouth. "Mikey says we're too much alike. That we both have to be in control. Is that going to get us in trouble?"

Cary shook his head. After a second, he pulled her hand away. "We're just going to argue a lot."

She laughed. "And that's okay?"

"It's okay with me. Lie down."

"No." She sat up completely, remembering something. "I need to see your tattoo."

Cary groaned.

She lifted up his arm. The tattoo was over his ribs. Faded, but still clear. A small anchor and block letters, all in black:

*HONOR.*

*COURAGE.*

*COMMITMENT.*

"They're the Navy's core values." His forearm was lying on his forehead. His eyes were closed again.

Shiloh stroked the tattoo with her palm and then her thumb. It was

350 · RAINBOW ROWELL

smooth except for a small welt along the anchor. "I've never thought of you as a tattoo person."

"I was fresh out of boot camp and full of myself."

"Do you have more?"

"No. I regretted that one."

"Why?"

He shrugged. "It should be enough to live it."

Shiloh stroked his ribs. "Symbols are nice."

He opened his eyes. He reached into the neck of her T-shirt and pulled out the dog tag. "When did you put this on a chain?"

"Freshman year. After you left."

He tugged on it. He looked sad. Then embarrassed. "You don't have to, but will you keep wearing it?"

"I'll wear it until you come home again," she said. "I'll let you take it off."

Cary made a fist over the chain. He closed his eyes. "I don't know why I love that idea so much. It makes me feel like a teenager."

Shiloh leaned closer. She kissed him. "Feel like a teenager, Cary."


Shiloh heated up their dinners and brought them upstairs.

"You're getting gravy on your sheets," Cary said.

"You think I wasn't going to have to change the sheets before just now?"

When they were done eating, she stacked their dishes under the bedside table.

Cary wanted her to sleep without her shirt. He wanted to hold her.

Shiloh wanted to touch his tattoo with her tongue to see if she could feel the lines. "Did the Navy come up with their core values after they met you?"

"Shiloh"—Cary's voice was serious—"Mikey told me something, and it's been bothering me . . ."

She was licking him. "What?"

"Did you really vote for Ralph Nader?"

She buried her face under his arm. "Why did he tell you that?"

"What were you *thinking*?"

"It made sense at the time! I'm sorry, okay?" Shiloh poked Cary's belly. "Did you vote for W?"

He brought his arms down around her. He was laughing. "No. I voted for Al Gore. Like a sane person."

## SEVENTY-ONE

CARY WAS USED TO GETTING up early and used to drinking coffee.

Shiloh's coffeemaker was fairly simple. He stood over it, rubbing his eyes. He was wearing his uniform pants again, and his undershirt. He needed two showers.

He heard Shiloh in the living room.

"I'm making coffee," he said.

"Thanks."

He looked up. Shiloh's mom was standing in the kitchen doorway, wearing a bathrobe.

"Good morning, Gloria."

She was smiling. Her eyes were laughing. "Good morning, Cary."

Cary watched the coffee brew. His ears and neck burned.

He poured Gloria the first cup.

## SEVENTY-TWO

SHILOH SENT AN EMAIL TO her divorce attorney, and on Monday morning, she got an email back:

*"Ryan doesn't want to amend the overnight agreement."*

*"Why not?"* Shiloh replied.

*"He doesn't have to say why not. You can try to talk to him. But as it stands, no overnight guests unless you're engaged. (I think this was something you wanted originally, Shiloh.)"*

Shiloh wanted to wear her diamond ring, but she really *didn't* want to have to explain the ring to Junie. She would explain it all—in stages— after Cary left, and in the meantime, she hoped, they could continue enjoying Junie's customary enthusiasm and goodwill.

Cary wanted to wait to tell his mom about their engagement until after he'd sold her house. He didn't want his sisters to know and make things complicated. Shiloh wondered if his sisters would be invited to the wedding. She wondered if she and Cary would even have a wedding. There hadn't been a good time to talk about it yet.

He'd taken her metal fan with him when he left Saturday morning. (It took him fifteen minutes to get her bedroom window closed.) He came back that night with a plastic fan and a few changes of clothes, which were still folded in a neat stack on top of Shiloh's dresser.

The kids were home Monday night, and Cary came over for dinner. After Shiloh put the kids to bed, she sat on the porch with him and made out for two hours. Shiloh got nine mosquito bites. Cary got a bruise in the shape of her teeth. (It wasn't even sexual when she did it. She just wanted to bite him.)

"What the actual fuck is going on with you and Cary?" her mom asked Shiloh as soon as she had the chance. It was Tuesday morning, in the kitchen, while the kids were in the next room eating scrambled eggs.

"I don't know," Shiloh whispered. "I don't *know* the actual fuck." She was washing a few dishes.

Her mom leaned on the counter next to the sink with her arms folded. "Are you sleeping with him *platonically*?"

"No." Shiloh pulled the ring out of her neckline and grimaced. "*No.*"

Her mom's eyes got huge. She took hold of the ring and bent close. "Holy shit."

"I *know*." Shiloh shrugged her hands. "I don't know. It was sudden." She was getting dishwater all over the front of her dress.

"I wouldn't call it *sudden* . . ." her mom said. She was still squinting at the ring. "How's this gonna work?"

"Not easily. I don't want the kids to know yet. Or Ryan."

Her mom nodded. "It's a pretty ring."

"Yeah . . ."

She let go of the ring and looked up at Shiloh. "Are you happy about this?"

Shiloh nodded again. She put her own hand over the ring. "In the moments when it feels real, I'm really happy."

Her mom smiled a little. "It won't be easy with anyone—it may as well be 'not easy' with someone you love."

"I love Cary."

"You always have, Shiloh."

Shiloh finally told Tom.

He responded by standing up and putting one foot on his office chair and one hand over his heart, and singing the chorus from "Carrie" by Europe.

"*Caaa-arr-rie, Caaa-arr-rie, things they change, my friend.*"

# before

SENIOR YEAR, WHENEVER SHILOH GOT bored, she'd look up at Cary across the journalism room, or across the courtyard when he was meeting her after school, or across the front seat of his car—and sing "Carrie" by Europe. Cary *hated* that song, and he hated it when Shiloh made pointless scenes. Shiloh didn't have a great voice, but she was loud. "'*Caaa-arr-rie! Caaa-arr-rie!*'"

Cary would roll his eyes. Sometimes he'd shout, "Enough!"

Shiloh loved embarrassing him. It was *never* enough.

One time, in journalism, Cary got fed up and jumped out of his chair, pointing at her. "'*Young child with dreams—*'"

Shiloh shrieked with delight.

Cary kept singing. It was "Shilo" by Neil Diamond—Shiloh was named after this song. Cary knew all the words.

He backed her into a corner, against the paste-up desk. "'*Held my hand out, and I let her take me—*'"

"This isn't working," she said. "It doesn't bother me—I love it."

Cary kept singing. His eyebrows were low. He did a great Neil Diamond.

Shiloh squealed—she really was embarrassed, no matter what she said. She was embarrassed, she was ecstatic. "Okay, stop! Stop! I love it too much!"

"'*Shilo, when I was young—*'"

## SEVENTY-FOUR

HE'D WANTED HIS FAMILY TO get here on their own—to see that this was the best way forward for Mom.

But they were all too self-involved and living too close to the edge. Desperate people weren't generous. Or considerate.

Angel was the most reasonable of them, even though she had the most to lose. She was living in Cary's mom's house with her three kids—the youngest was a little older than Gus, the oldest was probably eight.

Angel was still with the kids' dad, but he only seemed to surface once in a while. Cary was half concerned that he was going to surface with a gun. Jackie's husband had already threatened to kick Cary's ass. *"You can try,"* Cary had shouted at him, *"but that won't pay the mortgage!"* (They'd been standing in their own front yard; Cary wasn't breaking his promise to Gloria.)

*Nothing* was going to pay the mortgage.

Cary's mom couldn't afford it without his help. That had become clear as soon as she gave him access to her bank account. She could lose the house to the bank or she could sell it.

That was it. That was the final word.

Cary was getting the house ready to sell.

Today he was packing up his mom's clothes. She already had all the clothes that fit her and that she liked the best at her new apartment, but he'd promised to let her sort through the rest of them.

Jackie had taken the dogs—after Cary had threatened to call the Humane Society. Cary was the mean old man. He was the landlord. He was the hard line.

It was hot in his mom's bedroom. Even with the window unit.

There was a dumpster in the driveway, and Cary had spent the week throwing out everything he found in the house that was still in a plastic thrift shop bag or a box.

*"Some of that stuff is worth something!"* Angel had stood on the porch and yelled at him. *"She has an eye for antiques!"*

*"Angel, it all smells like dogs and cigarettes."*

*"Not the ceramics!"*

Jackie and Don had eventually shown up, pissed off and probably drunk, and climbed into the dumpster to save things. Cary let them.

None of his own stuff was in the house. Not in a way he could find. His room in the basement had flooded a few years ago. Fortunately he'd taken his ROTC medals and his yearbooks with him when he got his first apartment. His saber was long gone. One of his stepbrothers had probably killed someone with it.

Cary had promised his mom that he'd set aside the family photos and all of her jewelry—the plastic necklaces and glass earrings.

She wanted her crocheted afghans and her coffee cups. And a drawer full of things that had belonged to Cary's dad—an engraved spike that he got when he retired from the railroad. A Zippo lighter. A cuff link.

Angel had a pile of things in her bedroom that she wanted to take for herself and another pile for Cary's mom. She kept calling his mom to see if she wanted something that Cary was about to throw away. His mom always said yes.

Angel's kids sat in the living room watching TV while Cary emptied the house. (While their mom squirreled things away. While their grandmother crawled around a dumpster, and their great-grandmother watched *Judge Judy*, five miles away with the shades drawn.)

Cary sat down on his mom's bed and held his head. He was exhausted. He was filthy. He had seven days of leave left, and even if he got this house cleaned out, he wasn't sure how he was going to manage putting it on the market.

His mom's mattress was shot. He could feel the springs. He should carry it right out to the dumpster—he was going to.

He didn't bother stripping the bed. He shoved the mattress off the frame. Maneuvered it up. Out the bedroom door. It was too big for Cary to lift by himself. He had to push and drag it. It got stuck on the staircase. He was going to have to force it. He squeezed between the mattress and the wall, trying to feel where it was caught.

"Cary?" Angel called out. "Someone's here for you."

"Who is it?"

"It's me!" Shiloh shouted.

Cary ducked, as much as he could, to see down the stairwell. Shiloh was standing there, holding Gus. She had Junie, too. He was supposed to meet them for dinner later. What time *was* it?

"Hi," Shiloh said.

"Hi."

"Do you need some help?"

"No."

Shiloh pointed. "I think it's stuck on this overhang. Are the dogs around?"

"The dogs are gone."

She set Gus down and pushed the mattress at an angle away from one wall, so it would come free.

"Step back," Cary said.

She did.

He pushed the mattress forward.

Shiloh leaned in when it got stuck again. She lifted up the lower end. "Where is this going?"

"Straight out the door."

"I'll open the door," Junie said.

"Juniper," Cary said sternly. "Stay back."

Her eyes got big and she scurried back.

"Set it down," Cary told Shiloh, dropping his end. "I'll go backwards."

They traded places. She squeezed his arm on her way past him. Cary opened the door, and they carried the mattress out through the yard and tipped it up into the dumpster.

"Thank you," he said.

He really looked at her. She was wearing a bright green summer dress and pedal pushers. She looked fresh. She looked happy to see him.

Cary brushed his hands on his pants. "Did I miss dinner?"

"No. I just missed *you*." Shiloh was already walking toward the house. "I wanted to say hi." She glanced back at him. "Is that okay?"

He followed her. "Yeah. Of course."

When they walked into the living room, Junie and Gus were standing by the couch, watching Angel's kids watch TV. Junie looked up at Cary and then looked down.

Cary touched her shoulder. "I'm sorry I used a sharp voice."

She looked back up at him. "Cary, do you want to get ice cream? We're going to get ice cream. Because it's a beautiful Saturday afternoon."

"I don't know. I think I still have work to do."

Shiloh was standing beside him. Angel was folding clothes on the couch.

"Angel, do you remember my friend Shiloh? And this is Juniper and Gus." He held his hand out to Angel. "This is my niece, Angel. And her kids—Bailey, Renny and Rex."

"I remember you," Angel said, eyeing Shiloh. "From the hospital."

"I babysat you once," Shiloh said. "Do you remember that?"

Angel nodded.

"You still have incredible blond hair," Shiloh said.

"Thanks."

Cary turned to Shiloh. "Where are you going to get ice cream?"

"We were gonna walk up to Kone Korner."

He looked at Angel. "Do you want me to take the kids?"

She seemed tense. Cary shouldn't have put her on the spot like that. It was hard to say no in front of them.

"Or you could come," he said.

Angel still didn't smile. "You can take them." She looked at the kids. All three of them were staring at her. Three pairs of yellow-brown eyes.

They scrambled up. "Bailey, you hold Rex's hand crossing Thirtieth Street."

"We'll walk down to cross at the light," Shiloh said.

He'd never once seen Shiloh walk down to the light.

"Go get your shoes," Angel said to the kids.

It was about eight or nine blocks to Kone Korner. Cary ended up carrying Rex across the street. He was a jumpy kid. He made Cary nervous.

Even though Cary and Shiloh had never walked down to the crosswalk before, he still got walloped with déjà vu crossing Thirtieth Street.

How many times had they run across this street together? Too many times to remember in any detail. So many times that the memories were like a wall slamming into him.

He bought all the kids ice cream cones. He let them all get dip. Cary was paying for everything lately. He'd never been a single man with a Navy salary—he'd always had dependents. There was always something. Always someone.

He couldn't touch Shiloh just now the way he wanted to. But she leaned against him while they were waiting for their cones. "Sorry I took you off task," she said.

"I'd probably still be stuck in that stairwell—Angel never would have rescued me."

Cary wanted to start walking back to the house right away, but Shiloh said the kids would drop their ice cream, and she was probably right.

The kids took up all the spaces at the single picnic table in the parking lot. Shiloh and Cary stood behind them, watching each other. She was eating a cherry-dipped cone. He wanted to propose to her again. He wanted to walk straight downtown and sleep on the courthouse steps and marry her at eight o'clock Monday morning.

They finished their ice cream and walked past Shiloh's house first. Cary promised he'd be over later for dinner. Then he walked back to his house with Angel's kids. He carried Rex on his back—Cary didn't trust him not to run into traffic.

When they walked into the house, Angel took one look at Cary and stomped into the kitchen.

He let Rex down and followed her. Almost everything in the kitchen was already packed up or gone. "Are you upset that I took your kids to Kone Korner?"

Angel wheeled on him. She had her hands on her hips. She looked like her mom for a minute, even though they didn't resemble each other. "I'm not your *niece*, Cary!"

Cary flinched. He found himself turning toward the door, like his mom might hear, even though she hadn't been in the house for months. "What?"

"Don't you dare lie to me right now!"

"I'm not going to lie to you—I just . . ." He looked at the door again, then back at Angel. "I didn't know that you *knew* . . ."

"I'm not a *moron*!"

"*Okay.*" Cary had one hand on his hip. He rubbed his forehead. "Sorry. I don't know how to navigate this—it's not something anybody ever talks about."

"Maybe I *want* to talk about it! Maybe I'm tired of pretending!"

"All right." He held up his palms. "Angel, all right. You're not my niece, you're my— You're my sister."

Angel crossed her arms. Her chin was pointed up. "We look alike, and we don't look like anyone else."

"I know," Cary said. He knew.

"You're my only whole sibling," she said. Angel had half siblings. And stepsiblings.

"I know," he said.

"And Rex looks just like your baby pictures."

Cary rubbed his forehead some more. "I don't know why you sound so angry about this—I wasn't intentionally keeping it from you."

"Because you treat me like I'm nothing to you, Cary! And I'm actually trying to *help* you—we're the only sane people in this family!"

Cary nodded. He nodded too long. "I'm sorry," he said.

Angel had started to cry. He didn't know how to react to it. It wasn't like seeing his mom cry. Or Shiloh.

"I'm sorry," he said again.

She wiped her face on her sleeve. "I always looked up to you . . . but you don't see me at all."


Cary didn't need another sister.

He didn't need more family.

He was stretched so thin.

He sat at the kitchen table and talked to Angel. He listened, mostly. She wanted to tell him how she'd figured it out. (*"And then Grandma told me she had a hysterectomy when she was thirty-five . . ."*) She wanted to tell him about their dad—and their dad's kids. One of them apparently looked like Cary. Suddenly the world was full of people with his eyes.

Cary tried to stay focused on this one person, sitting in front of him.

For the first time, he asked Angel what her plan was, where she was going from here.

She said she was moving in with her mom and Don. She didn't have a choice. She was on a waiting list for housing assistance, but it would take a couple months. She could afford rent, but every place wanted a two-month deposit.

*I can't take this on,* Cary wanted to say to her. *I can't take you on. I can't be tied to this house and everyone who ever lived here, for the rest of my life. Siblings, aunts, cousins, neighbors, dogs, ex-husbands.*

But he listened.

And he couldn't deny that it was Angel who had convinced his mom to stay at the assisted living center . . . Angel who was moving the needle in ways that Cary couldn't. She *was* the only other halfway-sane person in the family. And she had three kids.

He kept thinking about Bailey, Renny and Rex.

And Junie and Gus.

Cary was stretched so thin, he felt like everyone could see through him.

He told Angel she could have his mom's car. And the TV. (He was always going to make sure that she got those.) And he told her that he'd pay her security deposit—she didn't have to pay him back. It was better if she didn't try. It was best that she didn't tell her mom about it.

Then he agreed to talk to Angel about his plans from now on. To strategize with her, regarding his mom. Her grandma. (Lois.)

"You really think Grandma doesn't know that you know?" Angel looked like she felt almost sorry for Cary. "I thought for sure that she'd told you a long time ago."

He shook his head. "I think she's been calling me her son for so long, she's started to believe it—she told me once that I was her easiest pregnancy."

That cracked Angel up. "Well, I guess that's true!"

Cary laughed, too. A little. He felt anxious. "I don't want to take anything from her. Especially now."

"I won't say anything to Grandma. I never have. I've never even asked my mom about you—I don't know whether Don knows . . ."

Cary nodded.

"My mom has your baby picture in her wallet," Angel said. Begrudgingly.

Cary didn't know what to say to that.

She went on—"I've never even seen a picture of myself from when I was a baby."

"You were cute," he offered. "You had tons of hair, and it was the color of cornsilk. You looked like Renny. Everywhere we went, people said you looked like a doll."

Angel smiled at him. Then she looked down. "I'm not going to make this an issue with Grandma," she said again. "But when it's just the two of us . . . Or the next time you're introducing me to a girlfriend . . ."

"There won't be a next time," Cary said. "There's only Shiloh. And she already knows you're my sister."

Angel looked up at him. She wiped her nose on the back of her wrist. "I thought you were going to lie to me. Or try to deny it."

"I won't lie to you," he said.

Shiloh had the kids that night, so Cary couldn't stay over.

He waited for her to put them to bed—then collapsed on her, pushing her back onto the couch.

She didn't ask him what was wrong. Just ran her fingers through his hair.

The next day was Sunday, and Shiloh came over to the house to help for a few hours. She left the kids with her mom. She brought Mikey.

Angel's boyfriend came over, too. He was a real creep—but he got all the dog shit out of the backyard by noon, so that was something.

## SEVENTY-FIVE

LOIS'S OLD KITCHEN WAS NEARLY empty. Shiloh scanned the cupboards for something she could make everyone for lunch. There was white bread and canned tuna fish, and some pickles in the fridge. She ran home for mayonnaise and better bread and potato chips and watermelon.

She fed Angel's kids first, then Angel and her boyfriend. Then she went to get Mikey and Cary.

They'd spent most of the morning cleaning out the back porch. When Shiloh walked out there, Mikey was trying to get Cary to tackle the basement with him.

"I checked it out," Mikey said. "It's a two-man job—there's all this machinery and greasy shit . . . Fuckin' Batman-villain territory. Like, Alan Moore Batman, you know?"

"Yeah . . ." Cary was frowning. He rubbed his face with his T-shirt. There was a picture of an aircraft carrier on the front. "I don't know . . . Maybe not today."

"But you've got me today," Mikey said, holding out his arms.

"Yeah . . ." Cary shook his head. His jaw was locked, and his eyebrows were tense. He was squinting at nothing.

"Mikey, why don't *you* start on the basement," Shiloh suggested. "And I'll help when I'm done in the kitchen."

"No," Cary said to Shiloh. "You stay up here."

Mikey was looking back and forth between them. "I'll just start on it now—I'm not hungry yet. I'll clear a path."

Shiloh took Cary by the wrist. "You, come wash your hands. I want to watch you eat."

"You don't trust me to eat?" He followed her to the sink.

"I trust you," she said. "I just really enjoy *watching* you."

Cary washed his hands. Shiloh washed hers again, too.

"Will you eat tuna salad?" she asked.

"Yes."

She handed him the plate with the biggest sandwich and the most chips. He immediately picked up the sandwich and took a bite.

Shiloh watched him. She really did enjoy it.

"Let Mikey take care of the basement," she whispered.

Cary looked in her eyes. He was still chewing. He nodded.

## SEVENTY-SIX

SHILOH AND MIKEY WERE BACK again Monday morning to help, and Cary decided not to fight it. Mikey went straight to the goddamn basement, and Cary didn't even let himself worry about it—he didn't even look down the stairs.

Shiloh had taken the day off work. She was out in the front yard, helping Angel load up a truck that Angel's boyfriend had borrowed so they could put some of their stuff in storage. (Cary worried they wouldn't have the money to get it out.)

Jackie was out there, too, going through all the new basement shit in the dumpster.

Mikey just kept dumping more on top. None of it was anything personal—it was all stuff that Cary's mom had thrown down there to get it out of the way. Or stuff that people had left at the house and never come back for. Old washing machines. Boxes of moldy kids' clothes. Broken glass.

Mikey said this was going to inspire some dark and beautiful art.

Cary was patching the drywall in the living room.

Shiloh came in, letting the screen door bang behind her, and said she was going to make sandwiches. She'd been feeding everyone for two days.

Cary set down the drywall knife and followed her into the kitchen. "You don't have to do this," he said, pushing her gently against the fridge.

"I thought you asked me to marry you."

"We're not married yet."

There was a hole in Cary's T-shirt. She poked his stomach through it. "You're crazy if you think I'm going to let you do this alone. I wouldn't have, even if we were just friends."

"I owe you," he said.

Shiloh pulled on his shirt. She was making the hole bigger. "How many times are you going to make me say this..."

"Hey, Cary?" That was Jackie's voice.

He gritted his teeth and pushed away from Shiloh.

Jackie walked into the kitchen, holding his ROTC saber. "Isn't this yours?"

## SEVENTY-SEVEN

SHILOH FELT LIKE THE DAYS with Cary were flying out from underneath her.

She wanted to spend every minute with him—she *did* spend every minute thinking about him. She was a zombie at work; she kept apologizing to Tom.

"No worries," Tom said. "Just—one day, you'll come in, and I'll be senior education director and you'll be assistant education director. And it won't be a problem. You can even keep your side of the desk."

"That seems fair," Shiloh said.

On the days when she had the kids, Cary came over for dinner.

"We may as well set a plate for Cary," Junie said one night, rolling her eyes. "He practically lives here."

"He's my best friend," Shiloh said, "and he leaves soon, to go back to work."

"Back to the ocean?"

"Practically."

Would Cary ever come back to this house? Would he ever want to spend another night in North Omaha? His mom's house was so *much*. By the time Shiloh started helping over there, Cary had already been cleaning for a week, and there was still a river of junk pouring out into the dumpster. Cary kept having to call the rental company to come empty it.

Shiloh got home from work Tuesday and spent an hour cleaning her own living room. She was standing by the window when Cary turned into her driveway. She watched him get out of his rental car and bound up the front steps. He was wearing olive-green cargo pants, a white T-shirt, and a baseball cap with the name of his ship on the front. He knocked on the door, then opened it and walked in.

"Hey," he said, taking off the cap. "Why are you smiling?"

Shiloh shook her head. "Hi."

"You should lock your door."

"I knew you were coming."

Cary walked over to Shiloh and pushed her down onto the couch, falling on top of her. He dug her necklace out of her T-shirt, and his face fell. "Did you lose your ring?"

"I'm wearing it," she said.

He went looking for her ring finger and kissed it. "Why are you wearing it?"

"I don't know, I just felt like being engaged."

He kissed her hand again. "Asterisk."

"Pfff," she said. "There's no asterisk."

Cary looked up at her, one eyebrow raised. "No asterisk?"

"Shut up," she said. "You know there's no more asterisk."

He smiled so wide, his cheeks turned to origami. "You don't think I'm a bad idea anymore?"

"I never thought you were a bad idea."

"You know what I mean." Cary was looking in her eyes.

Shiloh worked not to look away. To be still inside the moment. "It's more like I'm past being rational about you."

He looked serious. "We should get married before I leave."

"No," she said, "*stop*. I want an engagement. And a wedding."

Cary kissed the palm of her hand. Then the inside of her ring finger. "Yeah, but what if something happens to me?"

"In San Diego?"

"I don't know, anywhere. On Thirtieth Street. I want you to get my death benefit."

"I'm not even a bride," Shiloh said, "and you've made me a widow."

"Are the kids with their dad?"

"Yeah."

"And your mom's at work?"

"She just left."

Cary started pushing up Shiloh's skirt.

"What are you doing?"

He was unbuttoning her jeans. "If you won't marry me, we can at least have sex on this couch."

"I said I'd marry you! No asterisk!"

Cary was pulling down her jeans. They were stuck on her hips. "Marry me tomorrow."

"No!"

He stopped, with all eight of his fingers curled into the waist of her jeans. "Do you want to have sex with me on this couch?"

Shiloh giggled. "Yes."

"No asterisk?"

She kicked him. "Just do it already."

"*Just do it already,*" he mocked. "We're not even married, and you're already tired of me."

"Why are you in such a good mood?" she asked, sincerely.

Cary picked up her left hand and kissed it.

Cary sat on the couch with Shiloh on his lap. (He sat on his T-shirt, which she thought was funny and also conscientious.) He'd never gotten around to taking off her dress.

They'd been having sex so often—whenever they were alone—that Shiloh didn't have time to fully charge her anxiety in between. She felt sort of half-dressed all the time. Only half wound up.

She leaned forward on Cary's cock and arched backwards, their fingers intertwined, rocking.

"I feel like I'm doing a lot of work," she said.

"Does it feel good?"

"Yes."

"Then it's still just your primary duty."

"Cary . . ." She was breathless. Because it *was* a lot of work. Because it was hot in here. Because it felt so good.

"Yeah." Cary was sweating.

"I'm sorry my house is such a mess."

He slouched deeper into the couch, pushing up his hips. "S'fine."

"Does it drive you crazy?"

"No."

"Will it drive you crazy to live here?"

"I'm not gonna live here."

Shiloh leaned forward. She put her hands on his shoulders. Cary held her hips.

"But I'm always gonna be like this," she said.

He looked up at her. "Like what?"

"Messy. Cluttered. Like your mom."

"Shilohhh." He groaned in a bad way. "Don't talk about my mom."

"Sorry." She rocked. "Sorry."

Cary sat up, he lifted her off. He was gentle. "What is this?"

"I'm kind of a hoarder," Shiloh said.

His face was still red. "You've got nothing on my mom."

"Give me time."

Cary squeezed her hips. "I like your house. I like the *you* part of it—all the pillows and old posters. It's comfortable."

"What if you like it *because* it reminds you of your mom, and then you grow to hate it?"

Cary groaned again. He let his head fall back onto the couch. Shiloh adjusted her hips, so she wasn't squishing him.

"Okay," he said, "you know what? Your house *does* kind of remind me of my mom's house. And it *does* drive me a little crazy. But I also like it. I feel at home here."

Shiloh shook him a few times by the shoulders. "Do you have some fantasy that it will be different when we live together?"

He looked at her. "Yes. Because we'll have a house with windows that open and decent screens. And I can do the dishes."

"We're probably going to argue about it . . ."

"Probably. But not for a while."

She frowned.

"You keep acting like that's a bad thing . . ." Cary said. "But every time you tell me that we're going to have problems in the future, all I think about is how lucky I am to have a future with you. Finally."

Shiloh looked at him. She was sucking on her bottom lip. She took off her dress.

Cary nodded at her. "Just throw that anywhere."


They took a shower together, and Cary asked if the kids had any toys that *weren't* in the bathtub.

The real reason he was in a good mood was that he had the paperwork to put his mom's house on the market. He was going to ask Lois to sign over financial power of attorney so he could handle the sale—but he wasn't sure she'd go for it. He wanted to head right over there to talk to her. Shiloh said she'd come along.

She put her dress back on and brushed her hair. She swept the front to the side with a barrette.

They stopped to pick up dinner from his mom's favorite Mexican restaurant—which delighted Lois. She clapped when she opened her door and saw the bags. She didn't have a kitchen table, so the three of them ate in the living room while Cary explained the paperwork to her.

The apartment was more crowded than the last time Shiloh had been here. Lois had wanted to keep a lot of things from her old house. There were boxes stacked in the living room and the bedroom. Shiloh could tell Cary was irritated by it.

Shiloh cleaned up after dinner. And Lois put on her glasses to take a closer look at the contract. "I just don't know . . ." she kept saying.

Cary sat near her on the couch. "Mom. What don't you know?"

"Well, honey, you know I love it here, and you make it all sound so good. But you're going back to your station. And I have to make it work with the people who are here."

"What does that mean?"

"What if I have to move back home?"

"You won't need to—I've explained it."

"But who will take care of me? Jackie doesn't have room at her house."

"Mom, I promise"—he was holding her hand—"that won't happen."

"Cary, I love you. But you aren't ever coming home."

"Yes, he is," Shiloh said from the kitchen. She was standing behind the little counter.

Cary and his mom both looked up at her. Shiloh looked at Cary. He wasn't telling her with his eyes to stop.

"We're getting married," Shiloh said.

His mom dropped the papers. She took off her glasses and looked at Cary. "Is this true?"

"Yes, ma'am."

"Shiloh, what about your husband!"

Shiloh walked into the living room. "I'm divorced, Lois. I've been divorced a long time."

"What!" Lois exclaimed breathily. "Is this true?" She touched Cary's face. "Are you giving me two grandbabies?"

He nodded. He looked tearful.

"Shiloh, come here! I can't get up that quick!"

Shiloh went to her. Lois gave her a big hug. And then Lois hugged Cary. She was crying. "Finally, my baby boy. Oh, I'm so happy."

Shiloh held out her left hand, to give Lois proof.

Lois took her hand and made more joyful noises. "That is beautiful! That's antique, isn't it? Is that white gold?"

"Yeah," Cary said.

Lois squeezed Shiloh's hand. "When is the wedding? Will it be in Omaha?"

"It will definitely be in Omaha," Shiloh said.

"The point is, I'm coming back," Cary said. "I'm coming home."


Lois signed the papers.

She talked to Shiloh about the wedding.

She made Cary go down to the dining room to get them real dessert, to celebrate. He came back with banana pudding and then stayed to make Lois test her sugars.

On the way to the car, Cary told Shiloh she could have her way whenever she wanted it, from then on. She'd earned it.

On the way to her house, he argued with her about waiting to get married.

## SEVENTY-EIGHT

CARY WAS LEAVING ON FRIDAY. There was no point driving him to the airport—he had to return the rental car.

They had dinner with Mike and Janine the night before.

Mikey was smug about their engagement. About Cary moving back to Omaha. Shiloh and Cary were Mikey's supporting characters, and he was pleased to have them where he wanted them. Or moving that way.

Cary went home with Shiloh after dinner. He brought his luggage. He kept her awake, making plans.

When it was time for him to leave the next morning, they kissed goodbye on her porch.

## SEVENTY-NINE

THE OCEAN WAS BIG AND blue and looked exactly like the pictures.

Cary told her she was under-romanticizing it.

Shiloh told him she wanted to try In-N-Out.


First Shiloh told Junie that Cary was her boyfriend.

Junie didn't like it. She'd run away rather than say hi to Cary over Skype. And the first time he came back to Omaha, Junie ran upstairs and slammed the door to her room.

It rattled Cary.

Shiloh was shrewd about it: the only way past this was through.

She made Junie's favorite dessert that night—strawberry shortcake— and eventually she came down to eat some.

Cary still seemed hesitant with the kids—the engagement hadn't changed that. Shiloh appreciated it. He didn't need to seduce her by seducing them first.

He eventually won Gus over by playing trucks with him for hours on the couch. Cary confessed to Shiloh that he was thinking about something else the whole time, and she immediately absolved him. "What were you supposed to be thinking about? *Trucks?*"


Lois's house sold, and Cary was so happy, he sent both Shiloh and Lois flowers.

Shiloh's mom wasn't happy about Shiloh's plans to move. Cary said they could find a house with a mother-in-law apartment, and her mom said she refused to be carted around like furniture.

The three of them argued about it one night over Skype.

"Mom . . ." Shiloh tried to be the voice of reason. "You know Junie and Gus can't share a room forever."

"We were going to finish the basement and put a room down there for Gus," her mom said.

"You're not putting Gus in the basement," Cary objected onscreen.

"I wasn't talking to you, Cary!"

"Mom, he's right. It was never a great solution."

"Gloria, we can get you a place with your own kitchen."

Her mom closed the laptop. "I don't have to take orders from that man. I'm not marrying him, and I never joined the Navy."

Shiloh laughed. "So, what do you want to do?"

"I want to stay here."

"I can't stay here, Mom."

She sighed. "I know."

Her mom started looking at apartments for retired people. The more she looked, the more enthusiastic she seemed. *"No more mowing. No more shoveling."* She was tired of the neighborhood, too. Everyone was ready for something a little easier.

## EIGHTY

SHILOH HAD ACTED UNIMPRESSED WITH the ocean, but Cary thought maybe it scared her.

His apartment in San Diego had never seemed as empty as when he was showing it to her for the first time.

She brought him a framed photo of her sitting on his lap at her table. "So you have a picture of us."

Cary already had their picture from college—when he was just out of boot camp—shoved into the frame of his bedroom mirror.

He was making headway with Juniper and Gus. It was probably only going to get harder with time—Shiloh said the only way out was through. He didn't tell her how much he still didn't want to be called anyone's stepfather. He already loved these kids, and he didn't want to be the person they hated most.

She finally told him about her divorce during a San Diego visit. She was humiliated. He wasn't sure if the kind thing to do was to look away from her while she talked—or to show her that he *could* still look at her.

Her ex-husband was a sociopath. Cary didn't want to know him at all; he never wanted to see that guy in Junie and Gus.

He didn't know what to say to Shiloh. He couldn't tell her that he'd never cheated on anyone—he had once, years ago, though the circumstances were gray. He hadn't always been perfectly honorable.

Shiloh didn't ask.

They were sitting on Cary's black Ikea couch. He kept his arm around her. "I'm sorry," he said. "I don't know how you got through that first year, when Gus was a baby."

"I don't know, either. My mom helped a lot."

"Is that why you got your tubes tied?"

Shiloh looked at him, surprised. "No—I had them tied when Gus was born. Ryan and I planned it. We were tired of birth control, and I was terrified of getting pregnant again accidentally. Two was already a lot."

"So you'd never want *three* . . ." Cary said.

Shiloh looked speechless. "My tubes aren't actually tied, Cary—they're cauterized."

He shrugged. "Doctors don't really try to reverse tubal ligations anymore. They suggest in vitro."

She stared at him. "You've been googling my *uterus*."

"No." Cary shook his head. "I've been educating myself."

Shiloh was biting her lip. "Is this something that's important to you?"

"If it was important to me," he said, "I would have brought it up sooner."

She nodded. "Good."

"I am merely setting it on the table for discussion."

She was upset. "I didn't know you wanted kids."

"I'm already going to have kids."

"You know what I mean," she said.

Cary rubbed her shoulder, refusing to flinch. "If you're asking whether I would like the experience of having a child with you—yes, I think I would. But I'm already getting what I really want, Shiloh. I want you."

"I'd like to set this question aside," she said.

"Okay."

"I'd like to stick a pin in it. A brass tack."

"Yep," Cary said.

"And you don't bring it up. I bring it up."

"Aye, aye."

"Don't be silly—I'm serious."

"'Aye, aye' is dead serious. It means 'understood and will comply.'"

"Oh. Then what do I say in return?"

"You don't say anything. You're the senior officer."

She brought it up two months later. She said three was possible, but not in a way Cary should plan on or even hope for. Three was not *impossi-ble*, Shiloh said.

Cary was going to have to invite his sisters to this wedding.

He put STRATCOM at the top of his preference sheet for his next billet.

He wanted to live near Mikey. In the hills. Among the trees. He wanted to put Shiloh there, no matter what.

## EIGHTY-ONE

SHILOH FOUND HERSELF ACTING LIKE her teenage self with Cary. Sounding like that old self. Shifting easily into old jokes and teasing.

There was a kind of mirth that Shiloh only ever achieved with Cary and Mikey, and now she was living inside that dynamic again.

She realized there was a tone of voice—deeper, rounder—that she never used with Ryan, that she used all the time with Cary.

And she made jokes she never would have made with Ryan, even though Ryan *liked* jokes. He was genuinely funny.

But Cary and Mikey were sort of *terribly* funny—there was nothing they wouldn't laugh about—and they made Shiloh terrible, too. There was a laugh she only laughed with them, throaty and fucked up. That laugh was back in her life, and it kept surprising her.

Cary made Shiloh feel like she was the same person she'd always been . . . But he *also* made her feel like she could be someone new. For all the ways they knew each other, so much between them was barely precedented—everything romantic or sexual.

Shiloh could start over.

She could be a different sort of lover with Cary, and someday soon a different sort of wife.

She'd thought, with Ryan, that she was lucky to have someone who didn't need to look in her eyes. She'd realized too late that he *couldn't*.

With Cary, Shiloh wanted to push through her own discomfort. To get over herself. To look directly at the sun.

## EIGHTY-TWO

SHILOH BROUGHT THE KIDS TO California for five days. Cary worried that he didn't have beds for them. He bought two air mattresses. He made sure he had whole milk and bread and other things he'd seen in Shiloh's refrigerator. Strawberry jam. Grapes.

He bought sand toys and beach towels.

He worried that his apartment felt less personal than a hotel room—and far less welcoming.

The kids were tired when they got there. It had been their first time on a plane.

Juniper was unusually shy, clinging to Shiloh. "Mommy," she said, raising the middle of her eyebrows, "is *this* where we'll live when you get married?"

"No, sweetie, you know this already—Cary is going to live with us in Omaha when he's not at work."

"Where are we supposed to *sleep*?" Junie fretted.

That was the first night that Cary slept with Shiloh under the same roof as her kids. He didn't sleep well. She kept getting up to check on them.

The next day was better. Juniper saw that Cary had framed one of her drawings—the first one. And Gus was reassured by the Disney Channel.

Cary took them to the beach and the zoo.

Shiloh had never been to Disneyland, which meant the kids had never been to Disneyland, which meant Cary got to take them all for the first time. He felt like a king on earth.

Because of the way the rides worked, it was always Cary in one car with one kid, and Shiloh in another car with the other. Or sometimes— Shiloh and both kids in a car, and Cary by himself.

They spent the whole day in separate elephants and pirate ships.

"I'm sorry," Shiloh said, between lines and rides. While they were all eating popcorn and waiting for a parade. She was smiling sadly at him.

"Why?"

"I know it's not fair to you, to spend so much of your life taking care of someone else's kids."

Cary licked his bottom lip. His eyes were very narrow. "I need you to stop calling them that, with me, even though it's true."

"Sorry." Shiloh slipped her hand backward into one of his hip pockets. It was a new habit.

"I'm so happy right now," Cary said. It came out serious. Solemn. He wouldn't blame her if she didn't believe him.

Shiloh looked in his eyes. "Really?"

He nodded. "Don't begrudge me this life."

## EIGHTY-THREE

THERE WAS A VERY FANCY uniform that Cary could wear to his wedding. A white coat and dark pants. His mom had been angling for it. Shiloh had initially agreed, but then she'd changed her mind.

On this one day, she didn't want to think about the Navy. She wanted to think about the man.

So Cary was wearing the navy blue suit he'd bought for Mikey's wedding. (Janine had been right after all—he *was* wearing it again.) He had a white rose boutonniere, and he'd grown his hair out as long as the Navy would let him. It was long enough to look blond again in direct sunlight. Shiloh couldn't get enough of it.

Shiloh was wearing a white lace, fifties-style wedding dress. A-line, tea-length, with white gloves and a little jacket. She'd hired a woman in the costume shop to make it for her. (Not Kate.)

Junie got to pick the color of her flower girl dress. She wanted pink. Gus wore navy shorts and suspenders, with a pink clip-on bow tie. He wanted to throw flowers with Junie instead of carrying the ring.

Shiloh and Cary got married in Miller Park and had the reception down the street in the youth wrestling hall. (Janine still had all the tulle and Christmas lights in her garage. Shiloh borrowed them.)

Shiloh hadn't wanted a bridal dance. She didn't want to dance with everyone watching her—it made her skin crawl.

*"But you're an* actress," Cary argued. *"People stare at you all the time."*

*"I don't want them staring at me when I'm actually being me."*

That meant the first dance of the night was Cary and his mom. Lois had *zero* issues with everyone staring at her. She was wearing a new dress. Pink, like Junie's. She left her walker at the table, and Cary supported her.

Shiloh watched from the side of the dance floor, holding Gus on her hip, even though he was too big for it.

Cary kept looking over at Shiloh. She'd honestly never seen him this happy. The lines in his cheeks hadn't disappeared all day.

Lois had picked the song for the mother-son dance—"Landslide" by Fleetwood Mac, which Shiloh hadn't been expecting. (She would have bet on something country.) It was making Shiloh cry. She swayed to the music with Gus-Gus. Junie was leaning into Shiloh's skirt. Shiloh put a hand on her head.

When the song was half over, Mikey jogged over to Shiloh's mom and dragged her out onto the dance floor, too. That made tears spill down Shiloh's cheeks. She hoped that Lois wouldn't mind sharing the spotlight—but, no, Lois was smiling. Everyone was smiling but Shiloh.

"Mommy, are you okay?" Junie asked.

"They're happy tears," Shiloh said.

"Mommy, you okay?" Gus said.

"I'm okay."

"Don't cry."

"Okay, Gus-Gus, I won't."

Cary hadn't wanted alcohol at the reception, not with all his sisters there and their grown kids. Shiloh had worried that would mean no one would dance. But her friends from the theater didn't need booze to make a scene.

After the first dance, Cary wanted to walk around and thank every-one personally for coming. Shiloh wanted to sit on the dark side of the room, gossiping with Tom and Daniel, and letting Gus eat more cake.

She'd loaded the reception playlist with songs about people named "Carrie" and "Carey." Plus "Voices Carry" and "Carry On Wayward Son." Every time one came on, Cary found Shiloh across the room and smiled at her.

That was her husband. (That had legally been her husband for months.

Cary was relentless—they'd gone to the courthouse two weeks after he gave her a ring.)

Three of Cary's friends from his early days in the Navy had flown in for the wedding. He was taking the opportunity to visit with them. He was the only one of them not in uniform.

Shiloh kept an eye on him.

Shiloh and Gus ate so much cake. Junie danced like a little maniac.

The reception was winding down when Cary came to Shiloh's table. "You have to dance with me," he said. "It's my wedding."

"He makes a compelling case," Tom said. Tom liked Cary. Tom liked anyone who could quickly get off book.

Cary took Shiloh's hand. She groaned.

Junie ran up to their table. "Mommy, will you *please* dance with me? I've been waiting all night!"

"She makes a compelling case," Cary said.

Shiloh stood up. She handed Gus off to Cary and took Junie's hand. All four of them walked out to the dance floor.

The song was "Babe" by Styx. Shiloh had always liked Styx. Even though they were a hessian band.

Shiloh held Junie's hands and sang to her.

Cary dipped Gus backwards and swung him from side to side. Gus loved it—until he didn't. "Gus wants to dance with Mommy!"

"*I* want to dance with Mommy," Shiloh corrected.

Shiloh took Gus, and Cary picked up Junie. The four of them swayed. Cary sang, too.

"This doesn't count," he said to Shiloh during an instrumental break.

Before the song was over, Cary was waving over Shiloh's mom to come get the kids. Shiloh let Gus go.

Cary put an arm around her waist and took her hand. The Styx song started over from the beginning.

Shiloh laughed. She laid a hand on his shoulder. "Oh, wow, is this *your* bridal dance?"

"Yes. I waited until people started to leave. No one's staring at you."

"You are."

Cary nodded, giving her a serious look. "Yeah."

Shiloh held the look as long as she could, then shivered, stepping closer and pressing her cheek against his.

Cary wrapped his arm tighter. "You okay?"

She nodded. "I'm happy."

He let go of her hand and hugged her with both arms around her waist.

Shiloh put her arms around his neck. "I'm sorry it took so long, Cary."

"Me too, Shy."

Shiloh closed her eyes tight. She bit her lip. She imagined herself holding him at every moment she'd known him, like a pearl-ended pin stuck through time and space.

"I want to remember this day," she whispered. "But I also want to have so many good days that this one gets lost in the plethora. Cary, I want to make you so happy that all your happy memories run together. I want the rest of your life to be a bright gold streak."

He pulled away to lower his eyebrows at her. "Shiloh, I'm not going to forget our wedding day."

"I hope you do," she said fiercely. "I'm going to make you feel so consistently good that the days lose specificity."

"Is that a threat?"

"Yes. I'm going to obliterate your memory. All you're going to remember at the end is a blur of milk and honey."

Cary blinked. His eyes were shining. "You should have put this in your vows."

"I was always heading your way, Cary."

He kissed her. It was a way of covering her mouth. "I know, Shiloh. You got here just in time."

# before

SHILOH HAD FOUND A WIDE-BRIMMED hat at the thrift shop. It was old, not just made to look old, and it had a black, gauzy bow.

She wore it one day to school, even though she couldn't wear it *in* school. She carried it around all day. Mikey thought it was cool, but Cary thought it was ridiculous.

A bunch of them stayed late that day to work on the yearbook, and when they walked out the front door, Shiloh immediately put on her hat.

The wind blew it right off her head.

It went rolling down the sidewalk, flying up into the air, then touching ground again.

Shiloh was too shocked to react until it was already too far away for her to chase.

Cary took off after it.

He ran all the way to Ames Street and around the corner.

Tanya and Becky laughed. "He'll never catch it," Tanya said. After a few minutes, the two of them walked to their cars.

That left Mikey and Shiloh. Mikey looked at her, with an eyebrow raised.

Shiloh ignored him. She watched the street.

After another few minutes, Mikey said, "Should we go after him?"

Shiloh looked down. It was colder than she'd expected. She wasn't wearing a coat.

They kept waiting.

"Holy shit," Mikey said.

Shiloh looked up.

Cary was walking up the hill of the parking lot. He was panting. He was holding Shiloh's hat.

"There's your man," Mikey said.

## ACKNOWLEDGMENTS

I COULDN'T HAVE WRITTEN THIS book without Troy and Bethany Gronberg. Thank you both for being so generous with your time and memories. I loved having an excuse to talk to you.

Thank you to Joy DeLyria, who rescued this idea from the scrap heap and helped me to see it in a new way. And to Stephenie Meyer, who cheered me round the first corner.

Ashley Christy's sharp eyes and sharp brain have shored up my books at their foundations. Thank you, Ashley, for making sure I make sense, and for sharing your very good instincts.

Thank you to Elena Yip for sharing her impeccable taste. And to Leigh Bardugo for sharing her impeccable judgment. And to Nicola Barr and Kassie Evashevski for never taking my books for granted.

I have two kids, and I used to thank them for being encouraging—but now it's something more. They're patient and insightful. They listen. Laddie and Rosey, I appreciate you very much, and I trust your reasoning.

I write Christopher Schelling's name on this page at the end of every book. He's my agent, and by now he expects it. But, Christopher, I am newly and deeply grateful for you each and every time.

Finally, thank you to my incomparable editor, Jennifer Brehl, and the team at William Morrow, who threw their hearts into bringing this book to life and to the world. I'm so grateful.